# TYNE

# TYNE TEES

## JOHN NICHOLSON
Nick Guymer Series
**No.6**

**HEAD**
PUBLISHING

Published by Head Publishing
Copyright © John Nicholson 2014

*Printed by Berforts Information Press Ltd*

*ISBN 978-0-9926640-9-1*

http://www.johnnicholsonwriter.com

*A doff of an especially large and feathery cap to my eagle-eyed editor, Janet, especially for her almost mystical ability to spot the words that aren't there.*

*Much celebratory whacking of the Corky Laing cow bell goes to Robert, for his editorial talents and understanding all the classic rock references, even the Captain Beefheart one.*

*A big thumbs up to Winty's Instant Grammar Referral Service and to Dawn for the cover art, lay out and all the best plot ideas.*

*You all make me look much, much better than I am.*

*A big thank you also to my readers. Your encouragement and support make the long hours slaving over a hot and greasy keyboard worthwhile.*

*Tyne Tees is dedicated to just getting through and surviving, any way you can.*

*"Got my head in the sky*
*and my mind knows what it wants*
*but my body just drags me down*
*And my world is something you can't see*
*but it's still very real to me*
*you can find it in the hole where I keep my soul*
*Way down inside me*
*there's a real man*
*Forget about my body and be a real man"*

# CHAPTER 1

'Do you take that woman in tight pants to be your lawfully wedded wife, then, Nick? There's still time to back out, y'know. She can be a bit of a sod, like...same as her bloody mother,' said Jackie Wells, letting out a rasping, wheezy laugh. She pulled on a cigarette and blew out a cloud of blue smoke, nodding at her daughter Julie, as she passed by with a tray of drinks. Condensation ran down the glasses of sparkling wine she was carrying. They looked very inviting. Nick almost reached out and took one; it was his wedding, after all.

'Yes I do, Jackie. I'm actually really looking forward to being Mr Julie Wells.'

He looked at his watch. Nearly noon. They were due at the registry office at 1.30pm. Everyone who was going to see them tie the knot was in their back garden, drinking.

Julie's mother was quite a sight. Her hair had been dyed the colour of coal, especially for the event. Not only that, she seemed to have drawn on her eyebrows with a marker pen and used a paint brush to put on make up. As a result, she had a face like a startled puffin.

'Eee, it's a mint drop of booze this, like,' said Jackie, drinking the wine down in a couple of big gulps, '...or a canny drop, as Conrad would say.'

Nick turned and looked at the man she was talking about. Conrad was a powerfully built Geordie. Six feet tall, broad and with big hands and big feet, even though he was in his early 60s, he still had the strength and muscle built up over a lifetime in the building and construction industry.

He and Julie had met her mother's boyfriend a few times, though 'boyfriend' was clearly the wrong description. It was hard to know exactly what to call him, but he and Jackie seemed to be getting on very well. They'd had the dubious pleasure of seeing the two of them singing a duet in the social club to a backing track of 'I Got

You Babe', amongst other 50s and 60s pop classics. They liked to call themselves Tyne Tees. Maybe it was a new career for them both, late in life, or maybe not.

'Aye, he's a nice fella, your Con, isn't he? A good laugh, like,' said Nick.

'Eee aye...he's that, alright,' said Jackie, clearly quite drunk already. They were going to have to carry her out of the registry office, at this rate.

'Now then, Nick. All set for your big day?' a voice said from behind him.

He turned away from Jackie and shook Terry Wells's hand. Julie's youngest and nicest brother grinned at him.

'Alright Tez. Yeah. Well, we bought enough booze to knock out a small army, so it should be a good day. Do you want a lager?'

'Better not. I'm one of the drivers, like. It's not stopped Kev, though.' He raised an eyebrow at his older brother, who had hold of two glasses of wine and was talking to his other brother, Ricky.

This was a degree of responsibility that Nick was unaccustomed to hearing from Terry.

'Aye, of course. Good lad,' said Nick. 'How about you, Jaz?'

'Oooh, go on then. Just a lager, thanks.'

He took a can of Budweiser from a big bucket of ice and handed it to her along with a glass. She smiled and nodded. 'It's exciting, this, I reckon,' she said, her long black hair blowing in the warm late summer breeze.

'Well, you two will be next, won't you?' said Nick. They grinned at each other in the way only two people who are massively in love can grin at each other.

'Mebees, aye,' said Terry. 'Her dad isn't keen on us, though. He reckons I'm not good enough for her.'

'That's nonsense and you know it,' said Julie, walking past with a tray now filled with empty glasses. 'Hiya Tez. Hiya Jaz. You look lush, you, Jaz. I love a bit of pearpull satin, me, like.' She dropped into her old broad Teesside accent to say it, laughing as she did so.

Jasmin laughed as well. 'Eee aye, I love a pearpull werk shert me, like,' she said, also in a cartoonish Teesside voice. She was an oval-eyed, small, willowy, Asian woman in her mid 20s, with smooth, supple, dark skin, dark hair and red, bordering on purple, lips. She wore thick black eyeliner which made the whites of her eyes look extra-luminous.

'I love the satin pants under the long matching satin top thing,' said Nick.

'It's an Asian classic, isn't it?' said Jasmin. 'And it covers a multitude of sins. Going to the toilet is a bit of a faff on, though.'

'Does her dad really not like you, Terry?' said Nick.

He shook his neatly cropped head. 'Nah. I'm too rough. Too working class, too everything he doesn't like.'

'It is infuriating. He doesn't even know you, really. He just hates the idea of me having a man from the Hardwick estate as my partner,' said Jasmin, '...but sod him. You can't help who you fall in love with, can you?'

They grinned at each other again.

'Eee, young love,' laughed Julie. 'Bless youse two.'

'Young? I'm almost 30, Jules, remember?' said Terry.

'When you're my age, that's young,' said Nick. 'And it's especially young compared to Jackie and Conrad over there.'

'I think they're great together,' said Jasmin, with a bright smile.

'I know. It's a bit weird, isn't it? Mam has become almost fizzin' human,' said Julie, her arched eyebrows raised in surprise.

Terry laughed. 'He's a canny old soul, is Con. A right old rascal if you ask me.'

'We'll need to get off in about half an hour, Nick. I'll just dish out one last round of drinks and then we'll get everyone in the cars,' said Julie.

He nodded. The people they'd invited around for pre-ceremony drinks were from Julie's side of the family, largely because he didn't have any family that he knew well enough to invite. Jeff and his girlfriend Rita were the only people on his side of the aisle. Not that there was an aisle. It was just going to be a quick couple of vows that they'd written for themselves, an exchange of rings and then back to the house for more drinking.

He was wearing the dark, fitted suit he'd bought for the Northern Sports Writer Awards a couple of years ago, a white shirt and a Middlesbrough FC club tie, largely because it was the only tie he owned, having been given to him as a freebie one Christmas by someone who worked in the club shop. You didn't need a tie to sit in front of a computer and type, and even if you did, he wouldn't have worn one.

It was quite a sight to see the whole of the Wells clan in one place at one time. Julie, the three brothers, Terry, Ricky and Kev, and Jackie, their mother.

'Nervous?' said Jeff, coming over and leaving Jasmin and Terry to talk to Jackie.

'Yeah, a bit, though I don't know why,' said Nick.

'It's a big day, man. As Best Man it's my duty to call the whole thing off if you get cold feet.'

'I think I'm more worried about the party afterwards. We'll have to carry Jackie out on a stretcher at this rate.'

Jeff laughed. 'She likes a drink, that one, and that bloke of hers is cut from the same cloth. A classic big drinking Geordie. You'd know he was from Newcastle even before he opens his mouth. He's just got Geordie written all over him. Looks like a cross between big Jack Charlton and Jimmy Nail.'

'Aye, I know what you mean. He's got quite a colourful past, from what I can tell.'

'Well, he's in the building game, isn't he?'

'Yeah. He's a joiner. He's working on that business development project on Prince Regent Street.'

'Is he? I always reckoned builders are the rock 'n' roll people of the labouring classes.'

'How do you work that out?'

'Well, they go all over the country on tour. Have trowel and spirit level, will travel. The northeast has always exported a lot of tradesmen. Like in the early 80s you couldn't move in Germany for brickies and joiners from this region. Also, like rock 'n' roll was before it became an extension of corporate culture, they're all shaggers and piss-heads, aren't they? Massive thirsts on them, builders, as yer man Con there is proving. That must be his sixth beer in the last hour and a half and he's still as sober as a judge.'

'Yeah, well, he's got plenty of place to put it, hasn't he? He's a big unit.'

'You're not wrong there. Hollow legs, his sort. I love his leather bike jacket though, eh. Good to wear that at a wedding.'

'There's a funny story about that. That old leather jacket is signed by the Rolling Stones. So he reckons, anyway.'

'Oh, aye?'

'Yeah, he says he saw them in 1972 in America, went backstage and got them all to sign his jacket. It's been his pride and joy ever since and it comes out on any big occasion. So we're quite honoured, really.'

'That'd be the S.T.P. tour as documented in the infamous and still unreleased *Cocksucker Blues* movie. That's pretty cool. Interesting rock factoid, ahoy.' He raised his finger aloft. 'I bet you can't guess who was the support act for the Stones on that 1972 USA tour.'

'You're right, I can't. Was it Savoy Brown or someone like that?'

'No, my tight-panted friend, it was not. It was, in fact, Steve Wonder.' He chalked up an invisible point to himself.

'That is top-notch trivia, Jeff. I'd rather have seen Stevie than the Stones.'

He grinned back at Nick and took a bow. 'So what's the deal with Conrad's jacket?'

'Well, the trouble is, it would appear Brian Jones signed his jacket, despite being severely dead for four years at the time. All the other signatures are there though, including Mick Taylor.'

'Ha ha. Does he know that?'

'He doesn't seem to. I can't work out if it's all a bullshit story he's made up and he signed the jacket himself, or if someone in the band or road crew played a joke on him, which in a way, would be an even better story. I've not bothered to point out the discrepancy to him. Seems rude to.'

'I hope it's a story he made up, I love an old bloke who makes up stories. So much more fun than sticking to reality. Reality is overrated, which is why I run second-hand record shops. Hey, Terry's lass is a cracker though, isn't she?'

'Jaz? Yeah. Have you not met her before?'

Jeff shook his head and scratched his beard. 'She's got a bit of class about her.'

'Her dad is Jimmy Patel, y'know.'

Jeff pulled a big wow face. 'The Jimmy Patel who's always in the papers? I didn't know that. You never said.'

'Did I not? Aye, he's the very same. Chief Executive of the Middlesbrough Industrial Development Organisation, to give him his full, long-winded and pompous title.'

'CEO of MIDO? Mido? The Boro have just got rid of Mido, haven't they?'

'Aye, they off loaded him to the Egyptian side, El Zamalek. They even got 450 grand in return. I thought they'd have to pay someone to take him away, like you do when the council takes your old freezer to the municipal dump.'

Jeff laughed. 'There should actually be a municipal dump for Boro's rubbish players. Well, that'll be a financial relief for the club, like. The cost of feeding that lad parmos was bankrupting us. It was like throwing coal into the boiler of the Flying Scotsman, trying to keep him well-fuelled.'

'I love a fat footballer. This era of footballers being professional athletes is very disappointing.'

'I want my footballers with a belly, a gambling problem and drunk in a hotel room with Miss Seaton Carew 1983. Some traditions are worth keeping,' said Jeff, looking around again at Jasmin. 'Yeah, Tez has landed on his feet with her, eh.'

'Yeah. They're really in love, but her father hates Terry.'

Jeff tutted. 'How could he hate Terry? He's a nice lad. What's his beef with him?'

'Too common, too council estate and too many rough-arsed, head-breaking brothers.'

Jeff shrugged. 'You can see his point, but Tez is alright; I've always liked him. Soft kid. I say that like I'm 75 and he's 15, but he does seem young for his age, doesn't he?'

'Yeah, I know what you mean. I suspect Jimmy doesn't like the idea of his family being in any way associated with Ricky and Kev, given those lad's history of doing jail time and generally being hard bastards. And Terry's been inside too, admittedly for being rubbish at thieving, rather than anything too unpleasant.'

'Hey, talking of the two meat head Wells brothers, I was thinking, how come neither of them have got kids? They're hardly the most responsible types. You'd think one of them at least would have knocked a couple of women up.'

'Funny you should say that, I was saying the exact same thing to Jules the other night. Neither of them have had long-term relationships, but even so...as you say...law of averages et cetera. She reckons that the Wells men have low sperm counts.'

'Really. They're all Jaffas, are they?'

'Jaffas?'

'Your Jaffa is your seedless orange, isn't it? Do try and keep up, old boy.'

'Oh, yeah. Aye, that's it. She reckons they put it about all the time and it's not happened once.'

'I wonder if Terry is the same, because if I know anything about women, and obviously, I don't, I'd say that Jasmin is mad on him. They've got the goo-goo eyes for each other, look. It's like no-one else is here. She might want kids and Terry there could be firing blanks.'

They were talking together and laughing.

'The way they are with each other is quite sweet, isn't it?' said Nick.

'I don't do sweet. But if listening to Todd Rundgren has taught us anything, it is that love is the answer.'

'Well, you can talk, you're very attentive to your Rita. Her belly is looking really big now.'

'I know, she's still got 12 weeks to go and she already looks massive. I think it must be quads in there...driving a Land Rover.'

'It's not, is it?'

'Nope. The scans just show one big fat bugger of a baby, unless there's another sneaky one in there, hiding up her arse or something. I think it's inherited my massive genes, so I pity the poor lass having to heave anything that big out of her. It's going to have to come out of the sun roof, I think. I hope so, anyway, it might ruin her shop front otherwise.'

Nick laughed and clinked his glass of water against Jeff's wine. They went quiet for a few seconds.

'I've not seen you for a couple of weeks. How's your head been, if you don't mind us asking, like? You were on good form, last time I saw you,' said Jeff, pointing at Nick's temple. 'All OK?'

Nick nodded. 'All fine. Yeah. Thanks for asking, Jeff.' He was going to mention really fancying a drink, but decided not to. It was probably just a passing thing.

Jeff nodded appreciatively. 'Good, good. Yeah. Err...still on the...?'

'...Phenibut pills? Yeah. They seem to be helping me a lot, most of the time, anyway. Hey, I'll tell you what, though...' he grinned at him mischievously.

'What's that? They're not giving you hallucinations, are they?'

'...no, man, but they've given me some serious trouser department action. I'm primed and ready to go most of the time and I can't get enough, once I get started. It's like being 18 again. Very odd. Nice but odd - and very distracting, at times.'

Jeff raised his bushy eyebrows. 'Gotta whole lotta love, eh? They're not blue, these tablets, are they?'

'Green actually. Raising your dopamine apparently increases the libido...and not just a little bit, either. Not for me, anyway.'

Jeff laughed. 'I thought Jules was looking slightly bow-legged, like.'

'Aye, I'm always tugging at her for it.'

'A sex pest, eh? I reckon that'd piss Rita off. She needs her kip. Does Jules not mind?'

Nick shook his head, impishly. 'Nah, not usually. It used to be the other way around, so she thinks it's funny, really, and she always humours me, even if she's not feeling up to the full 12,000 mile service.'

'Hey, you're not popping a woody on me right now, are you?' he said, stepping backwards with a look of mock horror.

'Well, you are looking very sexy today, big boy.'

'Sodding hell, it must be very strong medicine if you think that.' He flicked his long curtain of greying hair down his back. 'Mind, if our mutual love of 1960s west coast acid rock has taught us anything, it is that, whatever the question is, drugs *are* the answer.'

'This is true. Drugs and tie-dye clothing.'

'Not sure Jules would have liked you to get married in tie-dye,' said Jeff, pulling on his beard. 'Mind, she's as smart as anything isn't she, in that cream suit, like? A proper ray of sunshine. Has she lost some weight? I hadn't noticed before, but you can tell in that outfit, that she has.'

'After she lost the baby her metabolism seemed to change a bit, so she has, yeah. Probably lost 10 pounds in the last three or four months. Not that she wanted or needed to. It just happened.'

Jeff nodded and stroked his beard. 'Well, I'd say she looks super sexy and glamorous, if I wasn't so scared she'd overhear me, tear me bollocks off for being a sexist pig and then feed them back to me in one of those bread buns that are in the kitchen. I mean, I'm low carb, I can't be eating bread buns.'

Nick laughed and slapped him on the back.

'You should see what she's got on underneath that suit, lad,' said Nick, conjuring a mental image of her in the new underwear she'd bought for the occasion.

Jeff shook his head at him in pity. 'It's like you're in heat, you. I didn't think one of my duties was to pour a bucket of cold water over you every half hour. I'll have to put you on the bromide, if you get any worse.' They set each other off laughing.

'Aye, well, I can't help it when it comes to Jules. I'm mad for her, aren't I? I love her so much, y'know, Jeff. Can't believe my luck to be getting married to her.'

'I remember when you first met her in Harrogate. She was in town for some legal thing at the conference centre and she came into Jack and Danny's bar. We were sitting there enjoying a libation and arguing about whether Grand Funk Railroad were any good. You saying they weren't, me saying they were. You were smitten with her from the first moment...what was it she said to us?'

'Oh, she butted into our conversation and said *We're An American Band* was their best album because it was produced by Todd Rundgren. Her being a big Todd fan, like,' said Nick.

'Oh, yeah. We both got the horn over her because of that, didn't we? Ha. Pathetic really. More turned on by rock trivia than by the sweet, sweet ladies.'

Nick smiled at the recollection. 'Yeah, I tried to chat her up and got totally tongue-tied, and thought I'd totally blown it. Turned out, that was what she liked. She called us up the next morning and we went out that night and ended up in bed. Genuinely, I think I fell 100 per cent totally in love with her that night.'

Jeff nodded. 'Well, you'd have to be blind not to see why, like. Just look at her.'

Nick turned to watch her talking to her mother and taking a half-full glass out of her hand. 'She had that Oxfam shop Nicole Farhi suit re-tailored by some lass she knew at University, so it actually fits her now, and some other lass did her hair into those long ringlets and bleached some strands.'

Jeff drank some wine and gestured with his glass. 'Is the suit meant to be that tight?'

'Aye, she said she wanted it to look a bit more rock 'n' roll. Is it too tight, do you reckon? The trousers *are* right up her arse. I think I can see her colon from here.'

Jeff looked at him like he was insane. 'It might not be PC to say it, but frankly we both know that too tight is rarely a bad thing on an arse like hers. And you look all done up like a pox doctor's clerk, as well.'

'That's one of your favourite expressions, isn't it? I bet if you had syphilis and went to a specialist doctor about it, the receptionist would be no better dressed than anyone else.'

'Well if so, they'd be letting the side down. I'd want a rotating bow-tie at the very least. Actually, you look more like a Boro footballer who's up in court for some heinous crime committed in a lap dancing bar in Redcar.' He flicked at Nick's Middlesbrough FC club tie.

'Ha ha...you can talk...I didn't know you could get bin liners in your size.'

'This suit, I'll have you know, is a vintage bit of tailoring. Took me ages to dig the bloke up who was wearing it.'

The both laughed loudly at that one and hi-fived. It was a happy morning and a bloody good day to get married.

Julie made a gesture to Nick to indicate it was time to rally the troops.

'Right, we'd better start herding these people into the cars, Jeff. You and Rita are coming with me and Jules.'

'Cool.' He held out his hand towards him, cocked at 45 degrees. Nick grabbed it in a mid-air grip. 'Good luck to youse both, man,' said Jeff, awkwardly.

'Cheers, big man.'

They gripped their hands together for about five seconds and it immediately became embarrassing.

'Right. Well, that's enough of that. Can we get back to being emotionally repressed now?' said Jeff, looking away from him.

'I'd like nothing better,' said Nick.

He and Julie herded everyone around the front to their cars, locked the back door and had a quiet moment together before leaving.

'Well, this is it, kidda,' she said, happily. 'You can back out now if you want.'

'Nah. We'll still have to pay the fee. Anyway, I'm looking

forward to being your wife.'

She put her hands on his shoulders and looked in his eyes. 'You'll make a lovely wife, what with the washing, cooking and wearing the frilly panties for me, when I come in from work.'

'A girl has to work hard to keep her man satisfied.'

She laughed. 'Well, there's no danger there. Owee then, missus. Let's do the dirty deed.'

'I thought we were getting married, but I'm up for a quickie, if you fancy it.'

He kissed her full on the lips and rubbed her backside, feeling in very high spirits.

She beamed back at him. 'You bloody would an' all, you randy get. Don't you worry, we'll have a right good session tonight. I'm already looking forward to it.'

'That's a nice thought to get me through a few hours of pouring drink into your mother.'

'Trust me. When this place is empty and they've all gone home, we're going to have a night to remember. I'll have had a few drinks and you know what I'm like when I'm a bit pissed.' She rubbed noses with him and pecked him on the lips. 'Now, let's get a shift on.'

He held her for one more moment and let out a nervous, shaky breath, a ball of emotion in his chest. 'I really love you, Jules, more than I can ever say.'

She responded without hesitation, putting a hand to his cheek, a radiant smile on her face. 'I really love you, too. More than you'll ever, ever know.'

Terry, Jasmin, Conrad and Jackie got into one car, Julie's brothers Ricky and Kev into an old Discovery and Jeff, Rita, Nick and Julie in Nick's car.

'You know where you're going, don't you, Tez?' said Julie, leaning into the window of a big old Mercedes, a car acquired by Ricky especially for the occasion. It looked like a cross between a tank and limo.

'Yeah, it's that road near the station, isn't it?'

Nick put his thumb up and got into his old BMW to drive them.

The motorcade of three old and once luxurious cars went into Yarm and up the High Street, looking like low-rent outriders for the President of a banana republic.

'Bloody hell, we look like a Teesside Mafia,' said Julie, turning around from the front seat to look at her brothers behind them, then turning back to see her younger brother's car in front, now stopped at the lights.

'In a way, that's right,' said Jeff, from the back seat. 'If anyone is the Teesside Mafia, it's your Kev and Ricky.'

Julie snorted. 'I think they've long since been deposed from that dubious fizzin' title.'

'They seemed like nice lads to me,' said Rita, a statement greeted by laughter from the other three in the car.

'Did I tell you, I met Eddie Cavani last week?' said Jeff as they turned onto Yarm Road.

'Who's he?' said Julie.

'The Cavanis are Newcastle's primo gangster family, aren't they?' said Nick. 'Last time I was at St James Park, a local journo was telling me about them and how they manage to get away running a protection racket.'

'Yup. That's them. Fingers in a lot of pies, including, I am reliably informed, actual pies.'

'So how did you meet him, then?' said Nick.

'He's a customer. Collects Beatles records, so he was in the Stockton shop to pick up a couple of South American EPs I'd got hold of. Always pays top money. He's a nice bloke, actually.'

'Unless he's menacing you for cash?' said Nick.

'No, he's not in the extortion and blackmail business. He's the white sheep of the family and has a regular job at an estate agents. Anyway, I was talking to him about opening a shop up in Newcastle.'

'He's an empire builder, these days,' said Rita with a smile up at the big man.

'A third shop, Jeff? That's amazing,' said Julie.

'Well, this interest in vinyl is only going to grow as kids realise that you can't fall in love with a digital file the way you can with a piece of plastic, nor can you roll a joint on a download. And the Stockton shop has done really good business in these first few months, so I might as well strike while the iron is hot, or the needle is in the groove, if you like. So I was talking to Eddie about it. He reckoned there's a small place on High Bridge that would be ideal.'

'Aye, but his family will want protection money, won't they?" said Nick.

'He said he'd make it sweet for me, because I said he'd get first dibs on any Beatles rarities that come in.'

'Ha. Who'd have thought you can fight organised crime with vinyl records?' said Nick.

'It's the future for policing in the 21st century. The abolition of crime through the sale of picture discs. Anyway, I'm off up there tomorrow to look at this new gaff. If it looks OK, I'll sign on the dotted line.'

'That's amazing Jeff. Well done,' said Julie, clapping. 'The Stockton shop does look mint, mind. Almost cool, in fact, though I know you'd hate that idea.'

Rita laughed. 'Jeff thinks anything cool is something that is definitely not cool, don't you?'

Jeff wagged his finger. 'Damn right. I can't be running a hip establishment. All my regulars would be scared off if they have to stand shoulder to shoulder with men in their 20s with Amish beards and buttoned-up shirts. Record collecting is largely for socially dysfunctional men and proudly so, not for those interested in passing fads. That being said, if studenty types with awful facial hair want to give me their money, I'll force myself to take it.'

Julie turned around and handed Jeff a small video camera.

'Here, will you film us, Jeff? I want to have some record of the day. The journey there, the whole of the ceremony and some of the drunken shenanigans afterwards. This is dead easy to use. You just press that button there to record and this one to zoom in and out. Got it?'

Jeff took the small oblong device from her. 'Yup. Cool. Smile for the camera, you beautiful people.' He panned around. 'Try not to crash the car, Nick. Oh god, look at you ladies, you're both so gorgeous. We're in a car with two glamour models, Nick.'

Julie turned around and pouted at the camera, laughing. Rita was cackling too. 'Stop making me laugh, Jeff, I'll drop this bloody baby if you're not careful, I can feel it moving around. Its leg will be hanging out of us at this rate.'

'Ah ha, well, that's what reinforced knicker gussets are for, my girl, to catch surprise offspring emerging from one's lady cave,' said Jeff. The car was full of loud laughter as they turned onto Yarm Lane and came to a halt at another set of lights, before turning left onto Prince Regent Street.

It was a bright blue and white Wednesday afternoon, so bright and blue it almost made the place look good. Almost.

'Eee god, we used to go to the Incognito in there, remember?' said Rita pointing up at a faceless building across the road that had once housed one of Stockton's premier nightclubs in the late 70s and early 80s.

'God, aye. The tears that have been shed in there by lasses drunk on Pernod and black after being dumped by some awful bloke...' laughed Julie. 'I used to think it was the poshest, most sophisticated place. We used to get dressed up in full war paint to go in there when we were 16.'

'Oh god, aye, we did. Remember Pharoahs as well? That place was minging,' said Rita.

'The carpet in Pharoahs was legendary,' said Jeff. 'Your feet would stick to it. It was a form of fly paper, designed to keep you in there drinking over-priced lager.'

'You never went there, did you?' said Rita. 'They played disco. You hate disco.'

Jeff raised a finger. 'Correction, I just said I didn't like it, in order to appear manly. You cannot be a big Uriah Heep fan *and* like disco when you are 16. I mean, you can't imagine me dancing to "Boogie Wonderland", can you? It'd have been illegal. Or it damn well should have been.'

'Ha, me and you both, Jeff,' said Nick. 'Mind, the chances of hearing any rock music in either place were almost zero.'

'You occasionally got a bit of Quo and early Queen if you were lucky,' said Julie.'That was when all the lads would stand around shaking their heads.'

'This is true. The rest of the time we just sat there and drank lager and lime and then went home and dreamed of all the girls we wanted to grope, but were too shy to even talk to,' said Nick.

'Aye, they weren't the happiest nights, those, were they?' said Jeff, turning to film up the road as Terry pulled away at the lights in front of them and accelerated away up Prince Regent Street.

'Bugger, I've stalled it,' said Nick, turning the key in the ignition.

'That's the ghost of the Incog doing that,' said Jeff. 'It's trying to lure us back in for one more dance to Tavares or The Real Thing.'

The 1980s Mercedes was now well ahead of them. Nick put his foot down to catch Terry up, but as he squeezed his right toe down a little, without any warning, a large grey 12-wheel concrete mixer truck pulled off a building site on the left. It didn't indicate and without even attempting to stop or slow down, rammed into Terry's old Mercedes. With a dreadful scraping crunch and screech, it ploughed into the car, instantly buckling the passenger side doors and turning it over on its right-hand side, pushing it across the street and then flipping it onto its roof. Sparks flew everywhere as metal from the cement mixer and the car ground into the road. The mixer dwarfed the car and barely seemed slowed by it at all as it pushed the upside down wreck into a wall on the far side of the street, finally coming to a halt, buckling the driver side door as it did so.

When you witness something so dramatic, so violent and out of the ordinary, it barely seems real for a few moments. In our media age, a little part of our brains thinks it's really a special effect or a reconstruction for dramatic effect, or some kind of CGI trickery.

For those brief moments, it isn't reality, it isn't horrible, it isn't fatal, rather it is somehow fascinating and exciting. Then the truth strikes you and the awful nature of what you are witnessing dawns, as the logic and the reality constructs itself in your brain and hits home with a terrible realisation.

Four or five seconds and it was all over. There was barely even time to shout or make a noise. The cement mixer had driven off the site and into the car, crushed it, flipped it over and pushed it into a wall, all in one powerful movement. Even as Nick slammed on the breaks, threw the BMW onto the side of the road, got out and began to run towards the smoking pile of crumpled metal and spinning tyres, the only words he'd heard were Julie's and all she'd said, as the mixer had struck the Merc, in a voice hoarse with shock was, 'Oh my god. That's killed them all.'

# CHAPTER 2

Nick's mind was in a blur, he shouted to Jeff, or to anyone, 'Call 999!' He sprinted to the ruined car. The cement mixer was jammed up against it. The driver was getting out and shouting and holding his head in his hands.

'Shit, I...err...the...the...brakes...they went on me...' He was obviously east European. High cheekbones, gaunt unshaven face and fair hair.

What do you do in a situation like this? What emotional and intellectual resources do you draw on? Keep calm, that was thing. Don't freak out. Try and save anyone that can be saved. The dead are already dead. You can't help them.

'Terry! Jasmin!' shouted Nick as loudly as possible. Surely no-one could have survived this carnage. A back wheel still turned from the impact. The smell of rubber and fuel filled his nostrils. Other people, some from other cars which had been stopped by the accident, ran to the scene to try and help. All was chaos and confusion. Voices called out from all directions.

'Can anyone hear me?' he yelled.

'Nick! Help!' It was Jasmin.

'Jaz! Are you alright?'

'I'm trapped! Help!'

Nick tugged on the crumpled driver's side back door, but it was buckled and knitted together with the frame of the car. The window glass had shattered everywhere. Sirens were already approaching.

She was crumpled over on her head, pressed up against the roof of the car, but she seemed quite calm, possibly in shock but at least not in pain.

'Jaz. They'll be here in a minute.' The truck was jammed up against the driver's door.

'Tez. Tez! Are you alright?' There was a moaning and then his voice. 'Think so...'

Christ, how the hell had he dodged that bullet? The truck's full weight was pressed up against that door and had pushed him and the steering column over the gear stick. He was virtually skewered on it. But somehow, in amongst metallic origami, he'd managed to be relatively unhurt.

Now there was more moaning and groaning. It sounded like Conrad's tarry, oaky voice. The sort of noise made when someone is slipping in and out of consciousness.

The car was pushed up against the wall so he couldn't even get around to the passenger side to look in the windows at Conrad and Jackie.

'Don't try and move, just wait until the fire brigade get here,' he said, because he'd heard people say it in TV shows, not because it made any sense to him.

Julie's voice shouted from behind him.

'Is anyone alive?' she said. It was a specific choice of words. It didn't seem possible that anyone would have survived it..

'Mam? Mam! Are you there?' She called out, getting down on her hands and knees and peering into the shattered back window. But there was no reply from Jackie. Julie reached and touched Jaz. 'Just relax as much as you can, darlin'. They'll get you all out safe and sound.'

A fire engine was approaching from the other end of Prince Regent Street. Two other men were trying to help, but there was nothing that could be done. The car would need to be hoisted up carefully.

The driver was distraught, staggering around with his head in his hands.

Ricky and Kev ran up to him.

'What the fuck were you doing?' yelled Kev, pushing the man in the chest.

'If they're dead, you're dead,' shouted Ricky, jabbing a finger in the man's face.

Julie got to her feet and ran over to them, furious.

'Get back! Go on! Get back! I'm not having this. Stand back

there, you big apes! Go on! Leave him alone, this is not the time for this!' She pushed her brothers with the flat of her hand and then gestured with a finger pointing to where they'd left the cars. 'Get back over there!'

They did as they were told, as they always did when confronted with their angry sister.

Jeff came trotting up and gestured to them to join him. 'Owee, lads, let the emergency services do their stuff.'

They walked over with him to a low wall where Rita was sitting.

Nick ran around the cement truck to the front of the car and peered into the shattered windscreen. Though it was compressed, he could now see Jackie's lifeless body, draped over the seat belt like a stuffed toy. Conrad was sprawled at an angle, his back to the door, not moving. Terry was folded up in a sort of 'w' shape, blood running from glass cuts on his arm. He seemed fully conscious.

'Hey Terry!' he waved at him, feeling an instinct to try and alleviate the terrible situation with humour. 'This is a very unconventional way of parking. You must teach me how you do it. The fire engines are here. They'll have you out soon, kidda.'

He rejoined Julie. 'Jaz is OK. I think Terry is as well.' He excluded Con and Jackie from his assessment. They'd taken the brunt of the hit from the truck.

She had her hand over her mouth, her eyes blank with shock. 'She's dead, isn't she?'

'We don't know that, Jules. She's probably just knocked out.'

Two firemen ran up. 'Right, I want all of you well back,' one said. 'We'll get them out of there.'

Jeff came up as they walked back down Prince Regent Street to allow machinery in to work on the stricken car. Nick turned around. Jeff's bushy eyebrows were raised at him. Without him even voicing the question, he knew what Jeff wanted to know.

He wobbled his hand in mid-air, so that Julie couldn't see it and made a throat-cutting gesture. Jeff blinked his eyes slowly to indicate that he understood.

'Shall I call the registry office for you? Tell them what's happened?' said Jeff.

'Yeah, could you? Thanks. We obviously can't get married today. Not now,' said Nick. 'That's right, isn't it, Jules?'

'What?'

'We'll have to postpone it.'

She waved the very idea of getting married away dismissively and went back to staring at the firemen who were getting out metal cutting equipment. An ambulance pulled up along with six police cars and then two more red engines. A large crowd of people now stood around watching. The police began to usher them back and began taping off the road in both directions.

There were deep gouges in the tarmac where the torn metal of the car had scraped along it, along with scuds of gold paint from the old Merc. It was amazing anyone had survived.

'He reckoned his brakes went,' said Nick, pointing at the driver, who was now talking to a police officer and was then led away to a police car. Jeff nodded.

'I reckon he started it up, put the mixer in gear and it just took off...he obviously couldn't stop the thing,' said Jeff. 'You know what the irony of this is, don't you?'

Nick felt fuzzy-headed from the shock. 'No. What?' he said, as firemen began to try to cut open the rear door on the driver's side, where Jasmin was trapped.

Jeff flicked his hair over his shoulders and pointed at the building site. 'That's where Conrad is working. He was telling me, back at your place.'

'What? That's the building site he works as a joiner on?'

Jeff nodded and raised his index finger. 'And there's more. That site is being developed by McGull's,' he pointed at a big sign which proudly stated, 'A McGull Development - Building Teesside's Future'.

'So what?'

'This is part of that development project that was launched all across the region last year to revitalise city centre business in

Stockton, Hartlepool and the Boro. McGull's got the contract for the work from MIDO... and who is MIDO run by?'

A cold horror washed over Nick. 'Jimmy Patel. Jasmin's dad. Hang on...you're not saying that that's why this happened?'

Jeff's hands were already up in apology. 'It's just a coincidence, that's all I'm saying...for now.'

There was a crunch of metal as something, perhaps the lock in the car door was broken. Voices yelled out. He could hear Jasmin's voice clearly now. The door was popped, opened and held by one fireman. Jasmin's head emerged as she half fell, was half carried out of the car.

Nick put his arm around Julie's shoulder. 'They'll all be alright, I'm sure,' he said without any conviction he was right at all. She shook her head slowly.

'She's gone. I can feel it,' she said, flatly. 'She didn't stand a chance. That thing...' she kicked her foot towards the cement mixer '...it just mashed that side of the car.' She shook her head again. 'I just hope Jaz and Tez are alright...and Conrad too, of course. But mam's carked it. She's deffo carked it. God, I hope she didn't suffer, the poor old shitehawk. I hope she was too pissed to even know. Oh god.'

He nodded. It was as though Julie was preparing herself to face the reality by her plain speaking. He kept his arm around her.

'Can you make sure the others are all kept away? I don't want Kev and Ricky all over this. They'll only make things worse, I can't deal with them, right now.'

'Yeah, no worries.' He glanced back down Prince Regent Street. He could see them all standing in a group, smoking and looking on, but now being kept back by three police cars that had blocked off the street.

There was nothing to be said or done, apart from tell the police everything they had seen and then just wait and wait and wait for the emergency services to do their stuff. What a bloody job. All day, everyday, cutting people from wreckage, alive or dead or halfway between the two, covered in blood. Lives shattered by a moment of madness or misjudgement was their everyday working environment. What sodding heroes they were.

They carried Jasmin out first, clearly the least injured of the four of them. She could walk unaided to an ambulance. Nick and Julie were allowed up to see her.

'Jaz, darlin', how are you?' said Julie, laying a hand on her arm.

She managed a watery smile; flecks of blood from small nicks caused by broken glass looked to be her only wounds.

'I think I'm OK. I hurt all over, but I think I'm...I'm alright.' She was so small-framed and without muscle that it seemed scarcely believable that she hadn't just shattered to dust on impact. 'I think Terry is OK as well. Thank god. What the hell happened? '

As she spoke there was a commotion of voices on the other side of the fire engines. From around the side of the ambulance came a big, barrel-chested Asian man in a dark suit, dark hair swept back, hawkish, dark eyes set into deep, dark sockets surrounded by dark rings. It was like he was a moving shadow.

'Jasmin! Jasmin! My girl. Are you alright?' As soon as he saw her, he hugged her to him tightly. 'What on earth happened here? Was it that Wells boy? Tell me.'

Boy? Terry was a long way from being a boy.

'No dad. It wasn't!' she immediately protested. 'It was that cement truck!'

'You don't have to lie for him, Jasmin. We know what *his* sort are like.'

'Hey, hey...it was nothing to do with Terry,' said Julie, her brow wrinkled into a severe look. 'That truck just ploughed into the car.'

But the man, who had to be Jimmy Patel, ignored her. 'Was he drunk? Tell me, Jasmin. Has he been drinking?'

'There's no call for that, mate,' said Nick, feeling angry that this bloke had jumped to conclusions before even hearing the facts. 'Like Julie said, the cement mixer ploughed into the car without stopping. It wasn't Terry's fault.'

But Jimmy Patel was in no mood to listen. He gestured at them to walk away from Jasmin, as though they were his minions to be directed. When they didn't move he jabbed a finger at Julie and then at Nick.

'I know what you people are like. Common thieves, violent thugs and worse. Stay away from Jasmin and my family!' He turned around. 'Come on Jasmin, let's take you to a hospital.'

'I'm going with the ambulance, dad,' she protested.

A paramedic stepped forward. 'We think she's OK, Mr Patel, but it's best she gets checked out.'

'I will look after my own daughter, thank you very much,' he said in a well-spoken, clear and very pompous voice. 'Come on. Let's get you away from *these* people.'

'Hey, you've got a bloody cheek, mate,' said Nick. As he spoke Kev Wells ran up and began shouting.

'I heard what you said, Patel. You don't slag off my family like that. You'll fucking pay for that! I heard you. And leave Terry alone an' all or you know what you'll get.' He held a big, tightly gripped fist at him.

'I'm waiting for Terry, dad. Please just go away!'

She got into the back of the ambulance and sat down.

Jimmy Patel looked at Nick and then Julie and then Kev, who was now quickly joined by Ricky.

'You're nothing but trouble, you people. Nothing but trouble. I warned her what getting mixed up with this family would mean. You're the absolute scum of the earth!'

'You're a fucking nutter, pal and if you don't shut your mouth, I'll shut it for you,' yelled Ricky.

'You are nothing but foul-mouthed swine,' hissed Jimmy Patel in a hell of a temper.

'Excuse me, but my mother is in the front of that car, fighting for her life, or she may even be dead. Have a bit of respect, will you?!' said Julie, getting right into his face, her jaw jutting at him defiantly.

'Good! Good! I hope she *is* dead. One less Wells in this town is by no means a bad thing.'

Julie pulled back her arm and slapped him in the face as hard as she could.

'You pig! Nobody speaks to me like that!' she yelled.

His head was knocked back by the force of the strike, which made a noise of a whip being cracked. It was a fantastic hit, no doubt about that. Full force, right from the shoulder.

The shock on Jimmy Patel's face and then the painful sting washed through his expression, taking him from surprise to shock, to embarrassment and then fury in a second. He immediately lashed back at her with the flat of his hand, cuffing her on the left side of her jaw.

'You whore, you bitch!' he yelled, almost too angry to get the words out. Nick was so shocked by what he'd done that for a second he couldn't believe what he'd seen, but Kev and Ricky were not so slow; they pushed past him and grabbed Patel by the lapels of his suit, both of them leaning into his face, Ricky with his hand on his neck while Kev was clearly about to head butt him in the face, yelling at him and he wrestled to get free.

'You're a fucking dead man!' said Kev. Three police officers ran up and intervened, just as he was about to stick the nut on him.

'Calm down, calm down,' said one of them. 'Go away, Kev, go away Ricky,' he said, patiently, familiar with them. 'Are you alright, Julie?'

She nodded.

'I take it no-one here wants to press assault charges? Good. Now go your separate ways and behave like adults,' said the square-jawed officer in a Hartlepool accent so strong you could have used it to chop logs.

Jimmy Patel stormed off, pushing past the police officers.

'I'm sorry Jules,' said Jaz from the ambulance. 'He's a bastard.'

She let out a sigh. 'It's not your fault.'

Nick stared after Patel, wishing he'd had a chance to give him a slap. What a prick. He put his arm around Julie. 'Are you alright? Does it hurt?' Her face was a little reddened.

She shook he head. 'I've had worse. What a vile creature he is.'

Lifting gear had been put in place and the car was slowly and gently lifted onto its side and then onto its wheels with a creaking, metallic groan. As it was righted, it was easier to see the three bodies left in there. All the windows were shattered and Jackie Wells's lifeless body flopped and then slumped with the movement of the vehicle. Blood had run from a head wound, but now seemed to be congealed a little. It was a terrible sight to see her like that, floppy and lifeless. Behind her was Conrad; he seemed to be alive, his mouth agape, his eyes squinting like a man trying to sober up.

'Oh god. Poor mam,' said Julie, her hand over her mouth, as she saw her mother's body. She turned away briefly, unable to watch them force open the crushed door and with paramedics in attendance, lower the body onto a stretcher. Two of them leant over her, one put an oxygen mask over her mouth.

Nick turned to Jeff who raised his big eyebrows and gave one shake of his head. No chance. She wasn't exactly the most robust of women at the best of times, being little more than leathery skin and small bones held together by strong nicotine, cheap wine and bitter cynicism. Julie walked towards the stretcher as they took her to another ambulance.

'I'm her daughter, I'll go with her,' she said to the paramedics who nodded their approval. 'Mam. I'm coming with you.' She leant over the body as though she could hear her.

'I'll drive over to the hospital, once we're done here,' said Nick. She nodded, her face a study in grim horror.

The ambulance roared off to North Tees hospital. Nick walked down to where everyone else was gathered and told them what was happening.

'Jimmy fucking Patel, what a fucking cunt,' said Ricky, pulling on a fag.

'Yeah. He wasn't happy, like. Thought Terry was to blame,' said Nick.

'I'd like to twat him until he stopped fucking twitching,' said Kev with a cold menace.

'Tez is alright though, isn't he?' said Ricky.

'Yeah. I think so. He's moving. They'll have him out in a bit. Jackie isn't so good...you might have to prepare yourself for some bad news lads...she got hit the hardest.'

They were expressionless. Death was nothing to these blokes. It really wasn't. They were not afraid of it in the slightest, not for themselves, nor for anyone else. That was what made them hard bastards. The preciousness and fragility of life that was a given in regular people's lives just didn't seem to mean anything to them.

'The mixer driver says his brakes went,' said Nick.

'Is he an Ivan? said Kev.

'Russian? No, Lithuanian, I'd guess.'

'Same fucking thing,' he said, coldly, blue eyes narrowed. 'You reckon mam's snuffed it, Nick?'

'She wasn't conscious. More than that...I dunno. She didn't look good Kev. Jules will let you know when you can go over there.'

'So who do you think is responsible, Nick?' said Ricky. He knew why he was asking. They were already, instinctively, planning some sort of revenge. It was all they knew.

'I think it was just an accident, man,' said Nick.

'Fuck off. That's no accident,' Ricky said, with a snort, a sneer and a nasty laugh, pointing at the carnage up the road. 'He fucking did that on purpose. I fucking saw it happen.'

'Aye, Rick's right. If his brakes have gone, he could have steered it away from Terry's Merc at some point. When he knew he was going to hit it, he could have swung it round on a hard left or hard right. But he didn't, he ploughed on and pushed them up against that fucking wall.' Kev threw the fag down and trod it into the pavement. 'I'm telling you now, that was fucking deliberate.'

'That cunt's getting it, him and Patel,' said Ricky, always the most hot-headed of the two.

'You can't say that, man. You've got to let the police work out what happened,' said Nick, realising that they might beat the bloke to death and ask questions later. 'It could have been an accident,. You don't know. It could have been.'

They didn't seem convinced.

27

'There's nothing you can do now, anyway. He'll be taken down to the station for questioning,' said Nick.

Soon the fire brigade opened the old Merc up like a tin can and took out Conrad and Terry.

'Terry! Are you OK?' shouted Nick as he was helped up the step into the ambulance. He seemed dazed and not quite all there, but he managed to put a thumb up.

'He'll be OK,' said Jeff.

'Yeah, deffo,' agreed Rita.

'He looks like he's going in and out,' said Jeff as they lowered Conrad onto a stretcher. He was definitely alive and was moving and saying random words, but exactly how alive wasn't obvious.

Nick rubbed his face. Two hours ago they were having a laugh and looking forward to a great day. Now this. It had shattered everything.

As the bodies were taken away, the police began to clean up the road and make it ready for traffic again. That was their main concern, keep the traffic flowing. God forbid anyone should be inconvenienced for long by someone's pain and suffering.

He turned to Jeff and Rita. 'Youse two can get off home,' said Nick. 'I'm going to the hospital to see Jules and find out if her mam is brown bread yet.'

'OK man, give us a call with an update when you can,' said Jeff.

Nick went over to Ricky and Kev. 'Wait to hear from Jules before you do anything, right? The hospital won't want a load of people in there. She'll ring you when there's any news. Right?'

'Alright mate,' said Kev, chewing at his cheek.

He left them and drove the three miles to the hospital. As he was pushing money into the parking meter, feeling it was deeply wrong to be charged for comforting people who were injured or ill, he couldn't help but think of his mother, who had died so recently. He'd visited her so often in this hospital, so many, many times that the place felt haunted by her. He'd stopped hearing her voice inside his head in the last few weeks, but here, her presence felt palpable once again. The antiseptic smell mixed with the odour of boiled cabbage and bed linen, the scuffed corridors and coloured lines on the ground. It all said mother. He made a low moan in his throat. Christ, he needed a bloody drink.

He found Julie sitting in a waiting area on the first floor. She was sipping from a cup of coffee and looked pale.

'Hey lady,' he said, with a thin smile. 'How's Jackie?'

She blew out air. 'She's alive. Somehow, who knows how, she's alive. No-one knows how she survived. They think she's got a broken pelvis and loads of other things...' she waved a hand.

'Christ. I thought she was a goner. I thought she'd died in the car.'

'I did as well. I thought that was it. I mean, don't get me wrong, she's totally fucked. She's unconscious and battered to buggery, but at least the old shitehawk is still with us. She must be the undead. There's no killing her.'

He put his arm across her back and rubbed between her shoulder blades a little.

'And what about Terry?'

'They're cleaning him up. He need some stitches. I'm just waiting to hear what they're doing with him and with Conrad as well. He seems the least physically damaged, but he hit his head on the frame of the car and knocked himself out.' She let out a wavering, tense breath. 'What a bloody thing to happen and what a bloody time for it to happen.'

'Yeah. Amazing coincidence, as well.'

'Coincidence?'

'Well the mixer was from the building site that Con is working on.'

'Really. Huh. The bloke seemed upset though, didn't he? I'm sure it wasn't his fault. I bet the vehicle was faulty, like he said.'

'Yeah. Ricky and Kev were...'

'...wanting someone to blame?'

'Yeah.'

'I'll ring them in a bit and tell them to call the dogs off.'

'I said you would, like.'

She took his hand. 'I was really looking forward to today and to getting wed and to our night of passion.'

'Well, we'll never forget it now, will we? Does Conrad have any family who should know where he is?'

She looked at him and shrugged. 'I've no idea, y'know. I don't know much about him except that he's been in the building trade all his life and he's obviously from Newcastle.'

'Where does he live?'

She stared into the middle distance. 'I don't even know that. We've only met him a few times and he never talks about that, does he?'

'He seems a cheerful soul, always up for a laugh.'

'Aye. And mam seems keen on him. Poor old bugger. Mind, he's strong as an ox, so I reckon he'll be alright.'

They sat quietly. It wasn't busy, but it seemed overheated and Nick soon found himself nodding off, so went in search of coffee. Downstairs there was a cafeteria which felt like a motorway service station. The people in there were a mix of relations of patients and hospital workers, all just passing through, one way or another. A mixture of bored, worried and happy.

He got them both a black coffee. When he got back, a nurse was talking to Julie.

'This is Nick, my fiancé,' she said as he came up and put the coffee down.

'Hello. I was just telling Julie, her mother is stable now, but very unwell. There's not likely to be any change in the next few hours, so you can get off home if you want. Pop in tomorrow evening or give us a ring for an update. She'll be sedated for a while yet, at least until all her x-rays and tests are back. If we bring her out, she'll be in a lot of pain. The shock is the dangerous thing at her age.'

'How's Conrad?' said Nick.

'Mr Scott?' Nick realised he didn't even know Scott was his surname. 'He's bruised his head and has concussion, but he's being readied for a bed on a ward and he'll be fine. He's got some neck pain and his heart was a little irregular, but nothing to be concerned about. The same goes for Terry, your brother. We'd like to keep him in overnight, but I think he'll be fine to leave in the morning. He's got cuts and bruises but is basically OK.' She gave them a reassuring nod and a kindly smile.

'And Jasmin?'

The nurse looked at a sheet of paper on a clipboard.

'She's already been discharged...or rather she's left...she was collected by her father within 10 minutes of arriving. Paramedics said she seemed shocked, but was physically fine. We wanted to do an assessment of course, but we can't keep people here by force. So that's you up to date.'

'Can we look in on Terry?' said Julie.

'Yes, of course. I'll let you know when he's all set. Shouldn't be long for him or Conrad.'

They sat back down to wait again.

'She was so nice,' said Julie. 'Imagine what it'd be like if we were sitting here worrying about having enough medical insurance to pay the bills, like in America. I still like to pretend to myself that this whole thing runs on a few drops of altruism and not on the drive to make profits and huge wages for the managers, even though I know that's increasingly not true.'

'Making profit out of illness seems little short of evil,' said Nick, arms folded. 'I can't think of anything less altruistic and more exploitative. I don't know how we've got away from thinking anything different.'

She sighed. 'We seem to know the price of everything and the value of nothing. It never used to be like that. Mam's generation knew. These days it's like everything, even health, is a commodity to be bought and sold. Every illness is a chance to make your bottom line look better.'

'Talking bottom lines, I'd like a pair of the pyjama-style outfits they all wear these days. In green if they've got it,' he said, watching as a nurse came by in a pale blue top, loose, elasticated pants and lightweight canvas shoes. 'I never understood the pervy thing about dressing up as a nurse. Why a nurse? It's just a skirt and a shirt, isn't it? I mean, what's so sexy about that over and above anything else?'

She snorted an approximation of a laugh and picked a crust from the corner of her eye. 'No, that one is a mystery to me as well. Same goes for firemen. Why do women fancy men in uniforms?'

'They probably don't. They just say they do because it's expected, along with thinking pink is a female colour.'

'Well, you're not without your inclinations, are you? As I was going to indulge this evening.'

'Aye, but that's really only because it's you. It's all about you, Jules, not what you've got on or haven't got on, per se.'

'My god, I've got you trained well. That was just about the most PC excuse I've heard of for perving. Good work, Guymer.' She gave him a sly sideways grin. It was nice to see: a shaft of normalcy in amongst the chaos and upset.

Half an hour later the nurse returned and led them into a ward. Terry was sitting up in bed in a white hospital gown. He had a few laceration wounds from glass on his arm and neck, a big dark bruise on his right cheek and a cut in his leg.

'Hey sis...'

She leant over the bed and hugged him. 'I'm bloody glad to see you again, Tezza. I thought that mixer had made jam out of you.'

'Nah. I was bloody lucky, though. Those old Mercs are built like armoured tanks. If we'd been in a Ford we'd all be brown bread. They told us mam is still out of it, like. I thought she was dead. Honest to god. When they tipped the car back up and I could see her properly, I thought she'd snuffed it. Where's Jaz?'

'Her dad has discharged her, but she's OK,' said Julie, sitting down on the edge of the bed.

'Her fucking father. I hate him. I thought I heard his voice when the fire brigade first came. I'll call her in a bit.'

'Yeah, he did turn up. Kicked off a bit. I hit him in the face, he hit me in the face. We sent him packing. But he probably came straight over here and picked her up,' said Julie, pleased to see Terry so sparky already. The Wells family were such tough, gnarly buggers. Even Terry, who was the least beefy, least macho, least alpha male of the three brothers, already seemed to be brushing off his close shave with death. Bruises and cuts aside, he seemed like his normal self, as though nearly dying was just par for the course. You had to admire it. They all had, Julie included, an iron-hard resilience to the ill winds that life threw at them which Nick envied.

'This really messed up your wedding, didn't it?' said Terry apologetically.

'We can get married another day. It doesn't matter,' said Julie.

'Aye, I suppose so. The nurse told me Con is alright an' all. They've got him in the next ward. We were sodding lucky, y'know. Only mam got battered by that truck. Just luck really. Luck and quality German engineering.'

'I'll go through and see the old fella then,' said Nick, 'just for a minute or two.'

Julie smiled at him. She'd got some of her colour back and lost some of the tension in her shoulders.

The adjacent ward had six beds in it. It was exactly like the one his mother had spent so many years in, on and off. If she'd been sitting up reading a magazine in the corner, he'd not have been surprised.

A nurse had just brought Conrad a cup of tea. He was sitting up, looking none the worse for wear apart from an egg-sized bump the colour of a Victoria plum on his forehead. His bright blue eyes smiled at him as he approached

'Aye aye, kidda. Come to see the auld bugger, have ya?'

'How are you feeling, then?'

'I'm alright. More than can be said for Jackie, though. Mind, I thought she'd got away when the bloody thing hit us.'

Nick smiled inwardly. He'd always loved the old Geordie expression 'got away', meaning dying - as though existence was something which held you, from which you could be freed.

'They'll sort her out, I'm sure. She's a tough old bird is Jackie, like.'

'Aye. She is and they tell me she'll be OK in the long run, so that's the main thing, isn't it? It's a terrible thing to happen, but it could have been worse,' said Conrad.

Nick sat on the edge of the bed as Con drank his tea.

'Mind, this wasn't a bloody accident, son. You know that, don't you?'

'Come again?'

'As soon as I saw it coming towards us, I knew...'

'Knew what?'

'That it wasn't an accident. I reckon they've definitely tried to kill us.'

He said it quite matter-of-factly and didn't seem overly bothered by this.

'Who has?'

He supped at the tea again, relishing it. 'Now, that's more tricky.'

'Jeff immediately spotted the truck came off the building site you're working on...'

'Correct.'

'...and that it's a McGull development which was awarded the contract by the MIDO...'

'...which is run by Jimmy Patel. Aye, aye, I knaw, I knaw. I've been piecing it together ever since I was in that bloody car. What's more, me and Paddy McGull, chairman of McGull Developments, go way, way back. That's how I got the job on the site.'

'But the driver of the cement truck said his brakes had gone. He was really cut up about it.'

'Brakes gone? So that what he's saying? That's rubbish, man. He could have at least tried to steer away from us if that'd happened, but he didn't. I knaw, I saw it all, it was all on our side of the car. Listen, in 1976 I was driving a 10-wheel wagon down the A1 and my brakes went as I was approaching Dishforth roundabout - you're too young to remember Dishforth roundabout, but it was a right bugger because it was always a bottle neck...'

'...I do remember it, as it happens. It was still there until the mid or even late 80s.'

'Whatever. Anyways, me brakes had gone. Totally knackered. I could've ploughed into traffic, but I didn't. I turned the truck into the verge and ended up in the ditch. Point is, son, I was going faster than that lad in the mixer was and I still managed to avoid crashing. Even if he didn't have time to avoid hitting us, he could've tried and he never did. He just bloody mowed into us. He's been told to do that. That's why. He's been told to try and kill us all and make it look like an accident.'

Nick looked at him and wondered if he was in his right mind. He seemed to be enjoying spinning the story. He was full of shit, surely. He was a storyteller.

'Why the hell would anyone want to do that, Conrad?'

'I don't know, do I?' He finished his tea and wiped his mouth. 'But you're going to find out for us.'

'Me? Why me? How?'

'Jackie's already told us you're a clever lad. You want to find out who tried to kill your Julie's mam, don't you? Now, first people you need to talk to are the Cavanis.'

Nick shook his head. 'Who?'

'The Cavanis, they're a...'

'...gangster family in Newcastle Yeah, actually, I do know,' said Nick, remembering Jeff had mentioned one of them being a record collector.

'Correct. Now, I've done a lot of work for them over the years and I might, only might, mind, have given them cause to be a little bit cross with us.'

'Tell me you've not screwed them over, Con, please.'

'I've not. I did accidentally on purpose lose a few dozen bottles of whiskey once and err...I saw an opportunity to resell some paint they were doing this place up with in the Toon, like.'

'Christ almighty, Con. Why did you do that?'

'It's not major stuff. I was short for the weekend, wasn't I?'

'And when was this?'

'Earlier this year.'

'Well, they'd have tried to kill you before now if they'd wanted to, wouldn't they?'

'Mebees they didn't knaw I was down here.'

'It's only 45 miles Con, not 4,500.'

'No, but see, if it's not them, they'll like as not know who it is. They've got their fingers in loads of things them, especially in the building game. If there's a price on my head, I want to know about it.'

'You're just some gadgee, Con, not Billy the Kid.' Nick looked at the old sod. He was tricky old bird. With twinkling eyes and a wonky, roguish grin, it was hard to take him seriously.

'Look, if it was just me they were after then fair enough, but it involves Tezza and that lovely lass Jasmin as well as Julie's mam, doesn't it? They've tried to get them. So next time you're up in Newcastle, the Cavanis run the Toon Trattoria down on the quayside, there's a good lad.'

'If they did try and kill you, why would they tell me the truth? I mean, they wouldn't, would they? I could be the police.'

That seemed to puzzle Conrad for a minute. He sat and thought, his brown skin looking like an old leather suitcase. 'You've got me there. You'll just have to use your initiative.'

Nick sat and thought. This was stupid. He was having a laugh, wasn't he? He was a dreamer and a spinner of yarns. One of those blokes who you don't believe 80 per cent of what comes out of his mouth.

'Mind, I wouldn't trust that Jimmy Patel as far as I could spit him, nor Paddy McGull, they could be up to something. Either way, I'm going to sue the arse off them for this.'

'Jimmy isn't going to hurt his own daughter, is he?'

'They're a funny lot, the Asians. They don't like their lasses. They're not above killing them one way or another if they've dishonoured the family.'

Nick ignored the racist generalisation. 'I'll see what I can do, Con.' He got up, not wanting to disappoint him, but basically

36

trying to invent a reason to ignore him. 'I'm glad you're feeling OK.'

Nick went back to Julie sitting on Terry's bed.

'How is the old bugger?' she said.

'Fine. A bit shook up maybe, but he'll be OK.'

Terry blew out air. 'He's a lucky get, him.'

'How well do you know him, Tez?'

'Con? Err...I've met him a few times, but I don't *know* him, like.'

'What do you make of him?'

'He's a canny old soul. Dodgy as fuck though, obviously.'

'Watch your language in here, Terry,' admonished Julie, with a frown, looking around at the other patients.

'What makes you say that?' said Nick.

'Well you can just tell. He's one of those building gadgees who is basically always on the move. Works for cash-in-hand and goes from one site to another like a gypo. As far as I can tell, he's been like that all his life.'

'Where does he live, do you know?' asked Julie.

'Aye. He lives in a knackered old house off Norton Road with half a dozen other blokes who work on the site. It's a doss house, really. The sort of place contractors put east Europeans up in.'

'That's terrible. He's in his 60s,' said Julie.

'I know. He's hard sod though, isn't he?' said Terry, with admiration. 'It's all he's known. Mind, I did wonder if it's why he's hooked up with mam. Plenty of room in the old house for him. You couldn't blame him.'

Nick rubbed his arm. 'Tez, he reckons that someone has tried to kill you four. He thinks it's not an accident. What do you reckon to that?'

Julie looked at him in disbelief. 'He's kidding you, isn't he?'

Nick shook his head. Terry looked less surprised, possibly because in the world he was brought up in, conspiracies about who was trying to get at whom were all standard stuff.

'Gadgees like him make a lot of enemies, don't they?' he said. 'They go on the rob, they shag someone's missus, you know...so it is possible. Who does he reckon is after him?'

'He doesn't know. Some Newcastle crime family, maybe.'

'The Cavanis?'

'Yeah.'

'They're into everything, them lot.'

'I've heard of them, I think. Who are they?' said Julie.

'They run restaurants mostly, but they've got investments in all sorts of things. Kev will tell you about them. He was in Durham with the loony they sent round if you didn't cough up the protection money on your shop. He's still inside for that, I think. Vicious, he was.'

'Sounds like a charmer,' said Julie.

'They're a weird family, by all accounts. Some of them are Grade A nutters, some of them are alright. They're mostly into extortion and people reckon they do a lot of blackmailing and that. Still, I can't see them trying to crush Con into Prince Regent Street.' He coughed and rubbed his sore shoulder. 'If they wanted him dead they'd just shoot him and dump him in the river.' He said it so casually. 'I think it was an accident meself, like. All I know is there's nothing I could do to avoid it - it just came off that site and drove straight into us, I tried to put my foot down as soon as it struck the car, but it was too late and that thing was fucking huge, like.'

Julie looked around and put her finger to her mouth again. 'Language, Tez. You're not in the club now.'

'Sorry, Jules.'

It was funny how she was matriarch to all three brothers and the only one capable of exercising any degree of control over them.

'Right, we'll get off. I'll come in tomorrow morning and see how you all are,' she said. 'They reckon mam will be kept sedated for a while, until they work out what's broken.'

Terry nodded. 'They've probably got to wait for her to sober up. Seriously man, she was nodding out on the way over as it was. Pissed as a...err...she was drunk, like. Sorry, Jules. It was your big day an' all.'

'We can have another big day, can't we?' she said, ruffling his hair.

'Take it easy, kid,' said Nick with a wave.

As they got to the car, Julie turned and put her arms around him in a tight hug. They held each other for a minute in the soft light of a late summer early evening. What a nightmare.

# CHAPTER 3

Back home it had the melancholic feel of a place all set for a party that wasn't going to happen. They got changed out of their suits into jeans and t-shirts.

The fridge was full of booze and party food.

'We can't eat and drink all this,' said Julie pulling the door open and staring at the piles of samosas, sausage rolls, mini pork pies and cans of beer. 'I wonder if we could take it to a homeless shelter or something? It shouldn't go to waste.'

'Aye there's that place on Bath Lane. We'll cart it over there in the morning.'

'I'm due into the Teesside Women Centre at 9.00am, can you do it? I'll take the spare beer and wine into work. They can use it for functions and such.'

'Aye, of course.' He made some tea while Julie sat replying to texts and emails from well-wishers who assumed they'd be man and wife by now. He loaded the cans into a box along with some red wine. He looked at a bottle of New Zealand Pinot Noir, one of his old favourites. Lovely and full-bodied and yet soft. A glass of it would go down nicely.

'There, that's everyone brought up to date,' she said, throwing down the phone. 'Sometimes I hate communication devices. We just used to meet up 'round someone's house or down the pub and that's how we told everyone our news. Now you've got to reiterate it for everyone about 20 times over. It's all very tedious.'

'If I could live without a mobile phone, I would. If we went back to the technology we had in 1973 I bet we wouldn't be any less happy.'

'Probably. As long as I don't have to go back to wearing sweaty nylon knickers or having brushed nylon bed sheets.'

As she spoke his phone vibrated. He made a face at her. 'See, if it was 1973, we'd still be having a nice chat, uninterrupted.' He peered at it. 'It's Jeff...hi, mate.'

'Now then. Just ringing you for an update. Are you still at North Tees?'

Nick brought him up to date and told him about Conrad and his idea about the Cavanis.

'Well, I'll tell you what,' said Jeff. 'Why don't you tag along with me tomorrow? I could do with someone to ride shotgun and we'll ask Eddie if he knows Conrad, and if he does, what he reckons to him. He's not going to say, "Oh yeah, we've just tried to kill him", but we'll get an idea. Personally, I think yer man is raving there. The Cavanis have their psychotic element, but I've never heard of them killing anyone. Not even a rumour of it. Violence and breaking shit up with a baseball bat, yeah, they do that. But no-one ever said they'd killed anyone. Eddie sort of implied they get most of their money from taking a cut out of various business and also from blackmail. They're a Newcastle crime family, not the actual Mafia. And if they were going to bump anyone off, would it really be an old bloke like Conrad? No, it wouldn't. Conrad loves a good story, doesn't he? It's an accident, but it's more glamorous if someone's trying to whack him. That's all it is.'

'OK, I'll come up with you. Can you pick me up? I've got to take all this party food to the homeless shelter first.'

'Alright, Batman. I'll be at yours for half eight in the morning. I'm meeting Eddie at 10.15am at this shop on High Bridge.'

As Nick was talking to him, Julie's phone rang and she took the call and walked out into the back garden.

'OK, big man, I'll see you tomorrow.'

He poured the Sencha green tea into two white china mugs, took them outside and set them down on a white wrought-iron table. Julie was walking around the perimeter of their lawn. He'd cut it recently and it still had that invigorating smell of freshly mown grass. She was twirling a long strand of her blonde hair around her left index finger and then stood, resting on one hip.

The sunny afternoon had turned into an overcast evening and a northwesterly wind was bringing rain. In the distance, the Cleveland Hills were already covered in low cloud. Even though it was early September, an autumnal feel was in the air. The rowan trees in the hedgerows were already covered in red berries, blackberry bushes were littered with ripening fruit and the big chestnut tree along the track from their house had tinges of rust and yellow to its leaves. Summer didn't seem to last long in the northeast, even in a good year.

Nick sipped at the tea and took in the peaceful, rural scene, wondering how long they would live there. It had already been over two years since they'd moved in. It was good living in the countryside and he felt it had been very positive for his depression and his moods in general, but he did find himself wondering if they couldn't have more fun if they got a place in town, especially now that he was feeling mentally healthier than at any time in his adult life, thanks to his drugs.

She rang off, picked some lavender and came towards him, sniffing at it as she did so, letting out a small groan as she sat down.

'Who was that?'

'Martha at Teesside Women. She was a bit reluctant to call because she thought we'd be having the reception. Then she got my email explaining what happened. It's good news, really. They're sending me to a refuge as the first part of my training to be a Women's Support Worker. It's a week long.'

'Oh, right. Well, that's good, isn't it? All part of getting a full time job with them, eventually.'

She nodded. 'Hopefully, aye. As long as they get their lottery funding later in the year. And if I'm any good. This is just one part of the training over a couple of years. Trouble is, it's residential.'

'Residential?'

'I've got to stay in the refuge in the west of Newcastle for a week. I sit in on all the classes and meetings. I've also got to start training in the Freedom Programme as well.'

'And you can't commute?'

'It wouldn't be practical because there's evening work and early starts. I'd be flying up and down the A19 just to come home to sleep for a few hours. Anyway, I think they see being there as commitment to the cause.'

'Well, that's fine. It's only a week. You'll enjoy a break from me tugging at your nightie and making a rod for your back.'

'Ha, ha. Yeah, there is that.'

'So when's this happening?'

'I'm due up there on Saturday.'

'Bugger. That means you'll miss the Ipswich game.'

'I know. Nowt I can do, though. I fancy us to win that an' all. 3-1, I'm going for.'

'I love your confidence. It's been a good start to the season for a change. Won three, lost one, drawn one.'

'Aye. I hope they keep Southgate as manager. I like him and his massive nose.'

'They'd be mad to get rid now, I reckon. So where's the place?'

'Fenham in Newcastle. Near Leazes Park.'

'Oh yeah, I know. I used to have a mate who lived around there. A journo who worked on *The Journal*. I used to sit next to him in the press box. He died before he was 60. Heart attack.'

'Watching Newcastle United does that to you.'

'I'm tagging along with Jeff tomorrow. He's checking out that possible new store on High Bridge. The estate agent is Eddie Cavani - of the Cavani nutter family. He wanted a bit of support and I thought I'd see if he knew Conrad.'

'That's nice of you to go with Jeff, but don't go getting mixed up in anything. I'm sure Conrad is full of shit. I mean, I like him, but he's obviously full of shit, isn't he?'

'Oh yeah. I wouldn't believe the detail of anything he told me. I'm sure he's just deluded or being mischievous in this murder plot thing. I'm excited for Jeff, though. It's cool having a mate who has lots of record shops. In fact, I literally can't think of anything cooler.'

She grinned. 'Yeah, I'm really proud of him. He seems to have really found his feet since the heart attack and now meeting Rita and having a bairn. Good on him. She is huge, by the way.'

43

'I know, I was saying that to him. He thinks it'll be a C-Section because it'll be too big to come out the front bottom.'

'Makes me feel queasy just thinking about it.'

They sat in the quiet and watched the house martins swooping around and sitting on telegraph wires in big groups, as they prepared for the long flight to Africa. It was a sign that summer was really over and the darker, cooler days of autumn lay ahead.

'Do you fancy moving?' said Nick.

She turned to look at him, surprised. 'Moving? That's come out of the blue. I thought you loved it here.'

'I do. It is lovely. Though we have had some shit times here, as well as good. Maybe get a fresh start somewhere else?'

'Where would we move to?'

'I don't know. Sometimes I miss not being in town and being able to slip out for a coffee or something, but then, I do love the peace and quiet here.'

'Yeah, but you lived in Harrogate, which is a lovely town; living in Stockton wouldn't be as nice, would it? I mean, I'm a big fan of Stockton, but it's a bit bloody rough compared to where you lived, down there.'

'Aye. It was just a thought. The great thing about renting is that we can flit from place to place as and when we want.'

'True. But work is a bit up in the air for me at the moment. And we're so skint we probably couldn't even get a deposit together.'

'Oh yeah, I forgot about that. Alright, forget I said anything about it. Shall we get an early night? I'm exhausted after everything and I'll have to be up early for Jeff.'

'Good idea. You don't want to have a big session though, do you?'

He gave her a weary smile. 'Can we save it for when we've had a happier day? Not even I feel like it after all this.'


'It's like I said, blokes like Con are, in their own way, rock 'n' rollers,' said Jeff, as he drove them up the A19 to Newcastle in his white transit van, after dropping off the spare food to the homeless centre. 'So it wouldn't surprise me if he's got up to all sorts over the years.'

'I like an old fella who's lived a bit,' said Luke, who ran Jeff's shop in Harrogate and had driven up to Jeff's early. 'Better than a boring old bastard who's gone nowhere and done nowt.'

He was a skinny, pock-faced lad in his early 20s with long, lank hair and unpleasant, skinny jeans worn with an old Pearl Jam t-shirt.

'You're not wrong, Lukey.'

'Do you fancy working up in Newcastle then, Luke?' said Nick as they went past the turn off for Chester-le-Street.

'I dunno. All my mates are down in Harrogate and Leeds so I'd be on me own a bit, but then people say Newcastle is a good place to live if you like drinking and rock 'n' roll and I fucking love both of them, so I reckon I'd survive.'

'If we get this shop, I'll need you to help us set it up.' said Jeff. 'And you'll need to help me pick a manager to run it. Get the right sort in. And you'll have to train him up, as well.'

'He? What if a woman applies for the job?' said Nick.

Jeff looked at him with weary disdain. 'Take your tampon out, Germaine. What do you think the chances of that are? I'll tell you, about a million to one.'

'You never know.'

'Oh, I'd employ a lass to run it in a heartbeat, but women and second-hand record shops are not a natural mix, are they? Rita thinks the Stockton shop is a vortex of bacteria. She won't go near the place. Says it smells of old men and death.'

'She's got a point. It does, like,' said Luke. 'That's why I like it, though.'

'It'll be different in Newcastle, though. You've got a lot more students and a bigger, broader customer base, some of whom will have a womb,' said Nick.

'Yeah, you might be right. We'll just have to see who turns up. Someone who has got big computer skills would be useful. Anyway, I don't even know if I'm taking it yet.'

'So does this Cavani bloke own the empty shop?'

'No man, he's an estate agent. He's the respectable Cavani. His brothers and cousins are the heed-the-balls.'

'There's always one in every criminal family who refuses to get with the programme, isn't there?' said Luke, in his broad West Yorkshire accent.

'Must be a great disappointment to his family,' said Nick. 'C'mon son, just kick one head in for me. No dad, I'm not so much as breaking a single finger. I'm a peace-loving man.'

'Ha, well, I dunno about that,' said Jeff.

'I think I sold him a Spanish copy of *Let It Be* the other month. Picture sleeve. He made me play it in the shop before he'd cough the money for it,' said Luke. 'Cheeky git. When we say it's in excellent condition, then it is. We pride ourselves on that, don't we, big man?'

'Aye. Anyone selling records that are worth a few quid plays them to check the condition, or they should.'

Nick laughed to himself. In the three years Jeff and Luke had worked together they seemed to have had a mind-meld and turned into something of a double act, both agreeing with the other on the way to run a second-hand record shop.

They parked on a meter in the city centre and walked down Grey Street, taking a right onto High Bridge. It was a small, narrow street which had always been home to independent clothes shops and pubs. Nick had drank in the Duke of Wellington pub that sat centrally on the narrow road, when he and Jeff had been students in the late 70s and early 80s.

The unit had been a shoe shop, selling designer gear and had recently gone bust. It had a big plate glass window, but was quite small inside. They peered in.

'Is this big enough, Jeff? It looks small to me,' said Nick.

'There's another room about the same size at the back apparently,' said Jeff.

'That'll be plenty big enough then,' said Luke. We'll get 12,000 records in there, easy, maybe 15.'

'Jeff!' A Geordie voice called out. They turned around. A man in a fine-cut blue Italian suit and white silk shirt grinned at him.

'Alright Eddie. I dig the threads. Is this you in your work clothes?'

'Gotta look the part.' He held out the jacket. It had a gold satin lining.

'This is Luke and Nick. So this is the shop, eh? It's in a good position.'

Eddie opened it up and gathered up the junk mail that had been pushed through since the last store had closed.

'It gets incredible foot fall.'

'Or, more accurately, foot stagger, as they come out of the Duke of Welly,' said Jeff, tugging at his beard.

'Aye, well, if I tried to tell you that you won't get a few piles of vomit on your doorstep now and then, you'd know I was lying to you. You know what this town is like.'

'I have added my fair share of vomit to the doorways of Newcastle, back in the day, like,' said Jeff.

The floor was stripped wooden boards. Through the back was another slightly bigger rectangular room, lit by strip lights. There was literally nothing in the space at all and nothing whatsoever to see. Some spaces have a good feeling and some have a bad feeling, apropos of absolutely nothing. Why was that? Why did you feel comfortable in some rooms and not in others? Whatever the reason, Nick felt good in this space. It just felt right. He could imagine it as a record store. In fact, it felt destined to be a record store.

'You've got to take this Jeff. It's just right,' he said.

'Aye. We're 'avin' it,' added Luke, nodding his head and looking around.

'It seems my wives have made up their minds for me, Eddie,' said Jeff, flicking his hair over his shoulders.

'Honest, man, you get thousands past here every day. You know what it's like on a Saturday. It's jam packed. And you get some top-quality fanny down here, on their way through to the Bigg

Market.'

'That does it. Get the bloody papers signed, Jeff,' said Luke, pushing at the big man. They all laughed.

'So it's still the price you gave me by email?' said Jeff.

Eddie Cavani nodded. 'You'll clean up in here. I'm telling you. The last shop was selling expensive shoes. Never had the market to survive. But you'll get all sorts.'

'Right. Let's go and do it then,' said Jeff, clapping his hands together. 'How soon can I move in?'

'If you cough out the money today, you can be in as soon as you want.'

'I have the wherewithal, my good man.'

Eddie Cavani looked pleased. 'I wish all my customers were as decisive as you, Jeff. Let's go and do the paperwork.'

They walked out of High Bridge, down to the office at the bottom of Grey Street. As they went Nick walked alongside the estate agent.

'Eddie. Do you by any chance know an old Geordie fella called Conrad Scott? Tall lad in his 60s. He's a joiner.'

Eddie Cavani laughed. 'Why are you asking about that auld rascal?'

'I just came across him the other day. He mentioned your lot. He's quite a character.'

'Aye, you can say that again.' He cracked his knuckles and laughed again. 'What's he got up to now?'

'Well, he almost got himself killed. A cement truck ran into the car he was in. He's in hospital now.'

Cavani tilted his head to one side and shrugged. 'Poor old bugger. It'd take a truck to kill him. He's as tough as old boots.'

'He said he used to work for your family.'

'He did. On and off for a few years. Mostly in the night clubs and restaurants. He's a bloody good joiner, and a bloody good drinker. That's his problem.'

'Thing is, he has a daft notion that someone is out to kill him.'

Cavani laughed. 'Does he now? Wouldn't surprise me at all. He's probably pissed off a lot of people over the years, but I always liked him. Strong as anyone you'll meet, as well. He could lift crates of beer bottles all day long. I wondered what had happened to him. Hadn't seen him for a few months now.'

'Any idea who might want to hurt him, though?'

They stopped at the offices of Richardson and Franks and went in. There were three rows of desks with neatly dressed men and women sitting behind them.

'I wouldn't know. Why don't you ask Mike at the Trattoria? He might have an idea. He paid him. Right, sit down, Jeff, and we'll get this sorted. You lads might want to step out for a beer. This is boring work.'

'Bloody good idea. Come on, Nick,' said Luke.

'I'll call you when we're done,' said Jeff, sitting down at Eddie's desk.

They crossed the road and walked down Dean Street.

'You get yourself a beer in the Crown Posada - it's one of Newcastle's old-school boozers. I'm just going down to Cavani's place.'

'Sounds like an Italian name, Cavani.'

'Yeah, I think they are originally. Though I think it's more usually Uruguayan - like Edinson Cavani, the footballer who plays for Palermo, and as far as I know the Cavani family have been here for a few generations.'

He left Luke at the pub and walked down past the old Guildhall, round the corner to the Toon Trattoria, a bog standard pasta and pizza place.

'Table for one is it, pet?' said a buxom young woman, her large bulbous breasts straining out of a tight bra under a white shirt. Her nipples stuck out prominently. They were very distracting breasts, thrusting up and out at him like two fat, smooth, round animals topped with a big, hard button.

'Is Mike in? Eddie said I was to come down and see him.'

'Mike? Aye, that's him at the bar through there, pet.'

'Cheers.'

49

He walked past the tables to a small bar which acted as a holding point for punters waiting for tables. Mike Cavani was very like his younger brother apart from a bigger, broken nose and a receding hairline. They shared the same dark, olive-skinned, very smooth, handsome looks.

'Hi, Mike,' he said, holding out his hand. He looked at him. 'I'm Nick Guymer. My pal Jeff is a mate of Eddie's. He sent me down here.'

A reference to a family member seemed to be enough for him to pull out a stool.

'Can I get you a drink?' he said, in a far less Geordie voice than his brother.

'Just a sparkling water, thanks.'

He got off his stool, went behind the small bar and took a bottle of San Pellegrino out of the fridge and pushed it at him.

'So what brings you down here, Nick?'

'I was asking Eddie about this old bloke I know called Conrad Scott. Do you know him?'

Mike Cavani smiled right away. 'So he's down on Teesside, is he? That's where you're from, judging by your accent. Let me guess, you're from Stockton, you've not got the full Chris Rea.'

'Good guess, Mike. Thing is, a cement mixer ploughed into the car he was in and nearly killed him.'

'What's he to you?'

'Nothing really, I hardly know him, but my fiancée's mother has hooked up with him...he was on his way to my wedding at the time, actually.'

'Huh.' He smirked. 'Trouble follows Con around. That's because he brings it with him.'

'He used to work for you?'

'Yeah, he was a good worker. Good with his hands and a big, powerful unit. Funny bloke as well. Always quick with a joke...'

'...but?'

'But he's a robber, a scammer, a cheat, a skiver...what else now? Oh yeah, he's a fighter as well.' The recollection seemed to bring a

50

hardness to Mike Cavani's eyes. Until that moment, it was hard to believe that he was part of a criminal family that was almost certainly only staying out of jail by various nefarious activities.

'So how come you employed him?'

'For all of the above reasons.' He gave him a thin-lipped shark-like smile. 'Let me guess, he told you the Cavanis were out to kill him. He said we'd sent someone in a cement mixer to crush him.'

'Yup, that's it, Mike. It seemed far-fetched to me, but as Jeff was meeting Eddie about this shop I thought I'd ask a few questions.'

'And what would you have done if I said, yes, we tried to kill him?'

He stared at him with hard eyes now. Nick looked away, feeling uncomfortable. The big, busty waitresses kept glancing over at them. She looked worried. Was she concerned it was all about to kick off? Or was her bra just too small for those huge tits? That must hurt.

'Err...well, I assumed he was just a silly deluded old bloke, so I didn't really think...'

'...no, you didn't think, did you? And you should've thought about it, because I don't like people accusing me or my family of trying to hurt an old man.'

'I wasn't accusing you...'

'A bloke like you could get into all sorts of trouble...and I assume you don't want any trouble.'

'Look, mate...'

Mike Cavani leant into him and jabbed a finger into Nick's shoulder. 'So just tell Con that we'll come and get him when we want him.' Nick looked at the finger. He didn't like people trying to bully him. Not even people like Mike Cavani.

'Alright pal, I know you're the hard man. No need to try and scare me, 'cos I'm not scared.'

'Well, you bloody should be.'

'Maybe so. But I'm not,' said Nick jabbing him in the shoulder in return, also with his forefinger, his tone flat and resolute. Cavani looked at his finger and then up at Nick again with his hard, dark eyes. Nick swallowed. Cavani wasn't a big bloke. Average height and build, he knew he could take him in a fight. One good karate chop to the throat and a kick on the balls would sort him out. But he wasn't the sort to do anything as dirty as fighting, he'd have someone do that for him. Someone much bigger.

Cavani stood up. Nick stood up. He was two inches taller. Cavani fixed him with a stare for a full 20 seconds then held out his hand towards him.

'Nick Guymer, I like you.'

'What?'

'I'm a good judge of men and you're a bit of a hard sod, aren't you? I like you. Not many would come here with your attitude.'

'No, I'm not a hard bastard and I don't care if you like me or not.'

'I like you even more for that.' He laughed and slapped him on his shoulder and fished a card out of his inside pocket. 'What do you do for a living?'

'I'm a writer. I write about football.'

'Are you now? Well you call me if you need anything. Scandal on players, managers, club officials. I can always give you something - for a fee, obviously. I have video, photos, you name it, whatever you want.'

Nick took it. 'I don't do that sort of journalism. I write about the culture and history of the game, not which centre-forward is going out with which scrap metal dealer's daughter.'

'Well, the offer is there. For the record, and you can tell Con this from me, we don't give a fuck what he's up to and we haven't tried to kill him because if we had, he'd not be alive now, as he almost certainly knows. He's spinning you a line to send you away from whoever it was that did try to kill him. That'd be my guess. This is his idea of a diversion tactic. Mind you, he stole booze from us, so he should think himself lucky I've not had him broken.'

'Why let him off?'

He shrugged. 'I've got bigger fish to fry than a silly old sod like him.'

Nick nodded. 'Alright. Thanks, Mike.' He turned to go. 'Have you any idea who might have wanted to kill him?'

'Me? Not a clue. Seriously. Call me sometime. We can do business, me and you.'

He nodded at Big Busty as he left. She smiled back at him as he left, her chest heaving up at him. At least her nipples had softened, though.

Luke was on his second bottle of lager when he got to the Crown Posada. It looked very tempting. A beer in the Crown Posada, god, how many times had he done that when he was a student? A lot. And now, his memories of them were all good, even though the reality was, sometimes it must have been boring.

'Jeff just called. He'll be done in five minutes.'

'Cool. OK, let's get back up there.'

'Did you see your man?'

'Aye. I'm pretty sure they had nothing to do with the accident, which was pretty much as I thought.'

'What was this Tyneside Mafioso like, then? said Luke, finishing the beer.

'Hard. Scary. He seemed to like me, though.'

'Useful mate to have.'

'Useful, possibly. Mate, never.'

On the way home, Jeff was already excited about opening his third store and was dictating a list of things to do to Luke, who made notes on his phone.

'Stock is going to be a bit of an issue; we'll have to go on a buying spree. Get some ads in *Record Collector*, Lukey. We're about 10,000 records short. We'll need lots of classic rock and metal for Newcastle. I'm going to try and get all those 50 year olds who used to go to the City Hall to see rock bands to resurrect their vinyl buying addiction, now that their kids have grown up and left home.'

'Good thing is, it doesn't need any decoration. Unlike the Stockton one,' said Luke. 'We need display racks, though, and lots of plastic boxes.'

'Shit yeah. Display racks cost a bloody fortune new,' said Jeff.

'Why don't you build them? Knock them together from MDF,' said Nick.

'Do I look like a handyman? Are you a handyman, Lukey?'

'I can't even change a light bulb. The only thing I'm handy for is emptying alcohol out of glasses and looking at naked women on a computer.'

An idea struck Nick. 'Why don't you pay Con to do it for you when he gets out of hospital? He's a primo joiner. He can probably knock a load of units together in a few days and he'll know where to get the wood cheap.'

Jeff held a finger aloft. 'That, my unshaven show pony, is a good idea. How much do you think he'd want?'

'I dunno, but it'll be a lot less than buying the units in and probably better quality.'

'But he won't want to come up here if he's crossed the Cavanis, will he?' said Jeff.

'They're not after him. That comes direct from Mike Cavani, so that might put his mind at rest. But he might not want to leave Stockton with Jackie being in hospital. Talking of which, I wonder how the old bird is doing,' said Nick, calling Julie.

She replied on the fourth ring.

'Hiya.'

'Hey Jules. We're on our way back.'

'Did he get the shop?'

'Yeah, he did. How's your mam?'

'I'm still at North Tees. She's still sedated, but they're going to wake her up later today. I'm going to stay here while they do that. Did you find out anything?'

He explained about his meeting with Mike Cavani.

'I didn't think it was likely,' she said. 'I was talking to Ricky and Kev earlier. They came in to see mam, but they've found out the name of the cement mixer driver and where he lives.'

'How the hell did they do that?'

'Someone in the police leaked it to them, probably in return for money or drugs. You know what they're like.'

'I hope you've told them to leave off him.'

'I've told them in no uncertain terms that they're not to go near him. He is Lithuanian. Poor bloke lives in a squat at the bottom of Dovecot Street – 198 is an old terraced house. He's there with some other east Europeans. He's called Mykolas Alekna.'

'Is he illegal?'

'No, I don't think he is, but I'm willing to bet his labour is being exploited for little money. These people are very vulnerable. He's not living in a squat to save money on rent, is he? He's obviously got nowt.'

'Do you want me to come to the hospital?'

'No. I know you don't like it. I'm just going to hang around so that I'm here when mam surfaces. They'll dope her up on morphine, so she probably won't even know where she is for a while, but I feel like I should be here, especially as I'll be away for a week from Saturday.'

'You're a good lass. Not sure she deserves you. How are Con and Tez?'

'Both very chipper. They'll be out later today, so they can take over mother-supervising duties.'

'OK. I'll see you later, Jules.'

He put his phone away.

'Are you going into the Stockton shop, Jeff?' said Nick.

'I certainly am. I said I'd be back by 3pm. Part-time Pete has to go by then. I need someone full time in there, really. Or at least four days a week. I'll put a notice in the window.'

'Are you staying up here, Luke?'

'Jeff's putting us up at Rita's for a couple of days.'

'Who's running Harrogate then?'

'Temporary Tony. He's 62 and an ex-copper. Loves the Kinks. Good bloke, isn't he, Luke?'

'Aye. He's super serious about it. Very reliable. Never seen him smile. I like that.'

'Well, it is in Yorkshire,' said Nick. 'It wouldn't be appropriate. One of the few things I don't miss about living in Yorkshire, especially North Yorkshire, is the propensity of the locals to be sour-faced miserable sods. It's totally different on Teesside. We're much more of a laugh.'

'That's is true, actually. Yer Yorky takes pride in being dour,' said Jeff.

'Rightly so,' said Luke. 'Being 'appy is overrated.'

'Don't go getting all Boycott on us, Lukey', laughed Jeff.

Nick said, 'Well, I'm going to have a word with the mixer driver. He lives in a squat down Dovecot Street.'

'You want some support?' said Jeff.

'Nah. I'll be alright.'

# CHAPTER 4

Jeff dropped him off on Prince Regent Street, right alongside where the crash had happened. As the van moved away, he stood looking at the marks on the road which had been left by the police to identify details of the scene. The road was scarred and there was blue paint from the car on the pavement and wall. How anyone had survived was a miracle.

He took a left down Dovecot Street past the building that used to house the Dovecot Arts Centre, whose bar was a familiar old haunt of his teenage years, past the old Radio Tees building, too. So much of the Teesside he'd grown up with had gone now. There were some newly built houses further down the road, but also a few old boarded-up terraces. Perfectly respectable, neat, tidy houses back in the day, they'd just fallen into disrepair and needed either knocking down, like most of the other old houses, or serious renovation. 198 would have been a lovely modest home to live in for most of its life and part of a community of, in all likelihood, mostly steelworkers. How times change. The denuding of the housing stock was an ongoing issue that needed addressing by large scale, social housing building and renovation projects, which for some reason never really got done properly. Dovecot Street was typical. A bit of new, a bit of old, a bit of derelict, it was all too fragmented and disorganised and as a result, no-one had a real emotional investment in creating a community, so it all felt very temporary.

The door had been green, but the paint had flaked off to reveal several layers of blue, red and black, the only legacy of the long-forgotten generations of 100 years of inhabitants. People who had come and gone, who had lived some part of their lives there. All those Christmas Days and New Year's resolutions; all the nights of passion and days of laughter. Times of hardship and joy, love and hate. All come and gone now and only the layers of paint to evoke them. And now, here it was, a squat for people who were trying to make something of their lives in a foreign country, all its old integrity of hearth and home evaporated. The original people, who lived in it when it was new, could scarcely have imagined this was its future. He let out a low moan in his throat to assuage the melancholy he felt.

He knocked on it hard. A radio was playing inside. It was turned down and he heard someone walking to the door.

A broad man with closely cropped fair hair pulled open the old door.

Nick smiled to make it look as though he wasn't going to be a problem.

'Hi there. I'm looking for Mykolas.'

The man looked at him with blue eyes that were as cold as they were expressionless. He turned around without saying anything and shouted the name.

The Lithuanian was a big man. Broad shouldered, over six feet tall and powerfully built. He had to have nine percent body fat or less, he was lean and all muscle. He raised his eyebrows with suspicion at Nick. This was what life was like for him, living in poverty in a country that exploited your labour for almost no money and left you at the mercy of gang masters and the other awful people. Whatever the rights and wrongs of immigration, on a human level, you had to feel sorry for them.

'Hi there. I'm Nick Guymer,' he said, holding out his hand. The man shook reluctantly. 'I was involved in the car crash yesterday. You were driving the cement mixer.'

'I told the police everything,' he said, very defensive, taking a step back.

'I know. I'm not here to give you a hard time. My friends and relations were in the car.'

'Oh. Sorry. Are they OK?'

'Three are. The old woman isn't very good at all.'

He looked at the ground and shook his head. 'I'm sorry about that.'

'Tell me, Mykola. Who do you work for?'

'McGull. I drive machine and truck.' His English was good, if a bit halting and broken.

'Yeah, I know that, I meant who is your boss at work? What's their name?'

'Site gaffer is Sam Thompson.'

'Right. OK, thanks.'

'You want job?'

'No. Have you been driving cement mixers long?'

'I work building sites all my life. Brakes were...' he made a noise with his lips to describe the malfunction.

Nick nodded. A woman appeared behind Mykola. She was in her late 20s. He turned around and shooed her away.

'Sorry for your people. I live here in this shit hole. You understand? I have to do what I have to do.'

Nick nodded, 'I know, man. We've all got to earn a living somehow. Thanks for your help, anyway,' he said, shook his hand again and walked back up the street at pace and turned right onto Prince Regent Street to the building site. Like many streets on Teesside it was a mish-mash of all sorts of different buildings from different eras of piecemeal development. A large lot had been cleared to make way for several modern industrial units. Foundations had been laid at one side and that was obviously what the concrete mixer was being used for. No-one was working though and no-one was around so perhaps work had been suspended as a result of the accident. There had to be a foreman's office somewhere nearby, but it wasn't on the cleared ground.

He looked around. On the adjacent William Street was a Portakabin. That had to be it. Knocking on the closed door he pushed on the handle and opened it. A middle-aged bald man sat at a desk with a set of plans unrolled in front of him, anchored by two paperweights.

'Can I help you?' he said.

Nick shut the door behind him. It was stuffy and had a waxy, sour smell about the place, possibly emanating from the man behind the desk. He had a white shirt on, cuffs rolled up, and thick, hairy forearms.

'Hi there. I'm Nick Guymer. Are you Sam Thompson?'

'That's me, yeah.'

'My family were involved in the accident with the cement mixer yesterday.'

The foreman took off his glasses and rubbed his eyes. 'How is everyone?' He spoke with what sounded originally like a Huddersfield or Halifax accent, now mixed with some northeast inflections.

'Three are fine. One not so fine.'

'I'm sorry to hear that. It was a terrible thing to happen. How can I help you?'

'Well, as you can imagine, there's likely to be some sort of compensation case...insurance and so on.'

'I assumed as much, yes...and understandably too, of course.'

He seemed a plain, decent man. Classic bloke born into the working class who had gone up the social scale by a couple of notches to make lower middle-class.

'How long had the driver of the truck been working here?'

'Not long. We use a lot of casual labour.'

'Have you ever seen an accident like this before?'

He got up and poured himself a coffee from a jug under a filter. He gestured to Nick to ask if he wanted some. Nick shook his head.

'I've worked on building sites since 1977 and I've never seen anything like it. A total one off. I've seen virtually every kind of accident you can have.'

'Why did it happen? Any idea?'

Sam Thompson looked at him squarely. He seemed very stressed out, deeply etched worry lines spread across his forehead and at the corners of his eyes.

'Brakes failure. Has to be. That's what Mick, the driver said.' Thompson shrugged. 'The police report will find any mechanical error.'

Nick nodded again. 'Has work been suspended, then?'

'We'll get going again on Monday. I'm just waiting to hear from the boss to get the go ahead.'

'From Paddy McGull?'

'Yeah. Look, I'm busy...is there anything else I can do for you?'

'Nothing. Thanks, Mr Thompson.'

He nodded at Nick. Looked away, started to say something and then stopped.

'What is it?' said Nick.

Thompson let out a breath of air and rested on the edge of his desk. 'I said I've not seen anything like this...that's not quite true. I was working on a project up near Alnwick on a new housing new estate right by the A1. We had a forklift roll down a slope and it knocked a man over. Almost killed him. The handbrake just went.'

'Just went? What does that mean? I know nothing about mechanics.'

'It just failed. There were some who thought it was deliberate because the forklift had been recently serviced, but that was never proven. The guy sued the company. It was settled out of court. So if that's a guideline for your family members...'

'How much did he get?'

'It was never disclosed, but I think it was a lot. Nearer a million than 500,000.'

'OK, thanks, Mr Thompson.'

'I really feel for your family. It was a terrible thing to happen.'

'Mr Thompson, Sam. Tell me honestly, do you think this *was* an accident, or was it deliberate?'

He didn't hesitate with his answer.

'It's almost certainly an accident. An unlikely one. But all the same...'

'OK. Thanks. We're lucky no-one has been killed. Not yet anyway.'

'Absolutely. Please pass on my best wishes.'

'I will. I'm often in town. My mate, Jeff, runs the record shop on the High Street, so I'll drop in again at some point and let you know how things are going.'

Thompson seemed a good man, albeit one who was under a lot of pressure. It made his mind up that Conrad was either deluded or mischievous in saying it was a deliberate attack on him. The old bugger was messing with him, trying to make himself look like a big man or a victim. Like he was important enough that anyone would want to kill him. He sucked in a lungful of air, took his second Phenibut capsule of the day out of his jeans pocket and swallowed it.

As he was walking away across the building site, a sports car pulled up. A well-dressed older man, probably in his early 60s, with close, expensively cut hair, tanned, wearing a dark suit and open-neck shirt got out and trotted up to the Portakabin and went inside. He squinted at the car's registration plate - Gull 1. It had to be the gaffer.

Nick got a lift home from Jeff and set about making some food for when Julie got home, frying steak and onions, adding some beef stock and vegetables and putting the whole lot in a slow cooker. Then he went for a bath. Julie called at just after six, waking him up out of a doze.

'Hey Jules. You just woke me up. I'm in the bath.'

'Ooh, that's a nice thought.'

'Not from where I'm sitting it isn't. I need you naked on the other side to improve things.'

'What, me, with my stretch marks and sagging tits?'

'Oh god, aye. And the rest of you.'

She gurgled a laugh. 'Don't think I don't know that you're touching yourself up.'

He let go. She knew him so well.

'Don't go making a mess in the bath, if you're going to knock one out, do it in the sink.'

'Thank you for that practical advice, doctor.'

'You're welcome; now, to lessen your ardour, I'll tell you about mam.'

'That'll definitely do that. How is she?'

'Dazed and confused would sum it up, but she's awake. She

needs a full MOT and a 100,000 mile service. You should see the list of things that are wrong with her. There's the broken pelvis and three other broken bones. She's got a ruptured spleen, a partially collapsed lung...err...torn ligaments in her neck...'

'...good god. It's a wonder she's even alive.'

'The doctor told me there's pretty much only one reason she's still with us...'

'What's that?'

'...the fact that she was drunk when the collision happened; drunk and only semi-conscious. And that meant when it hit, she was relaxed and all sort of floppy. That reduced the impact on her.'

'Being floppy is a good thing in a crash?'

'Seemingly. Aye. So the long and the short of it is she's going to be in hospital for a long time.'

'Is her life in danger, though?'

Her tone was unflinching. 'Oh aye. She could definitely cark it at any moment. The doc didn't exactly put it in those terms, but he made it clear that she's very weak and all sorts of shit could go wrong with her, yet. The next 48 hours are the most dangerous, he reckoned. But they always say that, don't they? No-one says it's the fourth day from now that we have to worry about, so...I dunno...we should prepare for the worst really, but my guess is the old shitehawk will cling on.'

'Yeah, I'm sure she'll pull through...'

'...aye, out of spite if nowt else. Sorry if that sounds wrong. I'm ready to come home. I'm really sick of this place.'

'I've got a beef stew on for when you get back.'

'Great. I need some proper food, they don't have proper food here, it's like shite school dinners. I don't know how hospitals think anyone is going to get well if they don't serve people nutritious food.' She groaned and distorted the phone with her breath. 'God, I need a drink. I'll see you in a bit.'

After his bath he dressed and made sure there was cold white wine ready for her and then went to Google the news story of the runaway fork lift truck that Sam Thompson had told him about. It was in the *Newcastle Chronicle* archive from 2004. He scanned it for details. The man hit was David Farley, 43, from Morpeth. He'd sustained a broken leg and several other injuries and couldn't work. There were details of how it had happened and a photo of Farley with his leg in plaster, surrounded by his workmates all with their thumbs up in the classic, local newspaper style. A search using his name produced one later story about Farley which briefly mentioned his out-of-court settlement with McGull Developments, eight months later.

Nick went back to the original story and looked again at the photograph. He hadn't noticed it first time. On the far left of the semi-circle of seven men, holding his thumb aloft and a big cheesy grin on his face was Conrad Scott. He looked just the same, but with a little more hair. Nick enlarged the photo just to check it was him, but there was no mistaking it. He scanned the caption, but it didn't detail any names apart from Farley.

So the old sod had been working up there, had he? Was that a coincidence or had he seen that Farley had got a big pay out and thought he'd recreate a similar accident here? The two incidents were not that similar. The fork lift had been unmanned. Its hand brake had slipped and as a result rolled down a slope. But even so. Maybe it inspired him.

Julie's car soon pulled up and the engine cut out. He poured her a glass of Chablis as she came through the door. The condensation ran down the pale glass of wine. It looked so attractive. Even the way the light played on it made it look desirable.

'Welcome home, dear,' he said, affecting a flat Yorkshire accent. 'I've got some of your special medicine here for you.' He took a big sniff of it and handed the glass to her.

She flung her bag down on the kitchen floor, took the glass from him, gave him a kiss on the cheek and collapsed onto a kitchen chair, drinking the wine as she did so. By the time she took a breath, she'd drank half of it.

'Oh god that's lovely,' she said, wiping the outside of the glass with her index finger.

He set about serving their dinner.

'It's just so boring in a hospital and the air is so stale as well. You just want to fling open the windows and let some fresh smog in.'

'Did Terry get discharged?'

'Yeah, he's gone home. He's badly bruised, but he knows he was really lucky, so it's like he's happy to just have that.'

'And Conrad?'

'He's left as well. He looked in on me and mam for half an hour. It was quite sweet, really. He was stroking her arm and cooing at her.' Nick pulled a cringing face. 'Aye, it was a bit like that. I felt a bit of sick come up at one point. But he was just being nice.'

'Where's he now?'

'He's at mam's house, isn't he? I couldn't let him go back to that shared house with all the other workies, god knows what sort of squalor that is. He's had a real shake-up and they said he had bruised ribs.'

'That's really painful. I had it once, I fell over onto a sofa while running to pick up the phone. Buggered me bottom rib on the left. Knacked like hell for a month.'

'He seems fine. I don't think he feels pain. But he was even more lucky than Tez really and he knew it. Owee then, tell me about your day up in Newcastle.'

He went over events and told her about the David Farley accident, too.

'It seems a bit of coincidence, doesn't it?' said Nick, as they ate the stew. 'Maybe he thought if he told me someone was out to get him, it'd make him seem important.'

'It can't have been deliberate. If you think about it, that Lithuanian bloke couldn't have been paid to drive into the car,' said Julie. 'For a start, the bloke wouldn't have known when the car he was in would be coming past. Terry was at the wheel, so Conrad couldn't control how slow or fast the car was going either, or whether he'd be able to take evasive action. On top of that, he wouldn't know how badly hurt anyone would be, whether Conrad would be killed or not. Nah, it just doesn't make any sense. It is just a coincidence. He's been on building sites for 40 years, so he must have seen and been around all sorts of accidents. He just likes making stuff up. It's like his bloody jacket story.'

'Aye. I suppose so. Hey, Mike Cavani gave me his card, y'know. Said we could do business.'

Julie pulled a face and drank more wine.

'Eh? Why? What sort of business?'

He shrugged. 'I think he appreciated my attitude. He tried to intimidate me and I wasn't for being intimidated.'

She cocked an eyebrow at him critically, but said nothing.

'But he did say Con was a bit of a rogue. So I shouldn't really believe anything he says in future.'

'Well, there you go then. I can't believe you did in the first place. He's a bullshitter of the first water, that gadgee.' She pushed the bowl away from her and let out a satisfied groan. 'Delicious. More booze please, waiter.'

He went to the fridge and got the bottle. Her phone buzzed as he did so.

'Hiya, Tez. No, I haven't. Have you tried to call her? Yeah, sorry, 'course you have. And you've been around her flat? Now, steady on Terry. You don't know that. Yes, alright, of course I will. I'll ring you back.'

She put the phone down and put her head in her hands briefly. 'It's like a fizzin' soap opera, my family. There's always some bloody drama or other. Terry can't get hold of Jaz. He'd spoke to her this morning. Her mother had taken her to the family house from the hospital and she had called their private doctor to check her out. She was supposed to meet him at his flat and she didn't turn up. Now he can't get hold of her. He thinks her father is holding her against her will.'

'Bloody hell. Her father was a bit of a sod though, wasn't he?'

'A lot of a sod. I never saw the like. Horrible. Typical abusive man, if you ask me. He was more bothered about calling out my family than he was in her welfare. I shouldn't have clouted him, but I'm glad I did. Mind, he had no doubts about hitting a woman, did he?'

Nick picked up his phone. 'He was a twat with a capital "T". What's the Patel home number?'

She found it in a text Terry had sent her.

It rang for a while and then a woman picked up.

'Hello?'

'Hello. Can I speak to Jasmin, please?' He affected a well-to-do voice, stripping out his Teesside inflections.

'Can I say who is calling, please?' she said in a posh, Indian inflected voice.

'Steve Hillage. Cleveland Police,' he said in the sort of crisp authoritarian voice that he felt all police officers should have, though few did.

Julie barked out a stifled laugh at the name he gave. She mouthed 'Hillage' and began playing an air guitar, head back, eyes closed in an imitation of the 1970s hippy guitarist.

'Hold on please, Mr Hillage.' He put his thumb up at Julie. Jasmin came on the line.

'Hello?'

'Hey Jaz, it's Nick. Sorry I had to lie to your mother to get past her. You'll have to pretend that I'm the police, right?'

'OK, officer.'

'Good lass. Right, are you being held against your will? Terry has been trying to get hold of you.'

'I don't actually have access to my phone right now, officer. It's broken.'

'Why don't you just leg it back to your place or to Terry's? Are they stopping you?'

She was hesitant, clearly trying to find a way to tell him what the situation was, without it being obvious to anyone listening.

'There are just some things that I need to sort out here. Family things. We're having a big family meeting. Would it be OK if I contact you after that, tomorrow? I'll happily give you a full statement then.'

'Nice work, Jaz. Are you OK, though? You're not in any danger?'

'I'm fine now. Thank you for asking, officer. I shall call you tomorrow.'

He rang off and put his phone on the kitchen table. 'She's OK. Something is going on, but I don't think it's serious. I suspect she's just trying to stop her parents freaking out any more after the accident. Keep them sweet for a bit, like. She'll call me tomorrow.'

'Steve Hillage, indeed. Ha!'

'It was the first name that came to mind, for some reason.'

'Aye well, you are a bit of an electric gypsy. I'll call Terry and let him know. That was good work.'

'This is why Newcastle's primo crime family want me on their books, y'see,' he said, with a laugh, putting dirty dishes into the dishwasher. 'Brains and brawn, y'see.'

She got up and rubbed his shoulders and arms. 'Do you feel like exercising one of your most well-developed, hard muscles, then?' she said, kissing his neck.


On Friday morning Nick wrote a couple of pieces for websites and his Saturday morning column for the *Yorkshire Post*; Julie went into the Teesside Women Centre to make arrangements for her trip to Newcastle the next day. He'd just finished eating a couple of lamb chops for an early dinner when Jeff called him.

'Hey, mate.'

'Now then. Fancy coming into town?'

'I dunno, I was going to take it easy after the stress of the last couple of days.' He could hear glasses clinking in the background. 'Are you in a pub?'

'Aye, the Royal Oak. Just a lunchtime livener.'

'I thought you'd given up the beer.'

'I have, I'm drinking vodka and tonic. And there's another bloke in here also drinking vodka.'

'Well, it is noon, so that seems likely.'

'I think you should check him out.'

'Me? Why me?'

'And I've also got a new full-time worker I need to introduce you to. It's someone you know.'

'Eh? Who?'

'All will be explained. Owee into town.'

Half an hour later, Nick parked up in the Castlegate Centre and walked up Stockton High Street to Jeff's shop alongside Stockton Parish church. The High Street was a strange place, really. Wide and handsome and grand in its own way and yet simultaneously run down, with more than a whiff of hanging on in quiet desperation about it. Small groups of young men stood around smoking and wasting away the day in ill-fitting sportswear. The ones that weren't underweight were overweight. None of them looked like they'd done a days work in their lives and it was hard to imagine that they ever would. A kid with a face that looked like it was covered in pink Braille squinted at him as he stood alongside, waiting for traffic to pass so he could cross the road. He pulled on a cigarette as he did so, looking him up and down with a vague air of confrontation. Nick glanced over and saw there were a couple of girls alongside the six men. One of them was, almost inevitably, heavily pregnant, but was still smoking all the same.

'What you looking at, like?' the kid said to him. The others all turned to look at his raised, aggressive tone. Knowing he hadn't been looking at him in any way whatsoever, Nick ignored him. The kid was just trying to impress his mates and the girls.

He crossed the road and walked up the High Street. The lad began walking alongside him, still smoking. 'Ignoring us won't make us go away, you prick.'

Nick stopped dead in his tracks and turned to him. His mates were coming up behind him.

'Look mate, I know you're just trying to play the hard man.'

'I am the hard man, son. I'm a very, very bad, hard man. And I didn't like how you looked at us.'

He was streak of piss wrapped in cheap, high polyester mix leisurewear and Nick knew could drop him with one punch if he had to. But who needed all the grief and grazed knuckles? He let out a sigh, shook his head and walked on, but the lad ran around in front of him, trying to block his way. Nick walked around him again. His mates were laughing and goading him on to be more confrontational. It was a kind of sport really; a sport only played by losers.

'You can't get away mate. I want an apology.'

Nick walked on, head down until he was outside the Royal Oak, just along from Jeff's store. The kid's mates seemed to find keeping up with him a bit too much like vigorous exercise and had stopped by Silver Street to light up fags. The lad ran in front of him again and pushed him in the chest this time.

'You scared, old man? Just say sorry and all your problems go away.' He danced on his toes in front of him in a manner which put Nick in mind of Bez from the Happy Mondays. This guy was certainly twisting his melon, man.

Nick held up his hands. 'Sorry mate.' He grinned at him. 'Take it easy, eh.' He patted him on the top of the arm in an attempt at a friendly gesture and tried to get past him to go into the pub, but the lad blocked his way and hit him hard in the chest with the palm of hand, this time.

'Not good enough,' the kid said, clearly, for whatever fucked-up reason, wanting a fight of some sort. Maybe he just wanted to be hurt. Maybe it was only pain which validated his existence. Nick knew he could make a mess of him. He was taller, broader and built like mid-weight boxer these days, but to do so wouldn't be fair. The kid was screwed up. Only someone whose life was chaotic would try to pick a fight with a stranger over nothing and especially one who was clearly bigger and stronger than you were. By getting the snot beat out of him, maybe he'd get some sympathy and that was the only way he knew how to get any human warmth in his life. Or maybe he was just a piece of shit.

'Look fella. I'm not in the mood for this. I'm just going to meet my mate. I don't know what this about, but you should just back off and calm down.'

It was no good. The kid picked up 'back off' as though it was another threat to him. He seemed only programmed to respond to things negatively, as though his human software was malfunctioning.

'Nobody tells me to back off.' He charged at Nick with his shoulder, knocking him back a couple of steps. Was that the best he had? It was like being pushed by a light breeze. But he still didn't throw a punch.

'This is really very bloody tiresome,' said Nick.

From out of the pub doorway, Jeff emerged, pulled a mad face at Nick over the lad's shoulder, grabbed him from behind and lifted him up off the ground, dwarfing him in size and height. Even as a radically slimmed-down version of himself, Jeff was still a big man at six feet four and 15 stone.

'Is this chap bothering you, sir?' he said, holding the kid in an iron grip at arms' length, as though he was a bag of dirty washing, which, in a way, he was.

'Yes, he's being a total arse, Mr Evans. Can you dispose of him for me?' said Nick, in a pompous voice.

'Certainly, sir.'

'Aiyazz, gerroff us,' the kid said, wriggling to get free, his feet still off the ground. His mates had now arrived and were laughing at him. It was all part of the day's entertainment for them. Their daft mate probably did this sort of thing all the time.

Jeff carried him down to them. 'I believe this creature is one of yours. Take him away before I break him, please.'

'Owee Jase, you mad bastard,' said the girl. 'Let's go and get some cider.'

As ever, the words of the female in the group seemed to have the most weight. He did as he was told, red-faced and humiliated.

'Cheers, Jeff,' said Nick as they walked back to the pub. 'I thought I was going to have to chin him just to get him off my case.'

'I clocked what was going on as I came back from the bogs. You get kids like him around here all the time.'

'I sort of feel sorry for him, in a way, for all that he was being a sod.'

Jeff pulled at his beard as they walked up to the bar. 'You're a bloody loss to the social services, you. He's a scum bag. Plain and simple. I've got no sympathy; you don't have to be a twat, even if you're destitute. The world is full of nice tramps.' He nodded at the barman. 'Double vodka and tonic please, Harry, and a sparkling water for my unshaven monkey boy here.'

Nick looked with envy at Jeff's drink. He could just taste the sharp, sweet and slightly bitter tonic and the warmth of the vodka in it.

'I know, but what sort of state is his life in that he's behaving like that? I mean, he is a scum bag, but Jesus man, he can't want his life to be like that, can he?'

'Oh, don't go over-thinking it, Aristotle. He's just a twat. You'll not change people like him.'

'We seem to be breeding a lot of them though. I don't like it.'

They went and sat down by the window. 'Back in the day, idiots like him would work in a factory or do some heavy-duty labouring. He'd be kept in line by all the older blokes who'd slap him if he got too uppity and at the end of the day, he'd be physically knackered and probably not even have the energy to kick off. That's how it worked. But he's got nothing like that, has he? He's got all this young energy and nowhere to put it, add in drink and drugs and you've got a whack job who is trying to pick fights for fun,' said Jeff.

'Aye. That's about right, I reckon. Glad I didn't give him slap, though. Wouldn't have been right.'

'Aye, but sometimes it's the best solution, isn't it? Sometimes, a man's got to do what a man's got to do, and get off your horse and drink your milk...and other John Wayne-isms. But anyway, disciplining the local chavs aside, look over there in the far corner. Recognise him?'

Nick peered into the far dark corner of the pub. A man was sitting with two women and another bloke. They were all in their twenties.

'He looks a bit familiar, but I'm not sure who he is.'

'That is the bloke who drove the cement mixer into your future mother-in-law.'

'Oh, yeah. So it is. He was nice enough when I went round there yesterday. Yeah, I think the girl alongside him was in the house as well. Is he why you got me down here?'

'I was at the bar about three-quarters of an hour ago, right. He was buying a round when this bloke comes in, slaps him on the back and gives him an envelope and then leaves. He looks in it and it's stuffed with money. He goes over to the other three and shows them, they all cheer and they order the good vodka off Harry and start on a piss up. I saw the wad, it wasn't his wages, it was a good chunk of money.'

Nick sipped at the water. 'So are you saying he's been paid for...for the accident? Me and Jules were talking about that last night.'

Jeff had his index finger in the air. 'That, monkey boy, is exactly what I'm saying. He's just a regular east European dude. He works like fuck for no money and lives somewhere not far from squalor. If he's getting a big packet of cash, it's not his wages, is it?'

'Maybe he sold a car or something?'

'Come on. The only things he owns are the clothes on his back. He doesn't have a car.'

It did sound suspicious.

Jeff went on. 'Conrad was right, that accident was no accident. Someone paid him to do it, for some reason.'

Nick dwelt on what he'd said. 'Well, if that's right, at least we know they didn't mean to kill him.'

'What do you mean?'

'I mean, let's just say you're right. Mickey there has been paid for a job well done, but no-one died. So, if he's got his money, that can't have been the objective.'

Jeff nodded and tugged on his beard. 'You're right. Good thinking. So what other reason is there?'

'To scare someone in the car? Maybe one of Rick and Kev's enemies has paid him to do it.'

'To threaten Terry and Jackie, like?'

'Maybe. Seems a bit weird that though, doesn't it?' said Nick. The whole thing seemed really odd.

Jeff scratched his head. 'If someone paid him to do it, he had to know which car it was and somehow be there at the right time. He couldn't just sit there on the off chance for days, could he?'

'That's what Jules said. Why don't we just ask him who paid him?' said Nick. 'He seemed genuinely sorry for what he'd done when I spoke to him. In fact, now I think about it, he said something like, "I have to do what I've got to do, because I live in a shit hole." Maybe it was a confession of sorts.'

'An admission of guilt?' said Jeff.

'Could have been.'

'He's not going to just fess up to it though, is he? I mean, he can't. We could just go to the police and then that's him in a lot of trouble and offski back to Skintsville, Lithuania.'

'True. Who's paid him? That's what we need to know. Was the bloke who brought the money familiar?' said Nick, drinking some water.

Jeff shook his head. 'He was white, in his 50s. Could have been anyone.'

They sat in silence for a couple of minutes. 'I feel like we should do something, but I don't know what to do,' said Nick.

'Me neither.' Jeff finished his drink. 'Owee, over to the shop and see my newest member of staff. I just took them on this morning.'

They walked up the street and into the store. Led Zeppelin's 'Trampled Underfoot' was playing as they walked in. There in front of the counter was a familiar shaggy hair cut. She looked up as they came in and ruffled the top of her hair and grinned at him with her gapped front teeth.

'Hiya, Nicky, boy,' she said.

Nick grinned at her. 'Miss Emily Davids. I might have known.'

She was wearing black leggings, black baseball boots, a

Ramones t-shirt, an armful of silver bracelets and a silver skull pendent around her neck. She held her arms out wide. 'Give me a hug then,' she said, with her light fluttering laugh.

He gave her a quick embrace and she kissed him on the neck. She smelled of herbs and felt small and bony. 'I saw the ad Jeff put in the window this morning, came straight in and that was that. I'm hired.'

Luke came out of the back room with a box of records. 'Alright Nick. This is Emily, she's our...'

'I know. We already know each other.'

'Ah, right. Does everyone know everyone else on Teesside? OK Emily, you can start by putting these in the racks. They've already been priced up.'

'Cool,' she said, still looking at Nick. 'How are you, anyway?'

'I'm good. You look great. Your hair is especially good.'

She shook it at him. It was a rich dark chestnut, shoulder length with a centre parting and a feathery ruffle on top.

'Where did you get that look from, Em?' said Jeff. 'It's so 1973.'

She went to the 'Q' section of the record racks and looked through, picking out an original gatefold copy of *Queen II*. She opened it up and pointed to drummer Roger Taylor. 'I took this picture of him to the hairdresser and said, give me that look. I loved it 'cos it's sort of male and female all at the same time and it takes no looking after. It's ended up a bit more scruffy than Roger's, though.'

'Getting your hairstyle off album sleeves is so cool. It's definitely the best hair we'll have in the shop,' said Jeff. 'Little known fact: I got my hair style from the 1971 Crufts show.'

She giggled. 'And how is the lovely Julie, Nick?'

'She's fine. We were due to get married on Wednesday actually, but we didn't...'

'...ooh, did you get cold feet?' she said eagerly.

He explained about the crash and her face dropped into shock.

'How shocking and absolutely terrible for you,' she squeezed his arm with her small, warm hand. 'I hope Julie's mum gets better soon.'

She took out some albums and began filing them alphabetically. Luke was watching her intently as she did so. If he'd had his mouth open with a string of drool dripping out, it couldn't have been more clear how smitten he was.

Jeff sat looking at the computer behind the desk. 'OK, Em, you're a teckie type, aren't you?'

'Not just a type, Jeff. I'm a total computer nerd. I'm the sort of nerd who laughs at jokes about cascading style sheets,' she said in her light, girlish, well-spoken voice.

'Is that something fashionable you'd put on your bed?' said Luke. She didn't laugh. Poor Luke. He was trying too hard.

Jeff went on. 'One of the reasons I'm taking you on is because I really want to expand my online trade, but keeping the database of records up to date is a full-time job. I want to be able to enter new stock into the database and then upload it in one click to all the platforms we sell on. But I have no idea how you do that. Have you any idea?'

She slotted a Thin Lizzy album into the 'T' section and walked behind the counter to look at the screen.

'Uh huh. I can sort that out for you. It'll take a while, but it's standard stuff. Make a list of the places you sell records and I'll hook them up to your database via a bit of software. Then, when you sell something it'll disappear from all sites at once and when you add something, it'll add to all of them at the same time. Is that OK?'

Jeff held her head in his hands and kissed the top of her head. 'You're an angel-headed hipster. That's exactly what I want. Can I get the same set up on the Harrogate computer and in Newcastle when we open?'

'Yeah, of course. I'll sort them all out for you.' She gave him a bright, green-eyed smile.

'I love you and want to have your babies,' said Jeff, making everyone laugh.

She pulled a face. 'I don't think that'd be physically possible,

Jeff. I'm so small compared to you, it'd be like a Chihuahua mating with an Afghan hound,' she said with a pained expression. 'I think that'd sting quite badly.'

'Not for me it wouldn't.' He pulled his hair forward over his face and began panting with his tongue out.

'So you're opening in Newcastle as well?' she said, laughing at him.

'We are. I signed the lease yesterday. I'm hoping to be open in a month or less, which reminds me I need those racks building. Where will I get hold of Conrad, Nick?'

'Jackie's house. Have you got the number?'

'Aye.'

'Blimey, you've got a lot of stock,' said Emily, looking at the database.

'That's only half of it,' said Luke, taking over record-filing duties. 'It takes forever typing in the info.'

'I can set up a barcode scanning thing so it hoovers up the info into the database automatically, but you'd still need to manually enter the old ones which don't have a barcode.'

'What's she like, this one?' said Jeff, pointing to her. 'That would be amazing, Em. Seriously.'

'I'll put it on my list of things to do. I'll need to buy some software, but it shouldn't cost a fortune. If it does I'll get a rip-off copy.'

'You've not got any software which will make talking to over-focused, possibly autistic men about obscure records on the Transatlantic record label any easier, have you?' said Nick.

'Of course I do, Nick,' she said. 'It's called vodka.'

They all cheered at that. She'd bloody need it as well. Some strange blokes inhabited old vinyl shops.

'Anyone want green or brown tea?' said Nick.

'Aye, proper brown tea, none of your cat's piss green tea stuff,' said Luke.

'I like green, if you've got it, I'll have one if you're making one,' said Emily. The look of disappointment on Luke's face was palpable, as he clearly felt he'd said the wrong thing again.

'I'll have old school stand-your-spoon-up-in-it Tetley's,' said Jeff.

Nick went into the large stock room and put the kettle on. As it was boiling, Emily came in.

# CHAPTER 5

'Is the toilet at the back?' she said, pointing at the back wall.

'It is, indeed.'

She skipped through and closed the door behind her, though it did little to mask the sound of a long, powerful piss. You'd think a petite lass like her would do a light dribble; this sounded more like a horse. Maybe piss holes don't vary with the size of woman. She flushed it and went to wash her hands in the sink.

'I bet you heard every drop of that, didn't you?' she said, giggling.

'I was just admiring its turbo-charged quality. Very impressive urinating. Professional, even.'

'Ha ha. Some people have said I'm a bit of a piss artist. And I've got good muscles down there.'

'A grip like a tyre fitter's hand, I'm sure,' he said, laughing. She made a face of mock horror and slapped at him.

'I'm good at parties if you forget to bring a bottle opener, put it that way.'

He laughed loudly. She'd been flirty and dirty when they'd worked together at the Teesside Blues festival in July.

'I've been hanging on for ages because I thought it'd be filthy in there, but it's alright, really,' she said.

'I probably should tell you that a man was murdered in that toilet earlier this year.'

'Good god. Why?' she said, eyes wide.

'It's a long story. He doesn't haunt the place, though.'

'Well, thank god for that.'

'Does Luke just run the Harrogate shop?' she said, sitting on the bench next to the kettle.

'Yeah, he doesn't get up here much.'

She nodded. 'Good. He's a bit...' she made a cringing gesture.

'Oh, he's a nice bloke, really. Funny. He's just a bit over keen to impress you, I think.'

'I noticed. He seems about 12 years old.'

'He's got a year or two on you.'

She kicked her legs to and fro. 'As you know, I prefer older men.' She raised an eyebrow at him. 'I've not forgotten, you know.'

'Not forgotten what?' he said, putting tea bags into mugs and pouring hot water on.

'You and me at my house. I still think about it in idle moments, usually when I'm alone.' She gave him a look.

He didn't say anything, but he could certainly recall her naked body all too well. She'd left nothing to the imagination.

'Do you think about me?' she asked, just as he was doing so.

'What has been seen cannot be unseen,' he said, doing his best to be enigmatic.

She giggled again in her most annoying teenagey way. It made him feel very old.

'Sorry, sorry,' she said, seeing his slightly weary expression. 'That was immature of me.'

He put the mugs on a tray. 'Come on, we'll have these through there.'

She slipped off the bench and bent over in front of him, thrusting her backside up.

'I've been a bad girl,' she said, laughing. 'You must spank me.'

He slapped her playfully on her small arse and couldn't help but laugh as well.

For Nick, it was quite a unique experience for a woman to behave like Emily Davids did towards him. If God had created anything better than being flirted with by an attractive woman, then he kept it for him or herself. It was good for maintaining self-worth, which was a crucial component in keeping depressions at bay, but on the downside, it was *very* embarrassing and he had no real idea how to react to it, nor what, if anything, it really meant.

'Tea is served, ladies and gentlemen,' he said, setting the tray down on the counter. The paper lad, a 16 year old, came in as he did so.

'Alright, Raheem,' said Jeff.

'Hey Jeff. Have you heard?'

'What's that?'

The kid thrust the *Evening Gazette* at him. 'Front page news.'

Jeff unfolded it. The headline was huge: 'Jimmy Patel Murdered'.

He showed it to Nick with a look of shock on his face. Nick's heart leaped into his mouth. His phone rang. It was Julie.

'Have you heard about Jimmy Patel?' she said, without introduction.

'Literally, just this minute.'

'Me too. I tried calling Jaz, but her phone went to voice mail. Did she call you as she said she would?'

'No, she didn't. How did he die, do you know?'

'They've not said. It just says he was found dead at the family home this morning. That's all they've said apart from the fact that they're treating it as murder. I tried calling Terry and Ricky and Kev, but they didn't reply either. I'm already, instinctively worried they're involved in this.'

'Not Terry. He wouldn't do anything stupid.'

'He wouldn't, but Ricky and Kev would do something very stupid on his behalf, wouldn't they?'

'You're jumping to far too many conclusions. Anything could have happened.'

She let out a tense breath. 'Yeah, OK, I'm nearly finished here. I'll be home in an hour or less.'

They all looked at him as he rang off. Jeff spoke first. 'Her brothers aren't involved in this, are they?'

Nick gave him a dark look. 'Let's be brutally honest, none of us would be surprised if they were, would we? Not seeing what they were like after the crash.'

Jeff pulled his lips into a pout and stroked his long beard. 'This is true.' He leant on the counter and wagged a finger in mid-air. 'Jasmin is in a suspicious accident with a cement mixer that was on a site whose contract was awarded by her dad and he's now dead. That's just too weird, man.' He looked around the room. 'I'm not just being overly conspiratorial, am I?'

'I don't know anyone involved, so I can't say,' said Emily. 'But it does seem a bit strange. A bit of a coincidence, anyway.'

Luke sat down on a stool. 'Who owns the building site again?'

'Paddy McGull,' said Nick. 'He's been in the building game around here for decades. I remember seeing McGull signs when I was a teenager.'

'You see them down in York and Ripon as well,' added Jeff. 'I think they're all over the northeast.'

'And this Jimmy Patel bloke, what's he do?' said Luke, fiddling with a strand of long hair.

'He's the Chief Exec of the Middlesbrough Industrial Development Organisation. He dishes out publicly funded contracts for building industrial estates or renovating factories. Anything that looks like it'll support business growth,' said Nick. 'They're building some new industrial units to be used by small businesses.'

'So Patel has given McGull a lot of money, in effect,' said Luke.

'Aye. Exactly. And where there's money, there's trouble,' said Jeff, drinking his tea.

Luke nodded and began speculating. 'So they fall out over something to do with the contract and McGull or one of his henchmen whacks Jimmy the P.'

'That'll be it,' said Jeff nodding firmly.

'You can't say that,' said Emily, horrified. 'That's a terrible thing to say about anyone. What's this about his daughter and Julie's brothers? I vaguely remember them from the festival. Weren't they, like, thugs or something?'

Nick explained about the crash and the confrontation on Prince Regent Street between Julie and Jimmy and her brothers.

Emily put her hand over her mouth on hearing that. 'My god, if I hit someone in the face, they'd hardly even feel it with my little hands,' she said.

'Believe me, Patel felt it. When Jules hits you, you stay hit,' said Nick. 'I was shocked that he hit her back, though. We were queuing up to hit him until the police intervened.'

'But no-one would kill someone's father, even if their brother wasn't allowed to see his girlfriend, would they?' said Emily.

'You don't know Julie's brothers Kev and Ricky - they're psychos,' said Jeff.

'That's over-stating it a bit. They've both been out of jail for a few years now, but they have a history of violence and general criminality. But I'd hope they were not murderers, even despite that,' said Nick, as much to comfort himself though, without an iron belief in what he was saying.

Jeff's phone rang.

'Hello. Oh, alright there, Con. How are you feeling then, mate? Yeah? Good to hear that. Yeah, well, they'll have another piss up, won't they, and do it another day.' He grinned at Nick and put his thumb up, then explained to Conrad about needing racks building for the new shop. 'Can you do that for us? I'm told you're a top-notch joiner. Aye. You know where we are, don't you?'

He put the phone down.

'He's coming down here to discuss it. How much should I pay him for doing those units, Lukey?'

'It'll cost 12 grand to buy them for the whole shop. Offer him 3 and settle on 5 and get him to put some shelves in as well. We always need shelves for books and the occasional CD.'

Jeff made a cross with his fingers 'Out, demon. We shall not be stocking Satan's favourite music delivery format.' Emily giggled.

'You're weird, you are. Really weird,' she giggled again. 'I think I'm going to enjoy working here.'

'Let's hear you say that after you've entered 1,000 albums into the database,' said Jeff. 'Can you get started on it right away, Em?'

She nodded and went around to sit in front of the computer

Conrad soon turned up, looking very bright-eyed and healthy, all things considered.

'Now then lads and lasses, how are we?' he said, rubbing his hands together.

'You don't look like you were in a big smash, Con,' said Nick.

'They build us strong in Newcastle, don't they? I'll be back on the site on Monday. Mind, Jackie is not so good. It's going to be a while before she's on the mend. So you need some shelves making do you, Jeff? It's going to cost you, kidda.'

'I didn't think you'd do it for free. It's for my new Newcastle shop.'

'Alright, then. No bother. Where in Newcastle?'

'High Bridge.'

'Hey, it's canny good, that. Very smart. You're quite the businessman, you, Jeff."

'By the way, the Cavanis aren't bothered about you, Con. I spoke to Mike yesterday, after you mentioned him.'

'Eh? Did you now?' He looked at him with what looked like suspicion, or was it surprise. 'You went and spoke to Mike Cavani, did you? Bloody hell, you've got some balls, Nick, I'll give you that.'

'Yeah. I said about your accident. It was nothing to do with them, Con. He was quite amused that you might have thought it was.'

The big man turned his mouth down. 'That's a bit of a shocker, that, like.' He said the words, but he didn't seem that shocked. In fact, he looked awkward. Nick squinted at him. What was going on with Conrad? He'd clearly spun him a line, not thinking he'd be found out, just as Mike Cavani had said.

'Talking of shockers, have you heard about Jimmy Patel?' said Jeff.

'Jimmy Patel? No. What about him?' said Conrad.

'He's been murdered,' said Luke holding up the newspaper.

The colour drained out of Conrad's face. 'Bloody hell. My god. Murdered. My god.' Now that was a shocked reaction. He took the paper from Luke and read the story, his thin, pale lips muttering as he did so.

'You didn't know him, did you, Con?' said Nick.

'I knew him alright, aye.'

'How come?'

84

'Just working on contracts over the years. Poor Jimmy. I wonder who's done for him. That's a right can of worms, that is, if you ask me.'

'Why do you say that, Con?'

The big man put his hands in the pockets of his black pants. 'A man like Jimmy had a lot of power, a lot of friends and a lot of enemies. He was a stubborn sod, really hard-nosed y'knaw? There'll be some blokes in the building trade that will be raising a glass to his murderer tonight, that I can tell you.' He shook his head, looking at the floor, then ran his fingers through his slicked back grey hair. 'Right, so I'd better go up to Newcastle with you to measure up and price this job for you, Jeff.'

'Can you do that now?'

He looked at his watch. 'Aye. I've nothing on.'

'Owee then, I'll drive us.'

He turned to Luke. 'How long are you staying open for, Lukey?'

'I'll stay open until you're back - whenever that is.'

'We'll be back at about eight, I reckon. What about you, Em? You don't have to stay beyond 5.30 if you don't want to, but I run a loose ship. As long as you put in 40 hours in a week I don't care when you do them.'

She looked up from the screen.

'Oh, I'll be here until at least then, just to get across this database and get it in some sort of order. It's a bloody mess, Jeff. You've got info in columns it shouldn't be in and other columns blank entirely. It all needs a good clean up, before I hook it into your Amazon marketplace, Music Stack and Gemm and eBay accounts.'

'I'm away home,' said Nick. 'See you guys.'

'Bye bye, Nicky, boy,' said Emily, giving him a gap-toothed smile. 'Say hello to Julie from me.'

He drove home, his mind in a whirl. Julie was already back.

'Where've you been?' she said as he walked through the door.

'Jeff's. Any news?'

'They've already arrested Kev and Ricky.' She looked at him

with anger in her eyes. 'They're questioning them about Jimmy Patel's murder. They picked them up early this afternoon.'

'Bloody hell. That was quick. How do you know?'

'Terry called me. They picked them up driving in Middlesbrough about a mile from the Patel's home in Marton.'

'Christ almighty. That doesn't sound good, Jules.'

'I know.' She pulled a down-turned mouth.

'But they didn't arrest Tez?'

She shook her head. 'He said they'd told him they'd gone round there to put the shits up Jimmy Patel this morning. Bloody idiots. Christ, those two are morons.'

'Have they done it?' said Nick, in his heart fearing that they had. They'd been so angry at him and clearly already held some grudges.

'I simply don't want to believe they've killed a man...but...but would you really be that shocked if they had? I wouldn't and I'm their sister.'

'Yeah, yeah, I would actually. They're violent but...killing, it's something else, isn't it? Would the fact he's Asian make any difference?'

'A racist thing, you mean? Ricky and Kev aren't racist. If they did it, it was because they hate him over the Terry and Jasmin thing and because he's been so horrible about the Wells family.'

'Even so. That doesn't sound enough reason to kill him. They can't have known him more than a few months. Only since Terry and Jaz got together. Well, surely the cops are just questioning them, that doesn't mean they'll charge them. Should we go over there?'

'Yeah, I can't sit here and wait.'

'Right. Come on then. I'll drive us over. Where are they being questioned?'

'At the Cleveland police headquarters over the back of the station.'

'Ah yeah. Bridge Street, isn't it?'

She shrugged. He put his arm around her. 'Come on Jules, it'll be alright.'

'Will it? First mam and now this. My fizzin' family is nothing but grief. I'd love to cut them adrift. Really, I would. They drag me down. They *always* have.'

'Look at it this way. If they have killed him, you won't have to deal with them for a long, long time.'

'Ha. True. Things are looking up already. Thanks, mister.'

'To get a silver lining, you need to have a cloudy day, baby.'

Nick took the A66 into Middlesbrough turning off onto North Road, the blue Transporter Bridge standing proud against the now clear evening sky.

'Jeff's getting Conrad to build his Newcastle shop record racks. He came over to the shop this afternoon.'

'Conrad did?' she said, surprised. 'He's made a quick recovery, then.'

'Aye. He's a funny bloke. I told him the Cavanis weren't after him, but he seemed surprised I'd even asked them. He obviously didn't think I would. He also didn't seem that cut up about Jackie being in such a bad state. He was laughing and joking as normal.'

'When I saw him at the hospital he was worried she'd die. But once they'd said she would likely pull through, he seemed very relaxed about it. In fact, not just relaxed, he seems very chipper. Very upbeat.'

'He was shocked when he saw the front page of the *Gazette*, though. That stopped him in his tracks.'

'He's up to something, if you ask me,' said Julie. 'I'll be glad to get away from my family for a week, though, I really will.'

'Are you looking forward to the work?'

She chewed her bottom lip. 'I'm a bit nervous about it, to be honest and it'll be the first time we've spent any time apart from each other since we moved back in together.'

'You'll be fine. You know it's something you really want to do, so just look at it as part of the journey towards your new career.'

'I could do without having to worry about my brothers, though.'

'Well, like you say, maybe you being up in Newcastle is for the best. You can't wipe their noses for them every five minutes if you're away from home. They'll have to do without you, whatever happens. You've done quite enough for them over the years. It's not fair.'

He pulled up outside the large modern building which housed the police headquarters.

'I know, but I'm not made like that, am I?'

They walked into the reception. A fat officer, red-faced, his belly pushing his shirt buttons to the limit of their tolerance looked up as they came in.

'I'm Julie Wells, you arrested my brothers this afternoon,' she said in a flat, resigned voice.

'Hello, Jules. I've not seen you for years,' said the big cop.

'Sorry. Do I know you?' she said, rubbing her forehead with a finger.

'Frank Connor. We went out a few times. Must be 15 years ago now. You went down to London.'

'Good god, hello, Frank. I'm sorry, I didn't recognise you. My mind is on other things. You've...you've changed...'

'...got fat, you mean. I know. I should do something about it...'

'You worked on the railways back then.'

'Aye. I became a copper soon after you left. You were going to stay in touch but...'

'...but I didn't. Aye, well, there were distractions.' She laughed a little. 'Oh, this is Nick Guymer, my fiancé.'

Nick saluted. From time to time they ran into Julie's ex-boyfriends around Teesside, largely because there were a lot of them. Some were still a bit in love with her, judging by the way they looked at her.

'It'd have been nice if we could have run into each other in happier circumstances,' she said.

'Yes, indeed. When I saw they'd been brought in, I wondered about you and where you ended up.'

'We live south of Yarm, out in the countryside. What about you?'

'Been married. Been divorced. Been married again. To Janice.

We've got a three-year-old girl and have just bought a house in Coulby Newham.' He nodded and smiled. 'Anyway, down to business. I'll find out what's going on and see if they're going to be held much longer. Jon Gaunt is in with them at the moment. Do you know him?'

'Gaunty? The lawyer? Yeah, I know him. He's defended them before,' said Julie.

He nodded, went through a door and Nick and Julie took a seat to wait for him.

'Well, that is a big lad,' said Nick. 'I didn't you know you'd dated anybody who was morbidly obese.'

'He was normal sized when I went out with him in '94. He must have put on five stone or more. Shocking.' She shook her head.

'He gorged on comfort food to ease his broken heart when you left him, y'see,' said Nick, grinning.

She made a yawning gesture at him. 'He was very b-o-r-i-n-g after a while. Mind, he had a fat cock on him.' She grinned back at him. 'Ha, ha, you've blushed.'

He shuddered. 'That's too much information, Jules. I don't share the dimensions of my ex-girlfriends' vaginas with you, do I?'

'Yes, you do. You said that woman from the *Northern Echo* that we met at that lunch last month had a huge fanny.'

'Brenda Collins. Aye. She did. It was more like pot-holing than making love, with her.'

She let out a yelp of amusement. 'And that's not the only time. What about that Linda Outhwaite lass?'

'Little Linda? Aye, sex with her was like trying to pick a lock with your cock.'

She bent double, laughter completely overtaking her in a long, rolling, woody gurgle. A long string of slaver fell from her mouth, making her laugh even more as she wiped at it. The tension and emotion of the situation seemed to have made her a little hysterical. Once she'd started laughing, she just couldn't stop.

'What's funny about that? It was like trying to dunk a baguette in a thimble.' He looked at her innocently and that just sent her off again, tears running down her reddened cheeks.

'Oh god. Sssh, don't say anything else, I'm going to wet me knickers.' She dabbed at her eyes with a tissue and sniffed her runny nose. 'Oh dear me, oh god. Think you're funny, don't you?'

'All I'll be able to think when Frank comes back is that he's got a fat cock. I might mention it by mistake.'

She punched him on the arm. 'Don't you dare,' she said, then thumping him on the thigh. She let out a small sigh. 'Had small balls though.'

It was his turn to slap her. 'Why would you care about his bollock size? You get nothing from the bollocks, big or small. Don't judge a man by his balls.'

'I just thought it was a bit odd. Usually if he's got a big willy, he'll have big balls as well, won't he?'

Nick laughed a little, 'How would I know? Big willy, indeed. How old are you? 13?'

She wiped her nose and coughed. 'Gerroff us, I'm just being polite. His whole tackle was like half a pound of offal. Not my cup of tea at all, I'm afraid.' She scrunched her face up in displeasure at the recollection.

'You're not supposed to make tea with it, Jules. That's where you've been going wrong.'

'Isn't that what tea-bagging is, then?'

He pushed her playfully, she pushed him back. Both of them were still laughing, as Frank Connor returned.

She stood up and brushed herself down and cleared her throat.

'They're taking a break. You can have a quick word with them if you want. Just yourself, though,' said Frank.

She put her hand over his on the desk. 'Thank you so much, you're very kind,' she said, a little obviously flattering him. He blushed from head to foot. Even his fat arms blushed. It was endearingly boyish, really.

He went away again to arrange things.

Nick got up and stood next to her. 'He's an impressive blusher.'

'I know. Always was. Hence the offal appearance downstairs, I imagine,' she made a repulsed face at him and mimed putting her fingers down her throat.

'That blushed as well?'

She nodded with an amazed face. 'Honest, man, it went a very funny colour. Talk about Captain Beefheart, I thought it might burst. Now, don't say anything to make me laugh again. This is a very serious situation.'

She cleared her throat and straightened herself out.

He soon returned, opened a code-locked door and let her through. 'Five minutes, Julie. OK?'

Nick watched him look at her arse in her old jeans as she went through. He couldn't blame him, he'd have done exactly the same, in fact, he still found himself doing it. Well, old habits die hard, sometimes. When Frank returned he had a brief chat with him.

'Do you live on one of the new estates in Coulby, then?' he said.

'Yeah. You live near Yarm? I like it out there, but it's too expensive on a copper's wage.'

'Too expensive for a writer as well,' he said.

'Is that what you do? What sort of stuff do you write?'

'Football mostly. For papers and websites, and I do books as well.'

'I love football. Big Boro fan. Me and Jules used to go and see them. Is she still a fan?'

'Yeah. Big fan. We go to most home games.'

He looked at the door that she'd gone through. 'She was a great lass. She's still very...err...looks great...well...y'know...'

'I know, mate. Well, she looks after herself. Eats low carb, plays badminton, drinks Chablis,' he said, with a nod. 'Seems to suit her.'

Frank Connor nodded and looked in the direction she'd walked. 'Yeah, you can tell.' He let out a sigh and went back to his work while Nick paced up and down, half an eye on the policeman. He had a round face and pouchy cheeks and a squashed nose. You'd never guess he had a fat cock, though. Small fingers, small nose, nah, you'd never know. He wasn't handsome at all. Strange thing, attraction, and very hard to second guess. Some people are just appealing to you at certain moments in your life and some just aren't.

'So how long have you lived in Yarm, then?' said Frank.

'A couple of years. We used to live in Harrogate. We were supposed to get married on Wednesday, but there was an accident, so we had to postpone it.'

'Oh. Sorry to hear that.' They looked at each other. Two strangers, with only the woman they'd fallen in love with and had sex with, in common. Weird thought. Very weird.

Julie soon came out of the back room she'd been taken to.

'Thanks, Frank,' she said, with one of her nicest smiles. 'That was good of you to arrange that.'

'No problem. If you leave your number I'll let you know if there's any other news.'

That seemed a bit odd, but she scribbled her mobile on a piece of paper and they left.

'He was just getting your number, you know. He still fancies you. Probably wants to have an affair.'

'I know he does, but having a copper who's soft on you can be very useful, so I indulged it.'

'You're quite the schemer you, aren't you? How were the boys?'

'Kev and Ricky? They're innocent. They did nowt. That's what they told me and what they've told Gaunty and I believe them.'

'Is that what they say?'

They got into his car.

'Yeah, and they're telling the truth.' She let out a relieved sigh.

'How can you be so sure?'

'Nick, man. I've known them my whole life. I've seen them lie when they're guilty and I've seen them lie when they're innocent and I've seen them tell the truth. They can't get anything past me and they don't even try any more. I asked them straight. Did you do this? And they both said without hesitation, no they didn't. They went there to scare him. He opened the door and tried to fight them or something. They think he was already stabbed or hurt. There was some sort brief grapple between them and then they left after telling him to lay off Terry and Jasmin. They didn't kill him.'

'Well, that's a relief. If you're sure.'

'I'm sure. But...and it's a big but...will the police believe them? I don't think so.'

'Have they got any evidence against them?'

'The lads said Jimmy got blood on them. They think he was bleeding when they grappled with him and had been fighting with someone because he was furious, you know, really wound up. They tried to get the knife off him that he was waving. So they've already said their prints will be on it. The police are still doing forensics, though.'

Nick frowned. That seemed a very odd situation. 'So how come they got picked up within a mile of the Patel house?'

She shrugged. 'They didn't have an answer for that. Someone who knew them probably saw them walking back to their car. Trouble is - and the lads acknowledged this themselves - they totally fit the bill for the murder. But, you know what they're like, half their brain is always ready to go to jail for something. It holds no fear for them.'

The A66 was quiet as they drove home.

'Look, as extreme as this situation is, you need to forget about it and concentrate on your job in Newcastle. You'll be being assessed so you can't afford to just phone it in.'

She slapped her legs. 'This is true. I have to put my career first. Those lads have given me enough grief for three lifetimes, they're not going to do it again, guilty or not guilty.'

'Good lass. You're not selfish enough, sometimes. You play mother hen to your family far too much.'

'Mother hen? I don't know whether to be insulted or not.'

'At this point, I feel like I should make a joke about the size of your egg vent.'

'Don't be a cheeky get. We've had enough talk about such things, thank you very much.'

When they got home Nick stuffed some chicken breasts with

goat cheese and wrapped them in bacon, putting them into the oven to roast while Julie packed a suitcase for her week away. While it cooked he went upstairs to give her a hand.

'Do you need anything ironing?' he said.

She threw a pair of baggy black Nicole Farhi linen trousers at him.

'Can you do those for me? And these two shirts, oh, and these t-shirts. I'll take these old jeans for dossing around in.'

He gathered them, set up the ironing board and filled the steam iron with water.

'Have you got a week's worth of knickers and plenty of socks?'

'Aye. I got a new 10-pack of black knickers from Marksies last week, so I'll crack them.'

'Clean jim-jams?'

She laughed. 'Yes, mother.'

'Take a hoodie and a jumper. It's September in Newcastle, so it'll probably feel like winter.'

That night, as soon as they got into bed, she pushed him onto his back and kissed him passionately, intertwining her tongue with his as she gyrated into his hips, her breathing deep and quick.

He rolled on top and pushed into her as she wrapped her legs around him. She was more excited than usual and soon arched her back, letting out a deep, orgasmic growl as her whole body tensed, then whispering dirty talk, digging her fingers into the muscles on his back and shoulders and buttocks, turning them both on more and more. She came again, yelping, her face scrunched in the delicious pain of ecstasy as he tightened his pelvis to hold back for a bit longer and revel in sheer pleasure. Pulling her legs up and wide apart, she grinned up at him, looking into his eyes as every millimetre of his skin prickled with the rush of powerful sexual electricity.

They embraced, wrapped around each other, a veneer of sweat and the smell of sex binding them together.

'Who's a good boy, then?' she said playfully. 'That was delicious.' She kissed him. 'Mmm, you are such a sexy sod. I'll miss your body this week. Your mind I can live without, but not this...' She kissed and rubbed his chest, back and shoulders.

'Feel free to fantasise about me while you're away,' he said, his face on the pillow next to her head, getting his breath back.

'I might do that. We could have Skype sex.'

'That'd make a right mess of my keyboard.'

They rested for a few minutes, then she reached for a tissue to clean herself up, but as he watched her do so, the naked curve of her hips and bare buttocks stirred his passions again. He reached out for her and rolled her over onto her back.

'Let's do it some more, Jules. You're irresistible.'

She stroked his cheek. 'So are you. I could eat you with a spoon. Just lie back, darlin'.' She gently rolled him over and without saying anything more, began kissing him all over, down to his groin, taking him in her mouth until he was fully hard again.

'For some reason, you taste of smoky bacon,' she said, looking up at him, gurgling a laugh. 'And you know how much I love smoky bacon.' He watched as she worked on him with her lips and tongue, her hands between her own legs as she did so, really enjoying her own lust. Oh man, it was good, so vital, invigorating and life-affirming to feel his own passion and share hers, as she brought them both to an intense climax again.

Afterwards, she lay flat on top of him as he embraced her, his hands caressing her hot thighs and buttocks. She tasted of himself when he kissed her and that was so erotic that he kept guiding her mouth back to his, lust rising in him all the time, once again.

'How do you feel, luv?' she said, her breath heavy on his cheek.

'Lucky. How do you feel?'

'I'm throbbing. It's ace.' She laughed and pushed his hair off his face. 'I'm supposed to be the one with the big sex drive, not you. I never thought those pills would have such an effect.' She kissed him again and then looked at him with wide turquoise eyes, her arched eyebrows raised. 'How have you gone and got hard again, already? I've never known the like.'

'Sorry. You just turn me on so much.'

95

She rubbed his ear as he kissed her breasts and belly. 'If you can keep giving it to me, I'll keep taking it,' she whispered, letting a little shiver of pleasure ripple through her, as he explored her always sensitive belly button with his tongue. As he slid down between her legs, she pushed her crotch onto his tongue. He was lost in sex, his whole physicality and mentality absorbed in and by it. It was everything he could think, feel, see and smell and it felt like he could do it all night as she rolled onto her belly and, grasping eagerly at him, guided him inside her.

Time just slipped away as they wallowed in the intimate pleasure they gave each other. Later, totally exhausted, he lay on the bed cooling off.

'I've never had so much great sex, man...not even off you,' said Julie, coming back from the bathroom with a glass of water. 'We're getting bloody good at it, now, I reckon. Ha ha. It's mint, like. It really is. My legs feel a bit wobbly. I thought my heart was going to explode, it was beating so fast.'

'I think it gets better as you get older. It's much more intense for me, is it for you?'

She drained the glass, sitting on the bed.

'I can tell that and it totally is for me, yeah. My orgasms last longer and are sort of deeper. No-one ever told me it'd get better with age. It's a nice treat. It's also funny that you're being more assertive with me, asking to do stuff. You never used to do that.'

'Is that OK? I don't want you to feel like...'

She put her index finger on his lips.

'...don't be daft, it's really great...really great...ha ha...you're like a porno Energiser bunny.'

'It feels great - like I'm really alive. Even now, looking at you sitting there, naked, I feel like I want to have another go. I just fancy you so much, but I absolutely can't. The spirit is willing, but the flesh is finally weak...at least I think it is.'

'I know what you mean, the more you do it, the more attractive the idea of doing it becomes. I've caught myself thinking about us going at it when I'm at work and feeling like touching myself up.

It's like being a teenager again. Eee, what are we like?'

'Don't start talking about touching yourself up, I'll be pawing at you for it again, if you do. You know what that does to me. I'm feeling a shift of blood, already.'

She laughed and looked at him. 'I might say the same thing to you, darlin'. I was totally loving your dirty talk. But my lips are now sealed.' She made a zipping gesture across her mouth and then did the same dramatic gesture between her legs.

'Shit shit shit...I'm late,' said Julie, scurrying to the shower. Nick squinted at her and then at the clock. It was 7am. Her train from Stockton station was at 7.20.

He dragged himself out of bed, noticing as he did that he stank of the musky, sweaty smell of sex. 'You'll never make it Jules. I'll run you up to Newcastle. Take it easy, OK?'

'Thanks luv,' she called from under the water.

An hour later they were on their way.

'We'll get there in plenty of time for your 9.00am start.'

She did her hair in the passenger side vanity mirror.

'Eee god, staying up all night shagging is what did it.' She kissed him on the cheek, happily. 'I slept so solidly.'

'Me, too. It was a quality session, that. Drained me of all my lust, for a few hours, anyway.'

'It can be a distraction, can't it?'

'Being horny? Totally. Yer Buddhists think it drains creativity. I think they've got something there,' he said.

'It's like that episode in *Seinfeld* when George stops having sex and becomes really intelligent as a result. Ha, ha. I love that. Sex makes us stupid. I think it probably does.'

'A lot of stupid things are done because of sex, that's for sure. So where is this refuge you're staying at?'

'It's in Fenham, up Barrack Road.'

'Right. I know that. Oh man, I feel funny about you being away.'

'Will you miss me?'

'Like crazy, yeah.' He turned to look at her. They'd only been together again for a little over two years, but it felt like forever. Life without her was unthinkable.

He pulled up outside a red-brick Victorian town house in the west end of Newcastle.

'This is it,' she said, looking up at it. 'It's unmarked for obvious reasons. Looks nice.'

'Me and Jeff had a student flat around here on Stanton Street for a few months in 1980. At least, I think we did, we were drunk the whole time.'

She leant over and kissed him quickly three times on the lips. 'See you, then. I'll call later when I get a moment. I'm only going to turn my phone on once a day, I'll get distracted by Ricky and Kev's issues otherwise, not to mention mam and Con, Terry and Jaz.'

'Good idea. Just sweeping it all up once a day is a good policy.'

'That's what I thought.'

She got out the car, took her bag out of the boot and then leant in before closing the door. 'See you, then.'

'See ya. Have a good week. Don't worry about anything else. You'll be great.'

She smiled. 'Thanks, luv.' She blew him a kiss, slammed the door shut and walked into the house. He watched her go, then let out a big sigh. For someone who had been a bit of a loner most of his life and certainly as someone who was very used to living inside his own head, having his life and happiness so intertwined with another person was still quite a shocking thing, when he thought about it. When they'd lived together in Harrogate for 18 months before splitting up, he'd not been well in the head and that same intertwining of their lives had, as a result, felt claustrophobic. But now it felt wonderful.

Rather than go straight back home, he drove into Newcastle city centre to get some breakfast and coffee, parking up in the Bigg Market on a meter. He took a walk down High Bridge just to get a look at Jeff's new shop again. He was surprised to see two men walking into the open door of the empty unit with planks of wood.

There, standing in the middle of the floor was Conrad, a fag in his mouth and a huge toolbox at his feet, directing the delivery of wood.

'Con! Alright mate. You've got going quickly.'

He looked up at him and broke into a big, sparkly-eyed grin. 'Alright Nick. What are you doing in Newcastle? Come up for the match?'

'I was dropping Jules off of at the place she's working at this week. Just came to have a look.'

'Aye, well, me and Jeff agreed on a price last night and I thought bugger it, I might as well get cracking this weekend. If I crack on I might get it all done by Sunday night, then it'll just need painting and Jeff can do that when he likes. So I got an early start and went over the timber yard.'

'Cool. Well, I'll leave you to it. How's Jackie this morning?'

'I've not called yet. I'll catch up later in the day. She's a tough old boot. She'll be alright. We'll all be alright.' He laughed and beamed a smile at him. 'I spoke to a solicitor yesterday. Fella on Norton High Street, nice lad. Reckons I can sue McGull Developments for our injuries and distress and that. So I've left it with him. Reckons it'll be worth a canny packet, mind. So everyone's a winner, Nick. Wahay!'

Nick laughed and shook his head. He was irrepressible. It was as though a bad accident was an act of good fortune. Then again, for all he knew, he was making this up as well.

He walked down to the quayside to a small Italian cafe and ordered bacon, eggs, black pudding and sausage along with a large black Americano. How the quayside had changed since he was a student at Newcastle Poly. Back then it was at its lowest ebb. The shipping industry had gone, but nothing had replaced it. It was run down and, unless you were going drinking in the Cooperage or the Red House, pretty much a place to be avoided. Now it was full of smart hotels, pubs and restaurants. The only thing to remain the same were the seagulls which still occupied any ledge they could which didn't have a row of spikes on it. The powerful stench of fish-scented guano on some corners still cleared the nostrils as much as ever.

As he waited for his food he checked his phone. There was a request for a piece from a football magazine and a text from Jeff saying he was paying Con £3,000 to do the work on the shop. That was a nice earner for Con if he could get it done across the weekend, even by the time he'd paid for materials and help.

'We meet again.'

Nick looked up from his plate of food. It was Mike Cavani.

# CHAPTER 6

Cavani sat down opposite him. 'I was just walking past and saw you here in the window. Very handy. I wanted to speak to you. What brings you to Newcastle again?'

He had hazel-coloured eyes which somehow made the whites of his eyes look extra-white.

'I was just giving someone a lift up here.'

'Ah, yes. Julie. The delightful Ms Wells.'

'How did you know that?'

He grinned a toothy, white shark's smile. 'You just told me. But not much happens in Newcastle that I don't know about, if I want to know about it,' he said, enigmatically. 'I was doing a bit of research about you, Nicholas Guymer.' He gestured to a waitress for a coffee. 'Impressive stuff.'

'No, it's not. I've had to fight my corner a few times, that's all.'

'Well. That's the way life is,' said Cavani, stirring cream into his coffee.

Nick finished his food, feeling resentful at having his lovely breakfast interrupted like this.

'Is that everything, Mike?'

'I'm worried about Jimmy Patel's murder. Do you know anything about it?'

'I know Ricky and Kev Wells have been arrested.'

He nodded. 'Yeah, but they're not guilty, are they?'

'No. I don't think so.'

Cavani shrugged. 'I know that. That's what my sources tell me. But the police are dumb fucks and they fit the bill nicely, don't they, so they'll get charged with it.'

'Why are you telling me this, Mike? Do you know who killed Jimmy Patel? Was it your mob?'

He looked insulted as though this was a massively outrageous suggestion. 'Certainly not, and I resent the suggestion it was...'

'Because you're whiter than white, aren't you, Mike?' said Nick, an eyebrow raised.

Cavani had a sardonic smile, which managed to look both menacing and amused at the same time.

'I shall ignore that and I'll put it down to the stress of the last few days. Let me tell you this though, Patel being killed is very inconvenient to us.'

'It's even more inconvenient to him.'

Cavani liked that and laughed. 'True. However, we invested a lot in Patel and now that's all been wasted. I'd like to know who was responsible for that.'

'Invested? He was on your books?'

'In a manner of speaking. No actual books are involved, of course.' There was the sardonic grin again.

'So, do you know who killed him, Mike?'

He shook his head. 'No. No idea at all. That's where you come in.'

'Me? You want me to find out who killed him?'

'If you wouldn't mind.' He said it in such a way as to suggest the possibility of saying no wasn't an option.

'I don't want to.'

'Hmm. Then you and me would have a problem and I much prefer having solutions to having problems. Problems such as having a good-looking fiancée who is badly hurt in a car crash. I'm sure you understand me. Nobody would want that.'

Nick's blood went cold and then hot as a quiet fury rose in his throat. He leant across the table and hissed at him in a low whisper.

'If you know *anything* about me, you will know that you do *not* threaten Julie. If anything happens to her, I will hunt you down and I will kill you myself and you know I will do that, don't you? Don't fucking doubt it for a minute, Cavani. You won't have any problems at all after I've finished with you, because you'll be a heap of ashes in the crematorium.'

Cavani wiped a fleck of spit off his cheek with admirable cool and finished his coffee. Adrenalin coursed through Nick's veins, his armpits prickling with anger.

'I like your attitude, that's why I want *you* to find out who killed Jimmy. But let's not fuck around, Nick. You don't have a choice. Or at least, not a choice you want to have to make.'

Nick's guts felt cold and heavy. How the fuck could he get out of this? There wasn't a way. He couldn't. He couldn't risk anything happening to Julie and they'd hurt her as soon as look at her, he knew they would. He'd have to do what he wanted, at least for now.

'I'll see what I can do,' he said through gritted teeth.

'Splendid. My good offices are open to you...'

'...your good offices? Pah. You're not the Minister of Trade, Cavani, you're a fucking gangster, let's get it right.'

'Nasty word, that. I'm a business man and you can only push me so far, Guymer. I like a bit of attitude, but I don't like disrespect and you're disrespecting me now, so a word to the wise - don't do that again. Ever.'

There was a quiet, perhaps psychotic, menace to his polite, well-spoken Geordie voice now.

'Call this man, he works on Teesside for me.' He pushed a card over the table at him. 'Ian Gow might be of some help. Call me as soon as you find out anything. You have my number.'

Cavani stood up and smiled at him. 'Give my best wishes to Julie.' He nodded and left. As soon as he was gone, the woman who had served him his breakfast came over and took his plate.

'You alright, pet?'

'Yeah.'

She looked at Cavani's back as he crossed the road. 'He's a wrong 'un, that one.'

'You know him?'

'Know him? He owns this place, pet. If he wants you to do something for him, then just do it.'

'Yeah?'

'Aye. He's a vicious twat,' she said it under her breath, barely audible.

The knot in his stomach didn't leave him as he drove home. He was so incredibly worried about Julie. It burned in his guts like an ulcer. Worried they might do something to her. Cavani had obviously done his research, maybe he'd even had them followed. Then again, he couldn't have known that they were coming up to Newcastle that day, as it was only a last-minute decision for him to drive her. And it was just an unhappy accident that he'd chosen that cafe to eat in. Calm down. Cavani wasn't omnipresent. He probably didn't even know where Julie was and was just trying to spook him. Nick had admitted driving Julie up, he'd fallen into Cavani's little trap. Even so. The threat of violence hung in the air like a curse. His peace of mind had gone and had been replaced by a sick churn in his stomach.

But it wasn't going to go away until he'd found out who *had* killed Jimmy Patel. Maybe he could find out. Most murders are committed by family members, that was the place to start.

Once home, he tidied up the bedroom and put some clothes in the wash, pulling Julie's pyjamas to him and breathing in her smell. Weird how people had specific smells. Hers was very distinctive; a musky, strawish-honey scent that was all her own. What was his smell? He could never know. Smoky bacon, perhaps. Ha.

After he'd done some Hoovering and put the kettle on, he called Terry, thinking his voice mail would pick up but, the man himself answered.

'Now then, Nick.'

'Alright mate. How are you?'

He blew air into the phone. 'Stressed out.'

'What's the situation with Ricky and Kev?'

'They're keeping them in for more questions tomorrow. They wouldn't bail them because of their prison records...a flight risk or whatever.'

'And what about you and Jasmin?'

'She's here with me at my place.'

'Do you have any idea at all who killed her dad? If you do, it's important you tell me.'

'Eh? No, mate. Jaz was the one who found him and called the cops, y'know.'

'Really? Listen, I'm going to come round. I'll be with you in half an hour. Do you need anything?'

'Some cans would be good.'

He stopped at the off licence and picked up eight cans of lager and then drove to Terry's housing association flat in Roseworth.

'You look knackered, son,' said Nick as Terry let him in. He thrust the drink into his hand. 'How do you feel after the crash?'

'Knocked about a bit, but alright. Just called the insurance company about that. Got to fill in a ton of forms.'

Jasmin was sitting on an old sofa with a mug of tea in her hand as he went in the living room.

'Hello, Jaz. I'm sorry to hear about your dad.'

She gave him a weak smile, hands cupped around the Middlesbrough FC mug.

'Have the police interviewed you?'

'Yes, and Terry as well. It was horrible. I feel like I'm living in a nightmare which I can't wake up from. First that horrible crash and now dad.'

She wore a look of deep distress and was shaking a little. Maybe she couldn't believe she'd killed her own father. Maybe she didn't mean to. Or maybe she was just still in shock after the accident. Everyone had to be a suspect.

'How did it all happen then, Terry?' he said sitting down opposite him. 'Run me through events.'

He got up and walked around the room, picked up an old cricket bat, twirled it around in his hands and put it back down against the wall and then stared, arms folded, at the cheap, nylon pattern green carpet. 'After I got out of hospital I couldn't get hold of Jaz. I knew she was at her parents' house...'

'...how did you know that?'

'...I guessed she was because she was collected from the hospital, a nurse told me. So I went round there but her dad wouldn't let me see her.'

'They weren't holding you prisoner though, were they?' said Nick to Jasmin.

She nodded. 'Yes, they were, sort of. Well, dad was. He'd locked the door and had taken my keys and phone. I was outraged at first, but then I thought I'd just sit it out and they'd soon calm down. I wanted to give him one last chance to accept me and Terry. I was tired of fighting him. A private doctor came round to check me over and said I was in shock and should rest, so I went to bed and tried to relax.'

'So what did you do then, Tez?' She glanced at him nervously.

'I rang Kev and he said they'd go and have a word in the morning and basically put the shits up him and that'd sort him out. I wish to god I hadn't agreed to that now. Anyway, they did.'

'So you've only Kev and Ricky's word about what happened when they went there?'

'Yeah. I talked to them for five minutes when they were at the station before they were formally arrested. Kev told me to call Gaunty. They told me Jimmy answered the door and was already bleeding.'

'OK. So what were you doing all this time, Jaz?'

'I was just on my own in my old room in the house. I didn't even see Ricky and Kev arrive. I didn't see or hear anything. I was lying on my old bed listening to music on my iPod and reading for most of the morning. I went down stairs at about 11am to make some tea and I found him lying on the kitchen floor with a kitchen knife in his heart. I screamed and then called the police. He was just lying there flat on his back with blood on the white tiled floor.'

'Was anyone else in the house?'

'No, I was the only person there.' She nodded as if to confirm the fact. 'As soon as the police came, they sealed off the whole place as a crime scene. They interviewed me for ages. I told them anyone could have come and gone and I wouldn't have known. The doors aren't locked and I listen to my music very loud. I had no idea the brothers had even been taken in until Terry told me, later in the afternoon. I assumed they'd think I'd done it, but they quickly seemed to be persuaded that I hadn't, probably as soon as they learnt the brothers had called around.'

'They didn't do it, Jaz. I'm sure they didn't,' said Terry. For some reason, he didn't sound that sincere. It sounded more like the sort of thing you say because you're obliged to say it.

'Jules thinks the same. She got in to see them for a few minutes and also said they were innocent,' said Nick. 'They also said they were confronted by Jimmy waving a knife and had some sort of wrestling match with him.'

She shrugged. 'Then he must have been stabbed after that. Like I said, I didn't even know they'd been to the house, so who did it then?' said Jaz.

'This might be an odd thing to ask, Jaz, but are you bothered he's dead?' said Nick.

'Not really. I'm shocked, but I won't miss him. I haven't been close to him since I was little. I know it's terrible to say this about someone who is dead, but I didn't like him. He wasn't a nice man. He was selfish and egotistical and controlling and aggressive. He controlled and abused mum for years and he wanted to control me and Terry.'

The oppressed wife. That was a very good motivation for murder.

'And where did your mother go?' asked Nick.

'Oh, she usually goes to Her Hair on Linthorpe Road. So before you think it, she probably has an alibi. I think it has to be something to do with his work. He had a lot of power to award lucrative contracts,' said Jaz. 'He knew lots of dodgy people, I'm sure.'

'I'm sorry to have to ask this Jaz, but why do you think the police have been so quick to dismiss you as a suspect?'

She was quick to answer.

'Judging from the questions they asked, it's because he was killed with some force, more force than anything I could do with my weedy arms. I mean, they probably do still suspect me, but as soon as Ricky and Kev's names were mentioned, they seemed to put me on the back burner.'

'I know what the police are like, they go with the path of least resistance. If it looks like Rick and Kev, that'll be good enough for them, but I reckon in the long run, they'll be able to prove their innocence. It won't stand up in court,' said Terry. 'There's good news about mam, at least.'

'Is there?'

'Yeah. She's sitting up in bed. I even had a quick word. She was groggy and on morphine, but it was good to hear her voice. She was pegging for a fag.'

'Can't be anything too much wrong with her then,' said Nick. 'I'll try and look in on her later, in lieu of Julie being here.'

'Oh yeah, she was going to Newcastle, wasn't she?' said Terry.

'Yeah, it's really important for her new career prospects. It's just for a week.'

He was interrupted by his phone vibrating. It was Jeff.

'Hey, big man.'

'Are you back in Stockton?'

'Yeah.'

'Swing by the shop, will you? There's something I want to show you. Nothing to do with records.'

'What is it?'

'Remember I was taking the video of the wedding day?'

'Oh, god, yeah, I had forgotten about that. '

'So had I, given what happened. I just looked at the footage and there's some weird shit on it. Come and see.'

He got up to go. 'Jaz. Think on about who might have wanted to kill your dad.'

'I've thought about nothing else.'

'Of course. Can you make me a list of anyone you think might have had a motive to do it or just whack job fuckers he might have known? Email it to me.'

'I really don't know anyone, Nick. I know you want to get Ricky and Kev out, but I really don't know anything.'

He parked down Silver Street, off Stockton High Street and walked up to Jeff's store.

'Ah ha, here he is,' said Jeff's as he walked in. Emily was still sitting behind a screen.

'Have you moved since yesterday, Em? You were in the exact same position when I left you.'

'I have had six hours sleep, a few wees and one poo, but apart from that, yeah, I've been right here,' she said, without taking her eyes off the screen.

'She's like some hi-tech kid out of a movie working to crack the Pentagon's computer which contains information about aliens,' said Jeff, walking out from behind her, patting her on the shoulders as he did so.

Opening up his laptop next to her, he found the video files he'd downloaded. Nick pulled up a stool and sat alongside Emily. Her screen was full of database records. She gave him a little smile.

'That doesn't look thrilling,' he said.

'It isn't. Organising the information isn't thrilling. Making it work with the right software to push it to several locations at once, is what is thrilling.'

Jeff spoke up. 'I think it's thrilling that we have three copies of Ten Years After's splendid album *Watt.* I didn't know that until you pulled the data together across the two stores. Admittedly, this is not what most people think is thrilling. I'll give you that. Right, look at this. Here we are in your car going up Yarm Lane and now sitting at the lights. We're turning right onto Yarm Road and Terry is in front in the Mercedes, see?'

'Yup. Jackie is in the front playing at being the Queen. Conrad is behind her, Jaz is behind Terry on the back seat.'

'Now, watch as we pull away at the lights.'

The video was really good quality and well focused. Julie waved at the camera as they moved off, Jeff had then panned to Nick at the wheel and then back to Julie. He held the frame and pointed at the screen.

'See there, Julie is waving at the camera...'

Emily leant over to look. 'She looks lovely as ever, how sickening.'

'...but behind her, in the car in front is Conrad and he's on the phone. Why is he on the phone?'

'Roll it back a little, Jeff,' said Nick.

He did so and replayed it. Clearly, Conrad put the phone to his ear as they left the lights and kept it there as they came to a halt at another set of lights, directly before turning left onto Prince Regent Street. He still held it to his ear as they pulled away from those lights.

'Now you stalled here, remember?' said Jeff. So they're away and out of view for a few seconds. When we next see the car in front, he's put the phone away.' Jeff stopped the playback again. 'Now, what I didn't realise, is that I've actually caught the crash on film. Not very clearly, mind, but see what you think. I'll mute the sound because it's just us shouting and swearing.'

All three of them leant into the screen and watched the action unfold, as Terry's car pulled alongside the building site, the cement truck drove off the site and into the car, rolling it onto its side, then on its back and pressed it up against the wall on the other side of the street. It was spectacular. Emily gasped and held her hand over her mouth.

'Oh. My. God. How did anyone survive that?' she said.

'The truck was powerful, but really not going at much of a speed. That's what saved them. Two things occurred to me,' said Jeff, rolling it back again.

'Keep your eyes on Conrad. Here, he's put the phone away and now...look...he's moved to the centre of the back seat. Jaz is right up against her door and she's no size, so there was plenty of room for him in the middle. Why's he done that? And now look, the truck comes off the site...he's gunning that thing as hard as he can.'

'How do you know that? 'said Emily.

Nick pointed to the cloud of exhaust emerging from the back of the truck. 'He's got his foot right down on the accelerator, but it's in a low gear and they take some getting going 'cos they're so heavy. That's literally as fast as it could go from a dead start, still not that fast, but shows an intent to get it going quickly.' He tugged at his beard stubble.

Jeff stopped the video again, just as the truck struck the car. 'At first I thought he'd just been thrown on his side, but if you look at him here...in the middle of the back seat, he's got his head in his hands, bent over in a semi-foetal position, as though he's trying to protect himself. Don't you think that's weird?'

Nick sat and thought about the implications of what Jeff was saying.

'Can you run it back to when you first see him after stalling,' said Emily. As he played it again, she pointed at the screen with her right little finger nail. 'Play one frame at a time, two seconds apart.'

'How do I do that?'

She leant over, held some keys down, selected something from the Photoshop menu and hit return.

'There. Now watch. He moves to the middle of the back, seat and Jackie also moves that way as well.' She paused it and pointed again. 'Look where she is now. She's gone from leaning on the door to leaning right over the gear stick.'

'She was pretty drunk,' said Jeff.

'Oh. OK, maybe she's just swaying then. Funny that it's almost co-ordinated with him.' She let it play frame by frame again. 'But keep focused on her now. She turns her back to the door as it approaches so that when it hits, her back is facing the truck. Is that just a defensive instinct?'

'If it isn't, you know what this means, Em?' said Nick.

'That they set up the crash. That Conrad called the driver to say they were on their way, and they both took as much evasive action as they could to survive it,' she said, in a quiet voice, adding, 'that is sort of cool, but very uncool at the same time.'

'When I looked in the windscreen, she still had her back to the door. I remember thinking that at the time. It could be the factor that saved her life.'

Jeff looked at Nick, Nick looked at Jeff, both of them astonished.

'Why don't you call Jaz and ask if she remembers him using the phone,' said Emily, returning to her database work.

Jeff pointed at her. 'That, my pixie-like angel from Montgomery, or wherever, is a good idea.'

Nick did so. 'Jaz? Hiya. This will sound odd, but we're just exploring an idea. Do you remember Conrad using his phone on the trip to the registry office, specifically as you turned up Prince Regent Street?'

She paused to recall. 'Err...yeah, he did. Actually, at the time I thought it was odd to make a phone call right there and then. And it was a strange call, anyway.'

'Why was it strange?'

'Because he didn't say anything. He selected a number, listened for a few seconds and then hung up.'

'So it wasn't ringing long enough to be picked up?'

'I think it was just that it wasn't picked up. He didn't say anything, anyway. Then we crashed almost immediately so I didn't think about it again. Is it somehow significant or something?'

'Yeah, I think it is. Thanks, Jaz.'

'It's a compo job,' said Emily. 'He'll sue the building firm and they'll get away with it, as well. No-one hurts themselves that much on purpose, that's how insurers view it, I'd imagine. They won't suspect it's a set-up.'

'You're right, Em. Last time I saw him he said he was going to sue them,' said Nick.

'My guess is that they didn't mean it to be that bad, but it wasn't really controllable. Either way, the money I saw the driver take, was for a job well done from Conrad,' said Jeff, his finger cocked at 45 degrees.

'Crafty old sod. He said everything was going to be alright when I saw him in Newcastle. No wonder he's so happy,' said Nick.

'If I was Jackie, I'd be mightily pissed off to be almost killed,' said Jeff.

'But on the upside, the worse the injuries, the bigger the compo,' said Emily. 'Now, can you be quiet while I get this done? It's very difficult and I need to concentrate.'

Nick and Jeff went and stood outside. It was a blank day of weather. Cloudy, not warm, not cold, not windy, not wet.

'What do we do with this, then?' said Nick. 'I don't even know how to think about it. One part of me admires the sheer gall of it and yet it seems...just...wrong.' He looked up at Jeff, who was pulling on his beard, a long curtain of hair draped down his back.

'It's a weird one. Proper shocking. What a bloody con. The bloke is well bloody named. Do we shop him? That's the question.'

'If we do that, we shop the driver, the Lithuanian geezer and he's only done it because he's living in dire straits. I mean, the poor guy has nothing. I don't want that on my conscience.'

Jeff nodded. 'Yeah, that's true. And we've also got to remember that Jackie has almost certainly conspired with him on this. So if we put him in the clarts, we put her in as well. Do we want that? Not really.'

'Nah. She's been punished plenty already. She's properly knacked. They probably thought there'd be a bit of whiplash, but he really gunned that cement truck, panicked and totally slammed the car.'

Nick crossed his arms and they stood watching buses pull up at the stop.

'Well...let's just let him get on with it,' said Nick. 'McGull's will be insured. It'll all get sorted.'

'Aye. Like with the Brian Jones signature, I'm not even going to mention it to him,' said Jeff. 'I'll almost pretend it hasn't happened. What a bloody scammer, though,' said Jeff, shaking his head. 'You've got to admire it, from an old geezer like him. Poor Jackie, though. The pain she's going through for it.'

'Yeah, well, they must have known the risks. It's one last big free pay day. Why the hell not? His labour will have been exploited for low wages most of his life. It's about time he got something out of the system. Any money he gets will all be spent in the local economy. Everyone benefits from a poor working-class scam in a way that no-one benefits from a rich middle-class one, where money is just put in offshore accounts and the like. More pressing for us now, is finding out who killed Jimmy Patel.'

Nick explained his unpleasant meeting with Mike Cavani. Jeff looked at him wearily as he did so.

'Bloody hell, Nick. How the hell are you going to find that out? And if you do, how will it get Cavani off your case? Because you know what will happen, if you do a good job for him, he'll put you onto something else, under threat of hurting Jules again. It'll never stop. He's done his research, heard you're good in a fight, seen what balls you've got and he reckons you're what he needs on his team.'

'Hmm, maybe. But what do I do about it? Patel was on their payroll and they want to know who has disrupted their nice little inside deals.'

'Alright. Say you find out it was his wife that killed him, Cavani might have her killed and, indirectly, that'd be your fault. Can you cope with that? You can't contain what he does with your information.'

'They wouldn't do that. They're muscle merchants, they've not got a rep for killing people. They're extortionists and blackmailers.'

'Well, I'm glad you're confident about that, because I wouldn't be.'

'Well, what the hell would you do, then?' he said, frustrated. 'I don't have any choice. I'm not risking them touching Jules. She's everything to me. Everything. I'd rather they hurt me than her. Whatever else happens, as long as she's OK, that's what has to matter to me.'

Jeff held his hands up and nodded. 'OK sure, I get you. I understand. You need some insurance in this, though.'

'Insurance?'

'Aye. Let me think about it. You need to get something on Mike Cavani so that you can keep him at arms length in the long run.'

'Well, while you're doing that, I'm going to find out who popped Patel. Once I've got that info, I'll have something to trade with Cavani. After all, I don't have to tell him if I can scare him off in some other way, but I'd like to know just in case we can't scare him off. It'd be nice to get Ricky and Kev off the hook, as well.'

'Well, I'm here for you - but in a macho, non-touchy-feely, sort of way, obviously.'

Luke walked up with a bag of Greggs sausage rolls.

'Now then,' he said stuffing one into his mouth in an explosion of flaky pastry.

'Are you off south today, Lukey?' said Nick.

'Aye. More's the pity.'

'He wants to get in young Emily's panties,' said Jeff, pushing the lad on the shoulder. 'He's no chance though. I've told him she likes older dudes, like you.'

'I'm so jealous. She's so gorgeous and you saw her naked. What's she like?'

'A normal human female, albeit one in minimalist underwear, if my memory serves me well. Now put your tongue in. The more you try and slaver up to her, the more she'll ignore you.' He was quite pleased with this sage, older man's pearl of wisdom, though whether it was true or not, he had no idea.

'Well, I've gotta go home anyway, so there's no chance.'

'Aye, but she's going to be around a lot in the shop here and you'll have to deal with her on the phone and that,' said Jeff, 'so if you pick up your game, you might have a chance.'

That seemed to encourage him a little as he went into the shop.

'He's absolutely no chance,' laughed Jeff.

'I know. Poor lad.' He walked away and waved a goodbye. 'I'll speak to you later.'

Sitting in his car, Nick called Ian Gow on the number Mike Cavani had given him.

'Yeah?'

'Is this Ian Gow?'

'Who's this?'

That was stupid thing to say if you were trying to pretend not to be Ian Gow, because if you weren't you'd have said straight away, "no, it's not". Maybe he wasn't that bright.

'My name is Nick Guymer. Mike Cavani gave me your number and said I should get in touch with you.'

The man let out a tense breath. 'Oh, right. He mentioned you, yes.'

'Can we meet up? There are a few things I'd like to discuss.'

'Yes. Where are you?'

'Stockton High Street.'

'Do you know the Dickens pub in the Boro?'

'Yes.'

'I'll meet you there in half an hour. I'll have a purple t-shirt on.'

Nick drove straight over, putting on BBC Tees to listen to the Boro's home game against Ipswich. He should have gone to see them, but he couldn't focus on the football, not with all this shit swirling around. Traffic was heavy and it took him the full half an hour before he'd got parked up off Linthorpe Road. Before going to the pub, he walked up to the hairdressers that Myra went to, the morning Jimmy was killed.

Her Hair and Herr Hair were wittily titled women's and men's hairdressers next to each other on Linthorpe Road. Both were modern-looking places, mostly populated with young men and women with interesting hair, in all shapes and colours. Her Hair was busy, as orange-tanned stylists, mostly in full make-up, washed and cut hair and talked about the inconsequential stuff of life, as though it was important.

'Hiiiiyaaa,' said a young woman on the reception desk, in an up and down Teesside lilt. She had asymmetrical hair coloured in burgundy, cream and black, making it appear like she had a post-modern impressionist sculpture balancing on her head. It was superb. She must have been spray-tanned and baked on 400 degrees for an hour, so deeply bread-bun brown was she.

He felt like he was on foreign soil in an environment like this, be it for women or men, but this lass seemed very approachable.

'Hi there. My friend's mother comes here to get her hair done...she's called Myra Patel. Lovely lady in her 50s, do you know her, by any chance?'

'Eee aye, 'course I do,' she said, all smiles and happy eyes. Maybe she was high on hair spray or maybe she just enjoyed her job. Or hopefully both. 'I know Myra. I'm so jealous of Indian hair. It's gorgeous, isn't it?'

'Beautiful, yeah. Do you remember when she was last in?'

She looked through a reassuringly still analogue appointments book which was full of blue Biro marks.

'Yeah, Janice did her first thing on Friday. We open at 8.00am and she was first in. Why, like?'

'My girlfriend loved what Janice did to her hair and wanted to come in and get the same thing done. Did it take long?'

'No, only about 45 minutes.'

'OK, thanks, I'll tell her to drop in and make an appointment.' The receptionist wiggled her fingers at him and he left with a wave.

So much for Myra's alibi of being at the hairdressers when Jimmy was killed. The police would surely uncover that fiction soon enough if they could look away from Ricky and Kev's guilt. Then again, Myra hadn't made that claim for herself, it was made for her by Jasmin. Something wasn't right.

He made his way into the pub to meet Ian Gow. The Dickens Inn was a semi-legendary Middlesbrough drinking emporium which, being right by Teesside University, attracted a lot of students. Over the years it had grown and grown and now resembled a cross between a garden centre and one of those pubs attached to a Travelodge. Its champagne and cocktails bar made it sound a lot more upmarket than it really was. At its core, its primary function in society was to be a place where you went to get shit-faced on the drink, alongside a lot of your similarly shit-faced contemporaries, much like any other pub in the north of England.

A man in a purple t-shirt was leaning on the bar. Nick held out his hand. 'Ian?' He was an older man, not much hair left, a pudgy, unhealthy-looking face with a glisten of sweat on his hair line. He wore a pair of brown slacks that were totally at odds with the purple t-shirt. In fact, it looked as though he'd been dressed by a blind man in a charity shop, or had picked the clothes out of a box of donations at a homeless shelter. His crumpled, grey leather shoes were possibly the worst he'd ever seen. Ian Gow didn't look well at all. He exuded an air of decay and unkempt dissolution that hinted at a life falling apart.

Nick ordered a sparkling water, got Ian Gow another pint of lager and took a table in the corner.

'So you work for Mike, then?' said Nick, 'How long have you done that for?'

'Couple of years.'

'Can I ask why?'

'He helped me out of some debt I'd got into.'

Nick could believe that. He looked like the kind of man whose natural home was a bookies, chewing on a small pencil, worrying over the 4.45 from Kempton Park.

'And you're still paying him back?'

'Sort of, yeah. He called me and said you're interested in this Jimmy Patel murder.'

'Yeah. I need to find out who was responsible, for Mike.'

Gow nodded, clearly knowing all too well what it was like to be obligated in such a way. 'I'll tell you what I know about him.'

He spoke in a classic, gruff, coarse Middlesbrough accent born out of a million cigarettes and even more drinks. It was a voice that made Chris Rea sound like a choir boy.

'It was Jimmy Patel's final say-so which awarded building and renovation contracts all over this region. The Cavanis paid him to push a contract to one of *their* builders.' He put inverted commas around the word *their* with his index fingers. 'Not all the time, just on significant projects such as building those Prince Regent Street units. Do you know them? Supposed to be part of Stockton's industrial redevelopment.'

Nick snorted a laugh. 'Yeah, I know them. Not because of Cavani but for an entirely different reason, also involving a dodgy bloke.'

'They made sure Patel gave that to Paddy McGull's company. McGull's get regular work from Patel that way.'

'Is McGull's a Cavani company as well?'

Gow shook his head. 'No. At least, not to my knowledge and I'm pretty in the loop for Cavani down here. They probably know what's going on, though.'

'So why do McGull's get the work?'

'Because McGull's use suppliers which are basically Cavani's companies. He calls it his Empire solution.'

'Empire? Why Empire?'

'Because when we had an empire, we used to force colonies to buy stuff made in the UK and boosted those businesses that way. Cavani's front companies get loads of trade from companies that they've made sure have plenty of work. So it's like that.'

Nick sat back, arms folded. 'It's a rubbish analogy that, Ian, because if Cavani was the empire, he'd be forcing people to buy his stuff and he's not forcing them...they just buy it from his companies, anyway...so it doesn't work.'

Gow looked at him like he was mad. 'You bloody tell him that, then. Whatever the fuck...I don't give a shit. I don't even know what an analogy is.' He said it as "anna-lodgy." He drank his lager and wiped his lips. 'Cavani said you were smart bloke, like. I reckon he's got you in mind for something big. He likes brains and brawn together and you look a fucking middleweight boxer, you. Fucking arms on you. Shit.' He looked at Nick's biceps almost in disgust. Nick ignored him.

'Let's get back to Jimmy Patel. From what I understand, he was quite an arrogant bloke and arrogant blokes tend to have a lot of enemies when they're in positions of power.'

Gow nodded. 'Yeah. The power had totally gone to his head. He'd been in the chief executive role for MIDO for five years and he thought he was king of the castle. So if you want to know who

119

killed him, I'd look first at people who reckoned they'd get a contract and didn't. They'd be the most bitter.'

'Who stood to gain most by his death?'

Gow drained his glass and took a sip out of the new pint.

'I've been thinking about that. His number two is Sheila Simmons. She'll get his job. So you've got to look at her motives.'

'What's she like? I've never heard of her.'

'I don't know either. She's a back-room woman. Patel was always in the papers, she never is. Wouldn't surprise me if she did all the real work and he took the glory, in which case she might be very bitter.'

Nick raised an eyebrow and drank some water. 'Good call. You don't strike me as an obvious feminist, Ian.'

He looked at him like he was insane for a second time. 'I'm not. I don't give a fuck about women.'

That much sounded very true. 'OK, so there's Sheila to consider, who else?'

'Patel has got two sons. Cavani reckons one of them, Lomash his name is, is gay. And your typical Paki dad really fucking hates a gay, doesn't he?'

'The Patel's are actually Indian.'

'Whatever. They're all the same.'

Nick wondered how much blatant racism and misogyny was going to raise its ugly head.

'So I reckon Jimmy has given this Mash lad a hard time, due to him being a bender and Mash has gone round there and done him.'

'Do you really reckon that's what happened?'

Gow nodded. 'If Cavani is right about the kid being queer, that'd be my best guess, aye. Not sure how you'll find out for sure, though.'

'How does Cavani know the kid is gay?'

Gow shrugged. 'I didn't ask. Best not to ask Cavani anything, if you can avoid it. He's got eyes everywhere. It's unbelievable the stuff that man knows. Someone will have fucked the kid and then reported back up the chain. That's how it works. Cavani's business is all about using information, backed up with evil fucking muscle.'

'What about his wife, Myra? Anything on her?'

'I don't know nowt about her. Paki wives are always slapped around though, aren't they? Same as the daughters. Them and the Ayatollahs. All the fucking same. Never happier than when they're kicking women around. Mind, they're onto something, stopping them from driving in Saudi.' He smacked his lips as he drank the lager, nodding at his own certain view of the world. Nick couldn't let it go without some non-racist counterbalance.

'To be fair mate, violence against women isn't exactly unknown amongst white blokes from Teesside, is it? And if you've never met a shit male driver, you've not been paying attention.'

'Aye, true. Probably why so many immigrants feel at home here, eh. They're embracing our wife-beating culture.' He laughed at his own quip.

Sweeping racist generalisations aside, Nick knew for a fact that Jasmin was no fan of her father and she had said that her mother had been 'oppressed' by Jimmy for years. That sounded like a decent motivation for murder, no matter where you were from.

'Where would I find this Lomash bloke, then? Any idea?'

'He works at that big designer clothes shop on Linthorpe Road.'

'Flashmans?'

'Aye. That's it. Wall to wall designer labels. Overpriced shite for pricks and queers.'

Gow was so deep into a world of dislike, mistrust and hate, that his whole language was based in bigotry and nastiness.

'I'm not a fashion expert Ian, but you don't look like the sort of bloke who shops for Armani that often.'

'Waste of fucking money. But aye, he works in there measuring blokes' inside legs, I should think. Ha.'

'I'll check him out. What does he look like?'

'What do you mean what does he look like? He's a Paki, isn't he?'

Nick rubbed his eyes. This was getting very wearying. It was as if it was still 1975. Gow was a pitiful human.

'OK, mate, thanks for your help,' said Nick, finishing his water.

'Best to keep Cavani happy if you want to keep hold of your knee caps.'

'They're not murderers though, are they? The Cavanis, I mean. They don't kill people.'

'No, that'd be too easy. They specialise in maiming and torture. It's one of Mike's favourite fucking hobbies, I'm told.'

# CHAPTER 7

Nick shook his damp hand and walked out of the pub and up Southfield Road to Linthorpe Road, taking a right and crossing over to the big fashion store - the well-named Flashmans. It was a classic 'cash for flash' Northern designer clothes store. It was a place to buy clothes that said you had money, or at least that you did have money until you bought the clothes that said you had money, after which, ironically enough, you had no money left.

A Versace shirt in the window in a vivid acid green and cerise Romanesque pattern had a price tag of £295. Who the hell had that sort of money on Teesside? Not many, not legally, anyway.

He looked at some of the jackets on a rack; none came in under £750. Ties were a minimum of £100. Wandering through to the casual wear department he picked up a £65 t-shirt and looked at it. Its single design element were the letters D & G. Dolce and Gabbana. That elevated it from a five quid shirt to £65. It was a triumph of marketing over material.

A quick glance around. There were four shop floor workers. Three white lads in tight shirts and lavishly coiffured, asymmetrical hair and one Asian lad with close cropped hair and a well cut grey suit. That had to be Lomash.

How to approach this? Just ask him, 'Did you kill your dad?' But before he could approach him, another salesman came over.

'Hey, how can I help you today?' he said as though he was an American, despite clearly hailing from South Bank or possibly the less sophisticated side of Dormanstown and giving the impression of being a drug dealer in a sleazy night club.

'I'm just having a look around, thanks mate,' said Nick.

The lad looked him up and down quickly and with, it seemed to Nick, a look of disdain for his choice of jeans and t-shirt.

'Are those Tommy Hilfiger?' he said, pointing to Nick's jeans.

'Err...yeah, I think they are.'

'Cool. We've just got some new Tommy jeans in over here,' he tried to lead him to the denim side of the store. But why would he want more jeans? These were OK for about four or five years yet. They'd cost him £1.60 at a car boot and he'd haggled them down from £2. A similar pair on a rail here were £110. Presumably you had to pay the £108.40 premium to buy your clothes in a bricks and mortar store rather than in a windy field. It didn't feel like progress.

Glancing over his shoulder he saw a middle-aged Asian woman walk in and go up to Lomash, who was folding dress shirts.

'These are a great jean for a guy of your age. A little bit rock 'n' roll, but not too fashionable, y'know?' said the sales lad. His words sounded vaguely insulting. What did he know about rock 'n' roll? He was about 20. Nick took the jeans from him.

'Yup, these are definitely jeans,' he said.

'We've got a denim shirt to go with them as well.' Christ, he was building wardrobe for him. Considering his bank account was £3,790 overdrawn on a £4,000 overdraft, unless these were car boot prices, the sales kid wasn't going to get his commission.

That had to be Lomash's mother or another family relation. They were nodding at each other and then the woman turned and left.

'Thanks mate, but I think these are out of my price range,' he said and before the guy could try and sell him anything else, walked out of the store onto Linthorpe Road. The Saturday afternoon shoppers crowded the pavement, but he could see the woman in the distance walking towards the town centre.

He took a chance and ran up to her. 'Mrs Patel?' he said, coming alongside her. She turned, surprised, her black eyebrows raised. She did have lovely, glossy hair.

'Yes?'

'I'm Nick Guymer. I'm a friend of Jasmin and Terry and I just wanted to say how sorry I was to hear about your husband. A terrible thing to happen.'

She stopped and her shoulder tensed up. 'Yes. Well. Thank you. Oh, Nick, Terry's sister's Nick?'

'That's right, yeah. It must be a difficult time for you. I know they arrested Ricky and Kev but...'

She closed her eyes and held her hands up to silence him.

'I don't want to hear it. I don't want to hear anything about it. I've told the police everything I know and that's it for me...I'm drawing a line, I'm walking away.'

And that's what she did. Walking at a good pace away from him. Was it worth asking her anything else? One thing was clear, she was not exactly grieving for her murdered husband, so he watched her go. She was upright, quite broad and very well dressed in trousers and a wool jacket. Was she a killer? Oh yeah, she could be, of that there was no doubt and if you were bitter and angry enough to not be upset by your husband's murder so soon after it had happened, it wasn't too big a stretch of imagination to think she put the knife into him. She was physically capable of it. She wasn't at the hairdressers when it happened, as Jaz had said, and she surely had lied about that on purpose, for some reason. Still, even if she didn't do it personally, she might have had someone do it for her. Someone like her alienated gay son, perhaps?

He put his hands in his pockets and wandered back up the road, deep in thought. He couldn't just speak to these people and magically ascertain who had killed Jimmy Patel, it was pointless to even try that. Cavani had been sure that Ricky and Kev would be charged with the murder. Was that just speculation or some inside information? He stood outside of Flashmans and looked at Lomash. He was just regular Boro lad of Indian heritage, not especially flamboyant, nor any sort of archetypal gay bloke. Maybe Ian Gow was wrong about him even being gay. This was the trouble with relying on other people's information, you never knew if it was true, a lie or a rumour assumed to be a fact.

As he walked back to his car, he checked his phone. It was nearly 5pm. The match would be over. He checked on the Boro score. They'd won 3-1. Julie's prediction was spot on. Pity he hadn't put money on it. That was a good result. Boro looked set fair for a decent season at this rate.

With no-one at home, he felt no urge to go back and sit in the quiet on his own, so he sat in the car for a while, watching people going home after an afternoon shopping, going home with friends and in couples to their homes and maybe getting ready for Saturday night on the town. When you're on your own, it is times such as these when you really feel it most, when people are going about the ordinary stuff of life with their spouse, partners or friends. You feel so outside of it and as a result, almost invisible. No-one cares what you're doing, no-one cares whether you're going home or not, no-one cares whether you're eating well or not, no-one cares whether you've had a bottle of vodka and a handful of pills or not. They're busy with their significant others and you are not one of those. You feel like you are on the outside of society. You are out in the cold and, it seems, they are all sitting around the fire, warming themselves from the glow of their friends and family.

He let out a low groan in his throat and reached into his pocket for a Phenibut capsule. This was ridiculous. He had no reason to feel alone in the world because he had Julie and they had a fierce love for each other. And yet, even though he'd only dropped her off a few hours ago, he was feeling lonely, the way he used to feel lonely before he met Julie and much, much worse, that feeling went hand in hand with drinking. When all the couples were going back to their love nests, he would go to a bar and drink. The drink was his friend, his partner, his love. The drink never let you down. The drink was always there for you, like a loyal and true friend should be. It put its arm around you and comforted you. And sitting there in the centre of Middlesbrough on a Saturday afternoon, he felt its siren call again more strongly than he had done for a long time. He'd been sober for nearly three years, but now he really wanted a fucking drink. It had been building up in him for a while. Little flashes of desire, small glimpses of that booze lust, but now it was in full effect and had moved into his psyche lock, stock and 10 double vodkas.

It felt shocking to have that urge again, because one way or another he'd educated it out of himself. He'd got used not being a slave to drink cravings and to the temporary dopamine boost it gave him. He had got used to being more even-tempered and stable and not drinking himself into a temporarily better frame of mind. Climbing off the roller-coaster of endless carbohydrate consumption had been the best thing he'd ever done to combat his depressive moods and quitting drink had been one big element of that.

But even so. He needed a fucking drink.

He wasn't an alcoholic, he was pretty sure about that. He'd done the AA analysis and had come out as emotionally dependent on alcohol, but not physically dependent, or at least not back then, in 2006. So why was this an issue now? The worry and pressure of Mike Cavani and facing it all alone was part of it. Having a big thing to worry about in your life is the most stressful thing because it never, ever leaves you. The burning concern is always there in every waking moment and no matter how much you try and distract yourself from it, you still find your mind fretting over and over, worrying on it and shattering your peace of mind. It was exhausting and yet it is impotent emotion, spent to accrue nothing at all.

He craved the warm friendship of booze and also of the places that served it to you without judgement. It was such an acceptable thing to do. You were greeted warmly at pretty much every bar in the northeast of England, at any time of any day. Being drunk was not just acceptable, it was welcomed. To always be sober made you an outsider. In fact, he'd used his empathy with being out of the cultural mainstream to help himself reprogramme his drinking lifestyle.

But that hollow craving in his stomach, that old, old feeling that said to his brain, make me feel good, fill me with drink. It was back with a vengeance now.

He chewed his fingernails, wondering how to cope, hoping that the Phenibut would rebalance him, but worrying that it wouldn't and that this alcohol lust was too strong to resist. It wasn't just the craving for the effect of the drink, though, it was the need to be part of something when you felt alone. Even if it was just to be part of the population who were going out for a drink - the sprawling anonymous, amorphous mass of people, all of whom would be out in pubs and clubs tonight, rubbing shoulders with each other. Doing what everyone else was doing, somehow combated the loneliness, at least until you were pissed, at which point you became maudlin about being drunk and alone. It was a lesson he'd learned and learned well, when he started boozing in pubs, before his 16th birthday.

As a couple in their 30s walked past his car, hand in hand and laughing, he couldn't stand it any longer. He drove out of the Boro to Stockton High Street, got his regular parking spot on Silver Street and walked to Jeff's shop.

As he was going inside, Jeff came bustling out.

'Aye aye, what are you doing back here?'

'Nowt, I was just...I dunno...just wondered if you wanted to go for a drink.' He felt awkward.

'Ah, I can't. I'm taking Rita out to that place in Hartburn village that only serves lamb.'

'The Lamb House. Yeah that's a good place. Me and Jules have eaten there.'

'Cool. I've got to get going, I'm late already. Emily is in there, she's still working on the database.' He jerked his thumb over his shoulder at the doorway.

'Right. OK, man, have a good night.'

Nick watched him go, the long mane of salt-and-pepper coloured hair blowing down his back. The Royal Oak looked tempting. Very tempting. Or any of the dozens of pubs within five minutes' walk. Stockton High Street was always said to be the widest high street in the country and once had the reputation of having the most pubs, though whether it was true or just folklore, was never clear. Such claims are made by many places. One thing was for sure, there were plenty of places to get pissed.

A queue of people at the bus stop outside the shop got on the 17 to Ingleby Barwick holding carrier bags. All going home to someone, or so it seemed. He let out a groan in his throat again and rubbed his eyes, his hair blowing across his brow. Now feeling very emotional and still with an irresistible urge to drink and drink heavily, he leant against the shop window and contemplated calling Julie or texting her. No, he couldn't do that. She was busy and he couldn't bother her. She'd just fret and that'd be no good at all. Too selfish and too self-absorbed. He had to cure himself of that. He had to get through this. But oh for that burn of booze on your throat and the warm tingle in your belly. The aroma of the alcohol in your nose and coating your throat.

He put his head around the door and looked in the shop. Emily was still in position behind the screen. Luke had gone south to Harrogate. She looked up and her face broke into broad smile.

'Hey, Nicky boy. Yes, I'm still here. Nearly done now, though.'

'You've really put some hours into that.'

'Once I get started on something I can't stop until it's done. You've just missed Jeff.'

'I saw him, actually.' He put his hands in his jeans pockets and looked around at the records on the wall in plastic sleeves. A gallery of rare vinyl from the last 45 years.

'Oh.' She smiled again and went back to her work then looked up again. 'Well, come in then, you can put the kettle on if you want.'

He stepped in feeling awkward and nervous. Marc Lewis, his therapist, always said he had to talk about his issues with drinking and depression. That swallowing the feelings down and fighting them on his own - his absolute natural instinct since being young - was very bad for him, very destructive. It led to him turning further and further inwards in a self-feeding, destructive cycle.

'Em...you know I quit drinking...'

'Uh huh.'

He sighed. 'The thing is, right now, for some reason, I really want to have a drink. I mean, I don't want a drink, but...but really I do. Sorry, that's stupid. I'll...I'll...I'll get going. It's nothing to do with you. Sorry.'

He turned around.

'Are you alright, Nick?'

He had his back to her and shook his head, feeling very vulnerable, his emotions close to the surface, sweating with nerves and worry. He heard her push her stool back and walk around the counter.

'Aw...shit. I don't know what to say to someone who...err...don't have a drink, if it's bad for you, Nick. Sorry, I really don't know what to say...I didn't know it was such a big, bad thing for you. I thought it was just a health thing.'

She took his hand and squeezed it, but that just made him feel really embarrassed. What the hell was he doing here? She was a kid. This wasn't her fight.

'It's OK. I'll get off,' he said, turned briefly and gave her a quick smile, raised his hand and walked out the door without looking back.

He had to be strong, come on you useless shit, get yourself together. Be brave, don't give in to this. It won't last. It'll pass. He groaned in his throat again. But walking down the street and taking a left into Silver Street, the BMW was parked outside a classic old Stockton pub, the Stag Inn. With wide windows either side of the door, the lights inside were on and gave the place welcoming glow on a grey, heavily clouded afternoon. The stupid thing was, most of the time he didn't really like pubs. He and Julie rarely went to them. They seemed part of the past. A past when they were the only places you could get hold of booze.

But it was a Saturday evening, home was dark and quiet and he couldn't face that, so he went into the Stag Inn, walked up to the bar, sucking in the familiar pub air; a comforting air that is the same the world over.

'Yes, fella. What can I get you?' said the bar man with a welcoming nod, as he mopped down the wooden counter with a colourful bar towel.

'Double vodka on the rocks please,' he said, almost biting his tongue as he spoke the words.

'Drop of the hard stuff, eh? Smirnoff OK?'

He nodded and put a £20 note on the bar. The barman pushed the small glass to him, took his money and came back with change.

Nick swilled the clear liquid and ice in the glass, staring at it. It was just a drink, it wasn't *that* big a deal. It wouldn't kill him. He'd had a hard day, he was under a lot of pressure, he was under a lot of stress...all the old excuses still worked. All the old reasons for getting drunk remained. They hadn't changed and they never would, not for him, not for anyone.

He took it to a table in the far corner beside the window and sat down. Just as he did so, Emily came in and looked right at him, skipped over, lifted the glass off the table and drained it in one, sitting down next to him with a smile and a shake of her scraggy hair. 'Oh god, that burns,' she said in a hoarse voice and a laugh. She looked at him with bright eyes.

'You don't need booze. I'll drink for both of us, so you don't have to,' she said, slipping off her small, black leather biker jacket and going to the bar, returning with a big glass of fizzy water for him and a pint of lager for herself. She was so petite that it looked huge in her tiny hand.

'A pint glass in your little paw looks like a litre,' he said as she sat down next to him. She grinned and held her hands out, palm down with fingers out-stretched.

'Pixie fingers, Jeff called them earlier. Hands so small they make even the smallest cock look big,' she said, and giggled at herself, then ruffled her hair up so the top strands stuck upwards, a habit she repeated every few minutes. 'So come on then, what brought all this on? I was worried about you when you left the shop so I locked up and chased after you. I saw you turn down this street. I'm afraid I don't know anything about addiction or whatever your problem is. Are you an alcoholic?'

He shook his head. 'Not classically, no, but I drank virtually every day since I was 16, until three years ago. I was diagnosed as emotionally dependent on it. It'd have killed me eventually, one way or another.'

She squinted at him and fiddled with the silver skull pendent. 'What does emotionally dependent mean, exactly?'

'Basically, that I couldn't cope with life without drinking. I used it to prop me up emotionally and to try and lift me out of my depressions, but in doing that, it made the depressions worse in the long run. Once, I'd had a big night on the piss and the next day I was so depressed and everything felt so pointless and so lifeless, that I couldn't see the point of living. I would have thrown myself out of my flat's window on the seventh floor if it hadn't been for a kid who was walking with his dad below. I couldn't let him see me splatter on the pavement. So I shut the window. When I'd got through the blackness, I stopped drinking to try and get better in my head.'

'God. That's just awful. And did it work?'

'Yeah. Not totally, but it helped a lot. Those days feel behind me now. But it seems old habits die hard, and something just triggered it this afternoon...in fact, I've had it a few times, in recent weeks.'

She sipped at the beer. 'Why was that?'

'I don't know. Julie is away in Newcastle, so I'm sort of on my own...that's not it, though.'

'Why is she away?'

'She's at a women's refuge as an observer, to sit in on the work they do. It's going to form part of her training so that eventually she can become a women's support worker at the Teesside Women Centre. She's there for a week.'

'Very noble work, I'm sure,' said Emily, sipping at the lager again. 'But how does that equal drinking?'

He shook his head. 'I don't know. It doesn't really. I was in the Boro, I was feeling lonely and I didn't want to go home and it just came on...it's not rational and there are no excuses. I'm sorry, I can't really talk to you about it.' He tried to look at her, but couldn't meet her eye. It felt like she was too young to understand the sheer size of the ball of existential pain inside of him. He barely grasped it himself.

'OK. So what would happen if you did drink?'

'I don't know. I'd be instantly pissed, I should think.'

She giggled a little at that. 'I can't drink either. I'm too small and light. I can already feel that vodka going to my head.'

'How much do you weigh?' he said, wanting to stop talking about himself.

'Eight and a half stone.'

'Good god. It's a wonder you don't just float off. You're not underweight though, are you? You look really healthy.'

She shook her head. 'I am healthy, I think, anyway. I'm just small boned and there's no fat on me at all. I don't know why, all I do is eat puddings and meat. It's just the way my body works. When I went through puberty I hardly looked any different. All the other girls were getting big hips and tits, but I just didn't. It was quite upsetting, actually.' She leant back on the seat and rested her head on a hand.

'It's a difficult time, your teenage years.' She nodded.

'It felt like I wasn't a proper woman for quite a while. I kept looking at my chest every morning and wanting it to grow bigger, but not much happened. Imagine what that's like when you're at a girl's school.'

He drank all of his water. 'Must be hard when everyone else's bodies are changing.'

'Not just hard, downright upsetting and worrying. Imagine if you'd been in the changing room with all your friends and their penises had all got bigger and hairy and you were still like you were when you were 13? You'd feel less than properly male, wouldn't you?'

'I guess so, yeah. The boy's changing room was a maelstrom of hormones and heinous smells at the best of times. Everyone was always checking each other out in the showers, but trying to pretend we weren't.'

'It was the same at my private school, only you couldn't get away from them all at the end of the day. I got bullied for not having big tits. I mean, how messed up is that? It's not like it was a choice I made. You never forget shit like that, do you?'

'Some kids are bastards. Some adults are bastards. Probably the same ones that were bastards as kids. Anyway, you grew up to be a lovely woman with breasts and everything.'

'Aw, thanks.' She looked down at herself. 'There's still not much to put in a bra, but I've long since accepted it. It's not like you get a choice in the body your genetics give you, is it? It's not like it's a moral failure to have small or big tits or a small or big penis, or whatever. I've always thought people who are sneery about someone because of such a thing are just horrible. It's like men who think big tits are better than small ones, somehow. Or like when you hear a girl saying her ex-boyfriend's dick is tiny or something and being nasty about it. I think that's terrible. We are what we are and one just has to make peace with that and accept it in others.'

'We are much more than our bodies, I think,' he said.

'We are, indeed. As nice as bodies can be, it is who lives in them that really matters.'

She seemed to have lapsed into a much more well-spoken posh voice, when recalling her public school education, in the same but opposite way that his father had lapsed into a strong version of his Hull accent when talking about rugby league.

'But you work out, don't you? So you're obviously body conscious.' She pulled the sleeve of his t-shirt back and squeezed the top of his arm.

'I lift weights and do resistance training. I don't know if it's working out, as such. It's just to help me relax and helps to give me self-confidence.'

'I'd never guess you felt like that. You hide it all very well. Does Julie like you doing weights? You're obviously in what a lot of people would think was good shape.'

'She likes me being healthy. I don't know that she's over bothered about the dimensions of my muscles.'

'So how much do you actually weigh, then? You don't have to tell me, if you don't want to,' she said.

'11 stone 10. Have been since I changed my lifestyle. It doesn't go up or down. It just seems to be my natural weight now.'

'Well, that's not that much more than me, considering you're about four inches taller. What does Jules weigh?'

'I don't know. She lost quite a bit of weight after she lost the baby...'

'What?' She sat up and looked at him with her small eyebrows knitted together. 'I didn't even know she'd been pregnant. How awful for her and for you.'

'Oh, yeah, well we don't talk to people about it much. No point, is there? She lost it in June. Her hormones seemed to change her metabolism. She's probably 10 and a half or so. Jeff was saying the other day about that. But she reckons obsessing with the scales and weight is all emotional fascism designed to bully women into an unrealistic body image and, y'know...I think that's probably right.'

'She's very political about women's issues, isn't she?'

He shrugged. 'Yeah, she's strong-minded and she's proud to be a feminist. I totally support her in that, as well. She's really opened my eyes, over the years. Made me see things differently.'

She sipped at the lager. 'Yeah, but it's alright for her to say stuff like that, she's got a great body and is good-looking. It's easy to say women shouldn't be hung up about their body image, when yours is ace.'

'It's just as well she's not here, because you'd now be in big argument with her for saying that. I think she'd say she was fighting for a world where you wouldn't be bullied for the size of your breasts or any other physical attribute that didn't conform to some notional standard of attractive. A world where girls don't wear pink and boys blue. Y'know...just a world that isn't mental.'

He picked up the empty vodka glass and swilled the melting ice around.

'Still want to drink?'

He nodded. 'Sorry.'

'You don't have to say sorry to me. I'm not your mother...or Julie.'

'Take my mind off it. Talk to me about what's happened in your life since the festival in the summer.'

She sipped a little more beer.

'I moved out of that horrible house in Marton and into a lovely little one-bedroomed, top-floor flat in Green Dragon Yard. It's just been decorated.'

'That's good.'

'Yeah. So getting a job at Jeff's is so handy. It's literally three minutes' walk away. Dad offered to buy me a place, but, as you might recall, I don't want his money, so Jeff's wages will pay my rent and leave me with enough to live off, if I'm careful.'

'That's so cool. Well done, Em.' He rattled the ice in the glass again. She reached over and put her small pale hand on his.

'Sssh. Calm down, you're so tense,' she said, perceptively. 'Yeah, so that database work is coming on nicely. I'll get all the platforms hooked up to it tomorrow, then Lukey can just feed all the new stock info into it and it'll populate all the marketplaces at once. After that, I'm going to sort out a barcode scanner and software.'

'That'll transform Jeff's whole operation.'

'It will indeed.'

He wobbled his leg up and down and scratched at his stubble. She looked at him and shook her head.

'You really do need calming down,' she said. 'Come on, we're going to my flat.'

'I'm not sure if that's a good idea, Emily.'

At her house in the summer, she'd stripped naked in front of him and all but pulled his pants off. Was going to her flat a good idea, given the short, but relatively intimate history between them? Nothing more had happened, but the answer was probably no, it wasn't a good idea. But was it better than being alone and fighting the desire to get fuck-faced on vodka? Yes, it bloody was. Much better than that. He had to get through this, he had to not give in.

136

What the hell was an urge, anyway? What did it mean? Was it a chemical thing? What drove you to crave or desire something so intensely? He crunched a chunk of ice from the glass. It had a watery film of vodka on it. Shit. That only made him want to drink more.

'We'll just have a little weed. You're going to drive yourself and me crazy, if you don't calm down. Come on,' she stood up and took his hand.

'I can't smoke dope either, man. It'll mess with me. I've got to be really careful.'

'OK, well, you can watch me relax then. It's doing you no good in here around all the alcohol, is it?'

That was certainly true. Maybe it was the best solution available to him.

It was a short walk to Green Dragon Yard, an old Georgian area set off the High Street which was home to one of the country's oldest Georgian theatres. In recent years it had been developed as Stockton's 'Cultural Quarter' and was also home to a recording studio as well as flats, a pub and a cafe. If Stockton had a hip place to live at all, this was probably it.

'This is just right for you,' he said as the entered the yard and looked around. 'It's funky and just ideal.'

She grinned and unlocked the door to the building 'I know. It's so cool.'

Her apartment was small, but newly finished with exposed brickwork. It had a small living room with a kitchen at one side of it, bathroom and a single bedroom. Clothes were draped on the back of a big sofa. A TV hung on the wall and a stereo sat in the corner.

'As you can see, I don't really do housework,' she said, taking off her jacket and adding it to the pile of discarded stuff on the back of a chair.

'Now, tea I think. You like green, don't you?'

'I'll have whatever you've got.'

'I've got green somewhere.'

He flopped down onto the cream-coloured sofa and looked around. 'I would have killed to live in a place like this when I was your age. I had a shitty, damp, old terraced house flat in an unfashionable shit hole in Elswick in Newcastle. I didn't even have my own bedroom.'

'Did you share?'

'There were eight of us in this big old house. I actually had a bed the kitchen. Yeah, seriously. I did.'

'Ha ha. That might be awkward.'

'You're not kidding.' He stood up and went over to where she was fussing with the tea. 'There was this one time where I was with this girl and we were having it off, as you do, and people kept coming into the kitchen, so we'd have to leap under the covers every time. We'd get a few minutes, then we'd get interrupted. Finally we got a good run at it and we're nearly there, you know?'

'Nearly coming, you mean?' she said, putting green tea bags into a glass pot.

'Yeah, we're both right on the edge and this girl, she was a real screamer as well...'

'I'm a screamer...I don't know how anyone isn't,' she said with bright green eyes, opened wide.

'Aye, you do look like a screamer.'

'What's that look like?'—

'I don't know. It's just an instinct.'

'Are you?'

'Me? A screamer? That's not a question often asked of men, is it?'

'Well, some of you don't make much, if any noise. In my limited experience, anyway.'

'Good god. I don't know how they keep quiet. I'm a groaner, if not a screamer, which has got me into some trouble over the years.'

'Thought so,' she said, pushing her tongue between the gap in her front teeth.

'Go on with the story.' She smiled to herself as she poured hot water into the pot.

'Yeah, well, this lad walks in and stands there just staring at us. He's about 18 and it's his first time away from home and there we are, sweating and grunting like two wild animals.'

She screeched with laughter. 'What did you do?'

'We both just thought sod it, we're not stopping now and kept on doing it. She actually looked over to him and waved. I said, "do you want some tips?" We were doing it doggy style on the bed, so both of us are naked, I'm on my knees behind her, she's bent over and we're going at it hammer and tongs.' He laughed at the recollection of it 29 years ago. 'The bloke was so embarrassed at seeing this frantic coupling, that he actually let out a small scream and legged it out the door, like he'd seen a terrible apparition. I thought he might stand there and give us some encouragement but no...he couldn't get out of there fast enough.' It was funny even so many years later and made him laugh out loud again.

Emily was laughing so hard a tear ran down her cheek.

'Oh god. I'd have stood and watched you, for sure.'

'I'm not sure he'd ever seen a naked body before that wasn't in *The Sun*. We were all much more innocent in those days, at least compared to now.'

She shook her head, still giggling at the story. 'Not that innocent, by the sounds of it.'

'Well, in spirit, at least. It was all new back then in 1979.'

'Oh, you said that like a jaded old man. You must have been a lot more extroverted then, though, to do that in such a public place. You wouldn't do that now, would you?'

'I had almost certainly been drinking and I suppose it was all new - being away from home and everything. I did go wild for a while, actually. For a couple of years at college, I was a proper hedonist, did a lot of drugs, drank a lot and had a lot of sex. I envy you, though.'

She raised her eyebrows in surprise, cleared her throat and blew her nose on a tissue after laughing.

'Me? Why?'

'Because you're so young and you've got so many days ahead of you and you've got all your youthful energy. You can rock 'n' roll all night and party every day.'

She reached out to a low glass table and picked up a tin, opening it up to take out a packet of Rizlas and a small packet of grass.

'But, as you must surely remember, it doesn't feel like that. You don't wake up aged 22 and think hey, I've got so many years ahead of me, instead you think, what the hell am I going to do with myself? What's my place in the world? How do I...y'know...just live?'

He looked out of her window down at the yard below. People were milling around, some going to the Green Dragon pub.

'Yeah. I've still not really worked all that out yet.'

'Maybe we never do.' She laid the cannabis in a thin little row, licked the Rizla edge and rolled it into a small joint.

'We used to roll massive spliffs. That's a slim little thing,' he said as she made a small roach from a piece of the Rizla packet.

'It's strong stuff. If we smoke much we'll be comatose.'

'I can't have any, Em. Drugs fuck with my head, the same way drink does.'

'Are you sure?'

'Aye. The theanine in the green tea will calm me down a bit.'

She looked up at him and smiled. 'OK. You don't mind if I do, though?'

'No, of course not. I'm just wondering if you've got any Grateful Dead records to listen to while you get stoned. That'd be traditional.'

'I have no idea who that is, but I daresay I shall learn, working at Jeff's. He's a funny bloke, isn't he? I mean, funny ha-ha.'

'He is. Always has been. The way he is now was exactly how he was when we were at school together. He's hardly changed.'

'I think he's a nice man. I feel jolly lucky to have met you both. One meets so few really nice people.'

There was her posh upbringing voice again.

She lit the joint, inhaled a little smoke, held it in her lungs and blew it out her nose.

'You're obviously a pro at this, Em.'

'I learned at my posh boarding school. Like I said, it was a terrible place. Only being stoned and listening to Iron Maiden got me through it. How do you feel now? Do you still feel like a drink?'

She swung her legs up on the sofa and rested her small feet on his lap, keeping an ashtray in hand.

'To be honest, yes I do. But maybe not as much as I did earlier. Being with someone has helped, I think.'

'I'm not just someone, I hope,' she said, narrowing her green eyes and squinting through the smoke she blew out.

He didn't know what to say to that, so he said nothing. Instead, he took her bare feet in his hands. They were cold so he rubbed them.

'What hot hands you've got.' She smiled and wiggled her tiny toes.

'You have very small trotters,' he said, massaging each toe individually. 'I give off a lot of heat, apparently. Jules says I radiate heat in bed. Useful in winter, but like sleeping with a boiler in summer.'

She lay back, her eyes closed as he rubbed her feet, distractedly. His phone vibrated in his pocket.

'Aw, I was enjoying that,' she said as he let go of her to look at it.

It was from Julie. The message read, "3-1.Yay! Had a good day, but am knackered. So emotional. Got to learn to turn them off to do the job. Food, drink & early bed. Love you so much. J x"

He wrote back. "Glad it went well. All good here. Love you too. N x"

'That's sweet,' said Emily.

'What is?' He said, putting the phone away.

'The look in your eyes when you're texting Julie.'

'What look is that?'

She pulled on the joint, making the tip glow orange for a second, and then shrugged in silence as though she'd decided not to say what she had intended to say. He held her feet again.

'She wouldn't like you being here, though.'

'You've really helped me. Jules would appreciate that. She knows only too well how I struggle, sometimes, like.' He felt awkward again.

'Any time. You're an odd chap, but luckily, I like odd.'

She finished the joint and rubbed it out in the ash tray.

'Any good?' he said.

'Mmm, I feel very mellow now.'

He looked at his watch. It was just after 8pm. 'I should probably get going.'

She pulled a face. 'Do you have to?'

'I don't have to. But...'

'I'll be on my own all night. On Saturday night. That's shit. I don't want to be on my own on Saturday night.'

'You've got mates you could meet up with, haven't you?'

She exhaled. 'I suppose so. It's just nice being here with you. I'm not interested in going out and getting drunk and I don't like dance music and all the shit they play in nightclubs. I like rock music and you can't go out to a club on Saturday in Stockton and hear rock music, or not to anywhere you'd want to go, anyway.'

'Jeff would greatly approve of this statement by one of his staff.'

'If you're just going home to sit on your own and I'm here on my own, that's mad, isn't it? Especially as you're still uptight about drinking. You need a chaperone.'

He got up and looked out of her window again. Opposite was another Georgian building also converted to flats. Lights now illuminated rooms. He put his hands in his jeans pockets.

'Please don't go yet. I get lonely, too, and I'm trying not to behave badly when I'm lonely,' she said, getting up and crossing the room to hold his hand.

'Behave badly?'

'Oh you know. Nothing special. Just picking up guys. Unsuitable guys. Guys who like vulnerable girls who are on their own. That sort of thing, you know? Sometimes it's the easiest way not to be alone. At least I know you're not unsuitable.'

He totally understood. 'OK, Em. I'll stay a bit longer.'

'Thank you, kind sir.'

She got up and went to the bathroom. Nick poured more tea and began tidying up the small room, stacking magazines and newspapers in a pile on the coffee table. She began running a shower as he did so. He picked up her leather jacket from the floor and put it on a hook by the door. The kitchen counter top was scattered with crumbs and stains, so he wiped it up with a damp cloth and put dirty dishes on a drainer. A clothes horse with knickers, vests and t-shirts on sat by the window in the corner. They were all dry so he folded them into a neat pile and put the clothes horse away in a storage cupboard, along with an ironing board. Getting rid of the clutter made the room look a bit bigger.

She came padding in with a towel wrapped around her. 'Oh you've tidied up. You'll make someone a good mother.' She picked up a vest and a pair of pants from the pile.

'I hope you didn't sniff these,' she said, cheekily grinning at him.

'To be fair, they're so tiny there's almost nothing to sniff.'

She turned around. 'Look at my new tattoo. Great, isn't it?'

A snake wrapped around a sword ran from her shoulder and down under the towel. She had quite a few tattoos on her back to the top of her arm. Normally they'd be hidden.

'You didn't have these a couple of months ago, did you?'

'No. They're all new. I'm thinking of getting a sleeve tattoo done when I can afford it.'

'The snake and the sword is amazing. How far down does it go?'

'I'll show you. I've got the best one on my bum.'

She let the towel fall to the top of her thighs, her back turned to him. The tip of the sword ran to the small of her back. On her left buttock was a cluster of blood red roses.

'Great, isn't it?' she said, looking over her shoulder at him.

'The tattoo or the buttocks?' he said, tempted to lay his hand on it.

'The tattoo, of course,' she said, pulling the towel up and wrapping it around her again.

'It's great, Em,' he said as she turned around.

'The tattoos or my bum?' she said, laughing.

'Both are great. Those girls who bullied you at school would be jealous, I'm sure.'

'Aw, thank you, kind sir.'

She pulled on a pair of knickers under the towel and with a glassy-eyed smile, turned away from him, unwrapped herself from the towel, pulled on a vest and then ruffled up her hair in the full-length mirror, turning to see how the left buttock tattoo looked in the red G-String.

'It's great ink work,' said Nick, feeling like it was a good reason to keep looking at her in her underwear. 'Great colour. You've got very smooth skin. This is another good thing about being young.'

She went into the bedroom and came back in a pair of pyjama bottoms. 'Now that feels much better. You can have a shower if you want.'

'No, I'm fine, thanks. Do I smell, like?'

She leant over and sniffed at his neck.

'Oooh you do, actually. But not in a bad way. You smell of black pepper. Must be the dope heightening my sense of smell.'

'Jules says I smell of black pepper as well, so I guess I must.'

'Have you got any tattoos to show me?'

'No. I don't. I never fancied it. Yours are great, though. They really suit you.'

He went back to the window and looked at the people below. 'I like being able to see people doing stuff and yet being removed from it. I miss that in the countryside. Where I lived in Harrogate you could see people walking their dogs on The Stray and people going about their daily business. I always enjoyed that.' He made his groaning noise in his throat, almost involuntarily.

She stood alongside him and looked down. After being quiet for a couple of minutes she spoke again. 'Why aren't you happy, Nick? You've got so much going for you, but you always seem to have a bit of sadness about you. I don't understand that.'

He replied quickly. 'It doesn't make any sense, really. It's a chemical and hormonal thing. But I'm much happier than I used to be, though sometimes it's still a struggle, like now.'

She turned to look at him. 'Really?'

'Yeah. The pills help me. Occasionally, I am properly happy. That'll have to do.'

She put her small arm around his waist and pulled him to her 'Poor you. Come here.' She hugged him, her head on his chest. She felt small and, if not fragile, then certainly delicate. But it was a nice gesture from her and it was a little bit of comfort to his worry about Cavani and everything else. He kissed the top of her head instinctively, as you would a cat that jumped up onto your lap.

He held her tightly to him in the gloaming of the day, dark shadows filling the small room, held her tightly for a few minutes of silence, zoning out in the quiet, breathing in and out together, feeling the warmth of her body against his. Relaxing. Maybe, he was getting vicariously stoned. She put her hands on his belly and then his chest and looked up into his eyes.

'Nick, I'd really love us to...'

But she was interrupted when across the yard, on the same level, in a top-floor flat, a light came on and a man stood at the window. Immediately, he recognised him from seeing him just a few hours earlier. It was Lomash Patel, illuminated by a bright main light as he stood in the window. In an instant another man was there. He pushed Lomash and then hit him in the face. Lomash held his face, looking shocked. The man then head-butted him, smashing his nose open. Lomash fell to his knees and out of view.

# CHAPTER 8

It was as unreal as seeing the car crash - almost as though glimpsing something on a distant TV.

'Did you see that? What the hell is going on over there?' He pulled away from her and pointed at the window.

'What's wrong?'

'A lad is getting beaten up over there in that flat. The top one.'

She turned with shocked eyes and looked. As she did so, Lomash stood up, blood running down his face, only to be beaten down once more, this time with a right-handed punch. She yelped out a scream and held her hands to her mouth.

'Shall I call the police?'

'Yes. How do I get into that building?' He pulled on his boots.

'You go out here, down to the lobby and then follow the corridor around. Keep going left. When you get to the third lift, that'll take you to those flats. There are stairs to the side of the lift.'

She grabbed her phone and dialled 999, as Nick ran out of her flat and down the stairs. Following Emily's instruction he rounded two corners and kept going left, out of one building into another through connecting fire doors. Sprinting up the staircase of the building which was directly opposite Emily's flat, he got to the top floor, panting for breath. Which bloody flat was it? There were three possibilities. The first was quiet inside. He ran to the second and put his ear up to it but as he did so, it was yanked open and a man ran straight into him.

'What the fuck?!' he yelled as they collided and both fell to the floor. Nick managed a glance inside as he fell and caught sight of a man, presumably Lomash, lying on the floor.

Before the man had a chance to fully get to his feet, Nick got hold of his legs and hauled him down, rolled on top of him and, straddling his torso, pinned him down by the top of his arms. He struggled hard and was strong, pushing him to one side and wrestling himself free. Nick noticed his knuckles were grazed and

146

bleeding and swollen from the fight. As the man got to his feet and began to run for the stairs, Nick lashed out with his right leg and tripped him up, sending him sprawling on all fours.

Someone came out of the end flat on hearing the noise from the fight.

'What the hell is going on?' she said.

Nick leaped on the man's back and hammered him to the ground, grabbing him by the hair and thumping his head into the hard-wearing, blue nylon hall carpet. The men yelled out in pain.

'Get off him,' the woman said. She was in her early 60s, neat grey hair, in a black cardigan and slacks. She ran up and hit Nick across the back with the flat of her hand.

'He's just violently attacked Lomash in that flat,' said Nick, between breaths, struggling to suppress the man, who was probably 20 years younger. 'Go and see if he's alright. Call an ambulance for him if he's not.'

He heard her go in to the flat and exclaim, 'Oh my god. You poor man,' and then call the emergency services.

'What the fuck do you think you were doing?' he said to the man who was bucking under him again, trying to get free. He gripped his hair tighter, making him scream.

'Fuck you,' the man gasped out.

The stairwell door was pulled open and two police in high-viz jackets burst in and grabbed hold of both of them.

'He's the bloke you want,' said Nick, as one of the policemen put his arm up behind his back. 'He's assaulted Lomash Patel in that apartment.' The woman came out at the commotion.

'This poor man is bleeding badly from his nose. He's taken a real beating.'

The stairwell door opened again and Emily came running in.

'Are you alright, Nick?' she said, her eyes flicking between all the people on the landing.

'Yeah.'

'Let him go. He's Nick Guymer. He was in my flat and he saw the man getting beaten up, so he came and stopped it,' she said, her flowery, girlish voice, indignant on his behalf.

The other bloke didn't argue. He just stood with his head down, sweating, a graze on his cheek where Nick had scuffed him on the floor.

'What's your name?' the first officer said to the man. He didn't reply. 'Come on, lad. No point in holding out on us. We'll find out sooner or later.'

'Dave McGull,' he said. Even just those two words revealed he was a local, stretching out Dave to Daay-vuh and pronouncing McGull with a deep, guttural 'u'.

More officers arrived with paramedics. They took Dave McGull downstairs while the medics worked on Lomash. Nick gave an account of what he'd seen to one of the officers. Emily stood by his side throughout.

They took him out on a stretcher. The poor lad's face was a mess. Bruised and bloodied and a sick purple colour. His eyes were so swollen he couldn't see anything, his top lip bulbous and red like a pound of ox liver.

After detailing what Nick had seen, they took his address and contact details and they were free to go while the police secured the open flat.

Back in Emily's flat she put the kettle on and ran her fingers through her hair, shaking her head.

'That was so awful. That man, oh my god, he was in such a terrible state. If you hadn't seen them, he might be dead. I've never seen anyone beaten up like that.' She made some black coffee for both of them. Nick rubbed his fingertips on his forehead, tracing the deeply etched lines.

'Do you think Lomash lived there? Have you seen him around?'

'Yeah, I have. He's always really smartly dressed. That's the only reason I remember him. He's usually in a fashionable suit and shirt.'

'That's because he works at Flashmans in Middlesbrough.'

'You know him?'

'I know of him. His father is Jimmy Patel, the man who was

murdered.'

'Goodness me. Has someone got it in for that family? That can't just be a coincidence, can it?'

'No. I wouldn't think so. Shit, that reminds me.'

He went to his phone and checked on a Google alert he'd set up for Ricky and Kev's names. There it was. A news story logged half an hour ago. 'Richard and Kevin Wells were charged with the murder of Jimmy Patel this afternoon, following 20 hours of interviews.'

Such a short news story with so much significance. Cavani was right. Of course he was right, why would he have said they'd be arrested if it wasn't going to happen? Cavani probably had men inside Cleveland Police in every station, in every town in the area. People who would give him a nod here and there, a tip off when necessary, all in return for a few free drinks at his clubs, women, maybe some cash or a holiday here and there. All very discreet. Nothing too big or too grand, just enough to make sure he was on top of what was happening.

'Julie's brothers have been charged with the murder,' he said, his lips drawn together.

'Really? Good god. Does she know?'

'She'll find out tonight or in the morning when she checks her phone. We were half-expecting it.'

She looked at him incredulously. 'You were what?'

'We thought...'

'I heard you. You knew they were killers? That's...that's awful. They killed that man's father in cold blood? Why did they do that?'

'Settle down, Em. They didn't do it.'

That didn't make her any the less confused.

'So why have they been arrested, then?'

'It just looks like them because they were at the scene shortly before it happened and got his blood on them.'

'Blood? Blood?! The police have got the wrong people? That just doesn't seem likely when they had blood on them.'

'Well, there's not much I can do about it just now. They'll hold them in jail on remand. They've both done time before. They'll cope. Sometimes I think they're never happier than when doing a short stretch.'

She shook her head in puzzlement.

'That's just sick. There must be something wrong with them.'

'Yeah. I'll be honest, they're not very nice people. That's understating it, in fact.'

'What does Julie think of them?'

'That they're not very nice people. She won't defend them if they've done anything wrong. She never has.'

He got a glass of water. 'I'm going to get off, Emily. I need to ask a few questions of a few people,' he said, his brain already ticking over and looking for a route through this.

'OK,' she said, ruffling her hair up.

'Thanks for being there for me in my hour of drinking need.'

'You're always welcome. I hope you feel better.' She pecked him on the lips and patted him on the backside.

As he walked back to the car outside the Stag Inn, the good news was that he no longer felt the urge to get drunk. The bad news was that felt like he should feel guilty about being with Emily at all, as though it was being unfaithful to Julie. But then he'd really needed help and she'd helped. She'd stopped him getting drunk and maybe ending up doing something far worse. He was so grateful for that.

He started the engine and drove to Terry's flat in Roseworth. The light was on. He rang the bell and tried the door; it was open.

'Terry! It's just me, Nick.'

He stuck his head around the living room door.

'Now then. Owee, in.' Nick went into the brightly lit, sparse room. He'd been watching the football on TV. 'You heard they got charged?' he said, his hands jammed in the pockets of a pair of poorly fitting cheap jeans. 'They're both in Holme House, though, so it could be worse.'

Holme House was a prison located southeast of Norton, where a lot of local remand prisoners went. It would make visiting them much easier. Terry genuinely didn't seem that bothered. Something that in any normal family would be a traumatic event - two brothers charged with murder - was very much taken in his stride. Nick knew that the two blokes themselves, though keen not to do time for something they hadn't done, would have no fear of getting jailed. It was just life to them. In fact, they probably expected it, either for a crime they'd committed. or as a result of being fitted up by the police as payback for previous crimes and misdemeanours.

'Where's Jaz?'

'At her mam's.'

'Do you know Jaz's brother, Lomash?'

'Oh yeah.'

'Do you like him?'

'Yeah...he's a bit...' he wobbled his hands at him.

'He's gay, you mean?'

But Terry surprised him. 'No. I mean, I know he's gay, but I didn't mean that. He's a bit, like, a bit nowt...do you know what I mean?'

'Insubstantial, you mean?'

He shook his head. 'I don't know what that means.'

'Like there's not much to him.'

'Yeah. That.'

'Do he and Jaz get on?'

'Not really. None of the family get on with each other, as far as I can tell, apart from Jaz and her mother.'

Nick sat down on a poorly sprung old sofa which looked like it had been reclaimed from the tip.

'So who is in the family? There's Jaz, Lomash and who else?'

'The mother Myra, an older brother Kal and loads of aunties and uncles, cousins and nieces. There's dozens of them.'

'What's Kal do?'

'He's a heart surgeon at James Cook Hospital. Really well educated.'

'Wow. That sounds like a big deal.'

'Jaz reckons he did the classic Asian kid thing of getting good exams, going to college, getting a big, well-paid job, nice wife and kids. He grafted like shit for it all. He's got a big house in Marton, not that I've been there. Apparently, he's got every bit of technology you can get. Home cinema, surround sound, 3D. Loves his kit. Probably has robots to operate on his patients.'

Nick laughed. 'But he doesn't like you?'

'Nope. He's a stuck-up get. Thinks he's better than me, just like his father.'

'And Jaz doesn't get on with him either?'

He shrugged a little.

'Not really, because they're two different sorts of people. They're united in hating their dad, but she's all arty and creative. He thinks she's flaky and not playing the game. Same goes for Mash.'

'By which you mean they're not studying hard, getting good jobs, married, kids et cetera.'

'And by being gay.'

'He's not a fan?'

'It's a big no-no for Kal. He's old school. Thinks it's immoral or whatever, you know...like everyone used to on the estate when Jules, Kev and Ricky were growing up. No shirtlifters allowed. Bloody mad, if you ask me. Who gives a shit whose hole you put your cock in? That's what I say. Nowt to do with anyone else, is it?'

Nick gave a snort of laughter. 'I reckon that's as pro-gay a statement as you could make, Tez, yeah. But the thing is, right, I saw Mash get, appropriately enough, mashed tonight.'

'Eh?'

'Where does he live?'

'Green Dragon Yard. He rents a smart flat there. Half his wages go on that place. Mad.'

'Aye. That's it. I was there visiting a mate and across the way I saw him getting the shit kicked out of him. I went round and got the bloke. They've nicked him now.'

'Fuck me. Really? I never heard that. Poor Mash. I mean, he's not up to much, but he's alright, y'know? I'd better ring him.'

'He'll still be in hospital. He got beaten up pretty bad. The bloke who did it was Dave McGull. Do you know him?'

'McGull? I don't know him, but he's one of the McGull Developments kids, isn't he? One of Paddy's lads.'

'I assumed that might be the case, aye. He was a powerful unit. He took some knocking down.'

'Give him a good slap, did you?'

'Nah. Well, I slammed his head into the floor a couple of times, just to placate him, like.'

Terry laughed and rubbed his hands together. 'Wish I'd seen that. So what was he on Mash's case for? Was it gay bashing?'

'He didn't say. I wondered if you had any idea.'

'Haven't a clue. There's some fucking bastards out there though, eh. I'd better tell Jaz, as well.'

'Does she like Mash?'

'She doesn't not like him. But they don't spend much time together. She says...what is it now, that she says? Oh yeah - "he's like a wet fart in a trance". She doesn't rate him, really.'

Nick snorted. It was a nice expression. He rubbed his stubble.

'They're not exactly a close family, are they, Tez?'

'No, but they had the fact they hated their dad in common. I'm amazed none of them actually killed him.' He scratched his head and went to look out of the window. 'He gave them plenty of reason over the years and was always giving it the big "I Am" and shouting the odds. I'll tell you this, not one of that family has cried one tear about him getting knifed. And before you say it, no, Jaz didn't kill her own father. Even the police have ruled that out. To get that knife right up under his heart you needed more power than she had. And anyway, she's a peaceful kid. That's why I love her. She's not involved in anything fucked up like what I grew up around. She's decent, y'know. Never broken a law in her life. That's all I want, Nick. Just a quiet life without bother. Get me head down, do me work, nine to five, and come home to a lovely lass for me tea. I've had a gut full of Rick and Kev's world of bastards. It's not me. It never was. Jules got out of it by going to university. I'm too thick to do that, but Jaz is my way out. Do you get me?'

Nick nodded, got up and slapped him on the leg. 'You're a good bloke, Tez. You deserve a good woman like her. Make sure you keep hold of her. Don't do anything to screw it up.'

He nodded and stood up. 'I'm scared I might do that, though. Even if I don't mean to,' said Terry, worry in his eyes.

'My mam always said to me, just be yourself. That's the best advice I can give you. God knows, I'm a fuck up as well, mate.'

He went to the front door. Terry followed him.

'So you don't know any of the McGulls, then?'

'Nope, but I'll tell you who does. Conrad. He goes way back with the boss man, Paddy. They've known each other for years. That's how he got the job on the Prince Regent Street site, I think.'

'Good call, Tez. I'll have a word when he's back on Monday. He's working on Jeff's new store fittings this weekend up in Newcastle. Where would he be staying up there?'

He thought for a moment. 'Probably at Janet's. That's his first wife.'

'They still get on, then?'

'I dunno what Con's relationships with his family are like, really. They're like the Patel's, there's bloody loads of them, I can't keep up with it all.'

It was nearly 10pm when he got finally got home to the darkness of rural Teesside. It was the first time he'd actually slept in the house without Jules being there and as he unlocked the door and went in, he realised he was quite nervous of being on his own in the countryside. Stupid really. He went around the house and put on all the lights as though illumination would be a companion.

He took out two cold chicken legs from the fridge, saw a bottle of Jules' special Premier Cru Chablis left over from the pre-wedding drinks, took it and without hesitation or even a split-second of thought, drank from it, gulping the cold alcohol down without stopping until it was all gone. Nearly a whole bottle down in one. Exciting, thrilling and yet familiar, the coldness numbed his lips slightly. It felt so transgressive and so wrong that he just stood there with the fridge door open, the empty bottle in one hand, now hanging by his side, the plate of chicken in the other.

What had he done? No, not what. Why? Why had he done that? He licked his lips. Mmm, wine, fucking lovely wine. He let out a yell, a noise, a roar. It felt good. It felt bad.

Finally, he kicked the fridge door shut and sat down at their kitchen table, shocked at himself. He put his fingers together in a pyramid and just sat in the quiet, feelings of guilt already rising in him. Julie would be so mad at him for this. He was no good on drink. He got depressed and pushed her away. That's what he'd been like in Harrogate. She'd be furious, not least because it was a waste of the good wine. But it was in him and kicked in quickly on his empty stomach. It felt like a visit from a really old friend; exciting, warm and comforting. For 10 minutes or so, it was overwhelming and emotional. It felt like coming home to a warm fire on a cold day.

There was no more booze in the house. He knew that for a fact because Julie had taken all the leftover stuff to the TW Centre for when they had a little do. But it didn't stop him looking, because there's nothing you want to do more when you've got a drink buzz on you, than drink some more, almost regardless of the consequences.

Quickly, he got more and more drunk as the wine flowed into his blood stream. Every minute that passed, he felt more dizzy, until it was unpleasant. He locked the doors and went to bed with a pint glass of water feeling a bit paranoid, feeling sorry for himself, feeling guilty and his heart racing. But before he could get into bed, a wave of nausea washed over him, making him break out in a cold sweat. Leaning over the toilet he threw it all up, retching violently, until there was nothing left in him. It was violent and horrible, but also a relief. He rinsed out his mouth and went to bed.

Alone, with the smell of Julie all around him, he lay wide awake fretting about what he'd just done, about Julie, Ricky and Kev, Mash, about what Cavani might do to Julie if he couldn't find the real killer of Jimmy Patel, about what Cavani would do if he *did* find out who the killer was. Booze is supposed to make you relax, but he'd not felt as tense as this in a long while. All his time, booze sold him a lie that it helped him deal with his problems but the truth was, it didn't, it actually made things much harder to deal with. It had all been a cruel deception.

At some point he must have passed out or gone to sleep because he woke up with a start and opened his eyes. It was still dark outside. He leant over to look at the bedside clock. 4.19am. His mouth was dry like sandpaper. Sitting up, he drank half a pint of water and then went for a piss. The whole place seemed twice as quiet as it ever usually did, if that was even physically possible. There were cracks and creaks of floor boards, the sound of wildlife outside, something knawing at some wood somewhere in the house - probably mice or a rat. Something ran across a beam in the roof, again probably mice. It was ridiculous. He got back into bed and put the World Service on the radio. That was better. It was so good just to hear a human voice.

His mind drifted to thinking about Emily and her tattoos and he found himself imagining making love with her, but then felt guilty about doing that in their bed. So he hopped out again, went into the bathroom and did what almost all men can do, virtually on demand, at any time of the day or night, he quickly and efficiently masturbated into the sink. Afterwards, he rinsed his hands under the tap and looked into the mirror. Bags under his eyes and heavy eyelids: utterly fucked. This was what drinking made you feel like, had you forgotten? But why did hangovers always make him feel horny? He'd noticed this since his teens, even when his head was splitting and he felt sick. Was anyone else wired this way, or was it just him?

Back in bed, he felt more relaxed now and went back to sleep for a couple of hours, waking up feeling like he'd had no sleep at all. Exhausted. Fuck it. This was no good at all. He'd forgotten how shit waking up after you'd been drunk was. No, not forgotten, the intensity of it had faded. But now, in the lovely early morning light that he normally so enjoyed and often embraced with a brisk walk around the fields, he couldn't enjoy it because of how he felt. It was a rubbish trade off and he immediately resented it. He wanted to have his usual early morning freshness feeling back, not this woolly bullshit headache feeling. His body was trying to tell him that drinking would make his life much worse, not better, and in the cool blue light of a Sunday morning, he heard that message loud and clear.

He texted Julie, feeling like he should admit boozing and say sorry to her for doing it, but deciding not to bother her with it when she was busy and also because he couldn't face her being mad at him. Instead, he just said, 'Have a great day', then went for a shower and ate some cheese and eggs. The house was nothing without her and as he wandered around from room to room, it seemed that the meaning had gone from the place. It was clear that he could probably pretty much live anywhere, in any circumstances, because how you feel about where you live is about what is in your head and not the about the place itself, beyond a few basic amenities. Without Julie's presence in the house, it was just a big empty shell and no matter how much he filled it up with stuff, it would still be a big empty shell.

It was just a few days away and shouldn't have been anything to concern him at all. But as he wandered aimlessly around the garden, hands in the pockets of his jeans, for the first time since they'd got back together, he realised the intensity of their relationship, the sheer full-on love they had for each other was such that, when separated, it felt like part of himself was absent and the best part, at that. In truth, it wasn't a very nice feeling at all, despite being based in love. It made you feel dependent and incapable of functioning properly. Life seemed shapeless and meaningless without her, so much so that it was a little scary.

Would Cavani really hurt her if he didn't find out who had killed

Jimmy? Would he *really* do that? Or was he just messing with his head? Cavani was clearly a nasty bastard, but what did he have to gain from hurting Julie? Did he need to gain anything? Maybe he was just psychotic and enjoyed having power over people like him. Why was knowing who had killed Jimmy Patel so important to him? Too many questions without any answers and no way to get answers.

His phone vibrated as he sat thinking about the situation. It was a text back from Julie.

"R & K - I knew it! Don't do anything until I'm home. Off to work now. Jx" She'd sent him an email at the same time. It said, 'Thinking of you'. with an attached photo of her hand over her crotch, one small tuft of pubic hair between her index and middle finger. He kissed the screen with a grin on his face. As his lips touched the phone it rang, making him jump and drop it.

'Hello?'

'Don't sound so shocked, it's just me,' said Jeff. 'I thought I'd ring from Rita's land line. Doesn't get much use, you have to make an occasional call just to keep the rust off the wires, y'know.'

'Ah, right. That's why I didn't recognise the number.'

'Sorry I had to go out last night...you know how it is. Saturday night and that.'

'You're alright, man. I ended up having an eventful night, one way or another.'

'Oh, aye? Well you can tell me all about it on our way up to Newcastle, if you've nowt else to do, that is. I've got to check on Con and I said I'd sub him some money. We can go to a carvery, if you want. I fancy a massive plate of roast meat and gravy.'

'Err...yeah, that sounds good. I'm at a bit of loose end without Jules, like.'

'Right, I'll be over in 20 minutes, then.'

As they drove up the A19, Nick filled Jeff in on what had happened to Lomash.

'Hang on, back this up a bit. What were you doing in Emily's flat?'

'I'd had a bit of an issue.'

Jeff looked at him with a frown from behind the wheel of the van and then gestured for him to say more.

'I wanted to drink. I've been wanting to on and off for a while.'

For a while Jeff was quiet and Nick didn't really want to discuss it, nor mention the Chablis he'd necked.

'So did you?'

'I bought some vodka, but she took it off me and got me out of the Stag Inn.'

'Old school pub, that. The sort of pub you really want to go in when it's raining on a winter's day. Do you know what I mean?'

'Yeah. So this bloke that was hitting Lomash...'

'...what's her place like, then?'

'Nice. Small. Those flats in Green Dragon Yard are smart, though. I wouldn't mind renting a bigger one there for me and Jules.'

'Really? I thought you were happy in the countryside.'

He shrugged. 'Just a thought. I miss a bit of life and energy, y'know? That's what was good living in the centre of Harrogate.'

'Aye. I know exactly what you mean. I miss that as well. Rita's place in Hartburn is all well and good, but being in the suburbs is some sort of living death. Not that Harrogate was exactly rock 'n' roll.'

'No, but you'd see people going about their business from my flat. I can see rabbits doing that from our house, but nowt much else. Anyway, the bloke hitting Lomash was Dave McGull. One of the McGull family. What does your giant conspiracy theory brain make of that?'

They passed the turn off on the A181 to Durham. Jeff raised an index finger off the wheel.

'McGull's got building contracts from Jimmy P. There's a falling out and JP gets whacked by a McGull. Lomash finds out and McGull's lad beats him up to shut him up...err...well...maybe.' He lost faith in the idea and shook his head. 'No, that all seems wrong.'

'I can't make any sense of it, but this Mash lad was given a proper kicking and I do mean, a *proper* kicking. He was a mess and I think he probably had concussion.'

'Hmm. Well that's no ordinary fight then, is it? He's gone there to really do him over. You don't really go to someone's house and give them a pasting, accidentally. '

'That's a great point. And Lomash isn't a fighter. He was into clothes and fashion and you could tell he wasn't that sort of bloke. I'm sure some gay blokes are real bruisers, but Mash isn't. What I saw from Em's flat was a bloke who, without provocation or offering any defence at all, was punched in the face and then head-butted and god knows what else.'

'That means McGull was either punishing him for something - for crossing him or the family - or he's warning him not to say or do something. Either way, it's obviously a deliberate act of violence.'

Nick nodded. 'I think you're right, but was it related to Jimmy Patel's murder?'

'You've got to keep Mike sodding Cavani sweet, haven't you? That's totally wrong that is, you can't let that evil twat have a hold over you.'

'I know. I'm working on it, believe me. Why does he care who killed Jimmy P? I'd like to know that.'

'Because they killed one of his bigger investments. They'd paid him substantial wonga to push contracts to various people who the Cavanis supplied. Presumably that income is worth substantially more than what they paid Jimmy. That's about the best theory I've got. Anyway are you sure Ricky and Kev aren't *actually* guilty? I mean, it does sound exactly like the sort of circumstances those two would kill someone in.'

'Jules reckoned they're innocent - well not innocent, obviously, but not guilty of the murder. No-one knows them like she knows them.'

Jeff looked quizzical and cocked his index finger. 'Ah but

mebees, on this occasion, she's wrong, son. The biggest mistakes happen when you're surest of your judgement. Didn't Confucius say that?'

'I think it might have been James Taylor.'

'Same thing. Those two brothers are fucked up, you know and I know it. They've always scared the shit out of me because they've both got that look in their eyes which says, one wrong word and there'll be trouble. Even if you think they're your mate, one word out of place and they'd turn on you. Look how they were at the crash the other day, they'd have torn Jimmy Patel apart and stuffed him back up his own arsehole if the police hadn't been there. They're fucking monsters, man. Really, when you judge them against regular, decent members of society, they're absolute fucking monsters. We're just used to them over the years, so we stop seeing them for what they really arc.'

Nick had to agree. He was 100 per cent right. Them being guilty was far from the least unlikely outcome of this whole affair.

'Well she might be wrong, but Mike Cavani told me he knew they were going to be arrested, but that they hadn't done it.'

Jeff thought about that for a while. 'He's bluffing you. I bet if you think about it, he responded to you saying R and K had been pulled in and to your assertion that they were not guilty, didn't he? He didn't initiate that statement, he just picked up on what you'd already said was the truth and confirmed it back to you. It's a classic trick, that.'

He cast his mind back to that meeting. 'You're right, he did. Clever sod. Also, when I said I'd dropped someone off in town, he said something like, "ah yes, the lovely Julie" and I said, "how did you know that?" Thus confirming it was her. He even said, "you just told me." Yeah. So that's obviously a technique he uses. Good spot, Jeff.'

Jeff saluted.

'There you go, then. You're busy wondering how he knows so much, but he's just pulled some mind games on you. See, this is the power of the psychology of crime. When you paint yourself as some sort of overlord, everyone assumes you've got much more vision and power than you really have. It's like he's the Wizard of Oz.'

'That'd make me Dorothy.'

'You'd look terrible in red shoes, you, like. The gingham dress, fine, but red shoes are a no-no for a man with your skin tone.'

They parked on Grey Street in Newcastle and walked up to High Bridge. Conrad was working in the shop with two other, younger, men. The shop floor was covered in sawn bits of wood and tools. A circular saw was set up on a work bench. In the back, resting against the wall, were already constructed record racks.

'Hey, this is looking good Con, lad,' said Jeff.

Conrad looked up from the bench and wiped some sweat from his forehead.

'Aye, with a bit of luck we'll get them all finished this evening. We'll have put a couple of massive shifts in, mind.'

Jeff handed over a packet of money with £1,500 in it. Conrad pocketed it swiftly and without counting it.

'We've nearly got them all made. Just need to get brackets on the wall and then fit the racks to them. You'll need to paint them, like.'

Jeff patted him on the back of his wet, black t-shirt. 'Top-notch work. I'm impressed. I knew you were top rank, but I didn't think you'd be this quick.'

'I wouldn't if I was working for someone. I'd stretch this out for about two weeks like any good Great British worker should, if I was on the payroll.' He rasped a laugh and took out a tin of tobacco from the back of his army trousers. Inside were some roll-ups already made. He lit one and leant against the window as the other two men went on working.

'I hear Ricky and Kev have been collared,' said Con, flicking ash from his smoke.

'Aye, what do you make of that?' said Nick.

Con shrugged. 'To be expected, given the circumstances. But those lads aren't killers, are they? Hard bastards, like. But can't see them doing for JP.'

'Maybe they are now,' said Jeff.

'Nah man, Ricky and Kev might kill someone in a knife fight on the docks after a bottle of brandy, but they'd not butcher a fella in cold blood.' He said it as though this was a morally superior stance to adopt and spoke of their good character - something they might want to be proud of.

One of his fellow workers brought out a cup of tea for him from a flask.

'What do you know about the McGull family, Con?' said Nick. 'You said once that you and Paddy go way back.'

'Oh, aye. We do. We went to the same school in Walker. He's done well for himself, has Paddy.'

'What about the son, Dave? Do you know him?'

Con picked at something in his teeth and nodded. 'Oh, aye. Him.'

'Is there a problem with him?' said Nick, seeing his reluctance to talk.

'I'd rather say nowt about that one.'

'Why's that Con? Owee, man, you can tell us,' said Jeff.

'It might not be, what is it now? Politically correct? Is that what you call it now?'

Nick looked at Jeff. Jeff raised his bushy eyebrows at him.

'Is Dave gay, like?' said Nick, on a hunch.

Conrad flicked his eyebrows up and tipped his head. 'Every sodding kid is gay these days. I've nowt against them meself, never have had, but that Dave lad, he was like the rough trade you used to get in every port when I was a merchant seaman. Nasty bit of work, if you ask me.'

'You were a merchant seaman? When was that?' said Jeff.

'Certainly I was. I'd gone all over the world by the time I was 25. Not bad for a snotty kid from the arse end of Newcastle.' He said it with pride. The purple and red bruise on his head from the crash glistened like a ripe plum in the sunshine.

'See, the thing is, Dave McGull has just been arrested for beating the crap out of Lomash Patel, Jimmy's son,' said Nick. 'I

163

actually had to stop him.'

'You did? I bet he took some dropping, like. He's a powerful lad. Mind, you're no stick insect yourself, kidda.'

'Yeah, you can say that again,' said Nick. 'He took some bloody holding.'

'Beating up the Patel kid, eh?' said Conrad flicking the remains of the cigarette into the gutter.

'A gay Patel kid, I might add,' said Nick. Conrad raised his black eyebrows and shook his head.

'When I was taken on the site on Prince Regent Street, I was told that Paddy and Jimmy Patel had fallen out, but I never found out why. I bet it was something to do with the two sons. I bet them two lads were up each other like rats up a drainpipe.'

Nick winced at the simile. 'You mean they fell out about their sons having a relationship?'

'Don't know for sure, I'm just saying there was definitely some sort of bust up between Jimmy and Paddy because the site was full of talk about it. Paddy is a live and let live sorta bloke, like. He'd not care if his lad liked shagging goats, but Jimmy, he was hard line. That might be your reason for them falling out. Them two lads probably had a lovers' tiff. One of them was probably on the rag. Ha ha ha! Now, I'll have to get back to work if I'm going to get this done by the end of today. Thanks for the cash, Jeff. I'll see you around, Nick.'

'Funny hearing old gadgees like him talking about gay blokes, isn't it?' said Jeff as they went back to his van. 'Makes him really uncomfortable.'

'Different generation, isn't it? It probably seems weird to him that it's all above ground and accepted by most people these days. It was all a hand shandy in the showers, in his day,' said Nick.

'Wonder if he had a go at it, on the long, lonely nights in the dark, Sargasso Sea?' Jeff waved his fingers in the air to represent the waves.

'That's where all the eels in the world go to mate, y'know? The Sargasso Sea.'

'Gettaway, is it? Mating eels? Is that some sort of gay euphemism?' said Jeff.

Nick laughed and was about to reply when he saw a black Mercedes pass them and pull up sharply. Someone got out of the passenger side door and turned to face them. Mike Cavani. Shit.

'Now then, gentlemen. How are we?'

Jeff sussed out who it was right away. 'My name's Colin Warnock, you must be Mike Cavani.'

'Fuck off. You're Jeff Evans. I'm not a dumb fuck just off the boat, mate,' said Cavani, with a shake of his head, his porcelain eyes cold and yet bright. 'Eddie told me you were taking that shop.'

'How did you know we were here?' said Nick. Jeff turned to him and made some sort of expression, but Nick couldn't work out what it meant.

'I told you Nick, not much happens in Newcastle that I don't know about. I have eyes everywhere, including outside of a women's refuge in Fenham. So what have you got for me?'

Nick bristled and must have gripped his fists into a ball, because Cavani raised his eyebrows at him and said, 'I wouldn't recommend that as a course of action, Guymer. That would be very, very stupid.'

He bit his bottom lip with his top teeth and stared at Mike Cavani, unflinching. He'd get him for this. One way or another, he'd get him. No-one was pushing him around for long.

'I don't know who killed him yet. I'll find out though,' said Nick, licking his dry lips.

'Good. I want a name and I want a name quickly. Very quickly.'

'Shouldn't you be paying off a copper to find out? They'd be better at it than I am,' said Nick.

'Think of it as a job application,' said Cavani returning to the car with his nasty little grin. 'Come up with the name and you get the job.'

'What if I don't want the job?' said Nick.

'Whether you want the job or not is my call, not yours. Don't be so recalcitrant, Guymer, you've got Julie's best interests at heart, haven't you?'

# CHAPTER 9

Cavani got into the car and it drove off.

'He's a fucking psycho him,' said Jeff. 'A proper "shoot a man in Reno just to watch him die" psycho. You do know that you bought into the idea that he's some sort of omnipresent being, don't you? You said, "how did you know we were here?" But he didn't say he did know we were here, he has a restaurant down the road, he was just driving past and saw us. That's all. He's not God.'

Nick bit his lip. 'Alright, but he knows where Julie is and that fucking scares me.' He ground his teeth in suppressed anger. 'We're going to fucking get him, Jeff. We'll have to be clever, but one way or another, we'll fucking get him. I'm not having that twat in our lives.'

'Get him? What? Kill him?'

'No. That'd be too easy. We'll get something on him.'

'Yeah. Like I said before, you need insurance with a shark like him. The good thing is he thinks he's the boss of you and that means he'll probably underestimate what you're be prepared to do.'

'Aye. I'll know it when I see it. There'll be a way. I just want to twat him in the face very hard, but that's no good with someone like him. I've got to be more clever.' He nodded to himself. 'In the meantime, I'm going to do what he wants, not least because I don't want Ricky and Kev going down for something they didn't do.'

Jeff flicked his hair over his shoulders and rubbed his hands together.

'Oddly enough, being menaced by a Geordie gangster has given us a proper appetite. Shall we go and gorge ourselves on roasted meat or do you want to go and visit Julie?'

'Meat please. I can't look in on her. She's busy and anyway, it'd look pathetic, wouldn't it? Like I'm a kid who can't get on without his mam for a day.'

They stopped off at a pub on the outskirts of Newcastle that did a carvery and loaded up on roast beef and vegetables and then headed home. As Jeff drove, he mulled over Jimmy Patel's murder.

'If Conrad is right and this Dave McGull lad is gay and Lomash is, too, could the fight you stopped be exactly as he said, a lovers' tiff?'

'It wasn't a tiff, man. It was a brutal full-frontal assault. It was about more than that.'

'Maybe Mash knows it was Dave McGull that murdered his dad and he's had the shit kicked out of him to shut him up,' said Jeff.

'OK, let's run with that. Why would a McGull kill JP?'

'Revenge for some business deal? Con said there was a falling out between Jimmy and Patel. He gets the son to do the deed,' said Jeff, looking in his rear-view mirror.

'Yeah, I like that in principle, but it seems so extreme. McGull doesn't rely on what Jimmy could give them by way of contracts for their whole business, so even if they fall out, it wouldn't put McGull out of business. I don't see them being that desperate or even that furious at him.'

Jeff let out a bark. 'Ah ha! I have it, Sherlock...'

'I'm Watson, you're Sherlock, surely,' said Nick.

'...I do like a bit of violin, a silly hat and an opiate, too. Listen, like you've just said, there'd be no point in killing Jimmy, just because he'd fallen out with Paddy and wouldn't push any more work their way and you're right, it is too extreme to contemplate murder if you don't get anything out of it. But what if by killing him, it put someone in his place who would return all those lucrative contracts to McGull's? That would be a proper, stone cold motivation for murder.' He took his hands off the wheel briefly, put his right-hand index finger on his nose and pointed to him with his left hand index finger. 'You dig what I'm saying?'

Sometimes an idea falls into your brain out of nowhere and explains everything. It's almost as if you have a second brain which is at work while you're using the first brain to remember how to boil eggs and what Vanilla Fudge's *début* album is called.

In a flash of realisation, Nick yelled out. 'Jeff! Yes! You've bloody well got it. That's exactly right. Forget the Dave and

Lomash thing, that's probably a side issue between them. The woman who will step into Jimmy's shoes is Sheila Simmons. She's his number two. If he had decided to not give McGull's any more work and she is prepared to, then we've got two parties who both get a lot out of his death. A double reason to have him killed.'

Jeff nodded furiously. 'It's a classic conspiracy. Two parties come together to achieve a single aim for two different reasons. Perfecto. We need to dig into Sheila's life and see if she's basically as bent as Jimmy Patel was, but I can give you an even more classic conspiracy.'

'What?' said Nick. 'It doesn't involve Area 51, does it?'

'Not even a single alien. From what Terry told you, all his family hated him, one way or another. So try this on for size - you've got the McGulls, the Patels and Sheila Simmons all happy he was killed. It could just be a *Murder on the Orient Express* deal.'

'What do you mean by that?'

'Everyone stuck the knife into him. They're all guilty.' He rolled his eyes dramatically at Nick.

'Come on, Jeff, this is real sodding life under the grey skies of Teesside, not some bloody Agatha Christie fantasy on an exotic train.'

As they got back into Stockton, Jeff parked up alongside his shop.

'Hey Em, have we been busy?' he said as they walked in.

She looked up from behind the wide computer screen. 'That depends on what you think busy is, I suppose,' she said, drinking from a mug. 'Hello, Nicky boy. Did you have a nice dinner?'

'What it lacked in quality, it made up for in sheer volume,' said Jeff, looking at the list of items they'd sold since she'd opened up at 10.30am. He broke into a smile and held up the sheet of paper to Nick. 'Look at this.'

'Is something wrong?' she said.

'Ha ha. Not at all.'

Nick looked at it. There were 20 items on the page, all neatly itemised by artist, title, label, condition and price.

'He doesn't usually have such an easy-to-read, detailed list.'

'Yeah, but surely if you list everything about what you sell, you can enter those into a sales database and then every quarter you can analyse what sells and what doesn't. In fact, I've set one up on your desktop and entered those items in. I didn't note the label numbers, I hope that's OK.'

Jeff applauded. 'I love this. It's like having the shop run by a grown up. That's brilliant, Em. Now you've started this, I'll have to keep it up.'

She giggled a little. 'I didn't realise it was that radical an idea. You are running a business, after all.'

'What did you make of the customers?' said Nick.

'Fine. Students, mostly, I think. Oh, there was chap came in and asked if you were around, Nick. He was called err...let me see...I wrote it down...Sam Thompson. I said you might be back later. He left his number.'

'Oh, you know who he is? He's the site foreman at Prince Regent Street. I told him I hung around here.'

'Have you heard anything about poor Lomash? It's not been on the news or online,' said Emily.

'No. We've had some ideas about that, though, ideas which Sam Thompson might be able to help me with,' said Nick, picking up the paper she'd written his number on. 'You've got lovely handwriting, Em.'

'It's copperplate, isn't it?' said Jeff, going into the back room to put the kettle on.

'It's just writing,' she said, shaking her head. 'You two are far too impressed by not very much.'

He smiled at her and dialled the number, walking outside to speak to Thompson.

'Sam? It's Nick Guymer.'

'Can you come to the site?' he said, without hesitation.

'I'm on my way.'

Stockton was quiet on a Sunday, though maybe not quite as

quiet as it had been in the 70s during his growing up, when life seemed to go on hold for 24 hours while everyone stared silently at the walls and waited for it to pass. Keep Sunday special? Hell no. Sunday was a gateway drug for depression, and even now it was still too quiet, still not alive enough to stop you feeling as though life was not really being lived properly.

As he walked across the High Street and down Dovecot Street, he saw a semi-circle of lads and lasses standing around what had been a great old pub called the White Hart when he was kid. A real old man's pub which served great Exhibition Ale and stayed open on a Wednesday afternoon under the market day laws, probably dating back to the 14th century. Now it was some shabby place dedicated to getting the underclass fuck-faced on tasteless white spirit mixed in pop for as little money as possible.

The gaggle of kids were in full 'we don't want to talk about love, we just want to get drunk' mode and he walked past them head down and at a pace. One of them called out to him. He knew who it was right away, the stupid kid who had tried to confront him before. He was in no mood to have to deal with him again. But it wasn't a choice he could make.

The kid ran over to him and, walking backwards in front of him, shouted, 'Hey prick! I told you to stop, you do what I tell you right, yeah?'

From back outside the pub his mates goaded him on, once again.

'Me and you have got some business to sort out, yeah? I never got that apology off you.'

Nick stopped dead in his tracks, catching the kid by surprise.

'Yes, you did.' A surge of adrenalin went through his muscles and he sucked in a gulp of air through his nose. He wasn't having this.

'Eh?'

'I said "yes, you did." I apologised to you outside of the Royal Oak.'

The kid was such a dumb fuck, he didn't even know what to say to this.

'Err...I never heard you, like...say it again.'

'Nah. I'd rather beat the fucking shit right out of you. Owee then, let's fucking have you.'

He pushed him in the chest so hard that the kid stumbled back and fell over, shocked by this turn of events. Clearly he was more used to intimidating people who wanted to get away.

'Fuck off!' he said, as Nick advanced on him, real bloody anger in his blood now. These fucking people pushing him around, who the fuck did they think they were? Time to teach pricks like this that there's only so far you can push decent people.

He saw the fear in the kid's eyes now, as he pulled him up from the pavement by his sweatshirt and held him in a tight grip, staring into his scared eyes. 'You owe *me* an apology. An apology for being a twat. Owee then, where is it?' Nick shook him hard. The kid was light as a feather. He could just throw the skinny shit away.

'F-ff-fuck off. I don't owe you nowt,' the lad said, now pulling to get away.

'So what you're really saying is please fist me in the fucking face? Well, if that's what you want, son.'

He pulled his arm back to hit him in the face, but two of his mates had run up and pleaded at him.

'Leave off him, mate. He's just a fucking stupid shit. He doesn't know what he's doing,' said one, seeing Nick wasn't to be messed with.

'He's fucked up on glue,' said another.

The kid stank of fags and just rank body odour. So he let him go. No pity for him this time.

'Take a fucking lesson, son. If I see you trying this shit on with anyone else, ever, anywhere...I'll tear you apart and stuff you back up your own arsehole. See?' He was pleased to be able use Jeff's graphic expression about Ricky and Kev.

The kid wiped his nose on the back of his hand, nodded and walked away.

'Cheers, mate,' said one his rescuers. 'We'll keep him in line, in future.'

Nick spat out a gob of foamy spit. 'Aye. See that you do.'

He walked on to Prince Regent Street, wiping his sweaty hands on his jeans, crossing over and walking down to the building site. Bloody punk kids. He'd quite fancied giving him a right-hander, but as his adrenalin level dropped down again, he knew it wouldn't have solved anything and he also knew he was just venting some of the aggression he felt towards Mike Cavani. It was perhaps a small victory, but it felt like a decent win all the same.

There was a light on in the site office. He knocked and went in. Sam Thompson was sitting where he had been sitting on his last visit, behind a desk, with sheets of architect plans in front of him.

'Ah, hello, Mr Guymer,' he said in his west Yorkshire voice. 'Thanks for dropping in.'

'Working on a Sunday, Sam?'

'Getting ready for everything getting under way again tomorrow. I wanted to speak to you because...' he paused and rubbed the gap between his eyebrows with an extended middle finger. The tension Nick had seen on his first visit was, if anything, even more extreme. '...because when you dropped in the other day, you said your family had been involved in the accident and I've been worried about it ever since.'

He felt guilty that the bloke felt guilty when he knew fine well how the so-called accident had happened.

'I feel responsible. I'm the site gaffer. It all comes down to me. You said, "one was not so good". How are they now?'

'They've got her drugged up. She'll recover though. It's good of you to ask.'

'I didn't know who to ask to find out about who was hurt, y'see. It's really kept me awake. I'm waiting to hear if I'll be disciplined over it. I probably will.'

'What sort of discipline?'

'Suspension probably. A fine, almost certainly. Or the company might just sack me.'

'No, surely not.'

This wasn't fair. A perfectly decent grafter like Sam Thompson, getting it in the neck because of Conrad's little scheme. Shit.

'Well. We'll see,' he said.

'Have you had the report on the mixer?'

'A preliminary one.'

'What did it show?'

'As the driver said, the brakes failed.'

'What does *failed* actually mean?'

'They were faulty. Some of the cabling was loose...'

'That sounds like they were sabotaged, Sam.'

'The police didn't seem to think so. Bad servicing, they said. Not the driver's fault. Whether it's me or someone on the servicing team, heads are bound to roll for this.'

It sounded like Conrad, or whoever he'd paid to fix the mixer, had known exactly what to do to make a truck's brakes fail, but not make it look like vandalism or something more sinister. Probably someone who learned how to do it on the building site near Alnwick where Conrad had worked.

Nick shook his head. It all seemed wrong. People's livelihoods were at risk here for Conrad's benefit.

Sam Thompson poured them both some coffee and gestured for them to take seats on two padded chairs at the other end of the Portakabin.

'Have you considered that the accident may have been engineered, as part of a fraud?' said Nick.

Sam Thompson looked at him out of the corner of his eyes and shook his head. 'This wasn't some sort of shunt and whip-lash injury claim, was it?'

'No, but all the same, people do weird shit for money, don't they?'

'It doesn't even matter what I think, it's what the company thinks that matters. They'll OK the insurance pay out just to keep things quiet.'

'I think you'll be OK. If the brakes were defective, you can't be held responsible for that.'

'I hope not. McGull's have been good to me over the years.'

'Talking of McGull's, Sam, do you know Dave McGull, Paddy's son?'

'Know? No, I don't know him. I know *about* him.' He said it in a way which suggested this was not a good thing at all, a look of harsh judgement on his face.

Nick told him about the fight with Lomash that he'd witnessed last night. Thompson looked disgusted and turned away with a sneer on his pink face.

'Dave is a nasty bit of work. Always has been, by all accounts. Lives off his dad's money. You know the sort, son of a rich man, never done a days work in his life...he's one of those. I feel sorry for that lad and for it to happen so soon after his dad was killed. Poor lad.'

'It did cross my mind that there might be some dispute between the families. A couple of people have said to me that Jimmy Patel and Paddy fell out, possibly over their sons' relationship. It might just be pub talk, though.'

'I've heard those rumours as well, of course I have, but the building game has always been riddled with gossip about who's doing what, where, when and how. It's the nature of the business. We've got so much casual labour, people come and go all the time and rumours abound, about someone doing something they shouldn't to the chairman's wife or daughter. Sorting the fact from fiction is very hard. All I can say is, I never saw or heard anything to suggest there was any bad blood between them, quite the opposite. And since Jimmy died, Paddy has been very...well...sorrowful, I think that'd be the word. He seems very upset by it.'

'So those pub rumours which said that there was rift between them over something, you'd say those were wrong?'

'I just saw Paddy after you left, the other day, it's not like he was close to tears over Jimmy's death - no-one liked Jimmy that much, but he wasn't dancing on his grave, either. I'm also sure he'll be

175

disgusted at Dave's behaviour over Lomash. That is just shocking. I hope they throw the book at him for that.'

'But you know that Jimmy looked, shall we say, favourably, on McGull when it came to dishing out MIDO contracts?'

Sam Thompson nodded, but then shook his head.

'I know what you're saying but we, that is McGull's, have always been very competitive. I know that for a fact. We put in low bids for public works contracts and that's how we get them. We put in low bids and use cheap immigrant labour. Paddy's done it that way for 35 years to my knowledge, certainly for the 18 years I've worked for him. I wouldn't discount the possibility that there was some sort of arrangement between them, but genuinely, I have no proof of it existing. Again, it could just be building trade gossip.'

Nick didn't push him any further. Maybe he was right. He finished his coffee.

'I'm pleased they've made such quick progress on the arrest for Jimmy Patel's murder, though. That was such a terrible thing to happen,' said Sam Thompson. 'He was an arrogant bloke, but no-one deserves to die like that.'

'Do you ever have any contact with his number two at MIDO, Sheila Simmons?'

'No, I don't, but I do see her sometimes. She's often accompanied Jimmy Patel onto sites to see how things are progressing. We've done six or seven MIDO contracts in the last 10 years, so I'm familiar with a lot of their people.'

'What's she like?'

He shrugged and pulled a face. 'Hard to say. Seems good at her job. Very thorough, from what I can tell.'

'She'll be taking over from him now then, I guess.'

'Yes. I would think so. They'll all move up one, I suppose. Still early for all that, though.'

Nick put his mug down and shaped to get up. 'Well, if that's everything Sam, I'll get off.'

'Aye. Thanks for dropping by, like I say, I've been worried that bloody accident had killed someone. By god, it's been a terrible few days. This accident, Patel getting murdered and now his son getting beaten up.'

'Bad things come in threes, that's what they say, isn't it?' said Nick.

'True. True. I can only imagine what Myra must be going through.'

'Myra?'

'Myra Patel, Jimmy's wife.'

'Of course, what sort of person is she?'

'Lovely woman. Intelligent and smart.'

'You know her?'

'Just from talking to her at various functions and events over the years, when the wives are invited along. You know the sort of thing.'

Nick didn't, but he could imagine.

'I always really liked her. She seemed better educated than Jimmy.'

'I've heard from many people that no-one liked Jimmy, least of all his family.'

Sam Thompson's body language suggested this was true. He nodded and spread his arms wide. 'Yes, he could be an arrogant, stubborn man and he had an aggressive streak, too. He wasn't above bullying people if he felt he needed to. But he was also very good at his job.'

Nick liked Sam Thompson. He seemed the solid sort of chap that the northern building trade was founded on: trustworthy and without side.

'He was also on the take from the Cavani family, you know. The Newcastle gangster family. I have that on very, very good authority.'

The colour dropped from Sam's cheeks, a little.

'Bloody hell, he wasn't, was he? Seriously?'

'Seriously, yeah. They paid him to award the contracts to companies that use Cavani companies for materials.'

'Companies like us?'

'Yeah.'

'I've heard of the Cavanis, of course, but we don't buy anything from anyone with that name. I'd know if we did.'

'No, of course not. They have loads of businesses that are a shell for their money, but you'd never know from the outside.'

Thompson blew out air and shook his head. 'My god. Is that gospel? Is that why those two blokes they arrested killed him? Are they the gangsters?'

'No, they're not. I think they're the wrong men.'

'Wrong men? Well I never.' He looked genuinely shocked by the news.

'So you know Myra? How well did she get on with Jimmy? Do you know?'

'They always seemed a distant couple, I suppose, when I think about it, but you never know what happens behind closed doors, do you? And she was good friends with Sheila Simmons too, of course, so if she'd known anything...'

Nick jumped and put his hand on Thompson's arm. 'Say that again.'

'What? That Myra was good friends with Sheila Simmons?'

'Good friends? How do you know that?' Sam Thompson looked around himself, a little flustered.

'Well...err...they'd always sit together at functions. They went to school together, I think. Some of the lads used to joke that they were a secret couple, lesbians like, because they were so tight with each other and because Lomash is gay, I suppose.' Nick must have looked very disapprovingly at this because Thompson added, 'Yeah, well, not very PC, but you know what these sorts of things are like. Dozens of men and apart from Myra and Sheila, the only other woman there was Joanne Gull, Paddy's wife. So they were all good friends, just because of that.'

'Well, thanks again,' Nick said, shaking hands, feeling like that was a very important bit of information.

He went back to the shop.

'I've got it,' he said, arms wide, as he walked in.

'Well, don't give it to me,' said Emily from behind the computer screen. 'These pants are too tight to get my hands inside to scratch it.'

'I had it once, but I put it down somewhere and it ran off,' said Jeff, his head in a *Record Collector Guide*.

'Everyone is a comedian, these days. Myra and Sheila conspired to have Jimmy killed. That's it. She gets rid of the husband she hated and Sheila gets the top job and they give their friend Joanne McGull the contracts again, which in turn means the Cavanis get their supplier's gigs back. Everyone is a winner. It's perfect. I've sorted it.'

He sat down and went over the new information from Thompson.

'If that's true and I like it as a theory...' said Jeff, '...it doesn't actually tell us who killed Jimmy. Only that they were accomplices to the crime.'

'They just paid some thug, didn't they?'

'I think it's an ace theory, Nicky boy. It all fits perfectly, but how will you ever prove it? Even if it's 100 per cent right, they're never going to confess to it. In fact, if they've done their planning properly, there will be no way to trace it back to them at all,' Emily said, still tapping away at the keyboard. 'You need to get hard evidence.'

'I'll get the evidence if it kills me.'

'That'd be pointless, wouldn't it? Getting killed is a bad idea, don't do that,' said Jeff, sliding out a mono copy of Jimi Hendrix's *Are you Experienced?* from its sleeve and grinning. 'Oooh lovely, it's a first pressing and in great condition.'

'Is that valuable?' said Emily, looking over.

'You bet your sweet and tiny tush it is,' said Jeff, looking at the sleeve. 'It's the matt one, if it was laminated on both sides, it would be worth twice as much. Still nice though.'

'Really? Wow. So how much is it worth?'

'A mono first pressing, matt sleeve, on Track Records in mint is £250. This is only in excellent condition - so we'll put it out at

£200, but if someone offers you £175, take it. OK?'

'Wow. Amazing. OK.' She leant over and kissed the sleeve. 'I love you, Jimi.'

'All the expensive items go in the plastic sleeves on the wall so they're harder to steal and we keep the records behind the counter on these shelves, see?'

She turned and looked. 'Gotcha, big boy, and the code on the sticker inside the sleeve matches the one on the record on the shelf.'

'Nowt gets past you, Em. That's right. He looked at the record again and held it up to Nick. 'This came in a box of 200 records from Hughes auctions rooms for a fiver, y'know. Bloody great music, as well.'

'Whoo hoo!' said Emily, punching the air. 'It's good, this, isn't it? Finding a rare record for no money, I mean. It feels like a little victory.'

'Ah, I see the vinyl drug is already getting into your bloodstream, my girl. We'll have you drooling over rare releases on the Verve Folkways label soon enough. You'll be a proper nerd by the time you've worked here for a few months.'

'I'm already a nerd. We live in the era of Nerd Rule, in case you hadn't noticed. Anyone who is anyone is a nerd,' she said, with pride.

'Excuse me. I'm solving a murder here, in case you hadn't noticed,' said Nick, banging on the counter.

Emily looked up at him with mock indignation. 'I'm sorry, sir, but rock 'n' roll comes before murder.' She grinned at him, pushing her tongue between the gap in her front teeth.

Jeff hi-fived her. 'You is talking my language, baby,' he said in a strange imitation of a southern American accent. 'But wasn't his wife, Myra, at the hairdressers?' said Jeff, starting to sift through some more records. 'That's a good alibi.'

'No she wasn't, I forgot to tell you. She was at the hairdressers at 8am till about 8.45. Jaz was wrong about that - or lied about it. Like I said, they could have paid someone to do it for them. She could even have given them a key to let themselves in, if the door was locked,' said Nick.

'I like it. Yup. But as my rock 'n' roll pixie here says, how the hell can you prove that?' said Jeff.

He took a record off the turntable and put it in its sleeve.

'What would you like to listen to, Em?'

'Some Zeppelin would be good, if you've got any.'

'Good question. It always flies out the shop.'

'I know. I've sold two albums of theirs already.'

Jeff looked under the counter. 'Ah, here we are.' He handed it to her. 'This is an old-school vinyl bootleg. Recorded live at the Kezar Stadium in San Francisco in 1973. It's a bit of a classic in the world of Zep bootlegs.'

'Is it actually illegal to sell it, then?' she said, inspecting it.

'It probably is, but I bet even if you called the police and told them, they'd refuse to arrest you.' He put it on. 'It's raw stuff, this. I love it.'

Nick was restless. Late afternoon was coming and late afternoon was when the momentum to drink used to build. The idea to have a drink had kept flashing in his brain all day. Just little instants, but there all the same. He knew planet booze was orbiting him again, he had to keep distracting himself from dwelling on it because he was almost certain he couldn't resist it for the rest of the week, until Julie got back.

'I can't sit here listening to records, I'm afraid. I said I'd go and see Jackie yesterday and didn't make it, so I'd better go now. I'll catch you two later,' he said and quickly waved a goodbye.

He had got out of the shop and started to walk down the High Street when Emily called and trotted after him.

'Are you alright? I can come with you to the hospital, if you like.'

'I'm OK, Em. Thanks.'

'Are you sure? Don't drop into a pub and start boozing. You know it's no good for you.' She seemed genuinely concerned for him. It was good of her to care. She was a good person and you didn't meet many genuinely good people. He looked back into her green eyes.

'I'll be OK.'

'But you'll be on your own again and that's why you wanted to drink last night.'

He hadn't told her about sinking half a bottle of wine when he got home. He actually felt ashamed of that now. He squinted up the street towards Stockton Parish Church. 'I do feel a bit twitchy about it, but I've just got to get over it.'

She pushed him in the small of the back with her hand. 'You don't have to fight it on your own. Come on, I'm coming with you.'

'What about your work?'

'Jeff said I can go. It's cool.' She grinned at him.

'Actually, I wouldn't mind some company at the hospital, I don't like the place at the best of times. Too many bad memories.'

While he drove them to North Tees hospital, he told her about his mother's long fight with schizophrenia and how she'd spent so long in hospital in a state of confusion.

'All of that explains a lot about you,' said Emily, as they parked up and went to Jackie's ward.

'You reckon? I suppose it must.'

'Do you want me to see her as well? I can just wait in the cafeteria,' she said.

'Err...yeah, that's good thinking, Em. Jackie is a shit stirrer and if I turn up with another woman...'

She held up her hand to stop him saying anything more. 'I get it, I'll wait for you.'

Jackie was in a ward with five other women. She was in the far corner drinking tea out of a mug, a magazine on the bed. She looked over at him as he walked up.

'I was wondering where you'd got to,' she said, before he had even said a word.

'Hello Jackie. How are you feeling?'

'Like shit.'

She did look like shit, even by her own gnarled and nicotine-stained standards.

'Julie said you were going to drop in yesterday.'

'I was, but I had to break up a fight and it got too late.'

'A fight? Was it to do with Ricky and Kev?'

'No. No, it wasn't.' He pulled up a seat. 'You know about them though, do you?'

'Oh, aye.' She sniffed wearily. 'They've got Jon Gaunt as their lawyer. They'll be alright. Gaunty is a good lad.'

'Jules is sure they're not guilty.'

She let out a wheeze. 'Not of that...mebees...' She shook her head. 'But they're a couple of wrong 'uns, them two. I gave up on them a long time ago.' She let out a wheezy sigh, 'If it's not this, it'll be something else.'

'Are you in much pain, Jackie?'

She looked at him with the turquoise blue eyes Julie had inherited. 'I'm on so many drugs, I don't know whether I'm coming or going, son. I'm bloody stoned, is what I am. Don't like it much. What day is it?'

'It's Sunday evening. Have you had any visitors?'

'Sandra. That's all. Dunno where Con is. Do you know?'

'He's in Newcastle doing some work for Jeff. He'll be back in the morning, I'm sure he'll look in on you.'

'Aye.' She put her head on the pillow and closed her eyes, talking to herself, muttering under her breath then snorting and waking herself up and looking around. 'Did I drop off for long?'

'Just a few seconds.'

'Bloody hell. I'm a wreck. Bloody crash has buggered me up good and proper.'

Nick didn't know what to say or do. He tried to think what Julie would do if she was sitting there. She'd take her hand, she was tactile, was Julie. So he did that. Jackie's left hand was cold and bony, but she gripped him tightly as he took hold of her.

'You'll be alright, Jackie. You just need to rest.'

'I know, son. I know.'

He had run out of things to say again because he was rubbish at talking to her without Julie being there. He'd always felt like Jackie thought he was insubstantial as a man and couldn't offer the right degree of maleness, though she'd always been nice enough to him, really, so he patted her on the arm.

'I hope you get a lot of compo money, Jackie. I hope all this ends up being worth it.' He hadn't meant it to come out like that, but it had and now there was no taking it back.

She opened her left eye and looked at him, but didn't say anything for a bit. Then she coughed, took a sip of water and said, 'Aye. So do I. It'd better be.'

And that was it. She had confessed. She didn't have to say anything else. He'd been right. It really was all a scam to get compensation money, but she'd paid a hell of a price, a price that she was surely never meant to pay. He grinned at her. She stared back and the smallest, thinnest of half smiles appeared at the corner of her mouth for a second or two. Crafty old bat.

He sat for 20 minutes talking about Julie, until she dropped off to sleep and then sat for a moment to see if she woke up again, but she seemed settled, so he said a quiet good bye and went back downstairs to Emily. She was eating ice cream from the cafe and looking at her phone.

'Hey, Nicky boy. How is she?'

'She'll survive. Tired, though. She's a really tough woman and I'm used to seeing her have a lot of energy. I feel really sorry for the old girl. She's whacked out on painkillers and will have a lot of rehabilitation to go through.'

'How old is she?'

'Late 60s. I used to think she was indestructible, now I'm not so sure.'

She nodded. 'They do a good ice cream here. Do you want some?'

'No thanks, Em.' Looking around, he shivered a little. 'Don't hospitals spook you?'

'Not really.'

'Have you never spent time in hospital?'

184

'Not really. I had my abortion in here, actually, but I didn't even stay overnight.' She scraped the bowl and licked her spoon.

It was such a personal thing to share, it caught him by surprise. She seemed very relaxed about it.

'When was that?' he said.

'First year at uni.' She nodded and turned her mouth down. 'Unprotected drunk sex in Freshers Week. Ooops. Silly girl. They were great here, though. Totally non-judgemental.'

'That was quite a thing to go through in your first year away from home.'

She nodded. 'You live and learn, don't you? I lived and learned to go on the pill.' Just occasionally, she seemed very grown up.

'Shall we get going, then?'

'Just a minute. I had a thought while I was eating ice cream. I get a lot of good thoughts while eating ice cream.' She pointed the spoon at him. 'I bet Lomash Patel was brought here, so I was just wondering if we could find him and have a chat. You were saying earlier about his mother and that woman conspiring to kill the father. He might know about that. Maybe it's why he was beaten up. He was beaten up by the son of Paddy McGull's wife, who is friends with the other two. That's just got to be significant, hasn't it?'

He nodded. 'That is good thinking, Em. Yeah, owee, let's go and find the men's wards.' He pointed at a sign which indicated the way. It was over on the other side of the hospital.

'I like how you say "owee",' she said as they walked. 'You're always saying it.'

'I know, my mother used to try and stop me. She thought it was common. It's a Teesside thing, isn't it?'

'There are lots of different variations, I think but you say it differently to the Middlesbrough kids I went to college with. Softer.'

'That's because I'm from Stockton, the accent gets softer the more west you go towards Darlington.'

'It amazes me how much it changes in such a few miles.' She

grinned up at him, walking fast to keep up with his big stride. 'It's brilliant.'

'You still like being up here, then? No plans to go anywhere?'

'No chance. I love it. I don't even know why. You just click with some places, don't you? I feel at home here and now I've got a great job, I can get properly settled in. I mean, I've been here for three years, but college isn't the same as actually being a resident, is it? You're always on the outside as a student.'

They walked down seemingly endless corridors, turning left and then right and then climbing some stairs.

'Funny you working for Jeff, though.'

'I think it's great. I really do. I'm not just saying that because you're best mates.'

'Hardly using your degree in Computing though, is it?'

She fiddled with the silver skull pendent. 'Well, I have plans to revolutionise his whole stock system beyond his wildest dreams and that'll just be the start. I'd like him to set up a proper mail order operation. That'll take some writing, but I could do it and operate it for him. I did my final year dissertation on ecommerce, so I'm sure we could transform him into one of the UK's best online retailers, in time.'

He laughed and nodded. 'Amazing. He'll be up for all that, I'm sure. It'll be great having you around, y'know.'

'Yeah. It'll be good to see you popping in and out. But err...' She paused and cleared her throat. 'But how will Jules feel about it? She's a bit funny about me.'

'No, she likes you a lot,' he said, dismissively. 'Ah here we are.' He pointed at the sign.

A nurse was at a reception desk.

'Hi there. We're here to see Lomash Patel,' he said. She looked down a list.

'Third bed on the right,' she said, pointing with a Biro. Emily smiled and nodded at her.

As they approached the bed, they both sucked in an involuntary gasp of air. He was in such a terrible state.

# CHAPTER 10

He looked like every local newspaper photo of someone who had been beaten up in a robbery at an off licence, with a swollen eye and a lot of discolouration on his face. He'd had the bridge of his nose stitched and the corner of his mouth, as well. He could only partially see out of one eye, his ears were swollen and there wasn't much of his skin visible that wasn't bruised.

Emily gasped and held her hand over her mouth as they approached the bed. He had headphones on and was watching a DVD, glancing up as they approached.

They both smiled at him. Emily did a little wave.

'Hey Lomash. How are you?' she said as Nick got two chairs. 'I'm Emily, this is Nick, he was the chap that came to your flat and stopped the fight. I called the police. Gosh, you're in quite a state, aren't you, you poor thing.'

The lad nodded. 'Someone said what had happened. I was out cold. Thanks for helping us.'

'I wish I could have got there sooner, Mash,' he said, sitting on the edge of the bed. 'How are you feeling, now?'

'I hurt.'

'I bet you do,' said Emily and put a hand on his arm.

'They've arrested Dave McGull, I think,' said Nick. 'Why did he do it, Mash? Any idea at all?'

He shook his head, but said nothing.

'Do you know each other?' said Emily, her hand still on his arm.

He turned his head to her, then back to the DVD and then back to her and nodded.

Nick wasn't sure how to approach this. If only Julie was there, she was so good at talking to people and being sympathetic. It just didn't come naturally to him at all; then again, Emily was about the same age as Mash, so that might help.

'Were you good friends?' said Emily.

He nodded again.

'Mash...was it about your dad's murder? Or was it about something else?'

But he obviously didn't want to talk. Not even Emily's gentle coaxing could make him open up.

'How long do they think you'll be in here?' Nick said.

'They've said a week or so,' said Lomash.

Nick stood up. 'OK, we'll get off. We just dropped in because my fiancée's mother is here after a car accident and we were visiting her.'

Emily stood up and put the chair to one side, leant over him and put a hand on his shoulder. 'Take care, I'm sure you'll get better quickly, you poor thing,' she said, with a nice smile and more empathy than he could ever have mustered. How could you just bring this sort of emotion out of yourself like that?

'They arrested two men you know...over your dad's...you know...' He didn't know if he should actually say the word *murder*.

He nodded again, but said nothing else.

'Right, we'll get off. Get well soon,' said Nick defaulting to a *cliché*, in lieu of an expression of genuine feeling.

'I don't think it was them,' said Lomash, just as they'd turned and taken the first steps away from the bed. Nick turned around.

'What makes you say that?'

He shrugged again.

'Well, if you think that, you can't let them go to jail for a murder they didn't do,' said Nick. 'They're in jail now. You have to tell the police.'

He shook his head again.

'Why not?' said Emily. 'Are you afraid to?'

Lomash touched the bulbous, plum-like swelling on his eye with his finger tips.

'I might get more of this.'

Nick sat back down, but Mash was still reluctant to talk, even if he wanted to. Fear of another, possibly even worse beating, was understandably inhibiting.

'Do you know who did kill your dad?' said Emily.

He made no indication either way.

'Let me just suggest something to you, Mash. Was Dave McGull trying to shut you up or scare you from telling what you know?'

He nodded straight away and more vigorously than he had to any other question.

Emily glanced at him. 'And that's why you don't want to tell the police?'

'Yeah.'

'Look Mash. It's my fiancée's brothers that have actually been arrested for the murder,' said Nick. That made Lomash look at him with some sort of expression - though quite what sort of expression was impossible to discern from underneath all the haematoma. 'So if you know it wasn't them, I'd really appreciate it if you could at least tell me why you think that and I'll take it from there. You don't have to worry that the McGulls will come after you again. I'll be really discreet. But we can't let innocent men go to jail for something they didn't do, can we?' Internally, he blanched at described Ricky and Kev as innocent, but their violent, criminal past needn't trouble Lomash.

Emily sat down on the edge of the bed and took his hand again.

'Please, Mash,' she said. 'Nick is good at finding stuff out. He won't let anyone know what you've said.'

His visible eye flicked to her and then to him. He licked his dried, cracked lips.

'I don't know who killed him, but I heard Sheila Simmons and my mum and Dave's mum talking about it in our kitchen a couple of weeks back.'

'They were discussing someone killing your dad?'

He kept hold of Emily's hand. 'About getting dad "out of the way" and then giving contracts back to McGull's, 'cos dad had fallen out with Paddy, over me and Dave.'

'Over you and Dave? Jimmy - your dad...didn't approve of your relationship with Dave?'

Mash shook his head.

'But Paddy did?' said Emily.

'He was alright about it. Dad was a bastard. Paddy wouldn't try and stop us meeting. That's what dad hated. That's why they fell out.'

'So how come the fight happened between you two?' said Nick.

'I told him what I'd heard his mother and mine and Sheila talking about. He went mad. Said I wasn't to say owt. I said I'd tell the police if they asked us. He went proper mad.' He pointed to his face.

'Did you say something to your mum about this?' said Emily. 'Did you let her know you'd heard her?'

'No. We don't talk much to each other. And...' he let go of her hand, '...I wanted it to happen. I only told Dave what I'd heard after it had happened. He wants us to shut it. But I hated dad.'

Nick stood at the end of the bed and jammed his hands into his old jeans' pockets, nodding. 'I totally understand. So you just kept quiet and hoped it'd happen? But how do you know Ricky and Kev, Julie's brothers, were not paid for by your mother and Sheila Simmons to do the job?'

'I don't, but something was going on that morning. Everyone was at the house.'

'At the house? You were there that morning? I thought only Jasmin was there?'

He shook his head. 'They didn't know I was there. I was in the rec room above the old garage. I saw Terry come first. Jaz let him in.'

Nick's heart leaped in his chest.

'Terry? You saw Terry?' said Nick. 'Are you sure?'

Mash nodded. 'Then Kal came.'

'Who's Kal?' said Emily.

'My older brother.'

Nick squinted at him. 'Who else was there then?'

'Err...Sheila and mum, Kal, Tez, Jaz and dad.'

Nick's brain was speeding to keep up with all this information. Emily looked over to him with wide eyes. Where did he start with all of this?

'Did the police interview you, Mash?'

'Not yet.'

'So they don't know any of this?'

'Any of what?' he winced as one of his injuries throbbed in pain.

'About who you saw arrive.'

He shook his head. 'I don't want to get involved. I never saw nowt. They didn't even know I was there. I'm not telling anything.'

'So where does the rec room look out on?' he asked.

'The side door.'

'So they all came in through the side door?'

He nodded.

'But Ricky and Kev didn't?'

'No, not while I was there, anyway. Anyone that knows the house goes in the side door. Anyone who doesn't goes to the front.'

'Did you see anyone leave?'

He took a glass of water from the bedside cabinet. It was hard to look at him because he was so swollen and clearly in such pain. Poor sod.

'No, but I left after mum and Sheila came.'

'When was that?'

'Must have been about 10am. Next thing I heard was later that day when Jaz called us to say dad was dead. Then I told Dave and he went mad and told me to shut up and not say what I'd heard mum and Sheila say.'

'And which way did you leave?'

'Out the back of the rec room. It's got a door onto the driveway and out to the street.'

Nick rubbed his forearm and rested his chin on his hand.

'So it's a separate building?'

Mash nodded. 'That's what it is.' He leant back, clearly very tired.

He signalled to Emily that it was probably best if they left.

'So who do you think did kill your dad, Mash?' said Nick, as a last question.

'Dunno. Dave obviously thinks it was something to do with his mam, that's why he did this...' he pointed at himself.

Nick nodded and put a thumb up.

'Get well soon,' said Emily, patting him.

'Just take it easy,' said Nick, awkwardly. Was that the sort of sentence you could leave someone on? It'd have to do.

Driving away from the hospital, the evening sun cast a soft, gold light.

'You know what this means, Em. If what he is saying is true, and obviously, it might not be, but *if* it is, everyone has been lying. Not just that, they've conspired to lie about being there when Jimmy was killed and they can only have conspired in order to cover up who murdered him. They were all there that morning, but only Jaz has said she was and even she had lied about everything else. They're not lying about that for no reason, are they?'

'No, well, he was telling the truth,' she spoke with a crisp, confident voice.

'Are you sure?'

'100 per cent. He was in no fit state to make up lies. He was in pain, Nick. Also, not to be rude, but he didn't seem like a really bright chap. I don't know if he was clever enough to work out a big lie and stick to it in those circumstances.'

It was a bit of a harsh critique of Lomash, but he was a bit wishy-washy and didn't seem the sort to twist and turn and scheme.

'Are you going to talk to everyone who said they were not there and confront them about it, then?'

The truth was he just didn't know what to do. He needed Julie's empathy, understanding and sensible head, but he couldn't tell her about all of this. It would just disturb her focus and this was not the time for doing that. She had a new career to think about.

He was especially disappointed in Terry, who he'd known quite well for a few years and had always thought was without side. Yet he'd lied through his teeth about where he was and how he found out about the murder. There was only one reason he'd do that and that was surely to protect Jasmin or himself. But if Jasmin really was somehow guilty of murder, however unlikely that seemed, why say she was there, when they'd lied about everyone else not being there? She could have disappeared as easily as they did. Her being there suggested she had to be innocent.

Probably better not to rush into doing anything just yet. Sleep on it and then try to come up with a sensible plan of action. He made a moaning noise in his throat, as a huge lust for alcohol began to wash into him, riding on top of the wave of all his problems and worries like a Halogen lamp shining in a dark night. Where did it come from? It was almost as though when the light level began to drop, it was creating this burning desire. A desire just to nip in somewhere and have a couple, like he'd done for so much of his life. Man, it felt like it'd be a great thing to do, even though the thought of feeling like shit afterwards ran in parallel. It wasn't just about booze itself, it was about reconnecting with your old self. The self you left behind when you stopped drinking. That old, old friend. But was he a friend, I mean, really?

'Are you OK?' said Emily, turning to look at him as he drove into Stockton town centre.

'Yeah. Fine.' Had he lied well enough?

'So what *are* you going to do now?' she said again.

'I don't know. I can't talk to Jules about Terry until she comes home at the weekend. As you and Jeff said earlier, the problem here is getting some evidence to prove this. Even if we could use Lomash's testimony, it's simply his word. He *could* be making it all up, or be mistaken. The most pressing problem is needing to give Mike Cavani a name.'

'Yes. That Cavani chap sounds horrid. I feel like you should be able to get the police to stop him threatening you like this.'

'Nice idea, but that's not how it works, Em. It should work like that, but it wouldn't. Going to the police would make everything much worse. He has people everywhere.'

She looked out of the window. 'You do need hard evidence to prove who murdered Mr Patel, but what actual hard evidence is there to be obtained? I can't see there is any. That house would have DNA of all of them in it, because it's the family home. I just can't see how it could be proven who killed him even if it was one of the family. As far as the police are concerned, they've got two suspects with blood on them. That's the only evidence. You can see why they've charged them.'

She had a good, logical mind. It had to be all that computing.

He turned off down Norton Road and made another involuntary growl in his throat, making her look over at him. Fucking hell, he really needed a drink. But she said nothing.

'Thanks for your company, Emily,' he said, turning to her and smiling. 'You were really good with Lomash. And it's been really nice having you around. It's good to be able to share this stuff and to try and work it out together.'

She didn't say anything, but reached over and patted his hand on the steering wheel. He gripped it and raised it to his lips. That made her eyebrows shoot up in surprise. What was he doing? He had no idea.

'Look, how would you fancy going for a meal?' he said. Distraction, that was what he needed.

'Really? I'd like that a lot, Nick. That'd be really nice.'

He didn't want to say he was worried about drinking. It sounded so weak, though, on one level, right there and then, it was all he could think about.

'Thank you for asking me,' she spoke politely, as usual, but now with a little surprise and hesitation.

'You don't have to. I just thought it'd be good. We've never had a meal together, have we? Not apart from hot dogs and burgers at the blues festival. It'll be nice to sit down and have a meal.'

'Yes it would. Well, if *you'd* like to...'

He smiled at her. She ruffled her hair up in the vanity mirror and grinned back at herself.

'I'd really like to...it's just that I did have a date with a chap.'

'Oh. Sorry, Em. I didn't realise.' He was so self-absorbed and self-focused that hadn't even occurred to him that she might be going out with someone. Of course she was going out with someone.

She looked at her phone and sent a text. 'There. Now I no longer have a date.'

'Aw, man, you didn't have to do that.'

'I'm not that fussed, if you know what I mean?'

'Is he not a keeper?'

'God, no.' She ruffled her hair up. 'I'd *much* rather go for a meal with you than a drink with him. So where are we going, Nicky boy?'

'What do you like to eat?'

'Meat and puddings, mostly. Anything, I'm not fussed.'

'Fish alright?'

'Sure.'

Half an hour later they were sitting down to eat a bowl of fish stew at a small restaurant by the riverside called Water's Edge. Small and smart and yet informal, it was exactly the sort of place you'd never have expected to find in Stockton a few years ago.

'This is actually really handy for my flat,' she said. 'It's only five minutes' walk away. We could go back there after this, if you like. We got rudely interrupted yesterday, didn't we?' A little protrusion of pink flesh poked through the space in her front teeth.

'Yeah, violent assault is definitely a rude interruption. And I really like your flat. I know it's not that big, but it's cosy. Ideal for a single girl like yourself.'

She nodded, eagerly. 'You didn't see the bedroom, but it's a good size. Plenty of room to stretch out. I've actually got a King-size bed in there. I'll show you later.'

'Cool. A King? You'll be a tiny speck of dust in the middle of a bed that big.'

She giggled. 'If I spread my legs as wide as possible, I can touch the edges with each foot and I can get my legs very wide, you know.' She gave him a cheeky look.

'Well, there's an image to conjure with,' he said, remembering her posing in front of him in her house in Marton. It had been quite a sight and not one which had left him in the intervening months.

They ate in silence for a couple of minutes. She kept looking up at him, a smile on her lips. He didn't know what it meant, but it was good to see. A nice big glass of white wine might have been even nicer, though.

'Yeah, all those flats in Green Dragon Yard are really good. You know what? I'm thinking of talking to Jules about us renting one. Could be really good for us.'

She stopped, looked down at her food and then up at him with a different expression now on her lips. He couldn't tell what it was, though.

'Really, Nick? Are you sure?' Her tone was one of slight incredulity.

'Yeah. I fancy a move back into town and I think it's a funky little place to live and it's not too expensive. We'd need a bigger place than yours, though. I've got a few thousand albums that need housing. I think Jules will like it.'

She didn't respond, ate a little more and then looked up at him out of the top of her eyes.

'I'm not being funny Nick, but I don't think she'll be keen on that move when she knows I live there.'

He looked at her and frowned. 'Why's that?'

She stared back at him, seemingly thinking he was kidding. 'You're taking the piss, aren't you? You really don't know why?'

'What? Too expensive, do you think?'

'Because I'll be on your doorstep and she knows I...'

'...what?' The fish stew was superb, with big chunks of white fish and prawns in it.

She leant forward.

'Nick, listen to me. After what happened in the summer, she can see through me. She knows I'm...she knows I'm *really* keen on you.' She said it in a whisper and looked at the table, embarrassed at having to actually say it. 'Can't *you* see that? What are you even thinking in your head? I don't get you at all, sometimes. Why do I have to spell it out to you?'

He instantly felt stupid. Why *couldn't* he see these things? He *should* have understood.

'I didn't want to actually have to *say* that,' she said, putting her spoon down, '...because I thought it was obvious and because now this is all *very* awkward.' She was flushed in her cheeks and now extremely, if quietly, annoyed. 'What *do* you want, Nick? I really don't understand. I thought...' she blew out air from her small nostrils. 'I thought this was something...' she made a gesture to him and back to her.

He looked at her, she was obviously upset and tense. What the hell had he done wrong? It was as though she was speaking a language which he couldn't understand properly.

'Sorry, Em. I'm not very good...err...I do really like you.' But obviously, that wasn't the right thing to say, either.

Her small face scrunched up. 'I think I'd better go, don't you?' She dabbed at the corners of her mouth with a napkin, somehow making this small gesture seem grand and dramatic.

'Err...no...I don't want that at all. I was enjoying this.'

'Yes, but it's not *all* about *you*, is it? *I'm* here too.' She paused and looked to one side in disbelief. 'God, you're so dim sometimes, you drive me crazy. Don't you understand what you've been doing? You don't, do you?' She shook her head. 'Sometimes, Nick, sometimes it's like you're autistic or something.' She shook her head again and walked out of the restaurant. He let her go, not knowing how to stop her, or even if that was something he should do.

'Trouble in paradise?' said the waiter, coming over to collect the bowls.

'I'm just useless with women, I think...and men too, probably,' he said.

'You and 99 per cent of all the other men,' he said with a sympathetic smile.

He sat and thought about what had happened. He just wanted to make it better instantly. The trouble was, underneath his unthinking surface, taking time to consider what she'd said, of course he knew Emily was keen on him. He'd sort of taken it for granted. And he also knew, if he was *really* honest with himself, that he felt very affectionate towards her, especially when she was being more grown up and less giggly and young. But it couldn't go anywhere. He'd also taken that as a given, but had continued to indulge her affection and hadn't, for a moment, considered how his behaviour might affect her. He hadn't considered, in his self-absorbed way, how she must feel.

He'd just been incredibly selfish and he needed to apologise.

He got his phone out and sent her a text. 'I'm really sorry, Em. Can we talk?'

After paying the bill and going out to his car, his phone vibrated.

'Yes, please. My flat.'

He walked around to Green Dragon Yard, trying to focus on what was the best way to handle this. He loved her flirting with him, he also had to admit that to himself, and in enjoying that, he'd led her on too much. That must be it. All he'd wanted was to have an attractive, exciting friend, though he also knew, if he was single, he'd have been in her bed long before now. That was an inconvenient truth.

She buzzed him in and he walked up the stairs to the top flat. She'd left the flat door open.

'Hi, Em,' he said, his voice at a higher pitch with the tension.

She had changed into a big sloppy off-the-shoulder grey sweatshirt, which went to her knees. She had obviously been crying a little. Oh, god. Not tears. He had no idea how to handle tears. Tears made his brain go cloudy.

He sat on her sofa and she sat down opposite him on a pouffe with her bare, pink knees pressed together.

'I'm so sorry. I really didn't mean to upset you. I'm not the best at human relations. I never have been. I don't know why. It's like I can't quite see how what I say and do, affects others. Not all the time, anyway.' He said it with genuine feeling, somehow finding the words, at last.

'I know that only too well. Honestly, for a man who is 48, you're like a teenage boy, sometimes. Seriously, you are. You're emotionally retarded and so wrapped up in yourself, at times. You're very unselfish in some ways, and totally selfish in others. It's...it's weird.'

'I'm too self-focused. It's something I've...

But she interrupted him with a stern tone. 'And before you start talking about yourself some more, for the sake of clarity, I will say this only once, right?' She licked her thin lips and stared at the carpet with her green eyes, the pupils dilated, her voice now more well-spoken, posh and public school than it normally seemed to be. 'I really like you and I know you like me. If you were single, even despite the age difference, we'd just go out, wouldn't we? Be honest.'

'Yes. Definitely.'

'And we'd come back here and we'd make love in my big bed - as I *thought* we were going to do tonight - because we're both attracted to each other and I'm sure it'd be great, wouldn't it?'

'Yeah. Definitely. We would.'

'But you and Julie are super close and as long as that is the case, neither of those things can happen. Is that right? Or do you want to have an affair? Let's not beat about the bush any longer, because I will have an affair with you, if you want. I'm single and I can do what I want. If you wanted to do that, I would.' She'd adopted a deeper, more bossy tone than her usual light, feathery voice.

'No. I couldn't do that to Jules. It'd be such a betrayal and I totally love her with my heart and soul. That's the truth of it.'

She nodded firmly.

'OK, now don't interrupt what I'm going to say. I need to say this. I *totally* accept your relationship with Julie. I really like her as well, and she's obviously a nice person. But that means you can't lead me on the way you have been in the last two days, because it's just not fair. We had a lovely time last night, until that awful fight. You were sensitive and funny and cheeky with me and you say such nice things just...just naturally. That's the nice Nick I like. And I feel flattered and just very attracted to you, right? I don't care that you're over 20 years older. You can't help who you're attracted to. Last night when I was holding you by the window, I thought something was going on. I thought maybe we'd make love, because it was a lovely, intimate embrace and I assumed you wouldn't have done, that if you weren't interested in us having a physical relationship, whatever the effect on your relationship with Julie would be.'

Oh god, she had thought so much, so many things must have gone through her mind and yet by contrast, he'd thought so little about any of it. It was really embarrassing how empty-headed he'd been.

She looked up at him squarely. 'I know you were turned on, it wasn't difficult to tell, so it wasn't a stupid assumption on my part, was it? But you didn't do anything and I was going to make a move, when the fight happened and that was that. The moment passed. I thought perhaps we were just interrupted. Then today, we've been getting on really well and you're tender and affectionate towards me again, and I think we've got some sort of connection, and then you ask me to dinner and again, I'm thinking, oh he's interested, he wants to have some sort of relationship, but then you start talking about getting a flat here with Julie, as though none of that has happened. It's too up and down for me. I don't know where I stand and I don't like that. If I hadn't just said something, we'd have kept going on like that day after day after day and, well, it's pathetic. We're not at school. We've got to be grown up and say what we want and not just...just...drift. Does *any* of this make *any* sense to you at all?'

She gave him a witheringly, disdainful look, as though she knew it wouldn't.

He nodded and apologised again and felt like crawling into a hole.

'I see what you're saying, and I love you flirting with me and saying *risqué* stuff and that...'

'...well, that's sort of how I am with people I like. It's my way.'

'...it's flattering and that's why I've indulged it, I think. Same with holding you and all of that, I've just been making myself feel good, or better, anyway. Tonight, I didn't say, but I was so scared of drinking again that I needed distraction.'

That was an insult to her and he knew that as soon as the words fell out of his mouth. It was just more self-focus.

'For god's sake!' she stood up and put her face in her hands and rubbed her face. 'Don't you see how *rude* that is? Shit. I want to be more than a distraction for your...your...your weaknesses. I'm not just a diversion to take your mind off *your* worries.' She pointed to herself. 'I'm here too, I live in this skin. I'm a person, not a bloody function for you and your life to utilise when you feel bad. If I thought for a moment you actually meant to be that crass and downright insulting, I'd kick you in the balls and tell you to fuck off and never speak to me again.'

He knew he just didn't have the emotional vocabulary to say what he really meant.

'I can see that I didn't pay much or any thought to what you might be thinking or feeling.' He held his hands together, wanting to get away from this situation, but also feeling like he'd messed her around and owed her an explanation, even though he came out of it looking like a twat.

'I've just been really selfish, because I have no intention of breaking up with Jules. The very thought of that makes me feel almost physically sick. But that's not to say you're not...y'know...important to me. That I don't like you or anything. I mean I want you as a good friend, Emily. I still think about what happened in the summer. You're great fun and obviously, you are...I find you...err...y'know...sexy.' It was one of his least favourite words. It sounded cheesy and cheap and shallow, but he didn't know how to express how he felt about her any better than that.

She sat back down and clamped her hands between her knees

and nodded, her frustration subsiding.

'OK. This wasn't meant to be me confessing undying unrequited love for you, or something like that, nothing of the sort. I just needed to sort out where we are going. So can we just go back to being mates and not lusting after each other, please? Not pretending we're both free agents who fancy each other. I'm happy to have you as a friend and now I understand it'll never be any more, I can just get on and I don't have to wonder if we're going to jump into bed. I might still flirt with you a bit - but not with the intention of getting in your pants. It's just how I get through the day. Right? Do you understand me, Nick?'

'I do. That's exactly what I'd like.'

'Well, that's settled, then. Good.' She stood up as though she had been a school teacher reprimanding a school boy and then, letting out a big sigh and groan. 'I'm sorry I lost my temper.'

'I'm sorry I gave you such good reason to.'

'Apology accepted. I suppose you can't help being an insensitive idiot. You are a man, after all.'

He paused for a moment to find the right words. 'At the risk of saying something unintentionally crass again, there's something really great about you, something really attractive and interesting. You give out a lot of positive energy. I might not understand what's going on in your head, sometimes, but I know this, we're going to be good friends for the rest of our lives and that's something to really be cherished. Something important, too important to fall out over.'

She smiled. 'Aw. Now that *was* nice.' She sighed. 'How can you find such lovely words like that but at other times be so insensitive? I don't think I'll ever understand you. You're an enigma wrapped in a riddle wrapped in snug-fitting jeans.'

He looked at the floor and shook his head. 'Sometimes I have access to my better self and sometimes, I don't. That's about as much as I can tell you.'

They stood looking at each other for a few seconds. Then she gave him her impish little grin.

'Well, alright. That's us done, then. OK? Now, I've only got one last request.'

'What's that?'

She held her arms out to him. He laughed a little, not really knowing what she meant, but very relieved the horrible atmosphere was over and pulled her into him. Immediately, she put her hands down the back of his jeans, gripped his buttocks and held him tightly to her, pressing herself into him for a moment. Then with a little smile, she took his hands, placed them onto her bare backside under the long sweatshirt, encouraging him to rub her buttocks and the top of her thighs, and briefly joined fingers with him to feel inside between her legs, for just long enough to get his passion properly rising.

'There. A last little grope,' she said, letting go of him. 'Now, time to move on.'

As he went back to the car, his mouth was dry and he felt emotionally and physically exhausted but hey, at least it had taken his mind off drinking. He laughed out loud as he turned the engine over. He'd so often thought that Emily was childish and seemed so young, but she had shown far more emotional maturity in the last half an hour than he was capable of. God, he admired her for that. She really had her shit together and had been totally right. If she hadn't said anything, it would have gone on and on. When someone is affectionate to you, it's so hard to resist, especially when you've spent a lot of time not really liking yourself. So that was that. Draw a line under it. She'd been totally right to do that. Totally. What the hell had he been thinking? Take a lesson: stop being so up yourself that you stop thinking about other people.

The house was dark and unwelcoming when he got home. Again, he went round putting all the lights on as well as the radio and TV, trying to fill it up with human warmth.

He put the Grateful Dead's *Skeletons in the Closet* compilation album on the stereo in the music room, turned it up loud and wandered around the house restlessly as it played, not really knowing what to do with himself or what to think about anything.

He couldn't settle despite having two football columns to write for submission in the morning, and he hadn't even bothered to study the day's results yet.

Julie called after 9.30pm.

'Hello hello, my favourite blonde lovely,' he said, loading a photo of her on his laptop, taken on Santa Monica beach earlier that year. In it she pouted, hair fastened up, pulling a model's pose in her black bikini whilst, somewhat incongruously, holding a can of beer and a huge burger. 'I'm just looking at you holding a large piece of meat,' he said.

She hooted a laugh. 'I didn't know you had any photos of me doing *that*.'

Her Teesside voice was like a ray of sunlight in the dark, yet the guilt about drinking the wine was still all over him like emotional cling film and he already feared telling her and he'd *have* to tell her. 'How's it all going?'

'I'm just about to go to bed. It's been another long day. So much to absorb.'

'Are you enjoying it, though?'

'That doesn't seem the right word. I'm sitting listening to women talk about how men have, one way or another, abused them. So it's pretty gruesome.'

'But you're strong. And you knew that'd be the case.'

'Oh yeah. I'm not squeamish about it. I want to be able to help and find solutions for them, so I've just got to learn to be empathetic, without being overemotional. What have you been up to?'

And there it was again. Guilt at drinking. Guilt at being with Emily. He put it to one side in his mind. That was over.

'There have been some very interesting developments in the Jimmy Patel murder. It's quite complicated, but it'll all keep until you get back.'

'Can it? Good. I can't be doing with thinking of all that at the moment. It's soaking up all my juices doing this up here. It's just all-consuming.'

'Have you been out to eat?'

'Yeah, I went to a Spanish place with Joyce and Nancy, two of the women who run this place, and Martha from the Teesside Women Centre. I had chicken breast in a tomatoey sauce sort of thing. It was a bit overcooked. What about you?'

'We went to the Water's Edge,' he said, without thinking.

'On the riverside? What did you have?'

'The fish stew. It was superb. They put loads of prawns and salmon in it.'

'That sounds better than my thing. Did you go with Jeff?'

If he lied now, he'd have to keep lying forever. And forever is a long time.

'No. You remember Emily Davids? Jeff's just given her a job in his shop - she's setting up a big online thing for him - using her computer skills. So I ended up going with her.'

'Has he now? Ha. Well that's a turn up for the books. Hey, she didn't show your her knickers again did she, like in the summer?' She laughed. He laughed.

'It wasn't *that* good a fish stew.'

She kept chuckling. 'Ha, ha. I'd think get my pants off for a good steak, or even some really juicy lamb, but not for fish. Fish is almost a vegetable. You can't de-pant for a haddock. It'd be immoral.'

'I think you would for a chub, Jules.'

She cackled into the phone, making it distort.

'I love a big chubby, me, like. Actually, I don't think I've ever had a chub, as it were. I like Popa Chubby, but have never eaten chub.'

'Good blues reference. I think the chub isn't very edible, actually. I'm hungry again, now.'

'So how is little miss tiny pants anyway? Still messing with her hair and looking like she's on *Top of the Pops* in 1973?'

'Yup still doing that and giving it the full '73. She's got a new boyfriend and a new flat in Green Dragon Yard, or was it a new dragon boyfriend in green yard?'

'There are plenty of dragons out there, that's for sure. As I can attest after this week up here.'

'She'll be great for Jeff's business, y'know.'

'God help her having to work in there. And I bet Luke will come up and he'll be dribbling all over her. Euwww. He's a nice lad, but you wouldn't want his hand up your skirt. He's the sort of lad who might have mince under his nails.'

'I certainly wouldn't, no. And I'm sure you're right. Oh, I went to see your mam. She's fine. Well she's not fine, but she'll get through. She was pretty doped up. Funny seeing her like that.'

'I've sent her a couple of texts.'

'She admitted it, you know.'

'What?'

'The accident. It wasn't an accident. It is a compo scam.'

Julie screeched.

'Eee, the tricky old shitehawk. I might have known.'

He explained what she'd said, feeling pleased to have got the Emily business over with.

'I was thinking how ironic it was that they set up an accident which accidentally was much worse than they had wanted it to be.'

'Well them's is the risks you run as a scammer.' said Julie, unsympathetic. 'My family. Good god. We must have criminality in our genes, but I just don't have the energy to worry about mam, or Ricky and Kev for that matter. They've all brought it on themselves, one way or another. I have to draw a line under them. Are you coping on your own?'

'Of course. Thanks for your last photo by the way. I enjoyed it. Twice. Very artistic.'

She gurgled a woody laugh. 'Did you, now? Dirty boy. I thought you might need a bit of visual stimulation, since you've got so much lead in your propelling pencil these days.'

'Very thoughtful of you. Would you like me to send you one back?'

'No need, luv. I've brought some with me.'

'You haven't, have you?'

She gurgled a laugh again. 'I have, aye. Those ones from the California hotel room with the mirrors.'

'Oh yeah. Ha ha...that was a night to remember. Well, don't make too much noise in the night.'

'Alright, luv. Make sure you clean up after yourself in the bathroom. Take care. It was lovely to hear your voice. I'll give you a ring in a couple of days.'

After ringing off, he found her photo again and pleasured himself in the bathroom, feeling like he'd just had her encouragement to do so. It was a poor imitation of real sex, but it'd have to do.

Afterwards, he did some weights in the small spare bedroom for half an hour. Now lifting a 25-kilo dumb bell in each hand and as a result, powerfully built around his shoulder and arms, he had a routine that he went through most days while listening to music on his iPod. It had all started as a way to combat depression. The endorphins that exercise released had sometimes taken the edge off his dark moods. Combined with the low-carb, high-fat diet he'd been on for over three years, he'd dropped from nearly 15 stone at his fattest, most depressed and drunk, down to 11 and a half, his body fat percentage falling from a blubbery 27 to a lean 12 per cent. As a consequence, he had really sharp definition to his muscles, if he flexed them, which he rarely did, because it seemed massively vain to stare at your own body in the mirror, and though he was more at ease within himself than he had been, he still couldn't allow himself to like how he looked.

But through doing increasingly heavy weights most days, for over three years, he had, almost accidentally, ended up with a middle-aged, pasty white, non spray-tanned and much hairier version of the young, waxed hard bodies featured in *Men's Health*-type magazines. He wasn't sodding well waxing off any body hair though, that was for sure. It didn't seem like the sort of thing northern men should do, not unless they were strippers, anyway.

Being stronger was often useful, but the really positive thing was that it somehow helped to boost his self-esteem and self-respect - always two bone china elements to a depressive's character and very easily shattered, that was the real reason he'd kept doing it, especially as he approached 50. It stopped him feeling like he was going to seed, the way his father had, and in some ways made him feel more male, more masculine, even. Hopefully, not in a blokey, macho way, but just in that he was physically capable and had some power and energy. Julie had never seemed that bothered about the aesthetics of his muscles, though often flattered him about his physique during sex talk, presumably just to make him feel good, which it did.

He had a shower to remove the sweat and stink from him and took some mint tea to bed at 10.30pm. It felt lovely being in bed, with the smell of Julie alongside him, the sheets cool and soft. He let out a big sigh. Sometimes getting out of bed, seems like the worse decision you make every day. It felt like he was properly home and protected from the world, when in bed. The urge to drink or do anything else was somehow removed and he finally relaxed properly, which in turn only seemed to make him feel distractingly horny, once again. It was getting quite ridiculous, now. Sometimes your body just demands attention, as though it is nothing at all to do with your conscious mind. He plucked a tissue from the box on Julie's bedside table and within a couple of minutes had done what needed to be done, then let the surge of endorphins send him off to sleep.

In a bizarre dream, he was filming Julie in her old Norton flat with one of those big old TV cameras from the 1960s which they used to push around on wheels. It was like a weird children's TV show. At first she was doing origami, making paper animals and was naked except for a pair of red football socks. Then she went into the kitchen and squatted on a litter tray like a cat and had a piss. It was his job to film this for some reason. Then the police arrived in a helicopter, hovering outside of the window, and he was required to take a big can of film to Leslie Brown's toy shop on Stockton High Street, which had long since closed, but which had been an important part of most Teesside kid's childhoods in the 60s and 70s. He'd just started to measure parts of her body with a ruler and put the statistics into a database when he woke himself up to get rid of the strangeness.

He began to surface from the surreal dream feeling confused, but realising that he was wrapped around the pillow Julie slept on, rubbing up and down on it, like it was her. Good grief, he was actually shagging a pillow. What the hell was wrong with him? He let out gasp of laughter as he woke up properly.

'Fucking hell...I am so messed up without Jules,' he said out loud, going downstairs to make tea. She was a much more stabilising influence on his life and on his mind than he'd realised before she went away. The digital clock on the stove said 5.58am. Nice and early, just as he liked it. He laughed again about the dream, as he poured hot water onto Sencha green tea leaves and went in search of some eggs and a chicken leg for his breakfast, opened his laptop, checked his email, opening a couple of Boro-related ones, trashing the rest, and began to write his pieces.

After so many years, even if he hadn't been paying much attention to the latest games, he knew so much about football that he could always manufacture a vaguely interesting angle on some news story.

He'd just sent the first piece off to his editor when he noticed the light next to the small camera set into the top of his computer was on. That only ever came on when the camera software was in use.

# CHAPTER 11

It had to be some sort of screw-up on his computer. He flicked at it with his finger, his preferred method of fixing anything on a computer, but it stayed on. Maybe it was always on and he just didn't notice, so he went to the bathroom, eased his bowels, got dressed in his old jeans and black V-necked t-shirt and came back down to write the second article. The light was off now. Relief. An illuminated light on your computer, or in your car, is always upsetting.

He made some strong coffee, took a Phenibut and sat down to work, only to be interrupted by the sound of email dropping into his inbox. Bugger. He usually closed it down so he could concentrate. Now he knew something was there, he'd have to look. You couldn't not look at email when you knew it was there. It was the same with social network sites. If you left them open you had to keep looking at things friends had posted, even if it was photos of someone's unexceptional dinner, some wild conspiracy theory or another video of a cat doing something. It all become oddly compelling.

It was from Emily Davids. The subject line said, 'I've got my eye on you.'

'Hiya. Glad we cleared things up between us, yesterday. I feel like it was really important for me to say all that stuff. I hope you understood why.'

He nodded. He did. And she had such nice manners. She went on,

'I'm just testing something. Your laptop camera was on about 25 minutes ago. That was me. I made that happen! Clever, eh? Remember that email advertising Boro tickets? That had a bit of code attached which you unwittingly opened. It means I can now turn your computer's camera on and off. I was hoping to catch you doing something obscene, but you were just sitting and reading and drinking coffee. Very dull. But now I know how to do this, we might be able to use it to get evidence. Call me.'

As he read, the light came back on. Bloody hell, she was full of surprises. He waved at her and rang her up. 'Aren't you the smart arse then?' She giggled.

'I'm very pleased with myself. It's not exactly original, but it's a bit of a hacker classic.'

'How do we use it to get evidence?'

'We get it onto Sheila Simmons's or Myra Patel's computer and then we spy on them. Of course, we might not capture them saying or doing anything...but if we did, it'd be 100 per cent primo evidence, of their conspiracy to murder Jimmy Patel.'

He nodded, admiring her thinking. 'It is a great idea. The best and only one we've got.'

'Hold on, I'm going to send the code to you as a file. There. Got it?'

An email appeared from her. 'Yeah. What do I do now?'

She took him through how to embed it into an email so that it opened automatically when the recipient opened the email.

'Right, now send it back to me.'

He did was he was told.

'OK, I've got that, I'm clicking on it now and...there, it's unpacked onto my hard drive.'

'How come our virus checkers didn't block it?'

'Because of how I wrote it. It thinks it's a picture, not a virus.'

She then sent him some more software which he installed. Step by step, she took him through how to make the virus he'd sent to her computer work. He made notes as she did so. Eventually, a window opened up and there was Emily, sitting in her flat on the sofa in a towelling robe, her hair wet. It was sharp and clear, if a little bright and overexposed. She waved and grinned her wonky gap-toothed grin at him.

'Wow, that's amazing,' said Nick. It seemed like a special kind of voodoo.

'It is great, isn't it?' She looked at her screen in order to watch him. 'I can see you clearly in your old blue jeans and black t-shirt.

I can even tell that you're dressing to the left, as per usual.'

'Very observant. I didn't even realise that myself, Em,' he said, checking himself. He was.

'My all-seeing eye knows everything! Can you leave your laptop on the table and then walk away from it? I want to see how much it'll pick up.'

He placed it on the kitchen table and walked backwards. 'Can you still hear me?'

'Yes.'

He walked further away. 'How about here?'

'I can hear you, but you've gone out of focus on the camera.' He walked back and sat down and picked up the phone.

'It's not that clear visually, more than about six feet away, but the sound is surprisingly good,' she said.

'I can probably find Sheila's work email easily enough.'

'When you send the virus to her, log onto this server I'm sending you details of, so she won't know where it's come from. It'll pick up some words from the email, so it looks right.'

'Thanks, Em. This is a great idea.'

'No worries.' She rang off, stood up and put the laptop on what he recognised as the kitchen work top.

He went back to working on his piece. The light was still on. She could still see him. He went to the camera software and turned it off and closed it.

A couple of minutes later, it came back on again. He grinned at the small round lens, stuck two fingers up and then turned it off again. It didn't come back on this time.

After he'd finished he made more coffee and had some thick cream and frozen cherries and sat reading a football website that he wrote for. Glancing at his tool bar, he'd forgotten to turn off the window that the virus had opened up on Emily's computer. It appeared to still be on her kitchen work bench. It was so spooky having access like this to someone's private life. She'd clearly forgotten it was on, though nothing was happening. Then she walked past, stopped and turned around, did something off camera and then bent over to pick some socks up out of a wash basket. It felt incredibly transgressive to be this intrusive. She took off her towelling robe and stood up close to the camera naked. Nick's heartbeat increased.

She was obviously getting ready for work. Not doing anything out-of-the-ordinary at all. She bent over and looked in the wash basket again, her small, round backside filling most of his screen. He felt quite dry-mouthed. The combination of nudity and everyday ordinariness was, somehow, almost unbearably erotic as she unselfconsciously pulled on underwear, t-shirt and leggings. After she'd dressed, her phone rang and she picked it up. 'Hello Robbie. Sorry about last night.' She ruffled her hair up as she listened. 'No. It was just a friend needed some help. Sorry, babe. Yeah, I'd love that.' She laughed her fluttery, flowery laugh. 'I've got to go, I don't want to be late for work. Totally, yeah, it's ace. I love it. The guy whose shop it is, is a real character. See you later, Robbie boy.'

He clicked the cross in the window, to close it. That was the fun over. And no, he wasn't about to make a trip to the bathroom. That would, for some reason he didn't really understand and didn't want to analyse, be wrong. As he went about his work, he found himself feeling a bit jealous of her boyfriend. She was right, he was like a teenage kid, sometimes. That was enough voyeurism. It could bend your mind out of shape. Yet, more crucially, it could put someone in jail for murder.

Getting Sheila Simmons's email address was easy, as it was on the MIDO website. He forwarded it to Emily. Then, checking his notes all the while, he constructed an email to send to her with the virus embedded into it. He used a discount coupon email which advertised mega cheap deals at local shops and hotels. It was the sort of thing everyone checks out for a bargain, or just as a brief, entertaining distraction.

Going over it again and checking he'd done everything as per Emily's instructions, he went to the anonymous server which she'd emailed a link to, logged in, uploaded the email and sent it to

Sheila Simmons.

Afterwards, he just sat there. It felt as though you should be able to tell what was happening, but there was no way to know if she'd opened it and that the string of code had unpacked itself onto her hard drive. She might not be using a laptop, of course. She may be on a PC without a camera, in which case it would be useless. After checking it three times he decided to go for his walk around the fields. The wind had picked up and was now blowing a stiff westerly, giving the weather a distinctly autumnal feel. Leaves were starting to turn on the trees with a big rowan now splashed with yellow and the horse chestnut's green canopy now bruised with rust and gold.

Perching on a wooden gate, looking east to the Cleveland Hills, the telephone wires were clustered with dozens of house martins, gathering now for their imminent migration to Africa. It didn't seem long since they'd arrived in April. Time passed frighteningly fast.

Maybe they'd be mad to give up living somewhere so nice and moving to a town apartment. Rural Teesside had a quiet, simple, loveliness to it that was a pleasure to be part of, especially early in the morning.

When he got back in and made more coffee, he checked the software again, but she still hadn't downloaded it. It was only 9.23am, though; she probably didn't start work until half past. His phone rang.

'Hello?'

'Nick. It's Mike Cavani.'

Nick's guts sank. 'What can I do for you?' he said.

'I need that name, Nick.' His tone was brusque. 'It's time to deliver.'

'I'm still working on it. I'm nearly there. If you're in a hurry, why don't you just get one of your police insiders to do this for you, Mike?'

'Because, I'm a nasty, vicious cunt who likes to make people like you scared of me. Are you scared?'

What was the correct response to that? It sounded like one of those questions a bully asks you to which there is no correct answer that will save you getting a punch in the guts.

'I know your reputation, Mike,' he said, trying to walk a line between telling him to fuck off and quivering like a jellyfish.

'Then you'll know not to ask why I do or don't do anything.'

'Sorry.' He fucking resented having to say that and silently vowed to get his revenge on this bastard.

'That's better. I want that name by 5pm or I'm taking Julie.'

The line went dead.

A wave of nausea washed over him, his hands prickled and went sweaty. What the hell did that mean? 'Taking Julie'. Kidnapping her? Killing her? What the fuck did it mean? Oh shit. He couldn't find out who had killed Jimmy Patel by then, he couldn't. It wasn't possible. Shit shit shit. Should he go to the police? Go and tell Detective Inspector Colin Harcombe? No. He was away, anyway. Also, Cavani had men everywhere, it'd get back to them in no time at all and god knows what that would provoke him to do. Should he warn Jules? He couldn't do that...what could he say? He'd just scare the shit out of her and put her off her work. And what was she supposed to do, anyway? Look out for men who look like their granddads might have been Italian for the next week?

This was clearly how men like Cavani worked. They ruled by fear of what they might do, far more than by what they actually did. They only needed to be ruthless, violent nutters a few times and then let those incidences reverberate an air of potential menace. He still wasn't sure that he knew what Julie looked like, but it just seemed likely he did. Then again that was purely because of his family's reputation.

Just give him a name. Any name. That was the idea he'd had and it seemed as good an idea as any. Give him Myra Patel...she had probably conspired to kill him, after all, according to Lomash. But, as Jeff had said, what if he then had her killed? That would effectively be his fault. He couldn't live with that.

He did a search online for the Cavanis. They hadn't been linked to any killings. Plenty of violence, but no actual deaths, which wasn't to say they were innocent of such a thing. But what was he saying? That they might torture her and that was alright? Above all, he had the gnawing feeling that this was some sort of test by Cavani and that a name, whether they were guilty or not, wouldn't be enough for him. He'd soon be back for more.

A mixture of fear and anger infested him as he paced around the kitchen, rubbing his temples. Cavani wasn't like the stinking kid on the High Street. He couldn't be physically intimidated and beaten down if necessary. He had to be more clever than that with him.

As he contemplated exactly what to do, he clicked on the virus software and the window it opened produced an image. It was working! He pulled up a chair and looked closely. Someone moved into view. They were sitting down. The picture was good and sharp though blurred when there was any movement. A woman was looking at the screen. It was certainly Sheila Simmons - he recognised her from press photos. In her mid 50s, she had shoulder-length, curly dark hair, a soft, fleshy face and bags under her eyes.

Even with all the stress from the Cavani call, this was still exciting to see. It was so clever. But quickly, it also became clear that it was very boring. She was just sitting there typing, clearly replying to emails. Then sitting back and drinking from a mug. He turned up the sound to see if the microphone was working. Yes. Albeit it was only picking up rustling and typing sounds.

Emily had told him how to record the video. He tested it for 10 seconds and all seemed to work. He left it running while he washed up his breakfast plates, the speakers turned up to 10 just in case she said something to someone. Nothing.

After drying his plate and putting it on the rack he sat down and looked at her again. She let out a noisy fart, lifting her right buttock to do so, followed my a small groan at the relief of the intestinal pressure. He couldn't help but laugh. This was everyone's secret life. We all like to think we're so different and individual but really, once on our own, we probably all behave very similarly. Certainly, Nick felt like this could easily be a film of his typical working morning.

She finished the mug of tea or coffee and then let out a small belch and sighed heavily. Another boring day at work is what it looked exactly like. There was a bang.

'Come in,' she said, looking up. Had the fart cleared? She'd be worried about that. Any of us would.

'Morning, Sandy.'

There was an audible, but indistinct female voice from across the room.

'Yes. We'll do that. No problem...no...I'm just working on the press statement...yup. OK, darlin.' She spoke with a classic Middlesbrough accent, stretching out the 'a' and not pronouncing the 'g' at all.

The door opened and closed and Sheila was back on her own and she went back to work with a sigh. The phone rang.

'Sheila Simmons...hello. Yes, we're going live with that at 11. I'm just finishing it now.' Clearly some sort of press release was being prepared. 'Acting Chief Executive. Yes. That's it.' She put the phone down, tapped at her keyboard some more. Someone else then came in. She let out a laugh and the door closed again.

There was no point in just sitting here watching this. He hooked up a terabyte hard drive to the laptop and began recording it onto the hard drive, and then called Emily.

'Hello, Nicky boy,' she said.

'Hey. Are you in the shop?'

'Yes. Is it working?'

'Like a dream. I'm recording her right now.'

'Cool. What are you going to do now?'

'I'm going to have a look around Jimmy Patel's house.'

'What? How are you going to do that?'

'I don't know yet. I just had the idea to go over there. It's not far from where you lived on Stokesley Road.'

'Oh, where is it? Mash didn't say.'

'Jaz told me a while ago. It's down The Grove.'

'Oh god, I might have known it would be. It's very leafy and expensive down there. The houses are massive and cost a fortune. It's exactly the sort of place that my mother would think, in her snooty London narrow-minded ignorance, didn't actually exist on Teesside.'

'The police might have it guarded as a crime scene, if they have, there's not much I can do. But I'd like to get a sense of the layout of the place, all the same.'

'It's not your worst idea, actually. See if you can confirm that Mash could have seen everyone arriving from the recreation room, as he said, and also that there's a way out of it, for him to leave without alerting anyone he'd been there.'

'OK. I will. Then I'm going to see Terry and have it out with him about why he lied about being at the house. I got a call from Mike Cavani this morning...'

'...Oh, shit. What did he want?'

'A name. Said he'd "take" Julie if I didn't give him a name by the end of today.'

'What?' Her voice went squeaky in disbelief. 'He can't do that. What does he mean?'

'I'm not sure. I'm scared about it though. I've got to do something...but I just don't know what.'

'You have to go to the police, Nick.'

'I can't do that. First, it would only force Cavani's hand into doing something. Secondly, it's just my word against his, if I complain.'

'I suppose so. Why don't you make up a name and a story about them. Say it's Frank Somebody who did it and he's left the country. Say anything, just to get Cavani off your back.'

'Great minds think alike. That's what I was considering doing, but he'd smell bullshit a mile off and I can't risk giving him a real name in case he wants to harm them. I can't have that on my conscience.'

She went quiet and then spoke up in an eager voice. 'I know, why don't you send him the virus?'

'Well...that had occurred to me as well. He must be doing dirty deals all the time, threatening people and such - so we could get something on him. Jeff said we needed some insurance and that'd give us it. But I don't have any contact email for him. It'd take too much time to find one. I think he likes to police his people by phone call, not email.'

'Hmm. But you have his phone number, don't you?'

'Yes.'

She paused for a moment. He could imagine her messing her hair up.

'I've got it Nick. I've got it. I'll bloody hack his phone. Yes! I can set that up! Everything Cavani does will be on his phone. Emails, texts, photos, documents. He'll carry them on his person, rather than leave them unattended somewhere on a computer or laptop, even. That's what a paranoid gangster would do, I'm sure.'

'Can you really do that?'

'Hold on, I'll just look it up...hold on...' she went quiet for 30 seconds. 'Oh, it's a piece of piss, Nicky boy. I'll have this done for you in 10 minutes.'

'Wow, are you sure?'

'Yeah. I just need to download it and send the hack to him in a picture. Then it'll give us everything that is on his phone.' She giggled and gave a yelp. 'This is sooo great.'

'It's not that great. He's a violent nutter. So make sure he doesn't know where the picture comes from, Em.'

'I won't. Send me his number and leave me to it while you go to the Patel house.'

The Grove was in Marton, set back from the A174; a little haven of leafy suburbia, most houses were detached and set back from the narrow, tree-lined road. Built piecemeal over the years, most of them probably dated from the first 20 years of the 20th century. It was possible to believe you were going down a quiet country lane, rather than a road in a suburb of southern Middlesbrough.

The Patel house was set at the end of a rough gravel driveway which was guarded by two mature oak trees and hidden from the quiet road with a dense hawthorn hedge. A sprawling property built in 1899, it was a classic Victorian half-timbered Tudor-style house.

Nick parked on the driveway, got out and looked around. It was very quiet, only the mumble of the dual carriageway in the distance broke the silence. Surprisingly, no-one was around at all. Then again, though it was a long road, the lack of density of housing meant few people actually lived nearby. He'd expected the place to be protected by the police. It was a recent crime scene, after all. But there was no sign of any police activity. They must have finished their work and locked the place up. The driveway curved around to the left and led in front of the house, then curved right into a large double garage. He went for a walk around the grounds, looking up to see if there were CCTV cameras by the door or watching the grounds. Nothing. They were surprisingly absent.

The recreation room had been built out of a pre-existing 1950s garage - a garage designed for much smaller cars. It stood alongside the new double garage, but it was an odd little building. The original core of it was still intact and had then been built up from, so that the room Lomash had been in sat on top of the now opened-up original garage space, which was in turn used to store a substantial log pile. A wide window looked down to an extensive back garden. A large side door to the house was clearly visible, perhaps 30 feet away. It was perfectly positioned to see people walking up to that door. There was a small door, but no window, facing to the driveway and the front of the house.

Nick crunched around on the small, pea-sized gravel and peered into the first window he came to at the side. It looked in on a kitchen. The kitchen where Jimmy Patel had met his rather stabby end. There were some marks on the white, tiled floor, which must have been left by the police to mark where the body was, but that was about the full extent of the sign that anything so traumatic had happened there so recently. It all looked expensively appointed and very tidy. The digital clock on the cooker still showed the time, as did a microwave in one corner. He was about to walk away when he noticed two red LED lights, one in each corner of the room. Cupping his hands over his eyes to try and reduce the reflection on the glass, he peered into the kitchen, squinting to see what those red lights were. They were only small, little more than pin pricks seemingly set into the wall. They had to be part of the security system. Some sort of laser beam that got triggered by movement. Odd that there were no CCTV cameras outside, though. Usually people wanted them just to suggest to would-be burglars that they'd be caught on film. Maybe Jimmy Patel didn't want any evidence of who came to the house because it would be too incriminating.

He walked to the back garden and then around the far side of the house, taking a side path that led back to the front, where he'd parked.

The front door was an almost medieval-looking thing, made of a massive slab of oak with big black Gothic hinges on it and a large black iron door knocker in the shape of a lion's paw. Standing at the door, it was impossible to be seen from where Lomash was. It was all exactly as he'd said it was. There was nothing to disprove that he could have seen people arriving at the side door and in many ways it was the natural door to go to. The front was one of those doors which looks like it is permanently locked or at least not often opened. The side door was clearly the one used to go in and out of day to day; you could see that just by the well- trodden gravel path to the door.

This was where it had all happened. If only walls could speak. As he drove away, he couldn't imagine Lomash had made that whole story up on the back of his beating. His story checked out geographically. The whole family had, in all probability, been there either when, or just before Jimmy died.

Twenty-five minutes later he parked up outside of Terry's flat and rang the bell. Someone looked out from behind the net curtain.

'Alright, Nick,' he said, opening the door a little as though not really wanting to let him in. Nick pushed past him anyway.

'Shut the door.' Terry did as he was told. 'Why did you lie to me, Tez?' he said turning around.

'Eh? I didn't. Err...about what?' Terry scratched his head and rubbed his eyes, as though trying to be casual.

'Don't fuck me around. You were at Jimmy Patel's house the morning he was killed.' Terry stared at him. 'Don't lie any more, Tez. I know you were. You were seen there. Why couldn't you tell me the truth? Eh? That's what pisses me off most.'

'No, no. You've got that wrong, Nick. Who told you that?'

'Never mind who told me, I know it's the truth, Terry. So, why don't you tell me what really happened there that morning? You've both lied about this.'

'Yes, we have, Nick,' said Jasmin, emerging from the living room.

'Ah, hello, Jaz. Right. Let's have it all out then.'

Terry looked at him with nervous eyes flicking to Jasmin and then back to him, his hands fiddling with his hair.

She gestured for him to step into the room. As she did so, his phone vibrated. He squinted at the text. It was from Emily. 'I now have everything on Cavani's phone. Have downloaded it to a server. Please come to the shop immediately. Important.'

Shit.

'Look, I have to go, something urgent has come up. Just tell me, you *were* there when Jimmy was murdered, weren't you?'

Jasmin spoke calmly. 'Both of us were. We found him together and then Tez left because of how dad was with him. It seemed best if he wasn't there. It was obvious someone had killed him. The police were bound to suspect Terry. He'd sneaked in to see me. We were in my room, came down together and found him dead.'

'And you two were there on your own?' he said.

She nodded. 'Yes. We were terrified. I told Terry to go.' She said it like it was truth.

Nick stared at her. The little liar. Talk about butter would melt.

But should he tell them he knew this was just a new lie? Or did he keep quiet and see how they wanted to play this?

'I can't admit it now because it looks even more dodgy, doesn't it? A Wells brother denying being at the scene of the crime,' said Terry.

'We didn't kill dad, Nick,' said Jasmin. 'Someone must have come in and did it and left while we were upstairs.'

Garbage, it was all garbage. What about the rest of the family? What about Ricky and Kev? They had Jimmy's blood on them. Terry and Jaz seemed to have forgotten that little fact. So they had to have been there, as well. Their lie was falling apart, but he just didn't have time to confront them with it now. He had to protect Julie and sort Cavani out, that had to be his priority.

'Both of you should think on, about what you've just told me and what it means for your brothers, Terry. You can't keep lying like this.' He pointed at both of them then left for Stockton High Street.

Twenty minutes later, he ran into Jeff's shop; Emily was sitting behind the counter at her laptop, Jeff alongside her.

'OK. What have you got for me?'

'It's not good news, lad,' said Jeff. 'Come and look.'

He walked behind the counter. Emily had downloaded the contents of Cavani's phone onto her hard drive.

'We've got his email and all contact info...so that's good,' said Emily. 'We can spy on him through the camera hack, in theory, at least. But in the photo file...look...'

Jeff loaded a slideshow of the photos. The first few were of a restaurant and cafe. He went cold and stared in horror. There was Julie, coming out of the refuge and walking down the street with three other women, one of whom he recognised from the Teesside Women Centre. There she was again with the three women in a restaurant, clearly having the Spanish meal she'd mentioned. There were 14 pictures in total. It was clear. They definitely *did* know who and where she was.

'My guess is he was going to send these to you later today,' said

Jeff. 'And put the shits up you.'

'Well, it's done that, alright.'

'There's also an email,' said Emily.

'Sent from Cavani to someone called Big G. 'Re our conversation. This is her. Be there today. She'll probably leave around 5pm.'

Nick swallowed down hard to keep his emotions in check.

'The bastards. Right, we've got to get up there. Well done on getting this, Emily.' He looked at his watch; it was still only 11.20am, plenty of time.

Jeff patted him on the back. 'Yup, of course we will. There's no way we'll let them touch her. I'll try and speak to Eddie Cavani, just in case if he can have any influence. Conrad is still up there, though. He didn't get finished and he's decided my money is better than McGull's money. So he's working on the shop. I've just spoken to him and told him what's what. Straight away he said he's going to get some of his mates to ride shotgun for us. They have access to large heavy tools and know how to use them, so don't worry.'

'Shit, you've been busy, Jeff. Thanks, man. Con, eh? He's up for a fight, is he? The old boy?'

'Not just up for it, "bring it on", he says. I think he fancies breaking a few Cavani heads and he doesn't want his Jackie's lass getting in any bother. They do this sort of shit all the time in the building game. They used to have to crack heads to get their money from dodgy contractors.'

Nick looked at all the files they'd downloaded, his mind racing.

'What's this yellow folder here, Em?'

She looked over.

'It's an encrypted folder.'

'So whatever is in there is super precious to him?'

'Might be banking details or anything that has to be kept secure. So you can pretty much be sure it's where the juicy stuff is.'

'Can you get into it?'

She shook her head. 'I've already had a look. It's password

protected and encrypted.'

'Can't you just hack it somehow?'

She shook her head again. 'You log into it, then you need the decryption key. So it's got belt and braces on. I can't do anything without his log-in password and then the encryption key...but I might be able to sort something out. I'll consult my hacker community.'

'You know, I really wanted to keep Julie ignorant of all this, so she can keep focused on her work,' said Nick.

'Not much chance of that. You need to tell her what's going on. She's got to know. I just wish we had Ricky and Kev on hand to crack heads,' said Jeff, tying his hair back in a pony tail. 'But springing them from jail as well might be a bit of a stretch today.'

Nick called Julie. Her voicemail picked up. 'Can you call me as soon as you get this, Jules?'

'Right, let's get up to Newcastle then,' he said.

'I'll keep you up to date with any developments here,' said Emily.

'Try and sell some records as well if you can,' said Jeff. She saluted him.

'Gotcha, Captain.'

They went up in Nick's car.

'That Emily is really something, isn't she?' said Jeff as he drove. 'Only had her in there three days, but she's changing the whole vibe of the shop. Having a woman in there, just changes everything. Makes it, I dunno, just makes it better and less weird. That's weird, as in the bad weird. Not the good weird. Do you get me?'

'Oh yeah, she just projects energy and positivity, I reckon. And on top of that, she's clean, which, let's face it, most men who work in record shops cannot always say.'

Jeff grunted and stroked his long, greying beard. 'You're not wrong, Batman. And better still, she's actually having a positive effect on sales already. We're 35 per cent up. Might just be a blip, but I bet it's not. Having a lass in there means women won't be scared off coming in.'

'And she's good looking, I think,' said Nick.

'Yeah. Not in a glamour model way, but she's got something, hasn't she? I don't know how these things work, but she's definitely got that sexy glint in her eye...' said Jeff, '...plus, a lovely little arse, which I have only noted for purely documentary purposes and not in any way for pervy lusting reasons, which, as you know, are anathema to a man of my strict moral code.'

Nick laughed a little. 'Definitely, aye. Actually, I had a bit of a thing happen with her the other night. Do you want details?'

'You bet I want details. Does it involve that arse?'

'It does a bit, yeah.'

Jeff punched the air and put his feet up on the dash board, hands behind his head. 'Yes! Give it to me, big boy. Leave nothing out. I want it all right down to the last buttock pimple.'

After making him promise not to tell Julie anything, he went over their last two meetings with her, including his difficulty with wanting to booze and the details of her tattoos.

'You can't tell her you know about those, though, not until she mentions them, anyway. She'll know I've told you, otherwise.'

Jeff whistled. 'She's been hot as a fox in a forest fire for you since the summer.'

'We sorted it out between us, thankfully. I was really being dishonest with her by sort of leading her on.'

'Well, who can blame you? What bloke wouldn't love her to cozy up to them?'

'I know, but that doesn't excuse it, does it? Not on many levels.'

Jeff shook his head and put the radio on.

'Don't give me your feminist bit, lad and don't get your panties in a wad about it. You didn't do anything. So she let you have a bit of a feel up and you did likewise for her. You know as well as I do, it's not sex until you expel bodily fluids into or onto the lady in question. A bit of dirty flirty is alright. It's not like you're being unfaithful. You're just sampling an amuse bouche, not eating the full dinner. I reckon you did exactly the right thing.'

'You do?' He looked at Jeff.

'Yeah, you copped a feel a couple of times, but knocked it on the head before you actually started anything more heavy. So you got a bit of excitement, but remained morally upstanding in your relationship with Jules. It's a win win. Most blokes would have steamed right in there. Between you, me and this hysterical rendition of a great Leonard Cohen song by someone off a TV show, I bloody would have...and more than once. She's bloody lovely, is Emily, though clearly, I would shatter her into dust with my giant body.'

Nick envied Jeff's simple conclusions. Everything always seemed much more complex in his own head.

'Anyway, sex, little lasses and their magnificent buttocks aside, sorting this shit out with Cavani is a little more pressing for us,' said Jeff, rubbing his large hands together and drumming on his legs. 'I was wondering, in my typically conspiratorial way, if Cavani was involved in whacking Jimmy Patel? I know he was their man, but it occurred to me when Emily was saying what the Lomash kid had told you, that he might be testing you to see how obvious or otherwise it is, that they killed him.'

'Well, I'm sure it was the mother and Sheila Simmons who conspired to have him killed. Perhaps it was Cavani who arranged the actual killing through their building trade connections. I'm recording her in her office right now. Hopefully, she'll let something slip. Can't help but feel it's a long shot though, and frankly, I couldn't give a flying fuck about any of that right now. We've just got to keep Julie safe.'

'Yeah, but remember, we've got to stitch up Cavani or you'll never get him out of your messy and frankly rubbish hair.'

'Totally, yeah. Alan Gow was a sad excuse for a man. Cavani had paid off his debts and now he's at his beck and call forever more. I mean, fuck that. I'm nobody's pussy cat and I never will be and I'm damn well not ready to play nice.'

'That's how they work though, isn't it? They do favours and then call in debts.'

227

'We have to neutralise him. Stop this game he's playing with me. If he thinks I'm going to replace his man on Teesside, he can fuck right off.'

'Well, Emily might find something on the phone that we can use against him, though from what I could tell, he's been pretty careful.'

'If there's anything we can hold against him - it'll be in that locked folder.'

As they got into the outskirts of Newcastle, Nick felt scared and he bloody hated feeling scared. He resented this imposition on his life and even more so on Julie's life. Simmering anger in his guts was a familiar and unwelcome returning visitor.

'Mike Cavani won't be there, will he? He'll keep his distance.'

'That's what I'd guess, like,' said Jeff. 'So what do we do? We turn up mob-handed at the refuge?'

'Discreetly mob-handed, yeah. I don't want them thinking it's a gang of angry, abusive men outside, come to claim their women back.'

Jeff snorted. 'Well, in a way, it bloody is.'

'I'll go in and see if I can see Jules and let her know what's going on.'

'Cool. Well, Conrad is at the new shop. He's got three mates meeting him there, so we'll drop off there first and tell them where to go.'

The shop was finished. As Nick and Jeff walked in, all the shelf units were fixed to the walls and the record bins in place. The only thing that betrayed the work that had gone on there was a heap of trimmings of wood and sawdust.

'This is great, Con,' said Jeff, shaking the big old guy's hand. He wiped his brow.

'Aye, it's a canny job, like. I've enjoyed doing it. So, we're off to bust a few heads, are we? It'll be like the old days,' he said enigmatically. 'My lads will be down in a minute.'

'You know it's the Cavanis, do you?' said Nick.

'Aye. Doesn't bother me or the lads. It'll not be one of the family, anyway, it'll be a couple of their goons. Big twat, called Baby G, does all their menacing in the Toon. He'll not get his hands on my Jackie's lass, divvant ye worry.'

'Con. You know you said to me in the hospital that the Cavanis might be behind that cement mixer crashing into the car?' said Nick, looking him in his twinkling pale blue eyes. 'Just to put my mind at rest, that was a load of old shite, wasn't it?'

Conrad tugged on a fag and grinned back at him with some pride. 'Aye. All bollocks that, like.'

'Fucking hell, Con,' said Nick shaking his head. 'I'd never even have run into Cavani if it wasn't for you saying that,' said Nick, pushing his hair behind his ears. 'All of this could have been avoided.'

'I knaw. Sorry, like. I wasn't to know you'd go and actually see the bastard, was I? But I'm here to help, kidda.' He gave him a stained, toothy grin.

'You could've pulled off a compo scam, without spinning me a bloody story. I'm hardly going to shop you, am I?'

'It's the way I am, isn't it? Always liked a story, me,' said Conrad.

As he spoke, three men looked in the door. One, tall at over six foot, one, broad and about 16 stone and one, a small pug-faced man, with a neck as thick as his head.

'Alreet, Con,' said the tallest.

'Aye aye, Bazza. Thanks for coming down.'

'Nay bother. Cavanis kicking off, are they?' said the short man, as though it was a personal insult to him.

'They're threatening to take this lad's missus,' said Conrad, pointing to Nick.

'Fuckers. Kidnapping? Why's that, like?' said the third, a fat man with a spider's web tattoo on his neck and NUFC tattooed on his knuckles.

'Mike wants me to find out who killed someone down on Teesside and basically, I can't.'

They looked at him blankly. 'Is that it? Fucking hell. There's got to be more than that. I thought you'd owe them money or summat,' said fatty.

Nick shook his head. 'That's it.'

Bazza, the tall man pulled on a cigarette. He was about 60 and looked like he'd slept outside for 55 of those years. With skin creased and brown like an old leather satchel, he didn't just look hard, he looked tough and somehow, that's different. Tough beats hard.

'That cunt will have summat else in mind then. He's not trying to break your balls over that. It's not worth his time. Are ye a smoggy gangster, then?'

'No, man. I'm just a normal bloke.'

'Well he must fucking fancy you then,' said the pug-faced man. They all laughed at that.

'Is he...is he gay? Is Mike Cavani gay?' said Nick, looking at Jeff, whose eyebrows were raised.

'Some say he's a right fucking bender, aye,' said pug face.

'Gettaway man, Mike Cavani is not a shirt lifter,' said Conrad. 'I'd bloody know if he was. I worked for them.'

'Hold on, hold on. I'm not gay, he knows I'm not gay. He's not interested in me for that reason if he is actually gay or even if he's bi-bloody-curious,' said Nick, feeling that things had taken a surreal turn. The men all laughed out loud at this, even though it didn't appear to be that funny.

'Howay then, let's get gannin,' said Conrad.

Nick called Julie again, but it went to voicemail, again. She must be in meetings.

Conrad and his mates followed Nick's BMW in a white van, out of the city centre and up Barrack Road.

'Those blokes looked meaner than a junk yard dog,' said Jeff, as Nick drove.

'Aye, they look hardened in battle, don't they?'

'Probably wanted by Interpol in 12 different countries, for cruelly inserting a spirit level, where no spirit level should be inserted.'

But Nick couldn't laugh. He was too tense, too worried, he repeatedly tugged at strands of hair, fiddling nervously with them. It was nearly 4.30pm when they parked up, down the road from the refuge. Conrad pulled in behind them. They got out and stood behind his van.

'Who are we looking out for, Con? The email we saw was to that bloke called Baby G,' said Nick.

'Aye. He's a big bugger. Fat cunt. Powerful, but someone with one leg could outrun him. He'll probably have someone in tow with him. We'll sort them out, divvant ye worry, son...come over and have a pop yourself, if you like. You look like you can handle yourself.'

'I don't want to be brawling in the street outside of where Julie is working, man,' said Nick. 'But if you need any extra muscle, just give us the nod.'

Conrad looked up the street, '...and there's Baby G, look, getting out of the black Merc. They've only sent two over...nay bother...we'll menace the fuck out of them and if they want trouble, we'll kick their fucking heads in, eh.'

Nick's heart pounded as he followed Conrad's gaze. Cavani *was* serious. They'd sent someone to snatch Julie. Only his anger was equal to his fear. He rubbed his eyes and tried to compose himself, feeling his emotions running high.

Conrad was the model of cool, though; in fact, he seemed in a very good mood. Violence seemed to cheer him. The three other men got out of the van. Each of them wore a workman's tool belt with various tools, such as hammers and spanners, slotted into it. It was a neat way to carry weapons that could put someone in a coma with a couple of blows. It also had the advantage of making you look like a workman and not someone tooled up for a fight.

Conrad spoke to them casually. 'Alreet lads. Don't look, but up the street is our target. He's leaning against the driver's side door of the black Merc.'

Nick tried Julie again, but there was still no reply. Maybe she wasn't even in the house. They made out they were working on something in the back of the van and kept an eye on Baby G.

'There's no point in scaring him off for an hour or two. They'll just come back later when we're not here,' said Nick. 'We need to show them that we're not going to be fucked around with and that if they touch Julie, now or in the future, then they're going to get a proper fucking kicking. Make them realise it's not worth the trouble.'

'I like hitting a fat lad. The blubber acts as padding on your fist. Never hurts punching a fat bloke,' said the tall man.

'Fat blokes always go down easily. Dunno why. You'd think they'd need a lot more fistin',' said Conrad. The other blokes laughed. It was remarkable how at ease with imminent physical aggression they were. It just didn't bother them, the way it bothered most regular members of society.

5pm came and went. No sign of Julie. Then suddenly, a cab drew up outside of the refuge and she got out with three other women, leant into the window and paid the driver. Nick's heart leaped at seeing her again. Dressed in her soft, ripped, washed out old jeans and a hoodie, her hair tied up, he just wanted to hug her to him to protect her. But this was not the time for that.

# CHAPTER 12

'Right, get in that fat get's face, lads,' said Nick, his mouth dry, expecting a move to be made at any moment.

'Howay, then gentleman, let us make our case powerfully, to the Great Fatsby,' said Con, adjusting the three thick gold rings on his right hand, presumably to better use them as an improvised knuckle duster.

They crossed over the road and walked slowly up to the black Merc.

'I like having a bunch of desperadoes to call on,' said Jeff as they watched them. 'Very useful. And they do look a gang of outlaws, don't they?'

'Totally. Bloody scary, I reckon. More scary than Baby G. He's rightly named, he looks like a massive baby.'

Julie didn't see them at all, but paid the taxi driver and the four women went inside the house. Conrad's gang strolled up to Baby G as the door closed behind her.

Nick and Jeff got into his car just as his phone vibrated. Julie. At last. He looked at it. No. It was a text from Emily. He read it out.

'*Have sent a keylogger to Cavani's phone. It's installed. As soon as he opens up that lock and encrypted file, I'll have the password and key. E x.*'

Nick read it out to Jeff. 'What's a keylogger?'

'A bit of software that records the keys you press and sends it to another computer or server and thus gives the hacker access to passwords and such. She's a smart cookie, that kid. You only hear about stuff like that in movies. Aye, aye, look up the street, we have action.'

The tall bloke leant into Baby G so he was right in his face. He was laughing, the others laughed. Two women were walking down the street, as a man got out of the Merc passenger seat, clearly to help his mate out. The pug-faced man turned to him as he advanced and, with a forearm like a pit pony's leg, whacked him in the chest, clearly saying, 'back off', and put his hand on a short-handle mallet which would, with one swing, break someone's head, like it was a chocolate egg.

'The short arses are always the most volatile,' said Jeff, with a snort. 'He's built like a five-foot-tall mechanical bull, made out of pig iron.'

More exchanges between the men took place. Con quite clearly threatened Baby G with a ball peen hammer that hung on his tool belt. That seemed to convince Baby G to tell them something. Conrad then ran down and leant in the driver's side window to talk to Nick.

'Right. This the craic. He's told us that those women that were walking down the street were Cavani's cousins. They've gone in the refuge and are supposed to get Julie outside somehow and that's when yer big fella was told to nab her. That's what he reckons, anyway. Now, obviously that's not going to happen, because we've put the wind up those two lads, but you might want to get in there and tell the lass what's going on. Now, I'll just menace the shit out of these cunts a bit more. Most fun I've had for yonks this, man.' He grinned with pale eyes shining.

'I never noticed them going in, did you?' said Nick.

Jeff shook his head. 'I saw them, but couldn't even tell you what they looked like.'

Nick's phone buzzed again. Emily was calling.

'Em? Is it important?'

'I'm in that folder. He just accessed it and I captured the keystrokes. Nicky boy, it's totally amazing.'

'What is it?'

'All sorts. Documents, agreements, photographs, videos. All of it is to do with criminal activity, from what I can tell, looking at it quickly. There are naked photos of people - male and female - clearly taken covertly. Sex photos, too. There are pictures of people meeting other people. I don't know who any of them are, but they're not on here for his entertainment. Also there are bank details, spreadsheets and what look like cash book records. I'll keep looking through it, but this is easily enough for you to use against him.'

'Em. You are brilliant.'

He rang off.

'Right, I'll go and see Jules,' he said, getting out. 'You wait here.'

There were raised voices from across the road where the two Cavani men were now trying, but failing to get back into the car, because Con's lads had blocked them off and seemed to be enjoying their frustration.

As Nick approached the refuge, the two women that had been walking down the street, the two that Conrad said were Cavani's cousins, came out and walked past him briskly without even looking at him or across the road. They obviously couldn't get Julie out, or had seen the problems outside and abandoned the venture. Nick felt about a foot taller and a ton lighter. But did they recognise him? He paused and pretended to fasten a shoelace, even though he was wearing boots with no laces. They walked down the street without looking around.

Where were they going now? He turned around and began to follow them, pointing to them as he passed Jeff in the car. He nodded. They walked down onto Barrack Road and then crossed over into Leazes Park. Keeping them in sight, but well in the distance, he kept pace with them. Not once did they turn and look at him, so presumably they had no idea he was there.

Then, suddenly they stopped by a park bench and sat down. He stopped too and found a wooden seat. They were 30 or 40 yards away and seemed to be chatting to each other amiably. One got her phone out and spoke into it. Within two minutes, a man joined them on the bench. Asian, thick set, probably early 40s and wearing a plain, dark suit, which was a little too big for him. He leant forward and rested his elbows on his knees and turned to talk to the two women. Nick took a photo of him on his phone, as focused in as was possible.

Not much happened. They sat for six or seven minutes and then all three stood up, the man and the dark haired woman walked off together holding hands, leaving the other woman to walk in the opposite direction.

Back at Conrad's van, Jeff, Conrad and the three blokes were all waiting for him.

'Everything OK?' he said.

'All quiet on the western front. The lads let Baby G and his mate go, under pain of death, or at least severe bollock pain, if they return,' said Jeff.

Conrad nodded. 'We told them that if we caught them round here again, there'd be trouble. Wasn't much more we could do than that...'

'...they knew we meant business, though,' said pug face. 'Me and the lads will have a tour around here later if you like, just to make sure they're not back. If they are, we'll just give them a kicking, to show we're for real. I think we should've just done that, anyway. Nowt better than a broken face to convince someone you're serious.'

Shit, he was a scary man, thought Nick. 'That's good of you, cheers man,' he said with a grin.

'Nay bother. I live just up the road in Fenham so I have to go past here, anyway,' said pug.

Conrad gave them a £50 note each, got in his van and drove them back into town, promising to see Nick and Jeff down on Teesside in a couple of days.

'Do you want to go and see Jules now?' said Jeff. 'Bring her up to date.'

He rubbed his chin. 'I dunno. Do I tell her and worry her, or do I keep quiet and risk something happening that she might be able to avoid?'

'Tricky.'

Nick flicked through the photos on his phone he'd just taken and showed Jeff.

'Don't suppose any of these look familiar, do they?'

He squinted and shook his head. 'The dark haired woman looks a bit Italian, so she could be a Cavani. Is the bloke Asian?'

'I think so.'

Nick groaned and rubbed his eyes, still a little worried that Cavani would send someone back to attack or kidnap Julie.

'She's probably not even going out again tonight, but if she is, she'll be in a group and in a public place. You can't just walk in and grab someone in a crowded restaurant. It's one thing in a dark street, but it's another in the centre of town.'

'Yeah. That's a good thought. Also, Emily reckons there's incriminating stuff on that phone, so I should make a call to Cavani and let him know I've got his balls in a vice and if he does anything, we'll grass him up.'

'That'll be a good call to make,' said Jeff.

'Actually, better still, let's go down to his restaurant and tell him in person. You up for that?'

Jeff drummed his hands on his legs.

'Aye. Let's do it. I fancy myself as Teesside's answer to Al Pacino. Can't let twats like this push you around. I'll pretend I'm your legal advisor and guru.'

'You'd have made a good guru in the 60s. You could've advised the Beatles.'

'Aye, I'd have advised them to leave those Ringo songs off the albums. "Octopus's Garden"? I don't think so, Mr Starkey, and while you're at it, we'll have those drumsticks off you as well.'

'Don't be beastly to our Ringo.'

'I'd also have told them to get a proper lead guitarist in. There's not a decent solo on any Beatles record except for on "While My Guitar Gently Weeps" and that was Clapton.'

'I know, I know...you've only told me this 427 times in the last 35 years. I know it's your little pet theory, Jeff. I'm still not buying it. George was great on "Taxman" and "Hey Bulldog", to name just two.'

'That's not proper lead guitar. Great songs, great melodies, great riffs, but low-grade lead guitar. I'm right. You know I'm right.'

'If you say so. I'll just ring Emily...Em?'

'Hiya. Is Julie OK?'

'Yeah. Fine. We're going to have it out with Mike Cavani. Can you tell me a few details of the stuff that's on the phone, so I when threaten to take it to the police, he'll know I'm not bluffing?'

'There's a whole folder of sex pictures of various people, which must be being used for blackmail. They've been taken by concealed CCTV-type cameras, judging by the quality of them and their angle.'

'Can you send me one of those pictures?'

'I'll do it now. Be very careful, OK? This man is up to all sorts of horrible things.'

The Toon Trattoria was quiet when they walked in. Mike Cavani was in residency at the small bar reading the evening paper. Nick strode over to him and patted him on the back with a slightly manic grin on his face. There was no point in being polite about this, you had to play it with big balls and pretend to be as big and bad a muthafucker as the twat you were dealing with. Maybe he was.

'Now then Mike. How are you, old boy?' he said.

Cavani looked up at slowly at him, with well-practised cool.

'Can I help you, Nick?' He looked between the two of them.

'No, you can't. We were just passing, so we thought we'd drop in. This is my legal advisor and guru.' He jerked a thumb at Jeff, who bowed slightly and held up a Vulcan 'live long and prosper' hand sign. Cavani gave him a smirk.

'I actually advised him to say *that*,' said Jeff, pointing to Nick, affecting a startled expression. 'I'm also handling security - do you feel secure, Mike?'

'Very.'

Jeff tugged on his beard and pointed at him. 'See. It's working already.'

Nick grinned at him. Jeff was very good at being a lunatic. It played to all his best cards.

'Come through to the back table,' said Cavani.

They sat in the far corner. Nick and Jeff on one side, Cavani on the other.

'So do you have a name for me, Guymer?'

'Garcia,' said Nick, off the top of his head, feeling confident, extremely arsy and very fucked off with this man for causing him so much worry and stress and for driving him to drink.

'Who?' said Cavani, his face set in a frown.

'Garcia,' repeated Nick.

'Who's Garcia?'

'Jerry Garcia,' said Nick.

'And who is he?' said Cavani, twigging that Nick wasn't being serious.

'He played guitar for the Grateful Dead...' added Jeff, grinning in a wilfully stupid way at Cavani, '...and also occasionally for the excellent New Riders of the Purple Sage...'

'...and also mandolin for the bluegrass band, Old and in the Way,' added Nick.

'Their debut album was the best selling bluegrass album in America for many years,' nodded Jeff. 'If you see a copy of that on Grateful Dead Records, Mike, pick it up - it's quite rare these days. More common to find it on Rounder Records, as I'm sure you know.' He gave him another strange look - somewhere between a man having electro convulsive therapy and someone with terrible indigestion.

'I'm sure you think this is all very witty,' said Cavani, sneering at them.

'No. But it is a name,' said Nick. 'And you wanted a name.'

Jeff leant forward. 'It is definitely a name. As Nick's legal adviser, I can confirm that,' said Jeff, nodding firmly, tapping the table with a big forefinger.

'Word to the wise, don't try and be clever, lads,' Cavani said, his eyes flicking from one to the other. 'It doesn't suit you and it's sure as hell pissing me off.'

'You just said you wanted a name. I've given you a name,' said Nick. 'So that's you and me square.'

Cavani slowly shook his head.

'I thought you could help me, Guymer. I thought you'd want to. I've told you what will happen if you don't. I've got a man on that, right now. Remember what I said, it's already past five.'

Nick immediately realised he hadn't been brought up to date with events in Fenham.

'Yeah, we met him, didn't we, Jeff?'

'We did. He was, what I believe a doctor would call, a big fat shite. Though, technically, we didn't meet him, some of our other representatives on earth did.'

Nick nodded. 'Aye and he was dealt with, along with his mate. They won't have told you yet because, unlike us Mike, they fear your wrath. Who do you think you are to be threatening me, Julie, or anyone else? Eh? What do you get out of that? It's pathetic. Did you think you were going to be the boss of me? If so, you're an idiot. Is this exercising of power a small-dick thing, Mike? It is, isn't it?'

'I'm guessing three inches,' said Jeff, measuring it out with his index fingers. '"Tiny is as tiny do", as the great Frank Zappa so accurately said. There's no shame in it, though, Mike. We are one nation under the all-seeing eye.' He began humming 'Ommmmm', 'Ommmmm', his forefinger pressed onto the thumb of each hand, his eyes rolled up into his head, leaving only the whites visible. Nick gave a snort of laughter. The big man was on fine form. It was quite a performance. Cavani wasn't used to people talking to him like this, nor behaving in this manner, and he really wasn't sure what to make of Jeff at all. It did appear that he was unhinged and might do anything.

'You don't want to make an enemy of me, Guymer, and if your big dumb arsehole mate here, thinks he's going to do business in Newcastle with that attitude, you can think again, my friend.' He jabbed a well manicured finger at them.

Jeff made an 'oooh' noise and raised his hands up as though clutching a handbag, making his front teeth protrude over his bottom lip like a deranged hippy rabbit. Cavani looked outraged at having the piss taken out himself like this and moved to stand up.

Nick leant over and shoved him down.

'Joke's over. Fuckin' sit down, Mike, we haven't finished with you yet, and stop looking like the biggest twat in the room. You're just a bloke, not some sort of god who must be obeyed. We're not impressed, are we Jeff?'

'I've been more impressed by things which have made less impression, Grasshopper,' said Jeff. Even Nick had no idea what that meant.

'You don't tell me what to do. You're going to regret this little show of bravado, both of you,' Cavani said, pointing from one to the other, standing up again.

'Not as much as you will when we publish the contents of the encrypted file on your phone, Mike,' said Nick, standing up, sucking in air, pushing out his chest and folding his arms, so that his well developed biceps protruded from the sleeves of his t-shirt. He gave him a little sardonic, thin lipped smile. 'Yeah, that's right son, we're the boss of you.'

Cavani, looked him up and down and stared back with flaming, angry eyes, trying to work out if he was just guessing or really knew what was on the phone.

Jeff held up a finger and cocked his ear upwards. 'I do believe that sound was the sound of a pair of pants being shat. Shall I call for a mop?'

'Now, sit the fuck down and let's pretend we're all grown ups,' said Nick. Cavani sat again. 'Since I've got your attention, I'd like a few answers. Failure to give me the answers will result in publication of your dirty secrets and if you doubt that we have this stuff, here's some proof.'

He showed him the photo that Emily had sent. Cavani's skin was olive coloured, but it went a sickly pale shade when he saw the photo of a woman with short dark hair performing oral sex on a pudgy middle-aged man.

'How the *fuck* did you get *that*?' he hissed, incredulous and bitter, momentarily losing his cool.

'We're wizards,' said Jeff with a beatific smile. 'We have magic powers bestowed upon us by other, even more hairy wizards. A word to the wise, Mike. Don't go against the wizards. We've got pointy hats and everything.'

'Now you know we're serious, my first question is this: Why the fuck are you interested in me, Mike? Why try and fuck me and my missus over like this? We're nothing to you. This poor bloke Patel got murdered, but why use that to bully me? You could find out who did it, easier than I can.'

Cavani signalled to a waitress to bring wine. She returned with three glasses. He was an evil thug, but a clever evil thug and he clearly knew when he'd been backed into a corner, so he went into charm mode, forgetting his previous threats and intimidations, as though they had never happened. Now he wanted to make friends.

He poured himself a drink, Nick put his hand over the glass after he'd poured one for Jeff and then Cavani laughed a little.

'Well, to start with, I was never going to do anything to Julie. If you've got access to my phone, you'll know I told Baby G to be there, but I didn't tell him to kidnap her. The whole thing was a set up to make you realise I was serious. My girls would have brought Julie out of that place, Baby G would have gone over, a photo would have been taken, so you could have seen what we *could* have done. If you'd come up yourself - which I assumed you would - you'd have seen my people on duty and also realised I was serious. You know how this game works now, I'm sure...one gets...shall we say, capital, with someone. Fear is the best capital to draw on. I knew you'd never work for me unless you had a good reason to, so I set about creating that reason. Really, you've sort of answered your own question by your little show here. I don't admire many people, but I admire you for setting this up. You're a good mix of sharp mind and powerful body, Nick Guymer. And you, my friend...' he pointed at Jeff '...you are a certifiable, Grade A, fucking lunatic.'

Jeff raised his right-hand index finger. 'No Mike, I just let you think I'm a lunatic, that's different...or did I?'

'Well, if you two will pull this on me, given my very well

deserved reputation, you could do it to anyone. I need that sort of talent on my team. How about it? Both of you. It'd be a nice income for you.'

'Bollocks. Don't try and flatter us. We're not impressed,' said Nick.

Jeff raised his finger again. 'Actually, I am impressed. I've always fancied being a gangster...but sadly Mike, I fancied being a gangster of love - you know, Johnny 'Guitar' Watson style - or even the Steve Miller Band's version. "Yes sir, indeed, Sheriff and that is your wife on the back of my horse."'

'I have no fucking idea what you're talking about, my friend,' said Mike. 'It's like you talk your own fucking language, man. Are you fucking high or something?'

'And right there, that's why we could never work together, Mike. You can't embrace your inner freak, or your outer freak either. Plus...you're a total twat...' said Jeff, raising a finger once more, '...and not in a good way.'

Cavani turned back to Nick, seemingly giving up on Jeff as a lost cause.

'Nick, seriously, we could do good business together, me and you.'

He drank some wine. As he was doing that, Nick's phone vibrated. It was Emily again. He took the call.

'Yeah?'

'Are you with him now?'

'Yeah.'

'He's been making payments to Kal Patel, Lomash and Jasmin's older brother. £1,500 a month for the last year.'

OK. Thanks.'

'Be careful.'

He rang off and tried to compute the situation.

'You're talking rubbish, Mike. You know I'm not working for you now, or ever. You were trying to co-opt me into your criminal way of life by threatening me and Julie, by being, essentially, a bastard. You wanted me to work for you, because I had to work for you, like Ian Gow does. Well, word to the wise Mike - we know you like that expression - I'm not a fucking pussy, I'm not Ian Gow. You can't do that to me because I'm an ornery fucker and I don't take kindly to someone making my life considerably more shit than it already is. So, I've made sure you can't do this to me or to any of my friends any more. And just in case you are in any doubt about how much I know about you and how much trouble I can make for you, I should tell you that I know all about your little payment to Kal Patel of £1,500 per month.'

Cavani had adjusted to this new reality now, and didn't look surprised at this revelation. His drank some more wine, smacked his lips and was obviously trying to work out a route through this.

'I'll put my cards on the table with you two. Jimmy Patel was on our payroll. He pushed big lucrative contracts to McGull. We supply materials to McGull's. With him gone, we lose a lot of revenue unless we can hook up another sweet deal. The deal we had with Jimmy was a licence to print money.'

All exactly as he and Jeff and Emily had worked out.

'Yeah, but you're still not being honest with me, are you? Jimmy was moving the contract. He fell out with Paddy McGull over his son's relationship with Jimmy's son,' said Nick. 'That's why you had Jimmy Patel killed, isn't it?'

'Hey, why would I kill Jimmy? I'd not gain anything from that. Anyway, the Cavanis don't kill people.'

'No, you get other people to kill people for you,' said Nick.

'Are we done yet?' said Cavani with a sigh.

'You're involved in that murder, I know you are.'

Cavani shook his head.

'You're crazy. I don't get into all that shit. You and the Big Lummox here should know that I'm all about information, not about violence - well, not much violence. A few incidents of severe punishment for transgressions is all we need to exert our influence in this town. I like to know who has done what to whom and why. As I say, it's a form of capital which I then draw down.'

'So who did kill Jimmy Patel?' said Nick.

'I don't know. Genuinely. That's why I asked you to find out for me. If I know, then it may be profitable to me...'

'...to blackmail the person responsible?' said Nick.

'Perhaps.'

'Why don't you just ask Kal? He was there,' said Nick. 'I know he works for you, so you must have got him over a barrel, somehow.' The last statement was a guess, but it seemed to be a good guess.

'He was there, was he? Interesting. Very interesting. I didn't know that. See, you've already been of help to me, I appreciate that,' said Cavani. He held up his hands again and stood. 'I have to go. Now, as long as you keep my phone info safe, we're cool. If anything happens to it and it finds its way to the hands of the police, then we are not cool and the gloves really come off and we go at it until someone dies. OK, boys?'

Nick held up his phone to him. 'Do you want to do a second take, Mike? I just recorded that. I'll add that to your collection of crimes, shall I? Threatening to kill someone. That'll add a few years onto your sentence.'

Cavani laughed out loud and genuinely. 'You're a clever bastard. I'll give you that. You ever need a career change, you come to me.' He began walking away, but then stopped and turned back to them. 'There'll be some point in the future when you'll need me, when I can be useful to you, when you need what I can give you. When that moment arrives, call me. I'll be glad to help.' He gave a little nod of his head, grinned and walked away.

As they made their way back to the car, Nick pulled at his sodden t-shirt arm pits.

'I stink of sweat,' he said, sniffing at himself.

'It's been a high-pressure day, dude. But we did good, man.'

'Yeah, you doing your best Wavy Gravy impression was suitably off the wall.'

'You spotted that security reference from the movie of Woodstock? I was pleased with it.'

'Yeah, man, you were on good whack job form. You did

genuinely look like a mad man, at times.'

'My inner loon likes to come out and play from time to time.' He rolled his eyes into his head again.

In the car, Jeff took out his phone and did a search for Kal Patel.

'Let's see what the eldest Mr P son does. Ah ha, here's a heart surgeon called Kal Patel.'

'That's him. That's what he does. Give me a look at him.' He leant over and looked at his portrait photo on the James Cook Hospital website.

'Jeff man, this was the bloke in Leazes Park.'

'Are you sure?'

Nick got out his phone and compared the portrait to the photo he'd taken of the Asian man in Leazes Park. 'Look, that's certainly him. What's he doing up here?'

Jeff looked, nodded and sat twiddling his beard and thinking. 'Why was he up here to see the two Cavani women who had been in the refuge? Why's he part of Cavani's gig up here?'

Nick looked at the photos he'd taken once again.

'He has to be having an affair with this woman, doesn't he? He's got his arm around her. It's not his wife. I know that might not mean anything...'

Jeff interrupted him. 'Ah ha...yes...' He jabbed his finger in mid air, as though pointing to the answer. 'Kal is having an affair with that woman, and we know those two women are Cavani women. So that's where the connection is. He's been working for Cavani and in the process has fallen for one of his family. But you saw how Mike looked when you mentioned Kal being at the house when the murder happened - he didn't know about it and given Kal is having it off with his cousin or whatever she is, he damn well wanted to know.'

Nick started up the car and began the journey south.

'We're getting close to who really did murder Jimmy Patel, I reckon. A lot of people had reason to hate him and plenty of incentive to kill him. Think about it. Myra, the wife, hates him and will inherit some money. Sheila Simmons gets his job,

McGull takes revenge on him for blowing out his contracts and for standing in the way of the two sons. Lomash gets rid of a father who bullied him for years. Terry and Jaz get free from the man who wanted to stop them even seeing each other, and meanwhile Kev and Ricky take revenge on the bloke who slagged off their family, hit their sister and was giving their brother grief.'

Jeff agreed. 'Aye. Remember what I said - it's a *Murder on the Orient Express* job, this one. Everyone hated him and had a motive. Actually, when you put it like that, Cavani is the only one who didn't have anything to gain by his death. OK, Jimmy decided to give the contracts to someone else after falling out with McGull, but killing him wouldn't have changed that. And anyway, I don't think they'd have someone killed for that, not least because Jimmy might have had a change of heart.'

'In the family, the older brother Kal is the only one who doesn't obviously have a grievance with his old man - not one we know about just now, anyway.'

'Well, it must be him then,' said Jeff. 'It's always the one who seems the least guilty, isn't it?'

'Yeah, except when it isn't.'

'Aye, except when it's someone else all together. I'll tell you what, though, that money Cavani is paying him, that's for something he needs and uses.'

Nick ran his fingers through his hair. 'He's this big respectable man. Worked hard, kept his head down, got his qualifications and the big, high-status important job.'

'That sounds like he's a really conservative bloke. Probably pushed himself as the respectable member of the family. His sister is hooked up with a rough kid, his brother is gay, which he doesn't like, his father is corrupt...so he'll have had a lot invested in being the upstanding man and yet he's involved with Cavani and having an affair. He's a massive hypocrite.'

'Yeah, I agree. When you look at it like that, maybe overall, regardless of who killed Jimmy, he's the one with the most to lose. Owee, let's go home. I'm drained.'

Emily was sitting on her own behind the counter when they got back to Stockton.

'Emily Davids, you are a workaholic. You didn't have to stay here so late. It's nearly 8pm,' said Jeff.

'My date will be here in half an hour, thought I'd keep working. How did it go?'

'Great. We totally stitched Cavani up with your help,' said Nick. 'I think we've got him off my back for good. The big man here played a blinder.'

'What did you do?' she asked.

'He did his best impression of a nutter. Honest, Em, he's a natural.'

Jeff took a little bow to each corner of the room. Emily laughed.

'I can believe that.' She gripped a fist and punched the air. 'Yay! One up to the good chaps.'

'Mind, we're still no nearer proving actually who killed Jimmy Patel and getting Ricky and Kev out of jail,' said Nick.

'Well it wasn't Cavani. From some of the emails and texts on his phone, he's definitely been trying to find out who did it, so I'm sure he doesn't know,' said Emily, yawning and scratching her head. 'But I've found an Excel spreadsheet with a list of drugs on it, alongside numbers and values. It looks like Cavani's documenting buying and selling them.'

'Interesting. Very interesting. What sort of drugs?' said Nick.

'They're brand names and I've not looked them all up, but I think it's amphetamines and stuff like that.'

'Ah, so it's brand named stuff. That means it's from a pharmacy. And who do we know will have easy access to legal drugs?' said Jeff.

'Kal Patel,' said Nick, pointing to him. 'And that's why Cavani is paying him the £1,500.'

'Almost certainly. So, Little Miss Kojak, have you got any idea who might have killed Jimmy the P?' said Jeff, looking at Emily's list of records sold and putting a thumb up, impressed with what had gone.

She got off her stool and stretched on her tip toes, arms out wide. 'Yeah, I think the whole family did it.'

Jeff pointed to her and looked at Nick. 'See? See? *Murder on the Orient Express*.'

She went on, 'I've been thinking about it all day and it was his family who hated him most. This Sheila Simmons person might have just gone along with it, because she gets a promotion or something.'

'That reminds me, I've got the hard drive running at home, recording her. It might have picked up a juicy confession,' said Nick.

'If anything is on it, will you call me?' said Emily. 'I'm *totally* obsessed with this now. I know it's been stressful for you, but I've never had more fun. So exciting to be hacking for a good cause.'

A man put his head around the door.

'Come in, matey boy, we're still open for the purveying of fine vinyl discs, to the discerning public,' said Jeff, waving at him.

'I've just come to pick Emily up,' he said, a little shyly. He was early 20s, with the makings of a beard and scruffy head of hair.

'Hey, Robbie. I'm good to go. Come on. I will see you gentlemen later and remember, text or call if you find out anything.'

After they'd gone, Jeff turned to Nick.

'Did you notice that?' he said.

'What?' said Nick.

'That lad.'

'What about him?'

'You really didn't notice?'

'Notice what?' said Nick, frowning.

'You must have...'

'Jeff man, how much longer are we going to do this?'

He leant into Nick and flashed his eyes at him.

'Young Robbie there, he looked just like you, only 25 years younger.'

Nick looked at the door, as if to re-visualise him.

'Gettaway with you. He did not.'

Jeff laughed loudly. 'I'm telling you. He was the spit of you, when you were in your early 20s. Emily is going out with you.' He pointed at him.

Nick shook his head. 'You're insane. It's been a sodding long day, I'm away home.'

The house was dark and though it wasn't actually cold, it felt cold in a deeper, more profound way, through lack of human activity. As he walked into each room, putting the lights on, he realised he'd just liked coming home because Julie was here or with him. He loved sharing his life with her and the countryside was beautiful, but the house itself he could take or leave and had no affection for. It wasn't homely enough and was probably a bit too big for them. They didn't have enough stuff to properly fill it or enough to adorn the walls and had no money to buy anything to do that. So he just had no attachment to it. And with her away, that was all too obvious. They had to move. He'd liked coming home to his Harrogate flat and he'd loved her flat in Norton, which she'd turned into a small but lush boudoir. Both those places had felt like a home. This didn't, so they had to move. In fact, now he'd had the thought, moving felt exciting, whereas staying here wasn't. How would Jules feel about it, though? She loved the countryside and enjoyed taking photos of the wildlife and of the natural world around them.

The fridge was empty except for their staple foods - eggs and bacon. Good. No choices to be made. Eggs and bacon, it was. There is much joy to be had in lack of choice. Who needs endless choice? The whole of western capitalism had been set up to deliver as much choice as possible, in everything, all the time - as though it was a moral thing to want as much choice as possible. But last time he'd been in a Waitrose there were 42 different bottles of extra virgin olive oil to choose from. That was ridiculous. Choice made life needlessly complicated. All you needed was a cheap one and an expensive one. Two, not 42. The rest just clutter up life and clutter up the world. Upmarket living didn't mean having so much choice, it meant being happy with a few.

After eating, he checked the computer he'd left running with the camera activated in Sheila Simmons's office. It was *still* running. Bloody hell, he had 10 hours of video to look through. But, as he sat for a few seconds looking at the screen, it was clearly no longer running in the Middlesbrough office of MIDO. It was in a house. A blue wall with a dado rail and a couple of framed art prints could clearly be seen. It looked as though it was on a laptop, which had been put on a coffee table. Turning up the sound didn't reveal anything. It was silent. No-one was in the house, so he loaded what had already been recorded and began fast forwarding through it. Every time she was on the phone or looked up to see someone enter the room, he stopped it and listened to what she said. It was all just business. She went out at 11am, presumably to do the press conference. By quarter past, she was back in her office and tapping away on her keyboard again. Nothing. He minimised the window and looked at the live feed again. There was movement. He paused the playback.

'I'll open a bottle,' a woman's voice said. There was a groan and exhalation of air, as someone sat down.

A minute later Sheila Simmons sat down on the sofa, directly in front of the laptop, holding a glass of wine. She looked to one side at her companion. 'Cheers,' she said, and drank from the glass of white wine. 'I'll just check my emails,' she said, picking up the laptop. The picture wobbled and blurred as she took it on to her lap. Now she was really close to the camera, surely she'd spot that the recording light was on. It felt like being a ghost in her room; an invisible presence.

Another woman's voice said, 'We should say something to the police, you know.'

'We can't say anything, Myra. You know we can't. We've just got to keep quiet,' said Sheila. Myra. She had to be with Myra Patel. No-one knew two Myras.

Myra's voice was quieter, but still distinct.

'It'll all come out, mark my words.'

Things went silent, as Sheila looked through her mail. The light from the screen cast a ghoulish blue glow on her face, as Nick watched her eyes flicking across the information on the screen. He held his breath, feeling as though if he made a noise, she would be able to hear and then see him.

Sheila sat back and drank wine, the computer still on her lap.

'I'm sorry Myra, but I don't trust Kal. I know he's your son, but I don't like him and I never have. He's involved with the Cavanis and they are terrible people.'

'I know. I wish to god Jimmy had never got tangled up with them and brought them into our lives. He was a greedy, greedy man. The more he got, the more he wanted. It was like he had a hunger for more and more money - an addiction, almost.'

'Well, Kal has inherited that from him, if you ask me,' said Sheila.

They sat drinking in silence for a couple of minutes. Then Myra spoke again.

'This Michael Cavani man, he says he knows the truth about how Jimmy died, he knows that Kal was there and now we've got to pay him money, or the whole thing will come out,' said Myra.

'He says he does, but he's offered us no proof that that is the case, so we don't know that he does. He might be bluffing just to get you to pay him money...' said Sheila, '...and by doing that, you're admitting guilt, which means, he'll feel he can then blackmail us forever. We can't give in to him.'

That sounded like a typical Cavani way of working.

'I think he really does know that we were all there - I bet Kal has told him - and now he's got us over a barrel,' said Myra, a worried tone to her voice.

'Keep calm, Myra. He knows nothing of our plot to kill Jimmy. Nothing. How could he? Kal didn't even know. Only you and me knew of our plans.'

Sheila leant forward and closed the laptop, shutting down the live feed. Damn.

Nick sat for a moment, realising it was he who had told Cavani of Kal's presence at the house. Cavani had used that information immediately and, in his clever way, suggested he knew much more about the murder than he actually did. Sorry, ladies. But crucially, now he had proof of Sheila and Myra wanting Myra's husband dead and now he had proof that Lomash had been telling the truth about everyone being at the house. It was all coming together.

He drew a family tree connecting them all together, with Mike Cavani and Paddy McGull as satellites of the Patels, then connected the Wells family to the Patels through Jaz and Tez.

Who did Ricky and Kev think had done it? Did they actually know the murderer and were taking the blame? Surely not. But they had Jimmy's blood on them. How did that happen? Had he really fought with them without anyone in the house knowing? That wasn't at all likely. But they'd be sent down for murder for 25 years; they'd likely die in jail. Would they do that for anyone? For their brother, maybe? Terry had a chance in life. Next to Jules he was the brightest and he had a nice girlfriend. He had the most to live for. Ricky and Kev were drinkers and womanisers and scammers, they'd never amount to anything and they damn well knew it. But Terry. Terry was different and much younger. He knew how to use computers, not like Emily, but he was proficient. He could get on. Would family loyalty go that deep? Would they really accept culpability for something he had actually done? He sat and thought for some time. Yes, they would. Virtually the only thing that was a constant in the brother's lives was family loyalty.

It was 9.30pm, but he called Emily anyway. She answered right away.

'Hello.'

'Em. Sorry to disturb you.'

'That's OK.'

'How can I view those documents from Cavani's phone online?'

'I'll mail you the link and password to the server. Any more news?'

'Cavani is now blackmailing Sheila and Myra, and I just saw them admit to plotting to kill Jimmy.'

She whistled.

'I've still got hours of the recordings I made of Sheila to go through. Things were getting interesting when she shut the laptop down tonight.'

'That is the drag about remote viewing. Look, do you want me to help you go through the documents? There are hundreds, thousands, maybe.'

'Err...well...you're with your fella Robbie, aren't you? I don't want to disturb you and it's late.'

'It's fine. I'll drive over to yours, then. Yes?'

'Well, I could do with an extra pair of eyes. I reckon time is of the essence on this. All the players are trying to work out what their next move is.'

'I'll be right over.'

Her old Mini came down the farm track within 25 minutes, bouncing up and down on the rutted mud and gravel.

'Hiya, Nicky boy,' she said, as he greeted her at the front door with a little arms length hug. She was wearing her black leather bike jacket, a blue plaid shirt and black leggings and some sort of black espadrilles. 'Isn't this quiet?'

'Yeah, some people assume Teesside is noisy and polluted. They don't realise it has lovely peaceful countryside as well.'

She stood and looked up at the sky. 'So many stars. Why do you want to move? It's just lovely here.'

They went inside and she threw her bike jacket onto the sofa and looked around. 'Where's your computer, then?'

'Come on, into my kitchen, because it's going to be raining outside,' he said.

'That's a rock lyric, isn't it?'

'An old blues tune. Can I make you a drink?'

'Do you have any hot chocolate?'

'Good question. I have cocoa and cream. That's the same thing, isn't it?'

'God, I don't know. I just drink the stuff out of a jar that you add hot water to.'

She sat down at his laptop, rubbed her eyes and ruffled her hair.

'You can't have been with your date for long,' he said, filling the kettle.

'No. We just had a quick drink and I made my excuses.' She pulled a face and shrugged. 'Just wasn't interested in him, really. Nice chap, but...' she shrugged and pouted a little.

It seemed best not to question her any more about him, largely because it was none of his business, was it? Or was it? Maybe he should ask about him, to show interest and concern in her. He was interested and concerned. But would it seem intrusive? What was the right thing to do? This was the minutiae of human relations that he simply had no idea how to judge and couldn't imagine ever learning how to judge.

'Now, let me see, you're OK for me to look on your laptop?' she said.

'Yeah, go ahead.'

'You've nothing secret you don't want me to see on here?' she said.

'Nope.'

She grinned up at him. 'You don't, do you?'

'No. Oh, I know what you're thinking. There's some photos of Jules in her bikini in California if you're interested in looking at a 45-year-old, semi-naked woman. You're thinking I've got a dodgy browsing history?'

'Well, you're a man and you're on your own.'

'Take a look.' He gestured with his hand to allow her.

She clicked on it and scrolled down the page.

'All very wholesome.'

'I am wholesome.'

'You really are, aren't you? Nothing x-rated on here at all.'

'I'm really not into all that.'

She shook her head and bit her bottom lip.

'That's so weird for someone of my age to hear. I don't believe there's any man, or probably any woman my age, who hasn't viewed some porn on their computer. It's part of our generation's culture.'

'You're probably right, but it's just not my thing. Never has been. Not since I was 16 or 17 anyway.' He mixed a paste of cocoa, cream and maple syrup. He didn't have any sugar. Then added hot water. 'See what that's like.'

She sipped at it and grinned. 'Oooh, it's delisheroony. Maple-choccy-tastic. Ta.' She tapped at the keyboard and brought up the server with the phone contents on. 'Right, you start looking on there and I'll load it up on my laptop.' She took it out of her shoulder bag and plugged it in.

'Let's have a look at *your* browsing history then,' said Nick, with a grin, looking over her shoulder. She opened it up.

'Rock music, drinking, hacking, software. You're as wholesome as I am, Emily Davids. How disappointing.'

'My biggest secret is that I'm really a good girl.'

He sat down to start looking at every item. 'I always thought you were, Em. Christ, there are literally thousands of text messages, aren't there?'

'And emails, too. We need to do a search of them for significant words.'

'Good idea. How about Kal and Jimmy Patel to start with.'

She ran a search with those terms in.

'There are 298 for Kal and 276 for Jimmy Patel. That's too many to go through. Let's try "murder"...oh, that's better, just 8. Let's look at these emails.' Her green eyes flicked through them, her top teeth biting on her lower lip, again

'Ah right. How about this? It's to KP - Kal Patel? And it says, "JP murder. Who did it?"'

'Is there a reply?'

'Yes there is, "Will try to find out". That's significant. If he was there, he already knew. He was lying to Cavani at that point.'

'When is that dated?'

'Half four on the afternoon Jimmy was killed.'

They spent the next two hours scouring messages for more information. Clearly, Cavani was making plans after the murder, trying to establish who the various contracts would now be in the gift of. There was discontent that Sheila Simmons would take over. She was described as "that noisy bitch friend of Myra Patel". No love lost there.

At midnight, they took a break.

'I think it's safe to assume that Cavani only discussed the really big stuff one to one with people like Kal Patel,' Nick said, leaning against the sink as he made them some coffee.

She nodded and leant back, hands behind her head. 'I'm pretty certain that we'd have found any email or text by now that accused anyone directly of the murder. There is evidence of him meeting Kal a few times and meeting Paddy McGull twice in the last two weeks and evidence that he thinks the Wells brothers didn't do it...' she read from the screen, '...this one is interesting, sent to his brother Peter; he says, "Wells brothers have been set up, surely?" To which his brother replies, "dangerous pair: stupid and violent. You never know".'

'So at this point, they don't know who is responsible,' said Nick.

She sucked her cheeks in and opened up another batch of text messages.

'Oooh look, you get a mention. This is very interesting. Listen. He sent this to Kal: "I met him. I liked him. Guymer surely knows these people. We need him onside. I'll rope him in". That was sent the evening of the murder. And here you are again. Now this *is* good. "Re Guymer's woman. Do nothing. Look the part. We want to scare him". Then there's that email we saw earlier with the photos of Julie in. Oh god, you know what? That whole thing you went through at the refuge, they were never going to take Julie, it was all just to put the wind up you.'

'Yeah, he admitted as much to me and Jeff.'

She found another text. 'This is from Baby G back to Cavani: "Did as you said, boss. They totally bought it. He thought Gloria and Jan were part of it. Came with some Toon nutters though".'

Nick laughed at that. He was right.

She took a slurp of the coffee as he put it in front of her.

He also took a drink and said, 'Cavani's only real interest in any of these people is the money from the supply contracts to McGull's. He's not bothered who lives or dies as long as the money keeps flowing into their coffers, so all he's doing, once JP was dead, is trying to keep the contracts with McGull. Nothing else matters to him. I think he only wants to know who the murderer is in case they can use that info to make sure McGull's get the contracts. If, for example, it was Sheila or Myra, then he goes to them and blackmails them into Sheila assigning the next round of contracts to McGull. But if it's, say, Terry, then it's of no use to them, because there's no money to be had from Terry.'

'Oooh, this *so* frustrating,' she said, ruffling her hair and piling it on her head, only to let it fall again. 'We've sort of sussed out what Cavani has been up to and I really think it's just distracting us. He's orbiting around this, buzzing around like a troublesome fly, trying to exploit things, but he's not responsible for the murder. He clearly doesn't know at any point who *is* the killer. We know the family and Sheila were at the house that morning. We know she and Myra wanted Jimmy killed. A plot to kill someone isn't a murder, is it? So we have absolutely no idea who was responsible for the murder, or who put the knife in.'

They sat in silence. Nick's brain hurt.

'You get off home, Em. It's late. I don't see we can get much more done tonight. I might go and see Ricky and Kev's lawyer first thing in the morning. I've got this idea that they're taking the rap for their brother. I mean, he and Jaz lied to me again, when I went to see them. They're not doing that for no reason.'

She yawned and closed her eyes a little. 'Oh, I almost dropped off there.'

'It's after 1am. Why don't you doss down here? We've got a spare room.'

She yawned again. 'Yeah. That's probably a good idea. Thanks.'

'Come on, I'll show you were it is.'

He got her a towel. 'Shower is in there, spare room is at the end of the landing. It's made up.'

She nodded and smiled. 'Night night, then.'

# CHAPTER 13

As he flopped into the bed, he heard her use the toilet and have a really powerful piss again, just like in Jeff's shop. It was strange someone being in the house, but it not being Julie. He was glad they'd had their heart-to-heart the other night or there'd have been a better than average chance of sharing a bed tonight. But then there was a knock at his bedroom door.

She looked around with a grin. 'Did you hear that?'

'Superb. I'm a big fan of your power pissing, as you know.'

She giggled. 'Can I use your tooth brush?'

'Sure. It's the red one.'

'Thanks. Aw, don't you look cute all tucked up in bed? See you in the morning.'

'Night, Em.'

He was so exhausted after such a tense, aggressive day that he fell into a heavy sleep immediately, not stirring until after 9am, going for a shower to properly wake himself up.

'Morning!' she called out, coming into the bathroom as he was under the water.

'Sleep OK?' he said.

'Yeah, it's a nice comfy bed, thanks.'

'Do you want the shower after me?'

'Yes, please.'

He turned it off, grabbed a towel and stepped out with a smile. She had the pink bath towel he'd given her wrapped around her.

'It can get really hot - so watch you don't scald yourself,' he said as he left, casting a quick glance behind him to see her stepping into the cubicle, naked, her tattooed back and buttocks towards him. Nice. She leant out and looked at him.

'I saw that. No peeking,' she said and pointed at him, but with a smile.

He boiled some eggs and put the recording of Sheila Simmons in her office on again as he pottered around the kitchen, stopping now and again to look at it. Christ, what a boring life it was to work in an office. How did people stand it? It looked so dull.

'I've no food, Em. So it's boiled eggs or nothing.'

'No cake?'

'No cake. You can't eat cake for breakfast, anyway. It's bad for you.'

'Muffins?'

'No muffins.'

'Danish pastry?'

'We don't eat anything like that, man.'

She shook her head. 'Well you should. Life without sugar is no life at all...but eggs will be fine,' she said, sitting down at the table, looking at the screen. 'Anything of any use?'

'No. She's just doing admin, typing, taking phone calls.'

He fished the eggs out of the water and into two egg cups and pushed them over to her. Just as he picked a spoon out of the drawer, Emily yelped.

'What is it?'

She had paused the playback and rewound it. 'Listen.'

He held his breath as she turned the sound up loud. Sheila's mobile phone rang.

'Hello, Myra.' There was a 20-second pause as she listened. 'Don't panic, Myra. It's all set up. No-one will ever know what really happened. The Wells brothers won't talk now that Kal has arranged everything with them.'

'It *is* a conspiracy,' said Emily, 'The whole family has got this stitched up between them to get the two brothers to take the blame for this murder!'

Maybe Jeff's *Murder on the Orient Express* theory, hadn't been so far wide of the mark, after all.

Nick dropped Emily off at the shop and drove into Thornaby to see Jon Gaunt, the lawyer appointed to Ricky and Kev. He'd defended them before. Unsuccessfully, as it turned out, largely because they were guilty.

The couple of times Nick had met him, he thought he was the

kind of bloke who would have got hippies out of jail on drugs busts in the late 60s. Just scruffy enough to suggest he had a hinterland that took in aspects of alternative lifestyles, he was, nonetheless, a firm-minded man who was often the solicitor called to a station to advise arrested or charged people as part of the Criminal Defence Service.

A grey-haired man with a face so without flesh that it looked like one of the skulls on a Grateful Dead album cover, looked up at him as he went into his office.

'Good to see you again, Nick. How is Jules?'

'Good thanks. I'll cut to the chase, Jon. I'm trying to find who is the real killer of Jimmy Patel. I'm sure it wasn't Ricky and Kev and I'm sure they've been set up to take the blame.' He went through what he'd learned so far, as quickly as he could. Jon Gaunt made notes in silence throughout, nodding appreciatively as he did so. When he explained about Kal Patel's relationship to Mike Cavani, Nick saw him underline Kal's name.

'What evidence do the police have on Ricky and Kev?'

'They had his blood on them, and the knife that was used to kill Jimmy Patel had their prints on. Circumstantial evidence, but good circumstantial evidence when married up with their history and the family disagreements with Patel.'

'What exactly did they say happened?'

'They say they went there at about 9am to have it out with Jimmy about Terry and Jasmin. They went there to scare him, let's be clear about that. They rang the front door bell, but no-one replied, then they tried the door, it was open. They went inside. Their prints are on the door handle, too, by the way. So they went in, Jimmy came at them screaming, wielding a kitchen knife. They say he was already cut somewhere. There was some sort of wrestling or grappling, that's how they got blood on them and why the knife has their prints on it. They pushed him away and left immediately, because those lads know trouble when they see it and obviously knew they'd be suspects. But a neighbour must have seen them go, thought they looked suspicious with blood on them and called the police, who duly picked up them up in Middlesbrough town centre. It's their belief that the killer had already stabbed Jimmy and was either still in the house or had left. He was in a right state and they say he was almost delirious.'

'So they don't say that anyone else was there?'

'No. Which somewhat contradicts your information, clearly. We have a problem. And if Sheila Simmons is to be believed - and why would she lie in a private phone call? - there seems to have been some arrangement made with them by Kal.'

'Could they be taking the blame for Terry? I mean. Terry killed him and then they've somehow agreed that they'd make themselves look guilty?'

Jon Gaunt made a face which suggested anything was possible.

'They could. Yeah. Given your information. They could. I see what you're saying. They take the heat off Terry, banking on a not guilty plea working for them. If it does, everyone's a winner. Let's be honest, it does look quite bad for them. They'd threatened Patel on Prince Regent Street after the crash and Jules had hit him. He'd hit her. I take on board all this research you've done and it's fantastic. I can use some of it - the video especially, to establish doubt of the boy's guilt - but Lomash's testimony needs standing up. He could be lying for any number of reasons about seeing people there. None of what you have found out actually clears Ricky and Kev and again being brutally honest, they look like the sort of people a jury likes to convict.'

Nick chewed his lip. 'Jasmin says she found Jimmy, didn't she?'

The solicitor looked at some notes. 'Yes, on the floor of the kitchen. He was dead by the time the ambulance got there.'

'That is certainly a lie. I think at various times that morning there were at least nine people in that house. Sheila Simmons, Myra Patel, Jimmy Patel, Jasmin Patel, Kal Patel, Lomash Patel and the three Wells brothers.'

'None were there when the police and emergency services arrived. That's a fact.'

'Yeah, they all legged it, it would seem, even Lomash in the rec room had gone. It seems very strange that Ricky and Kev are having this wrestle with Jimmy alone in the house. I just don't buy it. They're all lying, except Lomash. That's what I think.'

'If true, it's a conspiracy of silence. They all knew they were there, but are all pretending they weren't. "Curiouser and curiouser, cried Alice".'

They looked at each other. A strand of grey hair flopped over the lawyer's forehead as he consulted his notes.

'The boys don't even mention Terry, but you said Terry had admitted he was there.'

'Yes, at first he didn't but then he did. I'm not sure I believe either story.'

'They don't mention anyone else. The boys have got their story and they're sticking to it, but I wouldn't worry about them just now. They're fine. They like it in jail. Well, not like, they find it easy to adapt to it. It would seem that they are not guilty, exactly as they claim, but not guilty in entirely different circumstances. We need to build this defence case comprehensively with hard evidence. We don't have enough hard evidence. Just the odd sentence here and there on tape doesn't stack up against blood and fingerprints and a strong motive. Thanks for your input. Keep me in the loop. This won't go to court for months yet.' Jon Gaunt threw his Biro on the desk. 'What a bloody mess this is, though. It's very tedious when your clients lie to you.'

Nick nodded. 'Everyone had a reason to want Jimmy Patel dead. One, some or all of those nine people killed him.'

'Maybe you should go to Detective Inspector Colin Harcombe with this. He's your buddy, isn't he?'

'I can't, he's in America on some sort of advisory secondment to the Florida Police Department. Anyway, I'd rather present them with a proven case to release Kev and Ricky rather than something based on speculation.' He stood up and shook Gaunt's long-fingered hand. 'I've just got to prove who did it,' said Nick.

'If you can, obviously, Julie's brothers are in the clear.'

'Well, I'm so far into this now, I can't walk away.'

'What's your next move, Nick?'

'I think I'd like to talk to Kal Patel, but I'm not sure he'd want to talk to me.'

Gaunt's eyes lit up. 'Oh yeah, Kal Patel. Something occurred to me when you said his name. You know Stockton Marina has just opened?'

'Yeah - not that those are two words I'd ever have thought would be put together - Stockton and marina.'

'Incredible, isn't it? To those of us of a certain generation, something about the very idea seems wrong and though I hate to be cynical, it's hard to see it being a massive success - though I hope it is, naturally.'

'Yeah, I do, too. I'll certainly park my yacht there when I get one.'

'Well, that's what I was going to tell you. I have a client who has a boat moored there. One of the first to use the place, in fact. He'd had it in Hartlepool Marina before that. I was with him when he sailed it down to Stockton and we were talking to a guy who moored his boat next to my friend. I'm sure he was called Kal Patel because when he introduced himself, I thought he'd said Carl and he had to correct me. He was about 40 maybe. Quite thick set. Thick hair. Indian guy. Well spoken.'

'That sounds like him. He has a boat in Hartlepool Marina? Well, he doesn't seem short of money.'

'No, it was a decent size and they don't come cheap. I can find out what it's called, if you like. Hold on.' He made a phone call. 'Harry. Just a quickie. That boat you were moored next to in Hartlepool, what was it called? *Sea Urchin*, that was it. The fella's name? Yeah, that's what I thought. Thanks, mate.' He put his thumb up to Nick.

'So what are you thinking, Jon? What use is it to us if we know Kal has a boat?'

Jon Gaunt shrugged. 'Might just be worth going over there and having a look around.' He returned to his computer and opened a file. 'I have contact info for everyone in this case. This is his home address.' He passed him a note. 'It might be worth going over there as well. If we're going to establish doubt about convicting Kev and Ricky, we'll need hard evidence of him stealing these drugs, not just an Excel spreadsheet. That proves nothing in itself. Hard evidence would blow the case open because at the moment, it looks like two well-known law breakers were in the house of one of Teesside's foremost citizens and his law-abiding, upstanding family at the time of his murder. That doesn't look good. But throw in a provably dodgy son and a lot of other grievances and we have better grounds for acquittal.' He shook hands with Nick. 'Anyway, it's a lovely morning, ideal for a trip to Costa del Hartlepool.'

Nick called on Jeff and they drove north on the A19 and then east on the A689 to the coast.

'So basically, we're looking for a boat which is stuffed full of drugs and a neon sign flashing saying "illegal stuff in here". That'll be dead easy to find,' said Jeff, fastening his long hair into a pony tail. 'The council have probably put out road signs to direct us to it.'

'It's a long shot, I know that. But if you think about it, given what we know about all these people, although we can't come up with his motive for killing his dad, except perhaps his share of an inheritance, he's easily the most dodgy of any of them. Lomash is a simple shop lad, Sheila and Myra plotted to kill him, but we know from what they said that it was still only a plot. If we discount Kev and Ricky as innocent, that only leaves Terry and Jaz. The police seemed fairly convinced that she wasn't physically capable of the murder given where and how he'd been stabbed...also, she just doesn't have that sort of temperament, does she? She's a bit of a hippy kid, I think.'

'Yeah, totally. She seemed quiet when I met her. I mean, she works in Stockton Central Library, doesn't she, so she obviously doesn't like the wild life. So that leaves Terry and Kal. Terry is basically a decent bloke but has a prison record. Kal doesn't, but is totally corrupt. Yeah, it's narrowing down a lot, isn't it? If we

266

assume Terry is basically a nice guy and wouldn't butcher some bloke, that just leaves Big Bad Kal.'

He parked outside a row of shops and they walked across a parking area to where the boats where moored in the marina. It was hardly Monte Carlo, but there were a lot of boats moored there of all shapes and sizes.

'I've always liked this place,' said Nick, as they reached the quayside. 'It's smart, isn't it?'

'Not what people think of when they think of Hartlepool, that's for sure. There's some money here. No monkey's though, I note.'

They walked from boat to boat, looking for *Sea Urchin.*

'I bet most of these people hardly ever sail the boat, they just get pissed in port,' said Jeff. 'There's no-one on any of these.'

Nick stopped and pointed to a large white and blue boat bobbing on the water.

'There it is. Wow. It looks like a big speed boat, doesn't it?'

'That's because that's what it is, I think.'

They walked right up to it. The cabin area below deck was separated from the elements by a wood and glass divide.

'This is bloody lovely, isn't it? I can could see me on this playing at being a salty old dog of the sea,' said Jeff, his foot on the edge of it. With a quick look around, he hauled himself on board. Nick checked no-one was looking too, but the whole area was devoid of people, so he followed Jeff onto the deck at the stern.

'Is this bit called a cockpit?' said Jeff, pointing at a semicircle of white seats, like a small sofa, in front of which were two big padded seats. The right-hand one was in front of a wood steering wheel and a panel of controls.

Jeff swung his legs over and onto the seated area and went up to the wheel. 'Is the one who steers it called the driver on a boat?'

'It's captain, isn't it?' said Nick, getting onto his knees to look into the below-deck area.

'I dunno. You can be a captain without having control of the wheel, I think. It's really posh this, look at it down here. There's a kitchen area and I bet those couches convert into beds.'

Jeff squatted down and peered into it. 'Nice. This isn't much smaller than my flat was in Harrogate. You could deffo live in here. There's not so much as a scuff mark on anything. It must be new, this boat, it looks fresh out of the wrapping. Sadly, no boxes of illicit drugs around the place, though. I was hoping some that were on that Excel spreadsheet would be stored here.' He peered a bit closer. 'What's that in the corner?'

He pointed at a small red light.

'I don't know for sure...' said Nick, '...but there were two of those in the kitchen at his parents' house as well. I assume it's some sort of security system.'

'Ah, yeah. It'll be a laser beam, as soon as you disrupt the beam the alarm goes off. I've seen them before. I was thinking of getting one for the shop just in case anyone breaks in to steal some early, rare Butterfield Blues Band records. Then I saw how expensive they are and decided against it.'

'If an alarm went off, there's no-one around here to hear it. The whole place is deserted. Owee, let's go, there's nothing to see here. Let's check out his house in the Boro.'

'Where is it?'

'Gypsy Lane, in Nunthorpe.'

Jeff stood up. 'Aye, of course it is, wasn't likely to be in South Bank, I suppose.'

It was only 20 miles from Hartlepool to Nunthorpe, a well-to-do southern suburb of Middlesbrough.

'You know what...thinking about it...that red light thing...that wasn't a laser. It was a regular LED light,' said Jeff, as Nick turned off the A19 onto the A174. 'Those laser security systems have more than one light. They create a network - a kind of grid that you can't step over or through. That's how they work - invisible beams that you can't avoid.'

'The one in the family home had two lights.'

'Even so, you could easily get around that.'

'Doesn't it fan out from the light?'

'Not the ones I looked at. I might be wrong, though. My days playing a technology expert in *Mission Impossible* are long behind me now.'

Nick took the A172 and then the A1043 into Nunthorpe. 'But if it wasn't a security system, what was it?'

'I'm not saying it's *not* a security system, only that it's not a laser security system.'

Gypsy Lane was full of big, expensive houses set back from the green leafy road.

'We're looking for the Elms,' said Nick.

'Must be some of the most expensive houses in the region here,' said Jeff, looking out of the side window. You could virtually buy the whole of Roseworth for the price of a couple of these gaffs. Aren't these elm trees here?'

Nick slowed down and spotted a carved wooden sign, indicating it was indeed the Elms. He pulled the car onto the pavement.

'Anyone at home, do you reckon?'

'There's a car in the driveway. Small thing. One of those so-called green hybrid affairs, that run off 750 AA batteries, or prune juice and farts. Looks like a runabout for the little lady, to me.'

'Aye, I reckon you're right. Rich blokes like him always have a little runabout for their wives. It's their way of exerting their macho bullshit.'

'Are you menstruating again, sister?' said Jeff, with a snort.

'I'll go and knock on the door, see if there's any reply. It'll be interesting to see what his wife is like. You stay here, you'll scare her. She'll think a bear has escaped from the circus.'

The front door was set behind an old late-Victorian wooden porch, the house itself a mid-Victorian red brick mansion, surely originally built for someone important in the new steel and mining industries.

He rang the bell and could hear it echo down the hallway. No reply. He rang again. Still no reply. Maybe she was in the back garden. He walked around the perimeter of the house, but there was no back garden as such, just a stand of mature oaks and some more landscaped gravel. He went back to the car.

'The coast is clear, Jeff.'

'Nice gaff,' said Jeff walking alongside him. 'Let's look in the kitchen window first.'

It wasn't difficult. The sash windows gave unobstructed views into all the rooms. The kitchen was done out in a farmhouse style around a big central wooden table. School books on the table suggested they had teenage kids.

Nick saw it first. A red light in the top corner of the kitchen. He walked around to the window which looked into the living room at the back of the house. Again, there was a red light in the corner. They could look into four rooms in total and the hallway too. In each room, a red light in the same place.

'Whatever that is, he's had it installed into his whole of his life,' said Jeff. Nick took out his phone and took a close-up photo of the small light and emailed it to Emily with the message, 'Can you find out what this is, Em? There's at least one in the top corner of every room Kal ever goes in.'

There was a large, red-brick, modern garage with a side window, so they checked that out, too.

'No light in here,' said Jeff, just tools, garden stuff and...and look, Nick...yes, get in! One, nil.' He pointed at a four cardboard boxes. On the side was written "Desoxyn". 'That must be Cavani's next consignment.' He typed the brand name into his phone. 'It's an amphetamine. Take a photo or three and so it's identifiably yer man's garage here.' Nick did so. As he was taking the last one, Emily emailed him.

*It's a recording light on one of these*. There was a link to a website specialising in miniature and concealed recording devices. *He's filming it all and laying it down to a hard drive somewhere*.

Nick showed Jeff.

'Shit, that means it's probably filmed us looking in all the windows,' said Jeff.

'Right, we've got to move quickly now. As soon as he checks these, he'll know we're onto him and have seen where his drugs are. He knows who I am, and that I'm not just some would-be burglar.' He looked up James Cook Hospital and called the switchboard.

'Cardiology unit, please.'

She put him through.

'Hello, Cardiology.'

'Hi, is Kal Patel in his office this afternoon, do you know?'

'Dr Patel is seeing patients all afternoon, yes. I'm afraid he'd fully booked. Who's calling, please?'

'I'm...' he cancelled the call, trying to make out he'd been cut off, so she wouldn't think it was an odd call.

'Fancy playing at Wavy Gravy again, big man?'

'I might play at Peter Grant this time, like in *The Song Remains the Same* when he's dealing with the bootleg poster seller. "It's my facking group!" I missed my vocation in rock 'n' roll menacing.'

'Right, this is the plan of action. The way I see this, it can only be Terry or Kal that killed Jimmy.'

'And he's probably got it all recorded, as well...' said Jeff, '...from two different angles. You said there were two lights in the kitchen.'

'Exactly. We'll play the Cavani con on him, and we'll try it on Jasmin as well.'

'The Cavani con?'

'We'll let them think we know more than we do and in doing so, they'll effectively confirm or deny the truth of what we'll assert, just as I did with Cavani. I'll record them on my phone, just as I did with Cavani, too. And that'll be more evidence.'

Jeff hi-fived him. 'I love how you're using the whole Cavani thing as an education in how to get information out of people without them even realising. Good work, Batman. Turning bad to good, like some sort of Teesside Buddha.'

'Aye, well, to have a silver lining, you need a cloudy day.'

'Which song is that from? I'm guessing it's something by Carly Simon.'

'Nah, it's a Guymer original, but it should be in song, shouldn't

271

it? It probably will be one day. So, first we go and see Jasmin and we tell her that Kal has got it all on video.'

Stockton library was a minute's walk from Jeff's shop. Nick left him with Emily and walked round.

It was so familiar from his childhood. He'd spent many hours as a teenager in there doing homework and just enjoying being around books. A classic 1960s Modernist glass, concrete and brick edifice, it had been done up a bit, but still looked a little futuristic.

Jasmin was working on the lending counter. Dressed in a black sweater and trousers, she looked tired, with bags under her eyes.

'Hi, Jaz.' She looked up and gave him a watery smile.

'Hello, Nick. What are you doing here?'

'Err...I came to see you. Have you got a break coming up? I need to talk to you.'

She looked at her watch, nodded and went to get her jacket.

'How are you doing?' he said, as they walked out of the library and round the corner to a cafe.

'I'm exhausted by everything,' She looked it, too.

He got them a coffee from the counter, consciously trying to be empathetic and understanding.

'Yeah, me too. Still, at least we're not in jail, like Ricky and Kev. Hey, do you think they did it?' He cringed inwardly, at his own lack of subtlety in asking the question.

'Killed dad? No.' She stirred a packet of sugar into her cup.

'Who did, then, Jaz?' Nope, still not any more subtle or empathetic. How did you do this stuff?

She shook her head. 'I don't know. A business rival, maybe. McGull, maybe. I don't know. I told that to the police. They went on and on about what dad did, and how he was notoriously corrupt, but he kept all of that from us, so we didn't have a clue about any of it, though we'd all heard about it for years.'

He nodded and blew out air. Any way he said the next sentence was going to be like dropping a bomb into the conversation. He knew he could think about it for a day and still not find a good way to say it, so he just said it. 'Lomash was in the rec room when

272

Terry arrived. That's why I knew you and Terry were lying to me.'

She gave him a puzzled look. 'Mash was in the rec room?'

'Yeah. He told me he saw everyone arrive. Terry, Sheila and your mother and elder brother, but he left before they all left and he didn't come into the house. And I know you didn't tell the police that all those people had been there, and I know you lied to me about it, too. I was just wondering why that was, Jaz?' He'd tried to make it sound non-threatening, but knew enough to know it still sounded confrontational.

She shook her head at him, her black eyebrows coming together in a scowl.

'I...I...I didn't know they were there. I told you I was in my room with Terry, then we found him there, dead, like we said.' But it was a poor lie. Nick ploughed on.

'You know that Kal has recorded the whole thing, don't you?'

By the shocked look on her face, no, she did not know that.

'Yeah, there are hidden cameras everywhere. He's got them in The Grove house, at home in Nunthorpe and even on his boat in Hartlepool marina. Seems a bit weird. A bit paranoid.'

Jasmin didn't look at him and just kept on stirring her coffee now. This life of crime, it wasn't one that she knew how to deal with. She was out of her depth.

'I don't want to talk about it. I don't have to tell you anything.'

'I'm not the enemy, Jaz.'

She looked at him with disbelieving, dark chocolate eyes.

'Shut up. You stupid man. Stop sticking your nose in where it's not wanted. No good will come of it. Just leave well alone and everything will be fine.'

She got up and left. He seemed to be getting good at having women walk out on him.

He walked back through Stockton Parish churchyard to Jeff's shop. Music was blasting out of the open door as he approached. Inside, Jeff was holding an armful of albums and slotting them into his racks.

'What's this, Jeff?' he asked, pointing at the noise-filled air.

'Journey's first album. Quite proggy, isn't it? Well before all the lighter-in-the-air,    balls-crammed-down-one-leg-of-tight-jeans, power ballads. This an instrumental called "Kohoutek" - there's nowt more proggy than a six-minute instrumental named after a comet, is there?'

Nick picked the sleeve off the counter. 'Morning, Em. Do you like this?'

'It's not heavy enough for me.'

As the record finished, she leant over the desk.

'Come round here and I'll show you this Excel spreadsheet which itemises the drugs Kal Patel has been supplying to Mike Cavani.'

There was a list of six drugs, mostly amphetamines including the one they'd seen in his garage, along with codeine and methadone. In a separate column were amounts and in another, a value. Presumably, how much Cavani paid for them and how much he sold them for. Each £1,500 purchased was yielding nearly nine grand. It wasn't huge amounts, probably a carton or two here and there, but enough to provide a steady profit for Cavani when sold on the streets. It was low-level drug dealing, probably done at some remove, but it was obviously just another income stream for the gangsters.

'So Kal Patel is as corrupt as his father,' said Emily. 'And has a lot to lose if all of this was to come out. People are driven to do extreme things when they've got a lot to lose. Maybe his father was threatening to expose him, so he killed him.'

'Yeah, I reckon you should grass Kal Patel up to the authorities,' said Jeff, dropping a copy of *Waves* by Jade Warrior into the 'J' section. 'He doesn't look like the sort who would do well in jail, unlike Ricky and Kev.'

'Do you think Kal could have killed Jimmy and then somehow got Ricky and Kev framed for it?'

'I think it's more likely that he'd pay them to take the blame,' said Emily, after a moment's thought.

'What makes you say that, Em?' said Jeff.

'My dad is rich, right? He's got millions. So when he wants anything done, his first thought isn't to do it himself, it's to pay someone to do it for him. Kal Patel is obviously well off, so if he needs to get away with something, maybe that's what he'd do. He pays the lads, gets them arrested and they take their chances in court.'

'I've been thinking about that. I could see them possibly doing it to protect Terry out of loyalty...but that's about it,' said Nick.

'Maybe, but imagine if he offered them a lot of money...would they really turn it down?' she said.

Jeff looked at him, eyebrows raised. 'She's got a good point there. I reckon they *would* take the gamble for enough cash.'

'I'd go to jail for a few months, if the price was right,' said Emily.

'You reckon? Could you stand that much lesbian sex though, Emily?' said Jeff, holding up an album by the early 70s American female rock band, Fanny, an eyebrow raised and a quizzical look on his face.

She hooted a laugh. 'For at least 50 grand, I'd give it a go. How bad can it be? You'd have to pass the long, boring days somehow, why not pass the hours becoming an expert in cunnilingus?'

'That is the first and only time I expect the word cunnilingus to be spoken or indeed performed in this shop,' said Jeff, laughing as Emily did a licking gesture at him.

'Well, let's go and see him, Jeff.'

'Righto. We'll do our best Cavani on him.'

'Aye, I'm not sure I'm any good at it, though. It didn't work on Jaz. She just stormed off, so we might have to try something else - play to our strengths more.'

Nick drove them to Middlesbrough and the James Cook University Hospital down Stokesley Road, past Emily's old house, past The Grove and on to Marton Road.

He paid to park his car. Exploiting people for profit because they were visiting sick friends and loved ones still seemed fundamentally wrong. Was no human instinct safe from the profit motive? Yeah, let huge corporations avoid paying tax, but charge people for visiting sick and dying people, that's the right thing to do, isn't it? This was all too often the world they lived in, where money was loved more than love. It was wrong and people knew it was wrong, but the common decency of the common people didn't seem to count any more, so you had to pay a fiver to park for four hours and fuck you for visiting vulnerable people, you schmuck.

He put his money in the machine, spat on the ground in front of it, to pointlessly register his disdain for the very principle of charging, and stuck the ticket in his window.

The cardiology unit was listed on the board, inside the entrance of the hospital.

'All hospitals feel the same, don't they?' he said. 'This is just like North Tees. I feel like I should be going to visit my mother.'

'I know what you mean. Makes me want a bed bath.'

'A bed bath?'

'Never had one when I was in after my heart attack. I always thought one of the few upsides of being in hospital was being sponged down by an attractive nurse.'

'You watched too many *Carry On* movies as a kid, you did.'

'I've always paid my taxes, surely the least I can expect is a free wash from the state.'

They followed the signs to the cardiology unit. 'So, what's our approach with this bloke?'

'I'd like a good look around his consulting room. I wouldn't mind betting he keeps a lot of the video recordings in there, or at least, all the important stuff. If I was him, I wouldn't risk having it out of my possession. If I could get five minutes to have good look around, we might get some hard evidence.'

'Aye, but how do we get in? You can't just walk in this sort of geezer's office, they're always behind locked doors with entry codes.'

Nick winced. 'Are they? I didn't realise that, I thought I could just stroll in there like at a doctor's.'

'No way. We need an appointment, but it takes months to get one of them.'

Nick tugged at his beard stubble with his right hand. 'I've got an idea. Like I said, we should play to our strengths.'

'Are we going to invite him to a pub quiz about 1970s rock bands, like?' Nick gave him a big cheesy grin.

'Well he might know something about Heart, I suppose.'

'Boom and indeed boom. He's here all week, folks. Please tip your waitress.'

They came to a halt outside of a set of swing doors, behind which was the cardiology unit.

'OK, big man, are you ready?'

'Of course, remember, I was the man who got backstage at Wembley to meet the Stones by pretending to be Keith Richard's guitar technician.'

'Aye, but then almost immediately got thrown out by the roadies for not being.'

# CHAPTER 14

Nick walked up to the reception. A nurse in her mid 30s sat behind it, with her hair fastened up. She looked tired and stressed out, her cheeks the colour of raspberries, her eyes circled with dark rings. Her phone rang. She apologised to him and took the call. It seemed to be a basic admin issue that she had to deal with.

'I'm sorry about that. How can I help you?' she said as she put the phone down.

'My friend here is not feeling himself. He had a heart attack a couple of years ago, we were just here to visit a friend and he feels very weak.'

Jeff leant forward and put his hands on his knees and blew out air.

'I'll be alright in a bit. I'm just a bit worried my stent has...y'know...un-stented or something,' said Jeff. 'I'm a bit short of breath. Feel dizzy.'

The nurse came from behind her desk. She was short and stocky with thick, heavy 1970s centre-half's legs.

'Why don't you take a seat?' she said, taking him by the arm to a row of chairs along a wall. A messy, gaunt, elderly man who had a creamy, yellow pallor, sat at the end watching Jeff sit down gingerly.

The nurse felt his forehead with the palm of her hand. 'You are rather hot.'

'I've got a tight feeling in my chest. Feels like indigestion,' said Jeff, letting out a gasp.

'Is there someone we could see?' said Nick. 'Just to make sure he's OK.'

'I shall see if that's possible. We're very busy.' she said, and scuttled away, now even more stressed out, poor woman.

'It's probably trapped wind,' said the yellow man, who had the air of a tramp about him. His white hair was plastered on his head and he wore a pair of tweed trousers that looked like they'd recently been found in a ditch. His eyes were bright, but he didn't look well.

'What are you in for then, mate?' said Nick.

'I've had a triple heart by-pass...and a new lung...and something else...oh yeah, they took me appendix out. Liver's knackered though.'

'Good god, they've made a new you,' said Jeff, with a grin.

'Aye, if I could get a new liver, couple of new kidneys and a new arse, then I might live until I'm 150.' He laughed, which seemed to provoke a tide of phlegm into his throat, making him cough.

'I didn't know they could give you a new lung,' said Nick.

'Oh no, they just fixed it. It collapsed due to me smoking fags and also getting me head kicked in.'

He said it like it was nothing.

'You've been in the wars then, you poor old sod,' said Jeff.

The bloke gave another black-toothed cackle. 'I love it in here, mind. I'd spend all day every day here if I could. Better than in the park.'

'You been sleeping rough?' said Nick.

He nodded. Poor old sod.

'You're a bit old for that game, aren't you?' said Jeff.

'I'm 68, like. Boro born and bred.'

'Can't they find you somewhere to live?'

He shuffled inside his clothes and shrugged. 'I don't like houses...they're not for me. Not now. Not after 25 years.'

'Well, fair play to you,' said Jeff, extending a hand out to him. 'You go your own way, mate. I run Jeff's Records on Stockton High Street, if you're ever in town and you need a cup of tea or somewhere to doss overnight, stick your head round my door. It's not five-star accommodation, but it's warm and dry and you can stretch out over two chairs if you want. Any time.'

It was typically generous gesture from the big man. In Harrogate his store had been a place for various waifs and strays to drop by. Jeff saw it as part of the gig and it was no different in Stockton.

'Good of you, Jeff. I might do that. The High Street, you

reckon?'

'Aye, up by the church.' He grinned at him. 'We do a good brew. What music do you like?'

'I used to like Johnny Cash.'

Jeff nodded. 'We've got Johnny Cash records you can listen to. What's your name?'

The old lad put his thumb up. 'People call us Dice.'

'Dice? Why Dice?' said Nick.

'I love to play dice.' He took a pair of wooden dice from his pocket and held them up.

The nurse returned. 'Oh, are you feeling better?' she said, seeing Jeff was sitting back in his chair and yawning. He'd forgotten he was supposed to be ill.

'Oh, err...I still feel as weak as a kitten,' said Jeff, 'and I've still got that tight feeling in my chest.'

She got a clipboard and a form.

'What's your name?'

'Jeff Evans.'

'Alright Jeff, I've got Doctor Hall to come along and take a look at you for a few minutes. He'll be here as soon as he can. If you're not well, we'll have to have a think what to do with you.'

'Oh, is Doctor Patel not available?' said Nick.

'Yes. I'd like to see him if possible,' said Jeff. 'He's been highly recommended to me.'

'He's my fella,' said Dice. 'You can have my appointment if you want. I'm in no hurry.'

'I'm sorry, we couldn't do that. You need to see Doctor Patel, Dice. He'll be free shortly,' said the nurse.

Her phone rang again; she took the call and then left again. She seemed rushed off her feet and could have used some extra staff. No chance of the car parking fees paying for that, it would seem. Probably paid for plenty more managers, though. That was the way of the modern world. More money for more managers to boss around the people who did the real work, without them ever having done the job they were telling those people to do and not really understanding what it actually entailed. It was no wonder things were falling apart at the seams.

Nick got up and walked down the corridor, looking for Kal Patel's office. It was around a corner. He listened at the door. Someone was certainly inside. A coded lock was on the door panel so you couldn't just open it, exactly as Jeff had suggested. He went back to Jeff.

'What are you up to?' said Dice, with a rasping noise that was part laugh, part asthmatic convulsion.

'We want to get Doctor Patel out of his office,' said Jeff.

'Are you on the rob?' said Dice, his old grey eyes sparking, clearly hoping they were. 'Drugs or summat?'

'What's he like, this Patel bloke?' said Jeff.

'Patel? Up 'imself. Looks down his nose at me 'cos I'm a dirty homeless gadgee, but he's bloody good at his job. Saved my bloody life.'

'I'm going to put on a bit of a performance, Dice. Right? If we can get Patel out of his room, try and keep him busy for a few minutes, alright?' said Jeff.

Dice nodded. 'I bloody love a good scam, me,' he said, rubbing his bony, blue-veined hands together.

The nurse returned. 'Doctor Hall won't be long, Mr Evans.'

'I really don't feel good,' said Jeff, leaning forward and edging to the front of his chair. Nick put an arm around him. Dice was grinning.

Then, with an authenticity born out of actually having had a heart attack and knowing exactly how it felt, Jeff slid to the floor, clutching his chest and letting out tight, sharp gasps, holding his breath to make sure his head went a funny bright pink colour.

'Oh my god...' said the nurse and ran behind her desk and picked up a phone.

Nick ran down to Patel's office and hammered on the door. 'Someone's having a heart attack here, please help, please!' he said, raising his voice to a panicky high-pitch.

Patel yanked the door open and ran out, didn't even seem to

notice Nick standing to one side of the door, his back to the wall, and ran up the corridor to where Jeff was lying prone and gasping.

Nick put his foot in the closing door, waited and stepped into the room, shutting the door behind him quietly.

The consultation room looked like a doctor's surgery. He looked around, his heart pounding with adrenalin. What could he find? A phone, perhaps. A computer? No, he couldn't carry that out and anyway, it was his hospital computer. A laptop? No, there wasn't one.

Patel had a large desk pushed up against a wall. Pulling open each of the drawers, he inspected the contents. Papers, pens, files. Nope, nothing significant in the desk. He pulled open a grey metal filing cabinet, but it was just full of folders and files. Nothing. His hands were sweating now. Not much longer. Come on. Nick turned a 360 degree circle in the office. Nothing here of any interest at all. Shit. He had to get out. As he went to pull open the door, there was a green quilted jacket hanging on the back. He frisked it and pulled out something from an inside pocket. It was square and a little bit bigger than his hand. A hard drive. A fucking hard drive. On it was a small white sticker: 'The Grove etc'. There was a commotion outside. Jeff was clearly doing a good job, but time was up.

He cracked open the door, peered out and quietly shut it behind him just as Kal Patel rushed around the corner and back into his office.

Nick rounded the corner. Jeff was lying on his side looking up at him, making a strange gulping noise. The nurse crouched to one side. A quick glance at Dice. He was nodding keenly at him. Nick held his hand in front of his belly, put a surreptitious thumb up at Jeff.

'You're looking a lot better, Jeff,' he said, holding a hand out to him.

The nurse could not believe what he was saying. She frowned at him, her puce cheeks glowing.

'He looks terrible...'

'No, I am feeling better,' said Jeff, getting his feet. 'It's a miracle. I'm fine. Thanks for your help.'

Nick winked at Dice and without even looking behind them at a surely astonished nurse, they marched out of the cardiology unit, and then half walked, half ran to the stairs.

'I've got a hard drive,' said Nick, panting, 'I think it might be camera footage...not sure, though.'

They got to the ground floor and headed for the exit. The automatic doors parted and they were outside and free.

'Bloody good turn you put on there, Jeff.'

'I was pleased with it. Always fancied doing Am Dram. Exit stage left, pursued by bear...I could be the bear, me.'

'I don't know if Patel clocked me and even if he did, if he'd know my face.'

'Cavani might have shown pictures of you to him. But he'd hardly expect to see you in there, would he?'

'No. But he'll know something weird was happening by now.'

They got to the car and stood for a few seconds getting their breath back.

Nick looked towards the doors they had just come out of. The doors parted and Kal Patel emerged, still wearing his white consultant's coat.

'Shit. There he is. He's looking for us,' said Nick, crouching down ' Get down Jeff, get in the car. You're the biggest sodding thing in this car park.'

But it was too late. He'd spotted Jeff, shouted something that was inaudible at that distance, pointed and began running towards them.

'Now would not be a good time for the car to fail to start,' said Jeff as they leapt into the BMW.

Nick turned it over and it started first time, as the good old beast always did.

'OK, let's get out of here. Now, if we go past him, play the innocent, we don't know anything about anything.'

'I just had a funny turn. And now I'm fine,' said Jeff. 'That's pretty much always true of me.'

'Aye. Your funny turn just happens to have lasted over 40 years,' said Nick, reversing out of the space and heading towards an exit.

'He's coming towards us,' said Jeff.

'Just pretend you can't see him,' said Nick. 'We're just chatting about something, and not paying attention to the Asian man who is coming up towards us on my side. I'm just pointing at something over there, quite casually, the way you do sometimes.'

'And I'm just nodding and agreeing with you, as though you're talking a lot of sense, which would be unusual for you.'

He turned and made a gesture at Jeff, who pointed in the opposite direction, making out they were having a discussion about something.

Nick had to come to a halt to pull out onto the main thoroughfare and go towards the exit, letting traffic go past. As he did so, he had to look to his right for any more oncoming traffic and saw Patel had made ground on them. Twenty yards, 15, 10. He was waving.

'Do we pretend we're not who he thinks we are?' said Nick.

'I'm definitely not who I think I am,' said Jeff. 'I could be anyone, for all I know.'

The traffic was constant, there was no getting away.

Five yards, four, three, two...he trotted to a halt in front of the car, getting his breath he held up his hands at them and then walked around to the driver's side.

Nick wound the window down a little.

'Can I help you?' he said with a smile.

'I know who you are. What where you doing in my office?'

'I'm sorry, I don't know what you're talking about.'

'Don't bullshit me, Mr Guymer. You and your friend here have stolen...'

'...you're clear,' said Jeff, spotting a break in the procession of traffic.

Nick pulled away without waiting to hear anything else Patel was saying. He stood and watched them go, hands on hips.

On the journey back to Stockton, Jeff inspected the hard drive.

'I hope there's something significant on here.'

'I think, judging by his reaction, there is,' said Nick. 'I wouldn't mind betting that those sex pictures Emily found on Cavani's phone were from some of Kal's concealed cameras. He seems like a bit of an expert in it.'

'Yeah, they looked like they were taken from that sort of angle, don't they?'

'I didn't know you'd looked at them.'

'Just for research purposes, old boy. I take no pleasure in the sight of naked cavorting. They were clearly covertly taken.'

'Do you reckon he's paranoid or something? Filming the house and his home and the boat. Seems really weird.'

Jeff scratched his beard. 'I was thinking about that. I think it's two-fold. First, he's bit of a pervert, so he has concealed cameras to watch people in his house - visitors and that.'

'What? So he invites over guests for the weekend and then watches them undress in the spare room?'

'Exactly. Same on the boat.'

'But at the family home?'

'Ah, that's the other thing. I think he put those cameras in the house so that he could keep a track on what Jimmy was doing and who he was doing it with. Think about it, we know Kal works for Cavani, Cavani needs dirt on people. Kal records his father and other officials doing dodgy deals or *in flagrante* with someone they shouldn't be flagrante-ing with. Cavani then blackmails them over it. Perfecto.'

'That's good thinking, big man. The more cameras he's got set up, the more chance he's got of footage that can be used by Cavani. I did wonder if he had one in his surgery, but there was no red light.'

'Well if he was caught with a camera in his consulting office, he'd get the sack, wouldn't he? Super pervy to be filming your punters.'

After parking, they hurried down to the shop to see what was on the hard drive.

The shop was busy as they got back in. Emily was taking a card payment off a young woman for a small pile of albums, a copy of Fleetwood Mac's *Rumours* on the top.

'Hello boys,' said Emily.

'Good grief, are you giving away hot pies, Em? It's so busy in here,' said Jeff, going behind the counter and looking at the long list of records that had sold that day.

'It's been like this most of the day. We've sold loads and I've taken some orders for new vinyl as well. I assumed you could get hold of it. I just wrote down all the details.'

'Cool, yeah. I can sort that out.'

She handed the card back to the woman with a smile and bagged her records. 'I hope you enjoy them,' she said.

'I'll be back for some more when I get my next wages,' the woman said. She was about 22 and smartly dressed. She was the polar opposite of Jeff's usual dishevelled, dysfunctional punters

'She was like a regular member of society,' said Jeff after she'd left. 'We never get them in here.'

'Well, you do now. You should also get bags printed with your shop name and address on. It'll be good advertising around town.'

After dealing with a couple of more purchases, things quietened down. When the shop was empty, Emily slipped off her stool and went in the back to put the kettle on and use the toilet.

'Right, let's hook this up to my laptop,' said Jeff, taking the hard drive off Nick. 'These things don't look much, but they hold a terabyte,' he said, looking for a USB cable.

'I have no idea how much that is - and even if you told me, I'd be none the wiser,' said Nick.

'Sounds more like something they'd sell at Greggs, doesn't it?' said Jeff. "Try our new cheese and onion Terabyte". That or it was some ancient dinosaur.'

'As opposed to the modern dinosaurs, like?'

Jeff wobbled his head at him sarcastically. 'Ha-de-ha-ha. Right, here we go, we have an active hard drive.'

It was full of folders of videos.

'Good god, there must a thousand folders on there,' said Emily, coming back and peeping between them to take a look. 'What is it all?'

'Video from Kal's secret cameras, I think,' said Jeff, clicking on the first one. 'Yup. Now, this is the boat, isn't it?'

They crowded around it and watched. Nothing was happening, no-one was there.

'How much is there of this?' said Nick.

'An hour. It's just monitoring, isn't it?'

'Why doesn't he have a motion detector so it films only when there is movement in the room?' said Emily. 'The bloke's is a rank amateur. Not that I've ever covertly filmed someone...much.' She scratched her head and raised her eyebrows.

Jeff ran it forward at speed, but there was nothing on it. The next five were exactly the same.

'Is there any way we can scan these to see which ones have any action on?' said Jeff. Emily shook her head.

'Not that I know of. I'll upload all these to a server and then run 10 or 15 of them together so that we don't have to sit through each one.'

She took over while Nick and Jeff had tea. They'd just finished when Emily made a whoop and raised her arms in there. 'Hands up, who wants to see two people having sex?'

'That rather depends on who they are,' said Jeff, walking behind the counter. 'They're at it on the boat. Oh dear. He's not in good shape, him, is he?'

'He's gross,' said Emily.

'In fairness, she's hardly the prize pig at the fair,' said Jeff, his eyebrows raised. 'Come and have a look at this Nick,' he said. 'It's like watching a steamroller flatten tarmac.'

Emily giggled. 'He doesn't like porn, Jeff, you know that.'

'This isn't porn. This is just sex. That's different,' said Jeff.

'That is a tiny penis,' said Emily, one thin eyebrow raised.

'Aye, like one of those mini chipolatas you have at Christmas,' said Jeff.

'Nah, you're alright. I have no desire to see such a thing. Do you recognise him or her?' said Nick.

He shook his head. 'Nah, it's probably some council official banging the Mayor's wife or something like that. Ooops, there we go, all over.'

Emily put her hand over her mouth and quickly turned her head away. 'That was quite gross, actually.'

'See. You'll corrupt yourself watching that, one way or another,' said Nick.

'Too late for that with me, I'm afraid,' said Jeff. He pointed at another of the films, also from the boat. 'We have action on this one here...' He stood, stock still, his face set in a frown. 'That's Jimmy Patel, isn't it?'

'He's with an Indian woman,' said Emily.

'Is this his wife Myra, Nick? I don't know her to look at.'

Emily let out a scream. 'He hit her! The bastard. He hit her! He slapped her in the face!'

Nick went to look. The image was from the boat and it was Myra. She was lying on a bed, naked but under a sheet, her head in her hands and crying. Jimmy Patel suddenly came into view, his large, heavy fat belly hanging over a tight pair of underpants. He brought his fist down right beside her head, punching the pillow in a downwards motion, his face twisted in rage.

'Is there any sound on this?' said Nick.

'No,' said Emily.

'That poor woman is terrified,' said Jeff. 'I can't look at this. He's fucking raging, look at him. He's lost it.'

Myra Patel was curled into a ball, as her husband shouted and screamed at her, pushing at her, pinching her skin and then, in one nasty little rabbit punch, hitting her hard in the stomach. The look of anguish on her face was unbearable.

Jeff stopped the video and put his arm around Emily, who was crying.

'If he wasn't dead, I'd have gone round there and kicked the crap

288

out him,' said Nick, disgusted.

'Bastard. How could anyone do that to their wife?' said Emily, 'I've never seen anything like that...it's disgusting. I'm glad he's dead. I hope she killed the fucking shit!'

'I think we can assume this was hardly a one-off incident,' said Nick. 'Julie's told me loads about this sort of abuse. It goes on for years, sometimes. The man hurts the woman in places that are not visible to the public. He physically and mentally tortures her to control her, but the outside world thinks he's a big respectable man. And you know what? I think this might be one of the reason's Kal had cameras put around the place. He wanted to get film to convict his father.'

'Convict or blackmail,' said Jeff. 'This is dated from January this year, so she must have put up with this for so long.'

Nick prowled the shop floor.

'Oh god, there's another one here of Jimmy Patel kicking off at the house in The Grove. It's in the kitchen,' said Jeff, pointing to another of the screens. Emily couldn't look and walked outside for some air. Nick sat on her seat and watched as Jasmin argued with her father. He swiped a hand at her, picked up a plate and threw it at her, only just missing, it shattered into pieces against a wall. She bent down and threw a shard back at him, then flew at him, fists raised, pounding into his chest and clawing at his neck with her nails. But he was too big and strong for her. Grabbing her by her arms, he flung her across the kitchen and into a wooden unit. She was clearly dazed, but struggled to her feet and tried to get away, to no avail. He pounced on her, picked her up like a rag doll and threw her down onto the floor again, like a wrestler would his opponent. He followed it up with a kick to her belly and then stormed out, leaving her weeping on the floor.

Jeff halted all the playbacks.

The two old friends stared at each other in silence.

'Are you thinking what I'm thinking?' said Jeff.

Nick nodded. 'That you don't want anyone to go to jail for killing a man like this?'

'I bet there are hours of this stuff and it won't even be the half of it. This was why Jimmy had to give McGull the contracts. Cavani was already blackmailing him with these videos. When he fell out with McGull it wasn't over Lomash's relationship with Dave, it was over these. He probably got sick of paying the money. That's why it was such a big deal to Cavani. Not just the supplier contracts, but the money Jimmy paid them to keep quiet about this.'

'Can you face sitting through these?' said Nick. 'I'm not sure I can.'

'Do we have to? Can't we hand them over to the police?

'Pound to a penny, the film of the murder is on there, somewhere,' said Nick.

'Which is why Kal hasn't shown the police.'

'It probably incriminates him, doesn't it?'

'Probably. He'd rather Ricky and Kev went to jail than him, obviously,' said Jeff. 'I'm sure he paid them off, just like we said.'

They stood in silence.

'I'd better check on Emily,' said Jeff. Yes, of course. Why hadn't he thought of that? Nick followed him out of the shop. She was walking in the churchyard, smoking a cigarette, which he'd never seen her do before, head down. Jeff went over and put his arm around her. His bulk dwarfed her. She was obviously upset. Should he go over and comfort her too? He didn't know. Probably not. One comforter was enough, wasn't it?

He looked up at the sky. It was a grey, overcast, mild and placid afternoon, a light breeze blew his hair into his eyes. As he brushed it away a car came at speed down the High Street, a black Mercedes sports car. It swung off the road, past the church and screeched to a halt in front of Nick. A cloud of blue rubber smoke emerged from the back tyres and drifted away on the wind.

This was trouble.

It was Kal Patel.

Dressed in a white shirt, tie now removed, and a pair of black trousers, he got out and advanced on Nick, his hand out.

'Come on! Give it to me. I know you took it. I know what you're up to. Hand that hard drive over.'

He pushed Nick in the chest. Nick took a step back, glancing over at Jeff, who was already on his way over.

'Steady on, mate. Given what we know about you, I think you should be a bit more polite, don't you?'

But he didn't listen. He pushed past Nick into the shop. Jeff ran in after him; pouncing on him inside the door, he put his arm around his neck and pulled him backwards.

'Settle down now, sir. Just because we've got an obscure Brazilian copy of *Revolver*, there's no reason go radge on us.'

But Kal was furious now. Furious like his father had been furious. He thrashed his arms around and elbowed Jeff in the chest, pulled a scalpel from his pocket, took a cover off the blade and slashed the air in front of them with it.

'Get back, you idiots. You don't know what you're doing. Where is that hard drive?'

'I ate it,' said Jeff, unimpressed, his arms crossed. 'Very tasty with Marmite on.'

Nick weighed up the situation. Emily had uploaded the hard drive to the server. They didn't need it. But Kal didn't know that.

'It's behind the counter,' he said, waiting his moment.

'Get it!' shouted Patel, holding the scalpel out at him. It was super sharp and could easily slice off an important part of a human body.

Nick edged around him, hands up, and went behind the counter. Kal Patel had turned slightly to watch his movement and in that moment, Jeff leapt forward, grabbed him by the hair and slammed his head so hard onto the wooden counter that the wood resonated a low hum. Kal Patel was instantly dazed. Jeff kicked the knife out of his hand, pulled Patel over by his shoulder and kneed him in the face, kicking out at him again as he fell to the floor.

Nick walked back around into the shop and picked up the discarded scalpel. 'Good work, Jeff. There was a touch of the Giant Haystacks about that.'

'I prefer to think of myself as Kendo Nagasaki, real name, Peter Thornley from Stoke. True fact.' He pulled on his beard and grinned manically and puffed his cheeks and breathed out heavily.

Nick hauled Kal Patel up and propped him against the counter. He had a massive swelling on his forehead and was clearly seeing stars.

'So what are we going to do with you, Kal? We don't take kindly to people threatening us, do we, Jeff?'

'No. Traditionally we take very badly to people threatening us, Kal. Traditionally we kick the crap out of people who do that, Kal. So you got off lightly with a headache.'

As they squatted down in front of him, Emily looked around the shop door.

'Is the coast clear? Oh my god, what's happened to him?'

'He stumbled and hit his head on the counter...and on my knee...and my foot, as well,' said Jeff. Kal mumbled something.

Nick held up the knife to her. 'He came at us with this. He wanted the hard drive.'

She looked at them with wide eyes. 'I don't understand...'

But her words were cut short as they came out of her mouth. There was a thud, she screamed and fell to the floor in the doorway of the shop.

Nick spun around. 'Emily? What's wrong?'

It was obvious what was wrong. She lay motionless and standing over her, holding a cricket bat, was Jasmin, her long, dark hair spilling over her shoulders.

'Give me it!' she screamed, her dark chocolate eyes expressing a blend of fury and fear. 'Give me the hard drive! I know you've got it. I'll hit her again! I'll bloody kill her! Give it to me!!'

Emily was unconscious. God knows what damage that bat had done to her small head.

Nick got to his feet. 'Alright, alright...I'll get it for you, Jaz. Don't hit Emily again, please, don't. It's behind the counter, I've got to go around there, OK?'

'What have you done to Kal?' she said, gesturing to her brother with the bat.

'He wanted the hard drive as well,' said Jeff.

'Fucking prick.' She spat a small ball of foamy spittle in his direction.

'I don't understand, Jaz. We've seen a few of the videos on here and some are of your father being a total bastard. Why do you not want those seen? They show him for what he really was,' said Nick, going behind the counter and disconnecting the USB cable from the computer.

'I don't give a damn about that. Come on! I need it. Now!'

'Did you kill Jimmy? Is that what it shows?' said Nick.

'Of course it damn well does. I didn't even know the bloody thing existed until you told me he'd filmed it. I knew then that he'd have to have it all stored somewhere.' She spoke with anger and frustration and fear in her voice. 'Hand it over, Nick, come on.'

'I still don't understand, Jaz. Did Kal call you and tell you we'd taken it?'

'He asked where you'd be and told me what you had taken.' She looked at him with a grim face and then stared at her prone brother with a fury that echoed her own father's fury and reached over towards him as he walked back around the counter and onto the shop floor, stepping over the still dazed Kal Patel as he did so. Emily was still lying on her belly, motionless.

He put the drive into Jasmin's outstretched hand as she held the bat above Emily's head, ready to drive it into her skull. She might not be that strong, but she didn't need to be to give her brain damage.

'We had a perfectly good plan which has all turned to shit because of you.'

'You shouldn't have panicked and lied about your mother being at the hairdressers when the murder happened, Jaz. When I found that out she was finished there before nine, I knew either you or she was lying.'

'I thought you were on our side, Nick, but you weren't, and Kal wasn't either. He was out for himself. The whole family is so

293

fucked up. So from now on I'm just looking after myself and Terry,' she sneered at him and turned to go. This was his chance, but Nick couldn't get to her easily because Emily was in the way, so he let her walk out of the shop doorway before going after her.

'Call 999, Jeff.'

He stepped over Emily and walked out of the shop to see Jasmin walking up to a smartly dressed man in a blue suit, shirt and gold tie. It didn't register at first. It didn't register that it was Mike Cavani, not until he cast a wave at him and gave him his best shark-like grin.

She gave him the hard drive and he slid it into his inside pocket with his nasty smile. It all fell into place.

'We meet again, Nick,' he said, as Nick approached.

He tried to remain calm. 'So what's the plan, Mike? More blackmail?'

'As soon as Jasmin told me about this,' he patted his jacket pocket, 'I told her it was something I'd pay well for and came straight down.' He took out a white envelope and gave it to Jasmin, presumably full of cash.

'Didn't *you* know Kal had it all on film?' said Nick.

Cavani shook his head. 'He provides me with images, I don't ask him where they're from. I'm not an all-seeing eye, more's the pity. So this promises to be quite a little haul and it solves a lot of problems for me...I was delighted to get Jasmin's call.'

'I didn't know you knew this joker,' said Nick to Jasmin.

'He rang me up earlier in the week to see if I knew anything. He left his number...' She didn't seem proud of herself, but her hand was tightly gripped on the money. 'When Kal called me and told me what you'd taken and how he had film of...of everything...in the houses and on that boat...' she paused and shook her head, her face set in a look of anguish and upset. 'He just disgusts me...*disgusts* me! I knew you'd be here. I said I'd come and get it if Mike paid me enough money. Like I said Nick, it's everyone for themselves now. I'm sorry I hit that girl. I just...I'm sorry...I panicked. I didn't hit her hard. I think she'll be OK...I hope so.'

Nick crossed his arms and stared at Cavani. He was such a sly sod.

'Why not just come down yourself, Mike? Why pay Jaz instead?'

Cavani looked at him with narrow eyes.

'You learn who to pick fights with and who not to pick fights with in life, Nick. I like to keep one step removed where possible and I thought Jasmin had a much better chance of acquiring the drive without fuss and so it proved. Don't look so cross, Nick. Everyone is a winner here. I get videos for my business, Kal stays out of jail for theft of drugs and many, many other crimes and maintains his image as a fine, upstanding man, Jasmin has some money, doesn't go to prison and can now marry Terry. Sheila takes over from Jimmy on MIDO, McGull's will get their contracts again and that suits me fine. Myra is rid of the husband who bullied and abused her, meanwhile Kev and Ricky get paid handsomely by Kal for taking their chances with a jury.' He held his arms out wide. 'The only loser is Jimmy Patel and he was bastard, anyway. Cheer up, Nick. This is a happy ending.'

He turned to his left and signalled to two people in a car. They got out and went into the shop, emerging a few seconds later with Kal Patel over their arms. He was conscious, but groggy. They put him in the back of the car and drove off.

'There now, it's all very neat and tidy. Obviously, you can tell the police the truth if you want, but you can see what the consequences will be,' said Cavani.

There was a cold, undeniable truth about that.

Nick nodded. 'Yep. Fair enough, Mike. We'll draw a line under this. For now, anyway. One thing I don't understand, though. Why did Kal offer to pay money to Ricky and Kev, Jaz? You're hardly a close family. What did it matter to him if you or anyone else was accused of murder?'

Cavani answered before she could speak.

'I'm disappointed in you, Nick. Surely you can work that out. Any investigation into his family would reveal Kal's little video business. The quicker he could get it all wrapped up, the better.

Ricky and Kev were perfect for that. Chances are they'd get sent down for it, even if he told them the exact opposite when he told them they'd get 150 grand.'

Jasmin nodded. 'He didn't want anything to come out about anything. Though I had no idea he was so...corrupt.' She spat the word out like it was dirt in her mouth. 'Stupidly, I thought he was doing me a favour, but he was really just doing himself a favour.'

'I see. Well, there's just one thing you should know then, Mike. We actually uploaded that hard drive to a remote server. So you're not actually taking sole possession of it. We still have it and we can use it as and when we see fit to use it.'

He laughed, nodded and held out his hand. Nick looked at it. He wasn't shaking his hand for any money.

'See, I was right to try and get you in my business. You are so sharp.'

Nick's mind worked fast and furiously to put together a solution to this once and for all.

'And we still have all your phone contents, as well. So while you're admiring me so much, here's what is going to happen. You're going to use your influence at Cleveland Police to get Kev and Ricky released after they have had their money from Kal. You don't care if they go to jail or not and I'm sure you can get the investigation set aside as a cold case, so that nothing else comes out. So make sure that happens and all the secrets inside your Pandora's phone box will remain a secret. If you don't, then I'll sell it as an exclusive to a national paper.'

He held out his hand. 'Deal?'

Cavani gave him a porcelain-eyed look, his head cocked on one side, then nodded.

'I'll make that happen. I love it when a plan comes together.' He gripped Nick's hand firmly. 'Don't be a stranger, Nick.'

Back in the shop, Emily was sitting up, rubbing her head. His heart lifted to see her conscious.

'Wow, are you OK, Emily?'

'I think so. My head is bloody hurting.'

'I thought she'd knocked you out.'

'No. It wasn't too bad. Reminded me of playing hockey at school. You'd often get a whack in the head from one of the more psychotic bitches when you fell over. I just thought it'd be best if I played dead. You read about people doing that when someone is shooting people or whatever. I didn't even know who it was.'

'I didn't bother to call an ambulance since Cavani's men took Kal away and she got up as soon as you left,' said Jeff. 'So what's the score? I assumed that was Cavani's men, anyway. If it wasn't, then someone came and stole him.'

Nick explained what had happened outside.

Emily squeezed her eyes open and shut and touched the bruise on her head. 'In a way, that is a brilliant solution to all this, isn't it? Like he said, everyone wins. Except me and my head.'

'Sort of. I'm not sure there are any winners from the world of pain, hurt and abuse that radiated from Jimmy Patel. But at least it's over now. Let's actually see how Jimmy P died. The video must be on here.'

He went to the computer and accessed the server.

There were hundreds of videos, possibly thousands, too many to look through. A thought occurred to him, maybe the one of the murder was one of the last ones. There had been nothing to film since. Maybe the red light's on the cameras didn't indicate they were actually on, merely plugged in and potentially active.

So he went to the last file, double clicked it and let it play.

The pictures were silent and revealing.

Just as Lomash had said, the whole family where there in the large kitchen in The Grove house, along with Terry and Sheila. Taken from one of the cameras in the corner of the roof, it immediately showed a raging Jimmy Patel, grabbing Terry by the shirt and shaking him. Terry was trying to prise his hands off him but Patel was bigger and stronger. Jasmin was trying to pull her father off him, but couldn't do it. Others shouted at him. Then Jimmy pushed Terry away and reached into the kitchen drawer for a big carving knife. Terry, seeing him get the knife, backed off.

Jasmin was gesturing at him and then towards the kitchen door. She seemed to be telling him to get out. Jimmy Patel started laughing and lunging at Terry with the knife. Terry had seen enough, turned and fled out the door. There were more scuffles. More pushing between Sheila and Jimmy this time, though she seemed to be trying to calm him down. Then Myra had a go at him, furious, her face contorted in a scream at her husband, him waving dismissively at her. Kal tried to take the knife out of Jimmy's hand; after they pushed at each other for a few seconds, he managed to pull it out of his father's grip. Still furious, Jimmy advanced on Jasmin, shaking her by the shoulders now, his mouth wide in a seemingly endless bawl of rage. Her mother tried to stop him hurting Jasmin. Sheila tried to stop him, but he simply pushed her away and had such a firm grip on Jasmin that, being a slight woman, she just couldn't get free. Then, in one move, Jimmy threw her to one side, casting her away as though she was a bin bag of rubbish, just as he had in the earlier video. Jasmin crashed into a kitchen cupboard and hit her head on the corner. It must have hurt like hell. Kal had put the knife down to help her up, but she got to her feet unaided, grabbed the knife from the bench and in a tearful rage, leaped at him with it, wielding it overarm, trying to bring it down into her father's neck, but her father jumped backwards out of the way and she stumbled forward as she swiped thin air. Now Kal and Myra grabbed him around the shoulders to restrain him. This attempt on his life didn't placate or calm him, it just sent him into an even greater boiling rage.

And then, in a fatal moment, it was clear exactly how he'd died. He got out of Kal's grip, turned around to face his daughter who was still holding the knife. He advanced on her and under the pressure of Kal, Myra and then joined by Sheila Simmons, all trying to restrain him, he fell forward, or maybe he was pushed. Either way, he lost his balance, falling onto the knife still held by Jasmin, cocked at a 45 degree angle. The big silver blade just slid silently into him, disappearing from view with a chilling finality. He immediately slumped forwards on the floor. It must have killed him almost instantly. His full weight falling forward had created so much force, far more force than Jasmin could have generated. He fell to the floor as a dead weight and was motionless. They all stood around looking at him in shock. It was an accident, but when it had happened, there was not a second of sympathy or regret. Jasmin looked down at him. Kal looked down at him. Sheila looked down at him, Myra looked down at him. They appeared to be silent for perhaps as long as a minute. Then Kal began directing them, pointing, wagging a finger and spelling something out to them.

Sheila and Myra then left by the back door. Terry reappeared holding his phone and stared, astonished at the scene. Jasmin went to him and he held her. She wasn't crying, she seemed to try and explain to him what had happened. He pointed to his phone. Kal nodded, talked to Jasmin and then left the room.

He returned a few seconds later. Following him were Kev and Ricky Wells. He was talking to them. They stood and looked at the corpse bleeding on the floor. Kev laughed and pointed at Jimmy's body, callously pleased to see him dead. Ricky made a sarcastic joke - or it looked sarcastic, anyway, knowing him.

Terry and Jasmin went out of the kitchen door and into the rest of the house while Kal talked to the brothers for some time. They went out of the kitchen to another room. All the video showed was the perfectly still body of Jimmy Patel, the knife protruding from his chest.

'Why didn't they just admit it was an accident?' said Emily who had been watching it alongside Jeff.

'Why take the risk if you can pay someone else to take it for you? Kal knew the only way to prove it was an accident was to produce the video and then questions would have been asked. Also, the video shows her attempting to kill him. She'd have gone down for that alone.'

'But she was provoked, surely,' said Jeff.

'Yes and that'd have reduced the sentence, but she'd still have been found guilty of attempted murder, and then probably manslaughter for his actual death. It'd be like Jimmy was getting revenge on the family from his grave. To have to do jail time after a lifetime of his abuse would be pretty sodding galling. That's why she didn't own up to it, I think. She felt like she hadn't done anything wrong.

'Now, it looks to me like Terry has called his brothers for a bit of muscle and when they turned up, Kal has done some sort of deal with them. They're not on screen right now, they've gone into the lounge or somewhere. They've still not bothered to call the emergency services. He had more to lose than everyone else. If there was a long investigation into the family and into that house all his schemes would have been unearthed. It was worth paying the brothers 150 grand for that not to happen.'

It was 15 minutes before they returned to the kitchen. One after the other, the brothers grabbed the knife handle and then dabbed some of the blood on their clothing. Then they left. It was quite clear what was going on. A price had been arranged. Terry came in with Jasmin, kissed her and left. She made a phone call, presumably to the emergency services. Kal said something to her, put his hand on her arm and then went into the hallway. The video ended at that point, as though he'd turned it off. Good. Nick had seen enough. It was sick and it was sad and he wanted nothing more to do with it.

# CHAPTER 15

As he parked up outside the refuge on Saturday morning, he looked to see if any of Cavani's men or women were around, but all was quiet.

Julie trotted down the steps from the house dressed in a grey sweat shirt and old blue jeans, baseball cap and baseball boots. He got out of the car and waved. She skipped down to him and they hugged each other tightly.

'Fizzin' hell, it seems like ages since I've seen you, not just a week.' She nuzzled into his neck. 'Ooh, I've missed your smell.' She sniffed at him playfully laughing, her hands around his waist. 'What sort of a week have you had?'

'A week like you'd not believe, Jules. It has been incredible. I've got some tales to tell you.'

'Yeah? Do I want to hear any of it?'

'It all sort of turns out alright. Sort of. Your brothers are set to do alright out of it, but Jimmy Patel was a bad man. Very bad.'

'Hmm, I figured that might be the case. I only clout bad men. OK. But the really important question is, can we make mad, passionate love when we get home?' She looked at him with a bright glint in her turquoise eyes, her arched eyebrows, raised in anticipation.

'We can have it here and now, if you want.'

She gurgled a woody laugh. 'Don't tempt me. A week of celibacy is a long time for us. I'm literally gagging for it.'

'Literally? Actually gagging?'

She made a gurgling, choking noise. 'See, I'm gagging. I'm parched. I'm a sexual desert in need of...of...'

'An oasis?'

'A Bactrian camel.'

'A Bactrian camel?'

'Yeah. Two big humps.' She laughed again. 'Come on then, let's get all this bad news out of the way - I assume it's all bad news -

and then we can have, what that high-brow philosopher Ted Nugent once called, wang dang doodle.'

'"Wang Dang Doodle" is originally a Willie Dixon blues, actually.'

'Is it? Should I make a willy joke?'

Man, it was so good to have her back. It felt like being whole again.

He had just about covered all the main issues as they got home. She peppered the journey home with expletives, exclamations of astonishment and groans of disbelief.

She put her bag down in the kitchen as he filled the kettle.

'I can't believe all this happened while I was away.'

'I'd have told you as things happened, but I thought it'd have ruined your week.'

'I'm glad you didn't. It would have. Let's just sum this up. We've got Cavani and Kal banged to rights via various criminal evidence on the phone and videos. So neither can touch us.'

'Correct.'

'We've got proof that Jaz accidentally killed Jimmy.'

'Aye. It's all on the film. It's quite clear.'

She nodded and sat down, pushing her hair behind her ears.

'And we've also got proof that Sheila and Myra were plotting to kill Jimmy as well?'

'From her own lips, yeah. Also recorded on film.'

'Can't blame them, really - the bastard. And we know Kev and Ricky are innocent, at least of *this* crime.'

'Definitely. They are gambling on getting found not guilty, incredible though that is. Does it surprise you? It is one hell of a gamble.'

'Oh god man, I don't know.' She put her head in her hands and rubbed her face. 'Those two are bloody crazy, so no, it doesn't, not really. They can't think long term about the consequences of their actions. They just see everything in the short term. 150 grand is riches beyond their dreams. It'll have blinded them to anything else. In fact, knowing them, they'll think they're being very clever and they'll also be planning a few visits to Kal Patel once they're out, to extort more money out of him. It won't stop at 150 grand.'

'They'll do at least six months on remand, possibly nine, depending on how long it is before Cavani uses his influence.'

'They can cope with that,' said Julie.

'Cavani will probably bribe or blackmail someone in the police after a month or two.'

'We can't trust him, though. He sounds like an evil shit.'

'He is. But I think he'll do it. We've so much on him that even his tentacles of corruption can't buy off everyone in law enforcement or in the media. He knows that he risks being exposed if he doesn't follow through on his promise and he knows we can prove in a few minutes that Kev and Ricky are innocent and broadcast it to the world, if we wanted.'

'I just can't see Jaz surviving in prison. And it doesn't seem fair. It was all Jimmy's fault. Thousands of women are in the same position as she and her brother and mother were...trapped in abusive relationships. I'm not going to have her sent to jail if there's another option.'

'I doubt they'd let her walk free. She tried to stab him in the head. Courts hate people trying to stab other people in the head. Even really horrible people.'

She stood up and banged the table with her hands. 'Right, then. Cavani was right, really. Everyone does come out of this in a better place, except perhaps Kal Patel. You've sorted it all out. I don't know how you did it, but you did. Bloody brilliant.'

'I don't either. I had a lot of help from Jeff and Emily. They were the clever ones.' He stood up and hugged her to him. 'God, I love you being back. The place seems alive now. Maybe instead of moving, we should just get a dog to keep some life in the place when one of us is away.'

She stuck her tongue out and, laughing, began panting like a dog. 'Well, it's time to give the dog a bone,' she said, pawing at him and barking.

Man, it really was great to have her back.

On Sunday morning, Nick got up to have a shower, when he remembered that the towel he'd given Emily must still be in the spare bedroom, so he went through to pick it up. He opened the door for the first time since she'd stayed overnight and picked up the pink towel which had been folded neatly and lay on the end of the bed...right next to a small pair of red knickers. She'd written a note on a scrap of paper, lodged in the crotch. 'A little souvenir for you. Enjoy.' Cheeky lass. And man, they really smelled of her too. He stuffed them in his jeans pocket and later put them in the bin.

Before they went to breakfast he got a call from Sam Thompson to let him know that McGull's were not taking any further action against him for the accident. Apparently, they couldn't pin the blame for the 'accident' on anyone with sufficient conviction. Nick smiled as Sam told him. That was a relief. In all the stress of recent days, he'd forgotten about Conrad and his little get-rich-quick scheme.

They went out to a little cafe in Yarm, ordering bacon, eggs, sausage, mushrooms, tomato and black pudding and lots of coffee.

'This is ace,' said Julie, as she stuffed a large piece of bacon into her mouth after smothering it in butter. 'After all last night's horizontal dancing, I need to get my strength up again. Good grief lad, there was a lot of fuel in your tank.'

'Abstinence and my pills are an explosive combo, I reckon.'

'You did explode, like. I tell you what, if we are going to move, we'd better get somewhere with a sound-proofed bedroom. Genuinely man, we'll get complaints.' She shook her head slowly and bit her bottom lip with her top row of teeth.

'Complaints and requests for home-made videos too, I should think. So what do you think about moving into town?'

'Into Stockton?'

'Yeah, or the Boro or Darlo, wherever.'

'If you want to, I'm happy to. I like it where we are now, but it is a bit big and we're not going to have much money any time soon, so a lower rent would make a lot of sense.'

'Yeah, I think that's going to be important. We'll have a look around, then. Oh man, I've not had a good feed all week. When you're on your own, cooking just seems pointless. I like cooking for us, but can't be arsed just for myself.'

'You said you had fish stew with Emily at that riverside place,' she said.

'Oh, yeah. That was good. We should go there.'

'You must have been at Jeff's a lot this week then, what with Emily doing all that phone hacking and stuff.'

'Yeah, it's been hacking central in there. She's been brilliant, though. I mean, I'd never have got to the bottom of it all, without her getting all of the info off Mike's phone. And she was really brave the way she took that blow to the head with the cricket bat. I mean, there's not much to her, but she's a tough kid under all the posh upbringing. Oh, I forgot to say, I hope you don't mind, but she came over the other night to work through all the video footage and the documents. We sat up till after 1am.'

She looked out the top of her eyes at him and paused. 'Why would I mind that, like? It's obvious she was crucial to all of this. I must buy her a little gift or something.'

'She'd like that. As I say, there's not much to her to look at, she'd float off in a stiff wind, but she's got a lot of guts and spirit. Must be living on Teesside that's put that into a kid who grew up in London.'

'She's super brainy, I reckon. Grade A student.'

Well...you know...I just thought it might seem a bit dodgy, her staying over.'

'Don't be daft, man.'

'She said the bed was really comfortable in the spare room.'

'Oh god, the sheets haven't been changed on that since when Jeff slept over. I hope she didn't catch the lurgy. I can't help but think that a degree in Computing Science is wasted in a record shop, though, y'know.'

'Aye. I know what you mean. I don't think she's very career-minded. She seems to want to follow her arrow wherever it points.'

'Well, in this day and age, that's probably for the best when you're 22.'

'She's been good for sales so far, he's nearly 50 per cent up this week. Some regular members of the public have been in to buy records. They never do that normally. I heard her talking on the phone to her boyfriend; she seems to love it at Jeff's and love Jeff, too.'

'And she still fancies you, I bet.'

His stomach knotted a little.

'I don't know about that.'

'Course she does. Why wouldn't she? Didn't she try it on, especially since I wasn't around?'

He wanted to be honest, at least to some degree. 'A bit, yeah. Well, she's quite flirty by nature, as you know, like. But there were a couple of times she basically said, if I wanted to get in her pants, I'd be welcomed with open arms.'

She grinned and gave a good-natured snort.

'Aye, open arms and open legs. Eee, she's a cheeky cow, that one. Mind, the way you're going on these days, you'd ruin her for anyone else. It's like being in bed with an oversexed jack hammer.' He flushed a little and she gurgled her laugh. 'Don't blush too much, lad. You've not heard me complaining, have you?'

'I don't know, you were moaning a lot last night.'

She chuckled to herself and looked over her coffee cup at him.

'If you're worried I'll be playing the jealous wife or something, then think again. It really doesn't surprise me that lasses fancy you, even a youngish lass like her. Nor that they'd try and get you into bed.'

'Doesn't it?'

'Nah. I also know that you'd never even notice they were trying to do it, half the time. Not unless they spelled it out in block capital letters. You don't read between the lines very well, luv.'

He laughed and nodded. She was so right. 'You know me, Jules, I can never tell what anyone thinks about anything. I'm amazed that anyone even likes me, of any gender. There have been times this week when I really needed some of your empathy and understanding. I just don't know how to do that sort of thing. I can organise a posse of brickies to beat the shite out of someone, I can face up to a Geordie gangster, and butt heads with a Stockton scummer, but reading the emotional subtext to a relationship situation is often beyond me, I'm afraid. But I've got one big confession to make, though.'

'Oh yeah? She didn't sneak into the room in the middle of the night and suck you off, did she?' she said with a mock laugh, as she poured them more coffee from a pot. 'Actually, her little mouth is probably too small to do that properly.' She looked at him over-innocently. 'You've gone proper red. Ha. I'll never tire of embarrassing you. The look on your face. You should be used to me and my filthy gob, by now.'

'I'll never get used to your low-down dirty mind, Jules. I hope I won't, anyway.'

'Well, I've been like this since puberty and I'm not going to change now, am I? So what is it you're confessing to, then?'

He paused to drink some coffee and then played with the spoon until he could find the right words.

'It's about drinking. I've been struggling a bit...a lot - all week, and before as well.' He squinted out of half-closed eyes at her, not wanting to see her reaction if it was negative. But it wasn't. Of course it wasn't, she leant forward with concern in her eyes.

'Really? Aw, luv. You should've said.' She put a hand on his. There was that easy empathy again.

He explained about how it had come on so strong when in Middlesbrough. 'I went to the shop, but Jeff was going out with Rita and I was parked outside the Stag Inn, so I went in and ordered a double vodka.'

'What was it like to drink it?' she said, picking bacon out of a back tooth.

'I didn't get to drink it. Emily had followed me in. I'd told her I fancied a drink, but probably shouldn't have one. So she'd shut up the shop and chased after me, came in just as I was about to knock it back, took it off me and sank the bloody thing herself.'

'Eee, what a good girl. Helping someone and getting free drink at the same time, that's a win win.'

'Yeah. It was really good of her. Anyway, to keep me out of boozy trouble we went back to her flat in Green Dragon Yard. She smoked a joint. I didn't want to risk dope either, and that's when I saw poor Lomash getting the crap kicked out of him. So it was quite fortuitous really.'

'That was nice of her to help you out. She's a funny lass, her. She's like part teenage girl, part mature woman.'

'I think it's called being in your early 20s,' said Nick.

'Seems a long time ago now. What sort of place does she have, then?'

'Small, but nice. Exposed brickwork and that. It was in a right mess. I even started tidying up. Anyway, when I finally got home, I opened the fridge up, took out some chicken, saw that bottle of Chablis and without thinking for a second, I drank the whole bloody lot down. Drank most of a bottle without stopping until it was all gone, gulp, gulp, gulp.'

She stared at him, a piece of sausage on her fork. 'Eee, fizzin' hell. Why did you do that after so long not drinking? There's always wine in there, but you've not wanted to knock it back, have you?'

'That's just it. I don't know. I just had to do it. I didn't even think about it. I just steamed in and sucked that mutha down. I'd struggled all night with it, in fact all this week and last, on and off I've been really wanting to drink. Apart from that time, I haven't had any, but I've really had the urge to and only being distracted by people has stopped me. Had I been on my own at home, I'm pretty sure I'd have got shit-faced.'

'Was it because I wasn't there to stop you?'

'Sort of. But it was because I was sort of lonely, I think. I reconnected with my old self when pubs were like friends to me. Places I could go to get away from the things that upset me. They shone out in the dark and were comforting and welcoming when home wasn't. Because our home was always dark and with no-one there for me, it felt like that again. I felt like I was that 17-year-old kid again and no years had intervened. Mind, I threw up and had a bloody terrible head in the morning, so it's not like I fell in love with it all over again, but I just had to tell you.'

'Well it's not like you were an alcoholic who would die if you had one more drink...'

'I was on the road to it. I'd not been sober for one night in 10 years, remember.'

'Alright. That is an unhealthy relationship with drink, I'll give you that. But don't freak out about it. It's not like you started hurting yourself again...you didn't, did you?'

'Self-harming? No. It's just that I might lapse again sometime and if I do, don't be too surprised and don't think too badly of me. It's really bloody hard when you get the itch...I mean, I know it's weak, but sometimes I am weak and I don't feel like I'm over it, or can conquer it once and for all. I thought I had...but I know now that I just haven't. I'm still that kid running from his pain, underneath everything.'

She cocked her head on one side and nodded slowly. 'One of the things I was learning about this week is about not being judgemental with people and just trying to deal with the situation they're in.' She put her hand on his again. 'It's a fight you'll probably have to go through sometimes, but I'll be here for you and if you do fall off the wagon, then you fall off the wagon. No-one is perfect. We're all human. We make mistakes and do stupid things. It's all a road to a better place, if you can let it be that and if you don't beat yourself up too much about it.'

'I thought you might be angry at me and feel let down. It feels like I have sort of let you and let me down.' He rubbed his neck, a little embarrassed. She reached under the table and patted his knee and thought for a few moments about what he'd said. He looked back at her turquoise blue eyes and hoped she could see how much he loved her. This wasn't like sitting with Emily. She was a nice, fun person, but Jules was something else...his soul mate or something way beyond superficial physical attraction. She understood him and no-one else had *ever* understood him. Proper understanding is such a rare thing in the world.

'I couldn't be angry at you over that. You do your best with the cards you're dealt. You've done so well to get to a better place in your head, to not get so down and to be as good a man as you can. Only I've seen the battle you've gone through to do that in the last couple of years and even I don't really know the half of it, of what you struggle through every day. So if you get pissed once or twice, I can't blame you or think badly of you. I know you're doing your best.'

His eyes glazed with a tear.

'Thanks, Jules. Maybe it was just a thing that I had to get out of my system. I have no rational explanation.'

She nodded and finished her food, putting down her knife and fork, quietly.

'I know I don't really ever say this, except when we're messing around in bed, but you do look great, y'know - physically, I mean. I know that's not a really important thing, maybe it's even a bit shallow, but I should let you know that more often than I do. You have *absolutely* no idea how sexy you are to me, which is also one of the reasons why you are so sexy.'

He hid his head in his hands in a mock horror way.

'And that's all happened because of how you changed your lifestyle to help your brain and, by the way, that's sexy too - wanting to understand yourself and grow as a person. I'm not done with the buff Nick Guymer humping on my bones just yet, so I can't have you getting a drinker's belly and coming to bed drunk, like me, can I? I need a few more of the fit, stallion years, yet. So keep that in mind when you get a thirst for drink on you. Alright?'

He laughed. She grinned back at him and pushed a long ringlet of blonde hair back behind her ear.

'But don't worry about this drinking urge. Just accept it as part of who you are. You were right to talk about it, though and it was good of Emily to help you out. Even if it was partly just an excuse to try and shag you.'

'Sometimes, it's like you're a grown up or something,' he said and looked out the window for a minute. 'And I really needed to hear that from you. Not the sexy stuff - though that's nice, too - I mean not being judgemental and just being understanding. It's *really* been bothering me.'

'Someone has to try and behave like an adult, don't they? Also I need to keep you healthy because I'd have to pay a top-notch gigolo a fortune to...' she dropped her voice to a hoarse whisper so no-one could hear, gave him her best lustful stare and said '...fuck me as good as you.' She winked at him and raised her voice back to her normal level. 'So, there's that economic consideration to bear in mind as well.'

Taking a sip of water, he nodded and smiled into the middle distance.

She went on. 'Well, look, you know my friend Annie, the one who used to run that theatre over in Richmond, she actually has a rented flat in Green Dragon Yard. She and her bloke Mark are moving out in a month or so - they've bought a house on Upsall Grove. We could probably jump in and get theirs. It's in our price range.'

'Is there a spare room for all the records?'

'Yeah, it's a two bedroom with a large living room and a tiny kitchen. We'd have to juggle things around a bit. It's on the top floor right near the pub. I've been there a few times. It's really nice. We'd have to sell or give away a lot of our old shite, because it's loads smaller.'

'I fancy living somewhere smaller with less shite.'

'Yeah, when you put it like that, it sounds quite good. It's got solid brick walls, so we might not disturb the neighbours with our sex noise too much.'

'I'll try and be a bit quieter.'

'Aw no, I like you panting and moaning like an old arthritic Afghan hound. I shall try biting on a stick, instead of shrieking like a banshee.'

'I swear you perforated one of my eardrums last night. It sounded like you were having an invasive operation being performed on you without anaesthetic.'

'That is *exactly* what sex with you is like, son. Ha ha.'

He flicked the Vs at her. 'And what about rescheduling the wedding?'

'Whenever you want, luv. Choose a date.'

'I was thinking. Maybe we'll hold off. Get moved first, that'll cost us a bit. We'll need to find a deposit. Then think about it next year.'

'Well, I might actually have a paying job by then at the Teesside Women Centre, so it'd make it all much more affordable. We could even have a honeymoon.'

'Aye, a caravan at Marske, maybe.'

'Or if we want proper glamour, Seal Sands.'

He laughed. 'Is that alright, then?'

'Yeah. Mam might have recovered by then, too. Poor old shitehawk.'

'She might even marry Conrad when she gets her share of the compo money. The Tyne and the Tees brought together at last.'

'Aye, the northeast, brought together over a massive, dodgy scam. That sounds about right, doesn't it?'

'Perfect,' he said. 'Absolutely, perfect.'

## THE END

## About John Nicholson

John is a well-known football writer whose work is read by tens of thousands of people every week. He's a columnist for Football365.com and has worked for the Daily Record, The Mirror, Sky and many other publications over the last 14 years.

## Other John Nicholson Books
*published by Biteback Publishing*

We Ate All The Pies -
*How Football Swallowed Britain Whole (2010)*

The Meat Fix -
*How 26 Years Of Healthy Eating Nearly Killed Me (2012)*

Books in the Nick Guymer Series
Published by HEAD PUBLISHING

Kindle/Paperback

http://www.johnnicholsonwriter.com